The Last Life

Also by Claire Messud

When the World was Steady

The Hunters

The Emperor's Children

Claire Messud

The Last Life

PICADOR

First published 1999 by Picador

First published in paperback 2000 by Picador
an imprint of Pan Macmillan Ltd
Pan Macmillan, 20 New Wharf Road, London N1 9RR
Basingstoke and Oxford
Associated companies throughout the world
www.panmacmillan.com

ISBN 978-0-330-37564-1

The author gratefully acknowledges the support
of the Virginia Center for the Cretive Arts, where
part of this book was written.

A CIP catalogue record for this book is available from
the British Library.

Printed and bound in Great Britain by
Mackays of Chatham plc, Chatham, Kent

Aug. 2009

For J.W.

With love,

Laurence and Philip

He who puts on wisdom, puts on grief; and a heart that understands cuts like rust in the bones.

– St. Augustine

It is only for the sake of the dreams that visit it that the world of reality has any certain value for us. Will not the dreams continue, when the reality has passed away?

– William Hurrell Mallock, *Is Life Worth Living?*

One

I

I am American now, but this wasn't always so.

I've been here a long time – six years at Columbia alone, and what seems an age before that – and have built a fine simulacrum of real life. But in truth, until now I've lived, largely, inside. These small rooms on New York City's Upper West Side are my haven: an ill-lit huddle of books and objects, a vague scent that is home. I've been waiting, although I could not, until he appeared, have given earthly shape to what I waited for. 'By pining, we are already there; we have already cast our hope, like an anchor, on that coast. I sing of somewhere else, not of here: for I sing with my heart, not my flesh.'

I'm not American by default. It's a choice. But it is a mask. Who, in the thronged avenues of Manhattan, hasn't known this? It is the same for the Korean saleswoman or the Bangladeshi businessman or the Nigerian student, for the Iowan nurse and the Montanan secretary, as it is for me: Americanness draws a veil, it lends a carapace to the lives we hold within.

Wherever we have come from, there ceased to be room, or words, or air; only here is breathing possible. The guilt does not evaporate: I live – how can I not? – with my burden of Original Sin. But in America, at least, where the future is all that binds us, I can seem familiar, new. And for a long time, seeming sufficed.

Now I find myself wanting to translate the world inside, beginning with the home that was once mine, on France's southern coast; with the fragrances and echoes of my grandfather's Bellevue Hotel, perched above the vast Mediterranean in its shifting palette of greens and blues and greys; and, as a starting place, with the high season of 1989.

2

The beginning, as I take it, was the summer night of my fifteenth year when my grandfather shot at me. In this way every story is made up, its shape imposed: the beginning was not really then, any more than was the day of my brother's birth, or, indeed, of mine. Nor is it strictly true that my grandfather shot *at me*: I was not, by chance, in the line of fire; he did not know that I was there. But it was an event, the first in my memory, after which nothing was the same again.

Those summer evenings were all alike. As Marie-José used to say, we had to make the time pass. Of its own accord, it didn't, or wouldn't: the days lingered like overripe fruit, soft and heavily scented, melting into the glaucous dusk. We gathered by the hotel pool, on the clifftop, after supper, watching the sky falter into Prussian blue, to blue-black, and the moon rise over the Mediterranean, the sea spread out before us, whispering and wrinkled. Every night the white, illuminated bulk of the island ferry ploughed its furrow across the water and receded to the horizon, the only marker of another day's passage.

Still almost children, we scorned the games of tag and cops and robbers that the younger kids delighted in, spiralling their pursuits outwards from the round benches by the parking lot to the furthest foliated corners of the grounds. Instead we idled, and smoked, and talked, and were so bored we made a virtue of being bored. And we flirted – although most of us had known each other for years, and had spent each summer swimming and playing together, for so long that we knew each other's skin and laughter and illusions like our own, we flirted. It made the time pass.

I can't recall now whose idea it was first, to swim at night. We spent our days in the water, in the murky, boat-bobbed brine of the bay, or in the electric indigo of the swimming pool, its surface skimmed with oily iridescence. We lived in our bathing suits, tiny triangles of colour, and worked (it was the closest that we came to work) on bronzing our skin evenly, deeply, so it held its tinge even through the winter months. We filed from beach to pool to beach again, up and down the tortuous paths, past the aloes in which, in earlier years, we had carved our initials, careful scars in the prickled, rubbery flesh. Why we felt the need to swim again, I do not know: perhaps because our water games were still those we had always played, a sphere into which self-consciousness had not yet intruded. We tussled in pairs on the pool's rim, struggling to push each other in, jumped from the overhanging balustrade into the shallows (although this manoeuvre had been strictly forbidden since a guest had cracked his skull attempting it), flaunted our elegant leaps from the diving board and, squealing, chased each other the length of the pool, the prize a firm shove on the top of the head and a spluttering sinkage.

Our games echoed in the trees. The higher our pitch the more we felt we enjoyed ourselves. In the daytime, the adult guests lounged in disgust by the water's edge, cursing our explosions and the rain of chlorinated droplets that they scattered; or else, stoic and frowning, they forged a measured breaststroke through our midst, their wake immediately swallowed by our flapping arms and legs. But at night the pool, lit from below, wavered, empty, avoided by the grown-ups who wandered through the distant hotel bar or dawdled, debating, over endless suppers, their voices rising and falling in the cicada-chorused air. The nearest thing to swimmers were the swooping bats that shot along the waterline in search of insects, attracted by the light.

And so, around ten o'clock one evening in July, or possibly even later, Thierry – the son of the accountant, a boy who never seemed to grow and whose voice obstinately refused to change, who compensated for his size with awkward arrogance and tedious pranks – suggested that we chase away the bats and reclaim the shimmering depths for ourselves. Familiar in the sunlight, the pool in the dark was an adventure, all shadows around it altered. We had no towels and, beneath our clothes, no suits, so we stripped naked, our curves and crevices hidden by the night, and plunged in.

We were a group of eight or nine, the children for whom the hotel was home and those for whom it was each summer the equivalent. Our gropings and sinkings and splashings were more exciting for our nakedness, our screams correspondingly more shrill. We didn't think of the adults: why would we? We didn't even think of time. The night swim was a delicious discovery, even though our heads and arms, when protruding to the air, were cold, and our bodies riddled with goose bumps. Ten minutes, maybe twenty. We weren't long in the water, and it is still difficult to believe we were so very loud, when my grandfather emerged onto his balcony, a dark form against the living room lights, with the bulge of the plane tree like a palaeolithic monster yapping at his feet.

He declaimed, his voice hoarse and furious. People were trying to think, to sleep. This was a place of rest, and the hour unconscionable. In short, we had no right to swim. We dangled, treading water, cowed into silence for a moment until someone – Thierry, no doubt – began to hiss across to me, half laughing, inaudible to my grandfather, about how the old prick should be silenced.

'Tell him you're here,' he whispered. 'Just tell him you're here and that'll shut him up. Go on. Or else he'll blabber on all night. Go on!'

Others – Marie-José and Thibaud and Cécile and the rest – took up his exhortation: 'Go on, Sagesse, go on.' Their voices lapped like waves that my grandfather, slightly deaf and still ranting, could not distinguish.

'Grand-père,' I shouted, finally, my voice high as a bell. 'It's us. It's me. We're sorry. We didn't mean to disturb you.'

'Get out right now,' he yelled back. 'Get out, get dressed and go home. It's the middle of the night.' Everyone sniggered at this: we believed that people who went to bed, who got up in the morning and went to work, were some kind of joke. 'Does your father know you're here?'

'Yes, Grand-père, he knows.'

My grandfather snorted, disgusted, a theatrical snort. 'Go home, all of you,' he said, and turned, fading back into the light, regaining his features and the high, greyed dome of his forehead.

We scrambled from the pool, a dripping huddle, muttering.

'Your grandfather, man,' said Thierry, jumping up and down with his hands clasped over the shadow of his genitals. 'He's something else.'

'It's not Sagesse's fault,' said Marie-José, putting a damp arm around me. 'But he is, you know, a jerk.'

'He's a bastard to work for, my father says,' said a skinny girl called Francine, her teeth chattering. Her father was the head groundsman.

'My father says the same,' I said. Everyone laughed, and just then a bat nose-dived and almost clipped the tops of our heads. We screamed in unison, and tittered guiltily at our screaming.

'Be careful,' said Thibaud, one of the summer residents, the son of nouveaux riches from Paris and the boy I had my eye on. 'Or he'll come back out.' He growled. 'Rottweiler.'

We dissolved again.

3

That was the first night. Marie-José dropped me at home on her moped; my clothes stuck clammily to my skin and my long hair was damp and viciously tangled by the wind. She waved and blew a kiss from within her bubbled helmet, and as she putted back along the white gravel drive to the road, my mother opened the door.

Our house, the home in which I had lived most of my life, had the same marble stillness as the hotel, the same capacity for echoes and light. You could feel people in it or, more likely, their absence, even standing in the foyer before the naked statue of Venus on her pedestal, with the brushed aluminium elevator door like another artwork beside her. The front hall stretched up two stories, and the air high above seemed to hover, waiting to be disturbed.

My mother could slip through the house without moving that air, when she chose to. Her face, too, could remain still – even when she spoke, even when she was nervous – like a terrified mask, with its sharp planes and dark, hooded eyes.

'Not in bed?' I asked, as casual as I could be, plucking at my tats with my fingers as I pushed past her into the living room.

She fidgeted with the buttons of her blouse, and spoke to me in English, her language and that of my earliest childhood, used now between us only as the language of confidences and reprimands. 'Your grandfather called.'

'He did?' I sank into the middle section of the huge, death-white sofa, aware that my jeans would leave two wet bulbs beneath my buttocks. I spoke in French. 'And how was he?' I put my feet on the coffee table, careful not to go too far even as I indulged in this act of war: I placed them on a large, perfectly positioned book, and did not touch, let alone smear, the polished glass.

My mother took silent note. 'Livid.'

I waited, busy with my hair, tangling and untangling it like Penelope at her loom.

'He's furious with you and your friends. All that noise! In the middle of the night, Sagesse! The hotel is full of guests, for God's sake.'

'It wasn't very late. All we did was go swimming. It's one of the rules, that we be allowed to. He didn't have to yell at us.'

'Your grandfather is under a great deal of strain.'

'He's a jerk is what he is, who yells at people just because he can. Some of them – Renaud, or Thibaud, or Cécile and Laure – they're guests at the hotel. What right does he have to do that?'

'Your grandfather—' My mother's eyes were pleading, her

hands open to the ceiling and then slapped, suddenly, with a click of exasperation, to her sides. 'I don't want to talk about your grandfather and what's wrong with him. That's not the point.'

'Oh no?'

'The point is an abuse of privilege.'

Small and neat, my mother had done her best to impersonate a Frenchwoman: her dark hair was pulled back in a tidy chignon, her blouses and skirts were cut in the latest fashion, and she favoured trim, navy cardigans that pointed up the slimness of her shoulders. But something in her face, in the shape of her head or the way that she held it, gave away her foreignness, the way a transvestite is betrayed by her wrists or the line of her back. Perhaps it was simply anxiety; my mother was constantly anxious. But the result was an inability to take command. Her scoldings were always halfhearted, as if she didn't really believe in them, as if she were criticizing herself and found the duty excruciating.

Then again, there was the awkwardness of my mother trying to assume the voice of her father-in-law: for too long, for ever, I had heard and overheard the railing, the whining, the fury – the range of melodramatic expostulations that characterized my mother's emotional expression – much of it directed against her husband's family, against the very man whom she was now forced to represent; and if not, then against the whole of France, in a sweeping, metonymical gesture that fooled no one. The criticism never fell where we all, silently, sinkingly, knew that it must, on the key to her imprisonment: my brother Etienne.

4

I could have begun with my brother, as easily as I could with the night when the sharp reports of my grandfather's rifle sundered the family (although they did this not immediately: rather, they established the hairline cracks, that worked more insidiously and perhaps more lastingly than would a neater, more decisive action). For that matter, I could have begun with my parents, with their meeting, in a café in Aix-en-Provence one April afternoon, when the sun was sinking and the parade of eccentrics, in imitation of the metropolis, marched the boulevard like puppets in a theatre for the sole benefit of this eager young American, on a year's release from her women's college where the turbulence of the decade had failed to stretch its tentacles, and of the handsome (so he was, she tells me), gallant young Frenchman who leaned forward to watch the delight in my mother's eyes. They were particularly entranced by the septuagenarian with platinum curls who made her daily way along the sidewalk, on tiptoe, swinging pink ballet slippers over one shoulder and clutching a miniature poodle, whose curls matched her own, to her breast.

Or, indeed, I could have begun with the squalling of my own birth, which occurred at the time of the fall of Saigon, a matter of record for each of my parents in their different ways. For my father because his colonial blood led him to grieve at the ultimate loss of another former outpost of French glory, when the final anguished battles of his own vanished Algeria were little more than ten years past. Whereas my mother – whose interest in and grasp of the political were always vague at best – saw the moment in a rush of nostalgia for America, that vast and only intermittently familiar territory, in pain and internally divided as she, in exile, was herself. She hailed, after all, from the rolling comfort of rural Massachusetts, and had never expected, just as America had not, to find herself so confused: in short, she identified. And yet somehow I, slippery and screaming, would grow up believing that none of it – not war, not America, not the old woman swinging her ballet shoes with such false carelessness – had anything to do with me. Stories are made up, after all, as much of what is left out.

Why was my brother's birth the more significant, when I already crawled in my playpen, my parents' grave error made flesh? Because some things are truer than others, more inescapable, less dependent on the mad or imagined confluences of the mind. And what happened at my brother's birth was one of these inescapable things. Those precious minutes between the first wrenching push that propels the infant's head downwards, out of the womb, and its arrival into the brutal fluorescence that marks the beginning of its life – in my brother's case, those precious minutes bled and fed into another, longer, more terrifying gap, in which the doctor and the midwife panicked, and presumably my gasping brother also, trying as hard as they could, all of them, my mother too, desperate but unknowing, to drag him into the world. Perhaps he himself hesitated, sensing the agonies before him, feeling that he would not, could not, go ahead with life. He cannot tell us. Deprived too long of oxygen, his tiny limbs, blued, curled in upon his torso, his waving baby's neck slackened, and his mind . . . who knows where his mind went, or where it is, or whether it rages still behind his grinning eyes? He relinquished in those precious moments all possibility of language: nobody will ever know what Etienne may think, as he hunches, strapped at the waist and again at the chest, convulsing cheerfully in his wheelchair, a thin, glistening trail of spit always reaching like a wet spider's web towards the ground. The doctors, almost immediately, pronounced him incapable of motor coordination and severely mentally retarded: little more than a vegetable, by the reckoning of the world.

For my parents, this was the clanging of their prison door. But for me, two years old when they came home with him, my path was already chosen. We were the same, I decided, cooing over the silent bassinet, and I, at least, would not abandon him. If he could not learn to speak, we would share what words I possessed. I would move for him, too, and bring home to him the smells of the park, the beach, the schoolyard. We would be fine. And from that moment, too, I despised him as much as I loved him: he was – he is – my limitation.

My parents rose to their fate with Catholic dignity, against the advice of many – including, I was eventually to learn, their priest. We kept him and loved him, or tried to; and having chosen his name beforehand – now so inappropriate as to be laughable – they stuck with it, which is how my brother came to be called Etienne Parfait. To me, and when I spoke to him, he was *plus-que-parfait*, more than perfect, pluperfect, an irretrievable tense in the language he would never speak.

5

To interrupt my mother's lecture, I asked, knowing full well the answer, where he was.

'Your brother is asleep,' she said. 'Of course.'

'And Papa?'

'Your father had to go out.'

I nodded. I was tired, and so was she.

'Listen, Sagesse,' she ventured, in conciliatory French, her hand reaching to smooth my crumpled hair. 'Don't do it again. Tell the others not to. I assure you, your grandfather . . . it's not the best time. He's not . . . Your father says things at the hotel are worse. Not business-wise, just . . . Your grandfather is under a lot of strain. He's being difficult. For everyone?'

'I understand.'

I didn't really understand. How could I, when all my days were ordered only by the weary pursuit of pleasure? I went up and kissed Etienne as he slept, the rasping suction of his breath a distraction from the irritation I felt with my parents. I cocooned his narrow, tousled head in the draped net of my hair and breathed in time with him, his smell of glycerine soap and faintly, too, of urine, mingling with my own chlorine and sweat. I put my mother's warning away in the padlocked box in my head where I stored such information. That is to say, I forgot about it.

6

I had good cause to forget. In the days that followed I, my mother and father, the Bellevue crowd, the entire town – we were all distracted by a local event of sudden national importance. Our town, long waning in significance, ugly duckling of the Mediterranean coast, did not often merit mention in the faraway Parisian newspapers. Accustomed to provinciality, we went about our business as if we were invisible, occasionally puffed with resentment at the metropolitans, but blithely unaware that our own scrabbling tensions might have resonance beyond themselves. In this instance – in this summer bombing, or, more accurately, in this failure to bomb – we brought upon ourselves a scrutiny neither anticipated nor welcome.

The morning after our unpopular swim, I trailed downstairs near nine to find my father still at home, eating his breakfast in a fan of sunbeams, the *Figaro*, zebra-striped by the light, held close in front of his shiny, new-shaven face.

Slit-eyed with sleep, dressing-gowned, illicitly barefoot (shoes were a rule in our house, if only espadrilles), I muttered a greeting and drifted past him to the kitchen, where the tiles were cool on my soles. There, arms akimbo, my mother stood eyeing the toaster, in which her preferred – her American – *pain de mie* was audibly crisping.

'Why's he still here?' I asked, filling a pot with water. 'You want more coffee?'

'He got in very late. I was asleep myself. Paperwork, something.'

I raised an eyebrow.

'And then this tragedy . . .'

'What tragedy? Not another heart attack?' The previous year a Bellevue guest had succumbed, in his bathroom, in an inelegant posture, to fatal angina.

'The bombing. There's been a bombing.'

'Where?'

'Here. In town. It's incredible. Right here.'

'Gosh.' I tightened the belt of my dressing gown.

'Just like Algiers, when he was a boy – it's the first thing he said.'

'What happened?'

'It's in the papers. They're not entirely sure, but they think they know . . .'

What they thought they knew at the start, which they eventually decided was fact, amounted to this: two young men and a young woman, locals, dirt ordinary, none of them over twenty, and the girl just eighteen, had built a pipe bomb in the basement of the home of one of the boys. The bomb had been intended, it appeared, for a nightclub much frequented by Arabs in the old quarter near the port. There was no doubt – given the young men's activities in the preceding months, including their disruptive attendance at a National Front rally and, more troubling still, their arrest for the random beating of a young Frenchman of Moroccan descent – what they were after. The girl, it was thought, was merely a girlfriend: her commitment to the nationalist cause was undocumented.

In any event, the trio had paid for their malice with their lives. Whether the timer had been ineptly set, or whether the bomb had been too sensitively wired, tripped by a pothole or a sudden braking, they had exploded only themselves and their black Fiat Uno, just outside the downtown shopping centre at 1:12 a.m., as indicated by the frozen watchface belonging to one of the young men. The agitators were in pieces, as was their vehicle, and the road that had been beneath it, cratered like a small quarry.

The mother of the dead girl, a leathery creature ravaged by smoke and drink, her hair in lank, bleached strings around her bony face, would inform the local paper – from which I gathered my information – that her daughter had never been in any kind of trouble, had had a sweet and gentle disposition, and had been – perhaps her greatest flaw – something of a follower. 'She knew right from wrong,' said her mother, 'but she trusted people. She believed what she was told.' She had been working for two solid years at the checkout of the central Casino supermarket, where she was affectionately thought of by her colleagues of all races. This tragedy came as a terrible shock to her mother.

On the very morning, it was also, clearly, a terrible shock to my father. When I jested, bringing my bowl of coffee to rest with both my hands, that there was slight cause for mourning – 'The bad guys did themselves in, right? So, big deal' – my father looked at me over his newspaper with an unreadable expression, his eyes wide and sombre, his flesh scrubbed to gleaming, and rasped, 'Don't talk about things you know nothing about.'

'Ex-cuse me.' I rolled my eyes at my mother, who busied herself with the crumbs around her plate.

'If you had seen what I've seen—' my father said. I knew, even at my tender age – even Etienne most probably knew, had he but been able to say so – that my father almost never referred to his youth, especially not to those dark years at its end, before he left Algeria for France, or certainly not in front of his children; and I thought, even hoped, that he might now say more. But he lapsed back into silence, his conditional clause hovering, tantalizing, in the air, then withdrew momentarily behind his newspaper, only to snap its pages into ragged folds and pull back from the table, sloshing the milk in its jug and causing a precariously balanced jam spoon to clatter stickily from its jar.

'I'm late,' he said. 'I'll probably be late tonight. Tomorrow's the Joxe dinner. And remember, the day after we're at Maman's.'

'How could I forget?' said my mother, who had licked the jammy spoon and stowed it on her plate.

He kissed us, dry, perfunctory kisses. His face at rest bore – was it a tint, an angle, a shadow? – an indefinable mask of sorrow.

My mother waited until she heard the engine of his black BMW, the crunch of the tires on the gravel drive, before she sprang up and proceeded to clear the table at great speed.

'No time to waste. Etienne must be done with his bath. Magda will have him dressed soon. Chop, chop!'

'Where are you going?'

'He's got his checkup at ten-thirty, and then I thought he might like a walk along the promenade. You know how he loves the gulls. Want to come?'

I shook my head.

'Not much, eh? You used to dote on your brother.'

'I still do. For God's sake, stop picking on me. Is it a crime to want my own life?'

'There's no need to use that tone with me.'

I sighed. She sighed.

'I'm meeting Marie-Jo a bit later. I promised.'

'Lunch at your grandmother's, then?'

'I told her yesterday.'

'Save Friday for me.'

'Okay. How come?'

'Market downtown. I thought we might stop by the *parfumerie* and pick out a couple of lipsticks, one each, for the season.'

7

On Friday I washed my hair for the outing, and braided it wet, knowing that at bedtime, unfastened, it would ripple down my back in rare wavelets, still damp.

I loved our trips to the outdoor market. Usually my mother made hasty forays to its smaller sibling near the beach, a few umbrella-shaded stands in a parking lot, with only one or two of everything – one florist, one dairy stand, a single woman selling discount sheets and towels. It was handier for my mother when she had Etienne in the car: she could park, and leave him, and see him even as she filled her baskets. To go into town, she had to leave Etienne with Magda, his nurse. It was an expedition, a treat, and she preferred to go with me.

The town market stretched the length of a narrow street in the old quarter, running downhill from a small fountain near the shopping centre to the plaza opposite the edge of the quay. The stands lined the asphalt on either side, and behind the stands, forgotten, lay the stores that remained even when there was no market, dusty, odd caverns selling Chinese herbal remedies, or curtain rods and broomsticks, or plate glass and mirrors cut to size.

The visiting hawkers arranged themselves in front of these sleepy shopfronts in an implacable order prescribed by long tradition, mysterious to the uninitiated. There were vegetable men and fruit women and stalls selling both, blushing mounds of peaches alongside plump and purple eggplants, exuberant fronded skirts of frisée salads cozying next to succulent crimson cherries, pale, splayed organs of fennel pressing their ridged tubes and feathered ends up against the sugar-speckled, wrinkled carcasses of North African dates. There were florists whose misted anemones and roses glistened as if it were dawn, and the cheese vendors' ripe piles, wares which, from behind glass, leaked their fetid and enticing stinks out into the crowd. There were olive men and herb men, buckets of pungent rosemary and spiky bay leaves, cheesecloth sachets of lavender, blue bottles of rose and orange water, and teas for every ailment – for tension and bad skin and insomnia and constipation. There were tables of candlesticks and salad servers and pickle tongs; there were great strings of garlic and waxy pyramids of lemons. At the bottom, near the quay, the fishmongers sold their bullet-eyed, silver-skinned, slippery catch, blood-streaked fillets and orbed, scored steaks, milky scallops and encrusted oysters, all laid out on trays of ice in the morning sun, their rank fishiness rising in the air with the day's temperature; while opposite them, in their own corner, a family of young brothers hawked cheap women's clothes and glittering baubles, shiny earrings and gilded anklets, leopard-print leggings and lurid synthetic T-shirts with sequin lionesses, or fringed white vinyl jerkins with matching cowboy boots, all manner of sartorial novelties whose rampant success could be gauged from the ensembles of the women out shopping.

We liked to start at the top of the street and walk down

slowly, sniffing and pressing and sampling and chatting in the gentle current of fellow housewives, the odd runty husband or wizened grandfather as notable as the yapping dogs among us. It was, above all, a parade of women: young Arab mothers with kohl-lined eyes, their toddlers clutching at their knees; bosomy Mediterranean peasant matriarchs in tight nylon dresses, women as wide as they were tall, their bare arms hefty and marbled like prime cuts of pork; elegant African women in vibrant tunics, their hair elaborately turbaned, with enviably glossy skin and haughty almond eyes; gaggles of girls my own age, limning adulthood, feet squeezed into spike-heeled pumps, budding breasts outlined beneath scanty tops, mouths ageless slashes of wet colour, more often than not twisting and grimacing to accommodate cigarettes or chewing gum or both at once. Whereas alone I might have smiled at such groups, begging tolerance if not approval, on my mother's arm I frowned, slightly, in their direction, as an oblique reassurance to her that I had no truck with such slatterns.

We had not reckoned, that morning, on the bombers' funerals. We hadn't thought twice about it. Not that the funerals were to take place downtown, or anywhere near the market; but the nightclub, the avowed target (notebooks discovered at the bomb builder's home confirmed it) was only a few blocks from the stalls. There was, in the town, much sentiment and much of it divided on the matter of the bombing. In addition to the regular gamut of French citizenry, there were many, like our family, white refugees from Algeria, some of whom sympathized passionately with the bombers; and many *harkis*, who feared the rekindling of old tensions; and many more recent North African immigrants, suddenly terrorized and enraged. As if to set fire to this dry tinder, the National Front (how like my mother, I note in retrospect, not even to have been aware of it!) had dispatched representatives to the funerals, a delegation from out of town to march in solidarity with the girl's mother and the other grieving parents. They weren't quite calling the dead youths heroes, but the phrase '*Morts pour la France*' had been bandied about and indeed was already, as we would have seen had we but wandered the alleys behind the market, spray-painted, along with swastikas, on the brickwork and stucco throughout the predominantly Muslim neighborhood.

We had not thought of it, and did not think of it, but as we ambled into the fray at the top of the market street we could detect, in the air, something askew. The shoppers leaned in to one another in their discrete groupings, with a corresponding edging away – so very slight – from those who were different. Some stallholders held hissed conversations; some pointedly ignored their neighbours. Even the market's children seemed knowingly subdued.

My mother, in her careful attire, her Vuitton bag on her arm, her chignon tight, did not resemble many of the other market-goers. It was not that, on that day, her un-Frenchness showed; rather, it was a matter of too successful an emulation of a certain type of Frenchwoman. We detected, in our slow and cheery perusal of the tables, a certain frost from their attendants, but attributed it to the fact that we looked too long and bought too little.

It was the olive woman halfway down on the right who surprised us: the olive woman next to the stall selling only Spanish melons. We lingered in front of her display, eyeing and sniffing the briny, garlicky, slick smell of the olives. She had fat green ones speckled with red chillis, and tight oval kalamatas, and little withered oil-cured black ones like oversized raisins, and tiny, slivery brown ones that looked more like pips than olives, and great bowls of *tapenade*, both green and black, and bowls, too, of *anchoïade*, pure salt, which I loved. My mother and I debated, *sotto voce*, which treats to carry home. My mother wanted to taste one type of olive she did not know – spherical, large and almost red – but the olive woman's evil glare dissuaded her.

The olive woman was vast, her shelf of bosom quivering beneath a fading black T-shirt, her moon-pale, dimpled arms crossed over her belly. Her black hair was hacked around her puffed cheeks, and her chin, a great bony jut in her flesh, resisted gravity's pull into the billowing cushion of her neck.

Above her lip quivered a dark caterpillar of moustache, which rendered her more, rather than less, frightening. Her eyes, shiny as her blackest olives, glittered hostility.

My mother, all grace, asked merely how long the reddish olives might keep in the refrigerator.

To which the woman, summoning her bulk, replied, 'You're not from here, are you?'

My mother shook slightly as she insisted, 'Yes, I am.'

'No you're not. I've not seen you here before.'

'I shop at the other one, the little market, by the beach.'

The olive woman snorted. 'If you live here, where do you live?'

'Up the corniche. On the hill.'

'Oh yeah? What street? Name it. I bet you can't. Name it.'

My mother, who had been in retreat from the outset, stopped. 'I don't think that's any of your business.'

'Maybe not. All right. It's how you're dressed.' The olive woman's mouth was set in a grim little gape. She did not have all her teeth. 'I thought you were with *them*. Flown in to make trouble.'

'With "them"?' repeated my mother, mystified.

'With the National Front. The way you're dressed. Here for that funeral. Are you sure you're not with the National Front?'

My mother shook her head in sharp, insistent little shakes as she backed away from the olive woman and her wares. It seemed that the people around us were cocking their ears, listening without wishing to appear that they were, guarding their opinions but preparing, if necessary, for a fight. As my mother retreated, and I with her, sinking into a hole made for us by the crowd, the olive woman glared, and raised phlegm, with a harsh ratcheting, in her throat. She spat vigorously onto the mucky pavement. 'That's what I think of the National Front,' she called after us.

My mother trembled; she was almost teary.

'Don't let it bother you,' I assured her, tucking my arm in the crook of hers as we resumed our downhill course. 'She was a crazy lady.'

18

'It's her intensity that surprised me,' my mother said. 'She was so angry, but why?'

'Because you're dressed nicely, that's all. Let it go, Maman. What are you going to do, buy your clothes here in the market just to please her?'

My mother brightened at the notion. 'A red sequin mini-skirt and go-go boots – what do you think?'

'I think I'd stick to buying fish.'

8

That evening we went to my grandparents' apartment for supper. It was always a production to take Etienne there, because the Bellevue, and in particular its staff block, had not been designed with wheelchairs in mind. No matter which path one took – whether around the main drive, past the main hotel and the pool, in a wide loop, or straight up from the gate to the back parking lot and the staff building beyond – there were steps. My mother and I together could lift Etienne in his chair, but the effort made both of us bead with sweat, and soiled our hands and rumpled our blouses, and my grandmother would silently frown upon us. Carting Etienne was much easier when it was my father and me – or better yet, my father and one of the gardeners, or Zohra, my grandparents' maid.

That day, however, my father had gone straight from his office in the hotel to the apartment, so my mother and I panted and struggled while Etienne, drooling onto his fine white shirt, bucked and crowed and tried to reach for our hair or our arms or our shiny necklaces, and we all arrived at my grandparents' door flushed and dishevelled.

'Come in, *chéris*,' urged my grandmother from within her cloud of Guerlain (a particular perfume concocted, appropriately enough, for the empress Eugénie). Even though we were the only supper guests, an evening *en famille*, she had powdered and rouged, had draped her neck with jewels and her body in flowered silks. 'The men are just sorting out the drinks.'

Apéritif was ritual at these family gatherings: even Etienne had his cup of orange juice, a special red plastic cup that had a lid with a straw in it, so that his dribbling could be more or less controlled.

I hadn't seen my grandfather since before the swimming pool incident, although my grandmother had roundly chastised me on his behalf the following day. I wasn't certain whether or not to apologize directly, to clear the air but possibly to elicit an indignant tirade, or to pretend nothing had happened and hope for the best.

In the living room, my father and my grandfather stood side by side watching a fleet of little sailboats tack across the vista, back towards the port, as the early evening colours, soft and roseate, fell like dust over the receding rocky headlands and the great bowl of the sky. Both men held their hands clasped behind their backs; both allowed their lower lips to ride up slightly over their top ones, in a vaguely smug expression, as if the splendid view were of their making, the bonny white blips of sail a diversion solely for their pleasure.

There the resemblance faltered. My grandfather stood a head shorter than his son, a dapper man in an old-fashioned suit with a blue handkerchief at the pocket. His frame was slight and his face, animate, almost ugly, seemed too big for his body. His nose loomed imposing and bulbous above his broad mouth. His ears, too, were large and fleshy, their pink lobes dispropor- tionately pendulous. He was fair-skinned, greyed, his tonsured locks cropped close. My father, swart, bulky and hairy beside him, emanated excess. Formerly muscled, he was now merely fleshy in the shoulders and neck, with a second chin sagging, incipient, below the first. Dark curls crept down his nape and under his collar, from beneath his cuffs along the backs of his hands – like a werewolf, I had teased him when I was younger, until my mother told me he was ashamed of his hairiness. My father's eyes were large and profusely lashed, but these were his only outsized feature: his nose was fine and straight and of medium length (his mother's nose); his mouth was a sensuous but restrained bow; and his ears – he was proud of his ears – lay small and flat, as if asleep, along the outline of his skull. The two men looked at once utterly different and the same, in their attitude before the ocean.

'Surveyors of the beyond?' enquired my grandmother with a brittle hoot, jangling her bangles. 'Will neither of my men pour us a tiny little glass of port? We're parched!'

We assembled in our specific places around the coffee table, my father and grandfather in facing armchairs, my mother and I on the sofa – which was particularly high, or deep, so that we both had to choose between dangling our feet above the ground and perching at the front of the slippery cushions: I always chose the former and she the latter – and my grandmother, with Etienne parked at her side, closed the circle, in a tapestry chair with carved legs and futile little armrests: a lady's chair.

Before sitting, I kissed my grandfather hello. He seemed preoccupied, and registered no displeasure. Indeed, he seemed barely to register who I was. But then, when drinks had been poured and I was quietly crunching potato chips from a blue bowl, I caught him frowning at me, his eyebrows, ever exuberant (their hairs were very long), working, as if the sight of me in the middle distance had provoked an aggravating memory.

My grandmother was telling a story about an aging Italian opera singer who had visited the hotel every year for a decade – a woman we all knew, who wore grand, flowing tunics and who annually pinched my cheeks between her curiously strong fingers – when my grandfather interrupted her.

'Our country, in this time, has a problem of manners,' he began. 'It is not a uniquely French problem – indeed it stems, in part, I, like many, would contend, from the influence of your country – ' he nodded at my mother ' – although not, naturally, from your own gracious influence. What preoccupies me, however, as a nationalist – and I'm not afraid to say it, implying thereby only a love and a reverence of my nation, culture and history above all other nations, cultures and histories, which is perfectly natural and in no way implies disrespect for those others — anyway, as a nationalist and a Frenchman, I am concerned with the manners and mores of this country, and of our people. And it seems to me — ' here his roving, appropriative gaze, which had been sliding like oil around the assembly, and beyond, to the Provençal plates on the wall and the darkening corner of sea he could distinguish from his chair, came to rest upon me ' — that the loss of certain basic courtesies among our citizens, and among our youngest citizens above all, does not, of itself, comprise the fairly innocent informality that well-intentioned liberals would have us believe. No. It is, I am convinced, a symptom of a far-reaching and truly distressing cultural collapse, one in which the individual places his own will and desire above the common good in ways we, who are now aging, would have considered unthinkable. Rudeness is, I argue, a symptom of the profound anarchy that our culture currently faces but refuses to acknowledge, a chaos in which everyone has lost sight of his place in a natural — or rather, civilized, which is far greater a compliment than the natural, civilization being what distinguishes us from mere beasts — hierarchy. What motivates good behaviour—' he paused and sipped his scotch, with a slurp rendered louder by our silence; even Etienne, whose eyes rolled to the ceiling and whose feet twitched, sensed that our grandfather's discourses demanded attention. 'What motivates good behaviour and what motivates excellence are the same thing: fear. Fear of God, fear of the rod, fear of failure, fear of humiliation, fear of pain. And that is a fact. And in our society, today, nobody is afraid of anything. Shame, rebuke, imprisonment — none of it means anything to anyone. Kids need to be taught,' he said, looking now at my father, who managed to meet his gaze without apparently seeing him, 'that their actions have repercussions, real ones. Kids should be a lot more afraid than they are.'

'Not just kids,' I said, nodding and licking the salt from my lips.

'You would have me believe that we — ' my grandfather's ire was a fierce steeliness in the quiet of his tone ' — that we, around you here in this living room, behave with as little regard for anyone outside ourselves as you and your little friends?'

Tempted to insist that my friends were not 'little', but wise to the cost of such baiting, I adopted my most innocent and childish voice, and said, 'Oh no, nothing like that. No, I meant the woman in the market today. Right, Maman?'

My mother, who sought only to slip invisibly through these evenings, glared at me and pressed her lips.

'What woman?' asked my grandmother.

'Yes, what happened?' My father seized on any strand that might divert his own father's discourse.

'It was nothing,' my mother insisted.

Etienne squirmed. My grandmother tilted his juice cup to his slippery lips.

'That's not true, Maman. You were terribly upset.'

'Carol, what happened?' My father leaned forward in his chair. My grandfather's gaze, from beneath his wild brows, burned my mother's cheeks.

'Oh, Sagesse makes a mountain out of a molehill. It was just one of the pedlars, in the market, who didn't like the look of me for some reason.'

'She spat at us,' I explained.

'Whatever for?' my grandmother asked.

My mother shrugged. 'Just rude, I suppose. She was a nasty, tough old thing.'

'She accused Maman of being in the National Front, in town for the funerals.'

'Probably a communist,' my grandmother said with a sniff. 'You didn't take it to heart?'

'Of course not. But she was very unpleasant.' My mother adjusted her skirt.

'As if – ' my grandfather took a breath and spouted ' – as if our country's troubles stemmed from the National Front! As if that were an insult! How absurd!'

'How do you mean, Grand-père?'

'I don't vote for Le Pen,' my grandfather said, 'but I'd defend any man's right to. For a start, because we – you too, my little girl, although you know about as much history as a spotted dog – we, all of us in this room, owe that man a debt. To the last, he fought for our country, he believed in our people, he understood what it was, what it meant.'

'Algeria.' I whispered it.

'That's right, my girl. Algeria. And anyone who votes for him, maybe they're merely repaying the debt. I don't happen to agree with a lot of his policies, and I think it's political suicide for representatives of the FN to come down here and associate themselves with a posse of undisciplined children, children who exemplify the very anarchical destruction – in this case, self-destruction – that I've just been talking about. Left, right – the politics don't matter. It's chaos, it's entropy, and anyone with any wit should keep away. But the FN's not the problem. People who think it is are misguided. It's just a symptom of the problem. Of the problems. Plural. The problems that this nation faces, overrun with immigrants – Arabs, Africans, the English-speakers, all of them – our culture assailed on all sides. Our children, for God's sake, building bombs for no reason! And our government – this decrepit, farcical liar who fancies himself emperor – our government has nothing to say about it, nothing at all!'

My father coughed and looked into his drink.

'Le Pen, at least – he says the wrong thing, I think, for our time and our moment, but at least he has something to say. At least he knows his own mind. That's what you should've said to the pinko fishwife—'

'She was selling olives, actually,' my mother murmured.

'Olives, fish, garlic, whatever. That's what you should've said to that peasant – at least he doesn't wait for advice from Moscow on how to respond to a local crisis. At least he has an honest response – a French response.' My grandfather grunted, sipped his scotch, rattling the ice cubes.

I sat deep in the back of the sofa, swinging my feet slightly, watching, as my brother, strapped in his chair opposite me, twitched and rolled his bright grey eyes. I was quite impressed by the firecracker I had so nonchalantly launched in our midst: I hadn't known I would provoke so fulsome a response, so ready a distraction from the pettiness of late swims in the Bellevue pool.

At supper, my grandfather said almost nothing, as if he were spent. He looked small, slumped over his *pissaladière*, then over his slices of lamb shoulder. He sipped indifferently at his rosé and stared out to the now-dark sea, and when my father asked him about the notion of a security guard at the front gate, he seemed not to hear. My father looked at my mother as if to say, 'I told you so,' and she raised a finely arched brow.

'Who's for more potatoes?' urged my grandmother, at her head of the table. 'More peas?'

9

When we got home that night, I helped my mother bathe Etienne and put him to bed, because Magda had the evening off. Etienne lolled, half asleep, as we put on his nightshirt, his limbs heavy and slightly damp in the heat, and we left him to the cool air that drifted into his darkened room with the tang of the sea still on it.

I, too, bade my good nights, and my mother returned to my father in the living room below, her heels resounding on the stone staircase. While I brushed my teeth, my mouth full of minty foam, I tiptoed onto the landing to listen to my parents' quarrelling.

'. . . These interminable lectures, as if we were all Sagesse's age – no, for God's sake, as if we had the wit of Etienne!'

I couldn't hear my father's reply, but could deduce it from what followed.

'How many years have you been saying that? "He's difficult," "It's a difficult time," "I couldn't leave him now" – come off it, Alex, what about *our* life? *Your* life?'

The bickering was as familiar as a dream. I returned to the

bathroom to spit and rinse, and brought my nightie from my room so I could change for bed and listen at the same time. It would not end until my father exploded, and won. I could practically hear the ice cubes in his after-dinner glass of scotch, which I knew he held, and put down, and held again as he paced the room, around the furniture, seething like an animal until he would have to roar.

I stood, barefoot, in my underpants, my nightgown frothy in my hand, leaning forward. My heart pumped and tingled in my extremities; my neck was rigid. I could feel my veins tightening. It was always this way. I was waiting for release. By witnessing their arguments, their hidden confessor, I unthinkingly believed that I controlled and contained them; I would not retreat until their voices subsided, until I was certain that no hand had been raised (none ever was), that nothing, tangible or intangible, had been truly broken.

'Enough! Your incessant shrieking!' my father's bass thundered. I imagined his face purpled, his curls quivering, his hands, in fists, held tight as though they might escape him. 'And how, exactly, would you have us live – with your taste for maids and nurses and luxury all around? Do you think it's so easy?'

My mother whimpered complaint. She would cry soon.

'Spoiled! You're nothing but a spoiled American daddy's girl, still, after all this time. You think it's easy? It's work, every second of it is work, hand-dirtying, mind-numbing. You think I like it? You have no idea. I survive it. And he taught me that – which isn't nothing – and we've built something. Christ, *I've* built something, part of it, a large part, even if it's all in his name now. But his name is my name, it's our name, it's the only thing that makes a life mean anything—'

My mother said something else, inaudible; but conciliation was beginning.

'It will be our life; it's the only life, the only place we've got. He won't go on like this for ever. It's mine – it's your due. For the kids, for our family name. Jesus, Carol, walk away? You want to walk away? Then, walk—'

I could tell she was crying; she would be trying to embrace him now.

'I haven't thrown these years away for nothing. Not all these years. And it's our place. It will be our place, and we'll make it ours.'

'Of course we will,' my mother was saying. 'Of course we will.'

The volume was ebbing.

'It's going to belong to us,' my father said, almost in his normal voice. 'If you'll just be patient.'

I slipped my gown over my head and prepared to retreat. They would turn out the lights now. They would come upstairs, maybe even together.

'Agree with him?' my father said. 'Don't ask me that. I don't even fucking hear him. I don't hear it, so how would I know?'

If they continued, I decided, it would be on the relatively quiet ground of politics, for which neither could muster much venom. I had ridden out the storm. I went to bed, pausing only to catch the soft, wet snores of Etienne's room, to make sure that he, too, was safe.

10

The second nocturnal swim, a week later, took place without me. I could not have prevented it, and could only laugh when Marie-José told me. She sat outstretched on her bedroom floor with her spatula and honeyed mire of melted wax, smoothing it in even swathes onto her long brown legs and tearing, with exaggerated winces, at the invisible fair bristles. She told me the story in between the stripping sounds, and waved the sticky spatula for emphasis.

'Your grandfather – Christ, girl, he's a madman. It was earlier, you know, than last time, so I guess we thought it would be okay. It must have been before ten, nine-thirty even, and we were trying – we saw his lights on – trying to be quiet. But I think it was Cécile, she was screaming like a pig in the water. I think—' She paused to slather the back of her left calf. 'I think she has a thing for Thierry. Don't laugh – it's obvious. You wouldn't think anyone could go for him, the shrimp. But she's no Vogue model herself.'

'And she's short,' I said.

'And he's older than she is. And I suppose she doesn't know him very well. So anyway – she gets on my nerves, that girl – every time he swam near her, she'd start shrieking, even though the rest of us were doing our best to shut her up. He was loving it, of course.'

'You think he's interested?'

'Probably. I mean, how often can he get a look in? None of us would touch him. And at school he's a joke.'

'You're starting to make me feel sorry for him.'

'Wait for this, then. Because you really will. Even I felt a little sorry. It was so funny. You see, we were trying, except for those two, to be quiet. Well, quieter. I mean, we were talking and stuff, but most of us didn't scream. And we were in the pool for a while, you know and he – your grandfather – he didn't come out. I think we figured that maybe they were entertaining or something, or maybe they were out somewhere else. I mean, all he had to do was tell us to be quiet.'

'So? What happened?'

The wax was cold and petrified on Marie-José's leg, but she was too caught up in her story to attend to it.

'Well, all of a sudden there's this voice on the bridge – ' there was a walkway over the pool from the courtyard above, with steps leading down to the water ' – saying, "All right, who is it?" And then, "I know which ones you are," and "Get out of the water." So we do, I mean, what choice do we have? We didn't hear him coming, you know. It was so weird.'

'What did he do then?'

We were both leaning forward, our bodies plumped in the grubby pink shag carpet that had always, since I knew her, covered Marie-José's bedroom floor.

'He turned on this monster torch. Huge, like a searchlight, and he shone it on our faces, and then when it landed on Thierry – I mean, he's never liked me, he thinks I'm badly brought up, but Thierry, he thinks of him as polite, you know, because Thierry always says "Good day, sir" in that brown-nose way. So he gets the torch on Thierry and he says "Come here" and Thierry steps forward. And then your grandfather steps back a bit, I guess, because the next thing is, he's shining the light on all of Thierry, you know? He's exposing him.'

'Geez. Jesus Christ.'

'So there's little Thierry, with his hands over his balls, twitching around and whimpering and completely humiliated.'

'Oh Jesus.'

'I felt for him, I really did. Even you would have, I swear. Your grandfather stood there, aiming this great beam of light on skinny Thierry, and he starts this interrogation. Like "Does your father know you're here?" and "Don't you have summer school homework and shouldn't you be doing it?" and "Is everyone here a resident, or are these little friends from town?" and "Do you have any idea what it's like to be trying to sleep or to read with this racket?" And Thierry tried to point out that we were next to the staff apartments, that the guests were hundreds of metres away and couldn't possibly have heard, but that just seemed to annoy your grandfather more.'

'And then?'

'In time he just turned off the light and left us to get dressed. I'm surprised we didn't all catch pneumonia, we were standing there naked for so long. In-sane. Thierry was pretty funny about it, considering. But I suspect Cécile lost interest, once she got a good look. I wonder whether it would've been you, if you'd been there?'

'Me?'

'With the flashlight. Whether your grandfather would've lit you up like a Christmas tree.'

'Naked? Don't be sick.'

We doubled over with laughter. Marie-José peeled the wax

29

off her leg with a scream and we found that, too, unreasonably funny.

'How was your night, anyway?'

II

I hadn't been at the poolside because Thibaud had, at last, asked me out. I say 'at last' because for the past three summers he had come with his parents to the hotel for a month, in their fat white Mercedes, from Paris. And for three summers I had eyed his black curls and his impish hazel eyes, had marvelled at the pattern of freckles on his brown back, had preened and tried to cast interested but veiled glances at him, my skills at twelve and thirteen fairly primitive, so that Thibaud could not help but know of my infatuation. But at twelve and thirteen I was still scrawny and flat-chested, and he, two years older, showed no interest.

A year older than me, Marie-José, whose breasts had burst forth by the time she was eleven, and who at that age had already reached her full, impressive height, she who learned early to flick the golden brown waves of her hair in an insouciant but enticing way, and who was to be caught, later that same year, with an eighteen-year-old army recruit in her little-girl's bedroom with its pink shag rug – Marie-José had been flicking and winking at Thibaud for a couple of years. Voice of experience to my thinner, unvoluptuous youth, she had assured me several times that 'the vibe wasn't there': 'I think he might be gay,' she'd said, pursing her lips in modest disapproval. 'Men have a way of looking, of appreciating, even if they aren't planning anything. I mean, your *father* looks like that at me.'

I had so long envied and feared her mysterious power that I usually accepted her judgments – the sexual ones, that is – without hesitation. But with Thibaud I kept faith secretly, and continued to tan my skin with the touch of his fingertips in mind, and to stuff my bra, which did not seem to fill out fast enough on its own, with carefully folded bulges of white tissue.

At last, that summer, he spoke to me as we climbed the cliff back from the beach one afternoon. I was not surprised, although it was so surprising. I had imagined the moment so many times that it seemed, on the hot gravel path, that I might have misheard. When, later in my own room, I played our brief exchange over in my head, I heard different nuances with each repeat, and felt tremors in my body that were half delight, half fear. He had asked if I wanted to go for a drink and I, feigning ease, had said simply, 'Sure, whatever.'

I didn't tell my mother. Even slight sins of omission, though, have a way of tripping you up, and it was upon hearing from my grandfather of the previous night's events, when she was expecting to have to punish me for partaking, that she discovered I hadn't been at the hotel, or at least hadn't been swimming with the others.

In fact, my evening with Thibaud had been disappointingly innocent. I don't know what I had anticipated, but I had felt my heart like a great snare drum beneath my lace-edged T-shirt. I wore my favourite one, the color of a rosy shell, showing off my slender arms to best advantage (it was not long since they had been skinny and without advantages at all). I wore my most presentable pair of Levis, their hems fashionably clipped at the ankle, and a thick black leather belt. I wore my sandals, my newest, all straps, and I carried over my shoulder a navy cardigan I had stolen from my mother. I hesitated a while over my hair, and ultimately chose to leave it loose, knowing that although it did not have Marie-José's Pre-Raphaelite wave it could nonetheless be played with nonchalantly, and that, windblown by the ride into town, it should seem, if clean, sultry rather than a rat's nest. I glossed my lips.

Thibaud, when we met by the hotel gates, said nothing about my appearance. He asked whether I had managed to get hold of Marie-José's moped for the evening, and when I said I had, asked me to drive it. He wasn't surly, just silent, and I couldn't tell whether he was nervous, or whether he regretted his invitation. He was a Paris boy, and wealthy; and this was only a summer seaside town, and I the hotelier's granddaughter, a gawky girl in jeans who idled year round in these beautiful but vacant surroundings. I was smart enough and afraid enough to recognize these facts, and the possibility that he had changed his mind.

But fourteen is not an age at which you ask outright for answers: not yet. Those in-between years are a haze of second-guessing and dialogues entirely of the mind. The possibility of human proximity seems greater than ever it will again, trailing still the unreflective clouds of childhood, the intimate, unsentenced dialogue of laughter or of games. Children do not have the words to ask and so do not imagine asking; not asking and not imagining, they eradicate distance: they take for granted that everything, someday, will be understood.

Adolescence, then, is a curious station on the route from ignorant communion to our ultimate isolation, the place where words and silences reveal themselves to be meaningful and yet where, too young to acknowledge that we cannot gauge their meaning, we imagine it for ourselves and behave as if we understood. Only with the passage of years, wearied, do we resort to asking. With the inadequacy of asking and the inadequacy of replies comes the realization that what we thought we understood bears no relation to what exists, the way, seeing the film of a book we have read, we are aghast to find the heroine a strapping blonde when we had pictured her all these years a small brunette; and her house, which we envisaged so clearly and quaintly on the edge of a purple moor, is a vast, unfamiliar pile of rubble with all its rooms out of order.

As I drove the moped down the corniche towards town, Thibaud with his hand on my waist, so tentative, and me without a licence to drive – as we took speed on the hill all possible interpretations of his reticence, from adoration to nervousness to distaste, visited me, bright as fireworks, each in its moment seeming wholly and uniquely true. But by the time we reached the café on the sea wall, I had run the full gamut and begun again with no certainty, while he had done no more than tighten his grip around me on the sharp turns in the road and try to keep the flailing strands of my hair out of his mouth.

The café, on the boardwalk directly above the beach, was popular with people from my school. Festively lit with multi-coloured lanterns and hung with bits of boats and plaster fish, it was more like a stage set than a café, and attracted a younger clientele. Thibaud and I took a table on the terrace, in un-comfortable white plastic armchairs still gritted with the sand of day visitors in their bathing suits. He ordered beer and I a Coke, and we talked, desultorily, almost dully, about the hotel and its guests and our friends. Only at the moment when, reaching for the ashtray, his finger brushed the back of my hand did I feel a current snake the length of my body and erupt into tingling, and with it that moment swelled beyond all natural proportion.

We had not been there long when four people that I knew – a year ahead of me at the lycée – wandered in and, after kisses and introductions, joined us. For an hour or more we exchanged the gossip of the summer: who had failed their exams and was incarcerated at home, the long summer afternoons, with their books; who had been injured on a motorcycle while on holiday in Corsica; who, we all suspected, had started running with the druggie crowd and was more often than not red-eyed and dazed; and what would happen to them all when September came (as if September were the end of real life, or its beginning; with the summertime one was never really sure); and which teachers I might have that these guys had suffered under, and of the worst one, a Monsieur Ponty, whose red-tipped nose signalled disaster and who felt himself free to rap the knuckles of the unprepared with his metal ruler.

Thibaud sat through these exchanges all but mute, his gener-ally mobile face fixed in a distracted half-smile. Finally, when he had drained his second beer, he leaned across and murmured a suggestion that we walk a while along the beach. We abandoned my schoolmates and the gaudy glimmer of the lanterns for the dark whisper of the shore. The beach chairs hovered in the gloom, their white canvas backs like the sails of tiny ships. Occasionally we passed other couples or groups walking, the fireflies of their burning cigarettes heralding their approach. We passed a huddle of gypsies plucking guitars around their fire in the rocks at the end of the bay, and one of them called out to offer us a drink, or a smoke.

We did not touch as we walked, a failure that seemed purposeful: I felt my restraint because I knew the lightest brush would result, inside me, in a report as forceful as a gunshot, and I would lose the thread of the conversation that, finally, we seemed to be having. These sensations were new in being real rather than imagined (although they fluttered still only in my mind): I was actually there, walking along the soughing sand with this tall and serious boy, the two of us like other couples. My brother, Etienne Parfait, would never amble on a beach at night with the moon floating in the water and the rank salt in his nostrils, wondering in every fibre, and anticipating a touch on the skin so strongly felt without its having happened that it took on the quality of a waking dream.

When Thibaud and I arrived back at the hotel, it was not late, but neither of us suggested that we seek out the others. We dawdled in the concrete cavern of the parking lot, beneath the flickering bleach of the fluorescent light, serenaded by the trickle of a forgotten garden hose and the occasional scurry of a lizard along the wall. I fiddled with my hair (which I knew by now to be a rat's nest) and he, hands in pockets, toed the ground. Eventually I said I had to go, although I didn't, particularly. He walked me out, along the alley of palms to the hotel gates; and stood there, shadowed by the street lamp, as I turned onto the road and started off in the direction of home.

12

For this catalogue of unspoken and ungrasped opportunities, my mother expressed grave disappointment in me. It was a disappointment – as much about the failure of our friendship, hers and mine, an alliance that we both had long lived by, as it was about my breaking any rules – whose depths I could glimpse in her decision not only not to tell my father, but not even to threaten to do so.

'All you had to do was ask,' she insisted, tight-lipped, as we set the dinner table the following evening, when I had heard the story of the pool from Marie-José, and my mother had heard it from my grandmother. 'How did you get into town? And who is this boy?'

'It's nothing. He's just a friend. I don't want to talk about it.'

'I don't know which is worse, you raising havoc with those kids up at the hotel, or sneaking off with . . . how old is he, anyway?'

'My age. Maman, it's no big deal. We met some friends for coffee in a café on the corniche, and that's all. I would've thought—'

My mother glared at me, her hooded eyes, which I had inherited, spitting light. She waved a knife in her left hand, feeling its weight. 'What would you have thought, exactly? Honestly, Sagesse, I've had just about enough. You can't imagine what . . . this is the last thing your father needs, to worry about you. The last thing I need. These days – I don't know. I don't know what to do.'

The slip from rage to misery was instantaneous, a familiar melodrama. The knife sagged, suddenly so heavy in her hand that she dropped it, with a piteous (and self-pitying) clunk, upon the table. And as the script of years demanded, I was beside her in a second, my arms around her, knowing that although I could not see her face, her chin had puckered, waffle-like, and her eyes were milky with tears. When I hugged my mother, I was always aware of how small she was, how close her bones were to the surface, her shoulder blades like spiny wings, quivering, prepared for flight.

'Don't cry,' I soothed, stroking her perfect hair, smelling her perfume and beneath it the faint, delicate odour that was her. 'Don't cry. It isn't anything. It was nothing. There's nothing to be upset about.' I drew back and watched her features struggle into a hesitant, damp grimace, the approximation of a smile.

'I'm fine,' she said, as much to herself as to me. She dabbed her eyes with her cuffs and resumed the business of arranging cutlery.

'I think it would be better,' she began again after a moment, 'if you didn't go out in the evenings for a while. You're hardly ever here. How much time have you spent, this summer, with your brother? And your father and I — well, your father's very busy, I know, but still, he'd like to feel he knew what his own daughter looked liked. At your age I was—'

'You were working in the summertime. I know. You had a summer job. But that was in America, Maman. Things are different here. It's a different century, practically.'

'Sometimes I think you ought to be sent to summer camp, if your father won't have you going out to work.'

I snorted. 'Nobody goes to camp, Maman.' I meant, only poor kids did, and not anyone from our town: who would leave, when in front of us stretched the enticements of the open sea, when we were already in the place where the entire nation sought to come on holiday? 'And nobody I know works. Nobody.'

'You lack discipline. All of you.'

'Papa says there's time enough for that later, that now is for learning.'

My mother shrugged. 'And everything, as we know, is always your father's way. We live your father's life, after all.'

'Speak for yourself.'

'Believe me, you do too. You just don't know it.'

Eventually my mother came back to what it was she wanted: I was to be grounded for a week. She did not have the force to command me, so her promise was wheedlingly drawn, a pact between friends, born of guilt. But I agreed.

At that moment, it did not occur to me that I was lying. I didn't mean to lie. Although if I had seriously considered the prospect of seven long evenings pacing the marble floors or riding up and down in Etienne's elevator; if I had taken the time to picture myself squashed into the dark, airless hours my parents inhabited after supper, I would have known that I couldn't do it, not for all the love I could muster for my mother. For Etienne, perhaps; but evenings were not Etienne's domain. Almost immediately after dinner he was whirred along the hall and up to bed, because somebody believed his mute, spastic body required more sleep than the rest of ours; or because the night was the only time my mother had to close her eyes to her burden; or because my father, aside from an awkward, sticky embrace and a sequence of horrified glances over the table, could not really bear the sight of his son.

Certainly I would not have done it for my father, for the fleshy, ingratiating, explosive man who wandered in and out of our days. When he was adoring, his hairy, perfumed arms would reach out to clutch me to him, his sentimental eyes would shimmer with emotion – and I was appalled. Littler, I had charged across rooms and lawns to seek out his broad lap and nuzzle against his chest. But somewhere I had noticed that his love was offered only in the wake of rages, or in compensation for a hideous absence, and it grew sour to me. Much later, I would regret my bitterness, my inability to bend to the generous swoop of his bulk and his tender blandishments – 'Ma belle', 'mon petit ange', 'mon trésor' – to concede to the only love he knew how to give. But by then it was too late. And at fourteen, short of a command, and possibly not even then, no word from my father and no love for him could have made me relinquish the pleasures of my friends. In any event, he didn't ask: he was hardly home that summer; and it was solely a contract between my mother and me.

13

I had promised, and I tried. She didn't ask me to give up my daytime routines, after all. They continued to blend into one another, bathed in sunlight and the cicada-song, scented with suntan oil and the dry, hot smell of the pines, interrupted only by the quiet hour of luncheon, which I generally took at my grandmother's table. Mindful for the first time of my figure, I picked miserably at lasagne, or at great slabs of steak, served by Zohra, my grandparents' aged Arab servant, whose wrinkles were marked out, forehead and chin, by blue tattoos.

Zohra's hands were gnarled and stubbed with work, and when I remember my grandmother's lunches, what I recall most clearly, aside from the half-lowered blinds which the unremitting glare of sun and sea strove to penetrate, and aside from the powerful, wet clacking of my grandfather's mastication, are Zohra's dark, trembling fingers clasped around my grandmother's porcelain serving dishes, looking edible themselves, warty little sausages on the edge of a mound of beans, or poking towards the mashed potatoes, or glistening at the tips where they had slipped, for an instant, into the platter's pool of *jus*. Zohra was always good to me, obsequious and secretive: since my earliest childhood, she had pressed gifts of chocolate or jellied fruits into my greedy palms, baring her wrecked teeth with delight and murmuring, 'Poor little one, this is for you' – a poverty she located not in my person but in the sad condition of my brother and in the austerity of my grandparents.

My grandmother was a formidable and beaky woman, whose aquiline visage, in its austere definition, distracted from the soft spread of her girth. Although she had peppered my childhood with her versions of our family's history, which I thrilled to hear, she was not the sort of grandmother who crowed over my every endeavour, whose bosom offered welcome refuge. Rather, she expressed concern through criticism: 'Sit up straight,' 'Don't chew with your mouth open,' 'Don't run in the corridors.' She believed that meals should be sedate times, given to the full enjoyment of our food and to the sound of her husband's voice.

When he was there, and in good humour, my grandfather told jokes or stories, spilled over with anecdotes from his work, or from their long, exceedingly long, lives; or else he prised the details out of my days like an expert fisher for pearls. When he was angry, the table quivered with his rage, whether audible or present only in his violent thrusts at the china and silverware. When he was not there – and in that gloomy week of my grounding, the week before the shooting, he was not there once, too busy in his madness to leave his desk, or if he did, then only to roam the hotel grounds and spy on his employees – then my grandmother and I would sit in near-silence, serenaded by Zohra's humming and cleaning in the kitchen. I would watch my grandmother eat, the way she brought her fork precisely to her mouth and pulled her lips back over her teeth in a snarl so as to protect her lipstick, the sinewy grappling of mouth and food beneath her cheeks, and the bald, froglike swallow at the end. She always paused between bites, and her eyes, then, would focus and glitter as she inspected her plate, or mine, or the line of sunlight on the carpet. When it was just the two of us, I hated those lunches, struggled through them only by peering, as often as discretion allowed, at the turquoise swathe of the pool beneath the balcony and counting the minutes until my friends began to trickle into view.

'Grand'-mère,' I would ask, often my first word of the hour, 'may I please be excused?'

She would nod, slowly, as if considering my request; and then, sometimes, smile. 'Go. Have fun, my dear. But remember, no swimming for an hour. Digestion. Remember.'

And as I gathered my towel and prepared to run, she cautiously, gracefully, folded her napkin and began preparations for her siesta.

Daily there followed, in that apartment, a trough of silence as deep as death. Zohra slunk away and left the shuttered rooms to the breathy seesaw of my grandmother's snores. On weekends, my grandfather would lie beside her with a magazine until he too succumbed, the two of them beneath the rosary-draped crucifix on the wall like curled offerings, Christ's ever merciful eye upon their wrinkled bodies. It was fearsome, as a child, to discover that the world could be so still during daylight: I had had to endure it, when I was smaller and my mother left me in their care for the day; or in the winter holidays, even at fourteen

– but at least in winter the wind cavorted angrily around the window frames and the raindrops spat against the glass, disrupting the unending rhythms of their sleep.

14

That summer, though, that week, the luncheon hour alone was sufficient penance: I was paroled before siesta, a criminal loosed onto the back pathways to the beach or snoozing – somehow a livelier sleep, with the breeze at our skin – on the bridge over the pool. Everyone knew that I had lost my night privileges, and they knew why. My date with Thibaud, which otherwise might have been a source of gossip and speculation only behind his back and mine, became everybody's favorite joke. Not even Marie-Jo would defend me. Thierry was the most insistent: 'Locked up for your lover boy, eh? Like Rapunzel in her tower. Thibaud, you'll have to go rescue the damsel in distress. Better hope the grandfather isn't standing guard.'

'Too much necking and you'll get your head chopped off!' was another of Thierry's cracks. Marie-Jo knew there hadn't been any necking at all, but she kept her own counsel, smirked. Later she said, 'Come off it, Sagesse, it's good for your reputation. Do you want people to think you're a frigid prude?' She laughed, not kindly. 'It's doing him a favour too. My God, what is he? He didn't even try? Not even a kiss? I told you, he's queer, that one. You'll see.'

She licked her forefinger and used it to smooth the arcs of her eyebrows. We were in her bedroom, she at her child's vanity table, gazing into the mirror, I on the edge of her bed, raking the carpet with my toes. She was ostensibly changing to play tennis, but sat for ages in her bikini, a woman on a little girl's stool, making faces at her reflection.

'Not a bad hoax, though. Marry a gay guy with rich parents, and then have your pick of lovers, rich or poor, all of them gorgeous and madly in love with you. And then you could blackmail him: "Darling, I want a fur coat. Or I'll tell your poor *maman* about Félix, or Jean, or Paul, or whoever" – "Darling, a diamond necklace" – fantastic!'

'He's not gay. Only you would think of such a thing.'

'Because I am a woman of the world,' said Marie-Jo, exchanging her bikini top for a lacy bra, baring her pointed brown breasts at me as proof of her assertion. 'There would be a sex problem though. I mean, for the son his parents would want you to bear him. It might be impossible, if he couldn't even—'

'Stop it.' I stood up and strode to the door. Marie-Jo was spinning out her jest as she rummaged in her drawer for her tennis skirt.

'Poor sweetie,' she cried, rushing clumsily across to hug me with one foot in a white sneaker and the other bare, her long body brown in its white underwear. 'You really like him.'

'It's not that. Of course I like him. You know I do. But also, I just . . .' I trailed off.

'Forget it. C'mon, I'm late. My racket's under the bed – grab it for me?'

The fact was, Thibaud had retreated. He didn't even seem to look at me any more, let alone try to swim near me or walk with me. And as I had no part in the night gatherings, and only Marie-José's reports of them to go on, I had no idea what Thibaud was thinking. More tormenting than my dreary lunches, or than my mother's heavy sighs at night over her English novels, was my mind's picture of everyone assembled on the steps under the oldest plane tree; and the accompanying soundtrack, the conversations that in my absence might – would, I was sure of it – stray to cover me, the questions Thierry or Renaud would ask of Thibaud: 'Can she kiss? Too much tongue or too little? Her tits aren't much, are they?' Over the years – over that very summer – I had played along in the grilling of other girls, or boys even; I knew I wasn't fanciful.

I hid one night, two, three, four, in my parents' leathered library, prone on the slippery black Danish sofa in the aquatic television light, watching old American cop shows and black-

and-white westerns dubbed clumsily into French. Ordinarily I spent such times lip-reading, trying to pick out the American dialogue beneath the sonorous French voices, gloating that it was my secret language, these words of two hundred and fifty million people but all of them far away. Discerning a sentence was a triumph, proof that someday I would escape my sultry palm-treed prison for a real life, with my American self (who existed thus far only in the privacy of my bathroom mirror), in English. But on those nights – one, two, three, four – I barely saw the screen, and certainly not the lips of the Americans upon it. I stared for hours and saw nothing but myself, walking along the town beach at Thibaud's shoulder, or sitting, our hands just touching, in the café by the shore. Like a sorceress with a crystal ball, I saw, too, the screeching, gesticulating crowd by the pool, in their cloud of cigarette smoke, and I heard them making fun of me.

On the fifth day I decided to take matters into my own hands. I didn't think of it as going against my mother's wishes, or betraying her trust. I knew that my parents, together, were going out for dinner that night, invited to the home of an aspiring politician on the other side of town. My mother was suffering, even at breakfast, from one of her nervous complaints.

'His wife is a terribly cold woman,' she confided. 'She preens like a peacock. Her hair is the most unnatural shade of purple – eggplant, you know? One of these women who ought to be shrivelling up from all those years in the sun, but somehow manages not to. God, if I tanned like she does, I'd look like a prune! But it's some French gene.'

'An evil one, of course, like all French genes.'

'Don't, Sagesse, I don't need it.'

Knowing that they would be out, that they would never know, certain that with each passing day I was further forfeiting any possibility of romance with Thibaud, I seized my chance. That day at my grandmother's table, I didn't wait to see the troupe assembling beneath me at the water's edge. No sooner had Zohra brought in the two leaky rum babas that were our dessert (it was a stroke of luck: I was known to loathe them) than I scraped back my chair and slipped my napkin into its ring.

'Already?' asked my grandmother, blinking at my request.

'We thought we might go down to the town beach,' I lied. 'And rent *pédalos*. If you don't get there early, they're all gone.'

'If you'd mentioned it before, I would have moved lunch forward. But all right. Be careful. How will you get there?'

'On the bus. Don't worry.' I was already standing. I knew that if she saw us at the pool upon waking from her nap, I would have only to say that the tourists had beaten us to it, and rather than wait our turn, we had come back.

'Don't swim, dear. Not for an hour.'

'Of course not.'

As I left she was spooning the oily sponge of her baba rather sorrowfully to her mouth.

I ran, the shortest way, through the shrubbery to the back path, to the hotel. It was a risk, loitering in the lobby – that my grandfather or even my father might pass through, that Cécile or Laure might come up before Thibaud did. I could see him, through the glass doors of the restaurant patio, at a large table, under an umbrella, with his parents. His mother was wearing a yellow straw hat with a vast brim and square sunglasses, and his father's thick back was towards me, bent over the end of their meal. Thibaud I saw in profile. He sat, expressionless and silent, turning from one parent to the other as they spoke, like the umpire in a tennis match, occasionally brushing his hair back from his face with an irritated hand. He kicked his sneakers idly against the legs of his chair. His mother asked him something, a fine trail of cigarette smoke wafting from each nostril just before she spoke, her cigarette clamped between lacquered vermilion claws. Underneath her hat, I knew she had eggplant-coloured hair, immovable and shiny: she was the type of woman my mother feared.

Thibaud shook his head in response to her question, and stood to leave. At the far end of the terrace, I saw Cécile and Laure winding among the tables, and I cursed my luck; but they turned into the restaurant. He came on alone, into the cool marble from the glare outside. He did not know he was being watched, but still his face gave nothing away. He was about to cross to the elevators when I called out.

'You don't often come in here,' he said.

'Too risky. Might run into my father and grandfather.'

'So what's up today?'

I had not prepared a lie. 'I never had a chance to thank you for the other evening. With all the fuss about the swimming . . .'

'No. And the fuss about me. Sorry about that.' He seemed almost to be laughing, so I did.

'Parents, y'know. They're all the same.'

'Mine don't care what I do.'

'You're a boy. And you're older. A bit.'

'I suppose.'

He fingered his room key, clacking the metal against the translucent plastic square with the number on it and HOTEL BELLEVUE in gilded capitals.

'You headed to the pool?'

'Of course. What else is there to do? I just . . . I wondered if you wanted to meet up tonight.'

'Tonight? But you're under lock and key, aren't you?'

I shrugged, in conscious imitation of Marie-José's nonchalant shrugs. I was fiddling with the ends of my hair, flicking a swatch around my forefinger. 'So?'

Thibaud emitted a strange blowing noise, like an attempt at a chuckle. This, I could tell, was not how he expected me to behave. 'What did you want to do?'

'It's difficult for me to go into town. I might run into somebody, it might get back to my folks . . . I thought we could meet here, maybe go for a walk. I don't know.'

'Why not? I'm not sure I can stand another evening with Thierry, anyhow.'

'Isn't he a jerk? You almost feel sorry for him.'

'Maybe you do.'

We fixed a time, and a place — by the round bench, where the little children played; none of our group would ever wander over there – and then I left him, a shadow slipping between the mirrored jaws of the elevator. I managed to duck out of the lobby just as Cécile and Laure were coming down the stairs from the first floor.

15

As my parents prepared for their outing, I danced attendance with rare goodwill. I zipped my mother's dress and cooed over her new shoes. I fixed a scotch and soda (the chink-tink of the ice cubes, the viscous liquor, the sizzling froth on top) for my father, and balanced it next to his toothbrush while he shaved. I propped myself on the edge of the tub and watched him, as I had done as a very small child, teetering in the steamy air. My eyes monitored the flesh at my father's nape, rolling and unrolling, damp curls appearing and disappearing, as he angled his chin for the razor. I was eager, and my eagerness felt wholly pure: for an hour, I was their golden girl. I asked about the dinner, and who would be there. I made jokes about the adults that I knew: the man with the funny shoes; the lech whose wandering hands, like heat-seeking missiles, found women's breasts when he moved in to kiss their cheeks. I imitated the owl-faced mining heiress who, slightly hard of hearing, parroted whatever was said to her to be sure she'd understood. I could sense my parents' surprise, and their pleasure. It seemed to me a sort of blessing, because I couldn't entirely believe that they didn't know of my plan, and in being so loving, forgive me for it.

At the door, my father stroked my cheek (a tenderness for which, in that moment, I loved him) and my mother hugged me with particular force. 'Be good,' she said. 'Have fun,' said I.

By the time I was myself ready to leave, Etienne was long asleep – I checked – and Magda had retreated to her apartment, from which emanated the anguished, overbright blare of some variety special. I stood in the kitchen for a while and listened to its rhythms. It would have been so easy not to go: the plunge into the seeping night seemed an enormous effort, a question mark.

Thibaud made me wait. Even as I cowered in the shadow of a dwarf palm opposite the designated bench, wondering whether to go home, he sidled up, all darkness.

'You came.' I smiled in spite of myself.

'Of course.'

'What do you want to do?'

'To do?'

'Well, we could hang out here, or walk down to the beach, or – I'd better not go into the hotel because—'

'As if,' he said. 'Let's walk.'

He took my hand in his. It squirmed there, dry, for a second, then lay still, eliciting in me riotous palpitations. I could not speak. He did not speak. He led me, or we led each other (everything between us seemed suddenly to be understood) by the most circuitous route possible to the *chemins de la plage*, to their starting point beneath the swimming pool, where, in the pool's foundations, a porthole like a Cyclops' eye gave vista to the wavering, illuminated water. Perhaps fifty feet above us, the others sprawled and chattered; phrases and whole sentences drifted down – Marie-Jo's laugh, Thierry's voice, breaking occasionally in its insistent chirrup.

From a bench cut into the rock we could map the coast and the sea ahead – the same view as above, interrupted at this lower level by the spikes and billows of the trees. The porthole, at our backs, watched with us.

'We can eavesdrop,' Thibaud said, gently scraping my palm with his fingertips. 'Let's sit a while. See if they wonder where I am. See if they guess.' We giggled, titillated at the possibility of discovery, at our spying communion. The voices, the whooshing rise and fall of the sea, my blood, the noiseless fingerings between us: as ever, I listened.

It was not long before he leaned into me and murmured 'May I?' and kissed my neck. Then it was no longer a matter of the time, or of the others, or of my parents: too immediate and consuming for any of them, his tongue strayed into my ear and onto my eyelids and into my mouth (like a cat, I thought, cleaning her young). It was an intimacy novel and exciting to me; I was at once in the moment and apart from it, able to register the sensation of his saliva cooling and drying on my cheek, the slight roughness of his chin, the surprising coarseness of his curls to the touch, his lemony smell, anxious even as I matched his embraces with my own fervour that my kissing was too zealous, too passive, or too spitty.

By the time we heard the others tramping to the poolside overhead, we were lying flat on the bench, me beneath him, my T-shirt rucked up the better to admit his nimble fingers, and a smattering of sharp gravel against my back. Our friends' proximity alarmed me, and I tried to sit up; but Thibaud dismissed my attempt, silencing me first with his hand over my mouth and then with his lips on mine. Our adolescent fumblings fumbled onwards, but for me the sounds beyond our bodies now intruded. We could hear their shuffling feet, and the slap of their discarded clothing on the railing overhead. We could hear their whispers (might they not then hear ours?), then the cascade of splashes as they dived, with the expert timing of showgirls, one after the other. A few droplets splattered through the poolside slats and showered down on us.

Thibaud would not be deterred. Fearing that one of them might slither underwater to the porthole to catch the view (another game of which we never tired), and might instead glimpse our entwined bodies, I advocated a remove, wanted us to tiptoe further seawards and plant ourselves invisibly in the undergrowth. But Thibaud, preoccupied with the buttons of my fly, would have none of it.

'They'll hear us if we move,' he hissed. And then again, more gently, his hand sliding from my navel, 'May I?'

'I don't know.'

'Don't know what?'

'If you may.'

'Have you never—'

'It's not that,' I said, although it was, at least in part.

47

'Have you let other guys?'

'Well, I—' There was, I felt, a right answer to this query, something between prude and slut, between 'no' and 'yes'. Honesty didn't enter into it. 'That's for me to know and you to find out,' I said.

'So may I? Go on.'

'Sh.' The others were clambering from the water, raining their drippings unpleasantly upon us, laughing aloud and jeering at Laure, whose clothes Thierry, in a gesture of love (poor Cécile) had thrown into the deep end. Wily Thibaud chose to take my silence as acquiescence: he slipped his hand uninvited into my underpants, and began, inexpertly, to mash his fingers in the folds of my sex, a manoeuvre he compounded by stopping my mouth with his ardent tongue.

'That's nice, isn't it?' he muttered in my ear as his finger crept, snail-like, inside me. 'You're not sorry?'

His hip bone crushed my thigh. His fingers were cold in so warm a place, and his manipulations felt exploratory, even clinical; or perhaps it was merely the unlikeliness of this boy's hand in this position – of me, of us, in this position. It wasn't unpleasant, nor was it particularly arousing. 'So this,' I thought, 'is what it's like.' Afraid, above all, of disclosure, I didn't utter a sound.

Our first awakening was the report of the gun. It burst, a massive cracking sound. We later learned that the bullet had struck the wooden railing just above us.

The initial explosion bloomed into wild screams and symphonic wailing. I heard my grandmother shrieking, 'My God, my God, Jacques!' and Cécile's voice, recognizable only by its pitch, a keening chant overlaying the others' yelps. 'Fuck, oh fuck, oh fuck.' I didn't hear my grandfather at all. His rage was concentrated entirely in the rifle blast; it had no other voice.

Thibaud was off me, and I was struggling with my jeans, still tingling and engorged. 'Jesus,' he said, and though nobody was listening for us, I waved him to be quiet. 'What happened?'

To my later shame, I didn't go to my friends. I couldn't.

Doomed on all sides: by my parents, if discovered; among my peers, an assassin by association. Thibaud ran off, but not before he promised not to betray me. Incredibly, the black sea glittered ahead, its rising and falling unabated, and I lurked by the porthole, listening.

'He's crazy. Completely crazy.'

'He'll pay for this.'

'You bet he will.'

'Christ, Cécile, you okay?'

'I'm hit – on the arm' – Thierry, in tears – 'I'm bleeding.'

'Look at Cécile's back, for Chrissakes!'

'Are you joking? Can you see anything?'

'Somebody get an ambulance! Call the police!'

'Can you walk? She can walk, I think.'

'Just about.'

'Call the fucking cops. Murderer. I'll get my mom.'

'Where'd he go?'

'Where can he go? They'll get him. We all saw him. Jesus fuck.'

'He's insane. He'll go to jail for this.'

'I'm bleeding.'

'It's a scratch, Thierry. Cécile, can you walk? Where are her clothes? Where are my clothes? We can't take her naked.'

'We shouldn't take her anywhere. Wait for the ambulance.'

'Don't be ridiculous. This is crazy. I can't believe this is happening.'

'Should we wash her off?'

'In the pool? Don't be sick. Cécile, Cécile sweetie, talk to me. Can you walk as far as the driveway, for the ambulance?'

'Who's going to tell her parents?'

'Fuck, her parents. Where are they?'

'In the hotel, you nit. Stop blubbering.'

'I think I'd better go to hospital too.'

'Whatever – look, I can't believe this. My God.'

And then the sound of Marie-Jo's mother, out of breath, almost hysterical, and close behind other voices, men's and women's, huge torches jerking and swinging and a dawning like daybreak overhead as they inspected Cécile's blood-dripped back under the glare.

'There's no bullet hole. The bullet's not in her,' said a man, someone's father. 'For God's sake, get her parents.'

I crept away, skirting the paths, ducking in the undergrowth at the sound of footsteps, hidden behind an oleander bush by the gate as the ambulance careened past, all blue lights and honking. Once on the road, I ran. I sped the half-mile as though invisible, as though I or it weren't there at all, as though I were guilty, with Thibaud's spit tasting now like blood in my mouth, and a voice pounding in my head with every footfall, 'It didn't happen. It didn't happen. This never happened. It didn't happen.'

And in the door, and up the stairs, and first I crawled under my bed and cried, and then I stood up and took off my clothes and went into my bathroom and brushed my teeth furiously without running the water (it didn't happen, it didn't happen), and I put on my nightgown and lay in bed staring out at the sinking moon, willing it all away, pretending I was asleep. But the lemony smell of Thibaud's skin was on my skin; and when my mother woke me the next morning (softly, softly, things were that bad), I knew it was all true.

Two

I

The Hotel Bellevue was my grandfather's house built on rock. It hadn't always been there, hadn't been handed to him, in its ice-cream-coloured glory, with its sculpted pathways and meticulous flora, all eyes to the sea in front of it. He had chosen the land in the late 1950s, already a man fully grown and fighting failure. It was scrubby terrain then, a naked clifftop on an unfashionable part of the coastline, with only a military barracks and a fort nearby, and a few isolated villas buried behind cypress trees further along the road.

He, too, was nothing, or so he later maintained, a man in the first flush of middle age whose early promise had been distracted and sapped – by his mother, by the war, then by his wife and children. When he stood on the clifftop and imagined his hotel there, he was turning the page on a thousand disappointments and turning his back on the country he loved. (This is only a manner of speaking, of course, because he set himself and his future to face his past: from his hotel, had his vision been God-like, he would have been able to peer over the rolling Mediterranean and, when his eye again found land, it would have been on the shores he had so recently left behind, where his son (my father) and daughter and wife and cousins remained. It would have been – would still be, if any of us could see so far – on Algeria.)

My grandfather's father was a baker, his mother a teacher, both of them born on the far-flung soil of what was then only newly France. My grandfather was born there, too, in 1917, the youngest of four children, although for many years I was told they were only three. Raised in Blida – a town I long imagined as dusty and forsaken, though it is in fact famously lush – he grew up largely fatherless, his square-jawed papa having fallen into his flour, struck down by a heart attack, when little Jacques was only nine. My grandmother came into the world not far from there but a society apart, the daughter of a moderately comfortable civil servant and his delicate French wife living in the city of Algiers. And my father: by the time he drew breath, as the Second World War laboured to its close (even, indeed, as mainland France regained its freedom), he had Africa in his blood, from both sides. The earth on which he planted his feet for the first time was France and yet not France; and he grew up believing it would always be home.

My grandfather lost that faith, not so early, but earlier than many. He never spoke of why, of how doubt crept into his frame and spread until it became certainty of a different fate; but history speaks for him. In the spring of 1958, he crossed to Marseilles to scout for a patch of land, taking leave from his position as the deputy manager of the St. Joseph Hotel, on another clifftop overlooking the Bay of Algiers; and he did so in the immediate wake of the tribulation that has since been titled the Battle of that city. He didn't tell his family of his plan, but assumed that in time they would understand, if only because they had seen the violence, because the daughter of one of their friends – the friend a stout matron with a spun-sugar coiffure, with whom my grandmother regularly played bridge – had lost her slender legs when the Casino bomb went off (the very bomb that disembowelled the unfortunate and misnamed band-leader, Lucky Starway), and was still, months later, propped in a hospital ward, trying to reimagine her future in the metal embrace of wheelchair.

The transaction, entirely a matter of borrowed funds, with a wealthy university comrade of my grandfather's as a silent partner, took some time; and the construction of the edifice – stylish, by the day's standards, an early forebear of those modern, terraced structures which have usurped the waterfront from Monte Carlo to Marseilles – took a good while longer, three years during which my grandfather shuttled back and forth between the colony and the *métropole*. By 1961, he had bowed out of his job at the languishing bastion of Algerian *hôtellerie*. The St. Joseph's employees were all, ostensibly, Swiss-trained; but this was and had always been a lie, and by that late date in the French colony's brief history, no promise of Swiss service was sufficient to lure tourists to those unsettled shores. The world's journalists swarmed the panicked city, but they searched out more modest accommodations, indifferent to the quantity of starch in their linens. Only a clutch of mysterious Americans, Mormon-like in attire and sobriety, clacked along the hotel's hushed corridors, and conducted their business in hushed tones. He, my grandmother and my Tante Marie installed themselves in the staff block in the specially designed penthouse – the very same – from which they oversaw the finishing touches on my grandfather's great plan.

Alexandre, my father, did not at once join his parents. For the very reason that his father decreed it, he refused, even then, to accept that he might have to. This was not the beginning of his rebellion: that had begun much earlier, and even through my child's eyes I could detect its vestiges in the continuing subterranean struggles between father and son. My grandfather, from the beginning, did not want my father, his firstborn, impediment to freedom and the shimmering success that Jacques, still so young, the war just ending, dreamed of. And if later he changed his mind and claimed his heir and tried to clasp him to his breast (a matter purely of speculation on my part – in our family, who would ever discuss such things?), by then it was too late. With regard to his parents, my father's heart, like that of the little boy in Hans Christian Andersen, had turned to ice.

My father, famously *beau garçon* at sixteen, with the pick of the young Algéroises fluttering their lashes at him and cramming furiously for his exams besides, refused the interruption – no, the cessation – of his life. He kissed his mother and his younger sister (whom he called, with the cruelty of adolescence, '*La Bête*') and sternly shook his father's hand; then turned on his heel and went home to his maternal grandmother (her dainty

Frenchness now long wizened, she had become, like a Catholic convert, more African than her offspring, and would prove more difficult to uproot than the statue of the black virgin at Notre-Dame d'Afrique), in whose benevolent care he remained till the end, and her end, which came more or less at the same time.

On new soil, a new man, Jacques LaBasse, my grandfather, wanted to accomplish in five years what others took ten to achieve. With unforeseen adversity on his side, he determined that the second half of his life would redeem the humble first. His wish, his vocation, was to build the three-star Hotel Bellevue not into a man's work, but into that of a dynasty; to have people – all people: the locals, the tourists, even those who never ventured to the Mediterranean shore – believe that it had always been and always would be there, a haven of order and quiet for France's *bonne bourgeoisie*. And up to a point, he succeeded.

By that summer of my fourteenth year, the hotel had followed the round of seasons more than twenty-five times, its fifty-three rooms filling and emptying with the regularity of the tides, each change in nature's dress bringing a different clientele: the British and the elderly in the off-season, when the mimosa bloomed or the autumn winds blustered; elegant Parisians and their boisterous children in the heat of summer; a few eccentrics, often alone, and the widows, in the winter months. Each July brought familiar families back for a week or a fortnight or a month at a time, depending on the depth of their coffers. Many of the children I played with in the summertime it seemed that I had always known, although, amoeba-like, the group stretched and shrank and altered. One or two had been coming to the Bellevue for so long that they had learned to swim in that very pool, had first been stung by sea urchins off the rocky beach below, and knew the secret hiding places in the grounds as well as I did. They had been there when the extra parking lot behind the tennis courts – paved over five years at least – was a grassy playground adorned with swing set and slides, and when the potato-faced *patronne* of the paper store down the road still dispensed sweets with one hand while clutching her three-legged, crazy-eyed chihuahua, Milou, in the other. It had been more than three years since a yellow *deux chevaux* had done away with the dog, which seemed, at the time, like for ever.

2

My grandfather's motives, in most things, were unclear to the family. He had always been deemed, by those who loved him, a difficult man and brilliant therefore, a man with a temper, a man gnawed upon by undisclosed demons. (Not that the ways of the family allowed for disclosure: his mystery was his power, and they were all too keen to grant it him.) Family stories spun him into life, stories that my grandmother told with reverent indulgence, or that my mother repeated with a sneer. (My father never spoke about his parent, except in the present. As in: 'Papa needs me to work late,' or 'Papa hasn't been sleeping well.' I sometimes wondered if he even knew the stories, or whether he had made it his business not to.) From these anecdotes I, the grandchild, was to cull the essence of the man, who was so resolutely divorced from them in his own person. What was strange to me then was that two women could tell the same tale and draw such vastly differing conclusions.

That same summer, only a month or so before the shooting, my grandmother had imparted one such story – a new one, that at fourteen, I was only just old enough to hear. When I recounted it again, to my mother, she finished it quite differently, and less kindly, and I now turned both versions over in my mind, as if they might provide some explanation of the sunken, unshaven old man who presented himself, docile, at the police station the morning after the shooting.

That noon my grandmother had filled our lunch, just hers and mine, with my grandfather's past, while he himself dined at the hotel restaurant with pot-bellied business associates, sucking garlic-stuffed olives and downing them with rosé. Not sentimental by habit, she was dreamy and softened by the vision of her darling in his youth. I'd like to say that at the time I was wholly under her spell, as I had been when I was smaller ('Tell me more, Grand'-mère, more!'), but I wriggled in my seat and twisted my napkin and kept my eyes on the chip of turquoise through the window, eager to rejoin my friends.

I listened nonetheless, more closely than was by then usual, because my grandmother began by shocking me.

'Your grandfather,' she said, 'was not the youngest of three children. I think you're old enough to know this now.'

I sniggered. It seemed such a preposterous statement. Her glare was grim, and her skin splotchy.

'Your grandfather was the youngest of four. His brother, Yves, was the eldest, and Paulette, of whom you've heard—'

'Yes, of course.'

'Was nearest him in age. But they had another sister, too. Estelle.'

'Estelle?'

'She was a good bit older than your father—'

'Grandfather.'

'Yes. And she disappeared when he was nine.'

The story was not about Estelle's disappearance, but about a reunion, the reunion between them many years later, when my grandfather was studying in Paris.

'He was summoned,' my grandmother explained. 'He wouldn't – he couldn't – have found her otherwise. He never even looked. He was aware, of course, that she and Paulette wrote to one another, secret letters that their mother didn't know about; he had always been aware of that. But home – and Paulette, Yves and their *maman* – was so far from the life upon which he had recently embarked, and Estelle was further still, but a faint flicker in the memory.'

That afternoon, she told me, a wet afternoon in November, the air made more melancholy by the leaden drizzle in which Paris excels, he had declined to join his comrades in their

Saturday round of the cafés and had set off in the opposite direction, towards the Jardins du Luxembourg.

His mind was full of home, but not of Paulette or Yves or *maman*, not of the crowded little house in Blida that he was delighted to have escaped. No, it was the glow of Algiers that illuminated his eye: the sparkling white buildings climbing the hillside behind the port, the azure glitter of the bay, the alleys of steps winding towards the sky, and the paths of the Jardin Marengo, scented by jasmine and passionflower, overhung with banana fronds – all these sites suffused with the blush of first love.

'I was his first true love,' my grandmother continued, her eyes on the sea's hazy horizon. 'Or so he has always said. And I became his wife. He seemed young when we first met – he's three years younger than I am, you know. I was teaching kindergarten in a small school in the city. He was staying with cousins in the capital. I was charged with the care of, among others, their daughter, the daughter of these cousins, and he, studying for his special university exams, volunteered one afternoon to pick her up. You know this. I've told you this before.'

Thereafter, his walk to the school became a daily break from his studies, and the child's tiny hand in his a quotidian pleasure. A pleasure, too, to pass the time talking to the little girl's schoolmistress, trying, with his wit, to catch her averted eyes. My grandmother was smitten; how could she not be? He was so handsome, and dark, and fierce, and she could tell at once that his mind was like a great force, a wind. She knew he would pass his exams, although he claimed he wasn't sure.

Eventually they walked together, two young adults, in the early evenings, and he learned the curves and rises of the city with her hand, not the little girl's, in his. When he returned to Blida they wrote daily; and when he was accepted to his *grande école* in Paris, the triumph was tinged with misery for both of them, almost an ache, at the thought that their future together would be postponed.

They parted at the quayside, he dry-eyed and hopeful, eager

for France. His letters that first autumn in Paris were full only of his yearning for my grandmother, she said, and into that yearning he fed all his nostalgia for their beloved homeland. Paris was dark, he convinced himself, not because it was a northern city where the sun rarely shone, but because she was not there. (Later he would learn that it was dark simply because it was dark, that in winter its days were as abbreviated as a stifled sneeze; but that in June, when the twilight spun out, golden, until almost eleven, that city, too, unfurled its wonders, love or no.)

That Saturday, the park was empty of its usual clamour of children and parents and young lovers. The splash of the fountains was indistinguishable from the splashing of the rain, and Jacques stood a while, watching the drops skitter on the surface of the pond. Heavy with water, the trees sagged, their branches beckoning in the wind, their leaves waxy. Potbellied benches squatted in the gravel, dripping as if bereaved.

His melancholia was willed, but he indulged it nonetheless. In Algiers, he thought, Monique would be at home with her mother, perhaps sunk in the velvet armchair by the window, bent over her embroidery, or over a book. ('I had written to him, not long before, about Proust,' my grandmother explained, 'whom I had just discovered, and whose enveloping sentences I adored. Upon receipt of my letter, he had rushed to the secondhand booksellers on the quay and acquired a dog-eared copy in four volumes. Each night in bed he read a dozen pages, and felt he was reading them with me. I felt it too. In Gilberte, in Albertine, so unlike his beloved, he found my face, and my eyes, the colour, he used to say, of the Mediterranean.') And was she reading? Probably, with the cadaverous marmalade cat snoring in the cushions of the sofa opposite, and her mother stretched out in the bedroom on her high, shiplike bed, in her stockinged feet. Later, when the sun was low in the sky, Monique and her mother might go walking, arm in arm; or perhaps they would be joined by cousins and aunts, for an afternoon of honeyed Arab pastries and conversation. He imagined her distracted, withdrawing from the chatter to pace the balcony and pause, chin in hand, gazing out to the harbour, towards France.

When he reached his building, the *bleu* with which the concierge smilingly presented him took him utterly by surprise.

'Perhaps a little girlfriend?' she suggested with a wink. 'Mind, now, that you don't bring her back here. I keep a respectable house.' She flicked at his shoulder with her duster, and giggled before retreating behind her curtained glass door to the thick crackle of the radio and her singleted spouse.

He could not imagine who might be writing to him from within Paris itself, and worried that the letter might contain bad news: he had not been thinking of his mother, or of his sister or brother, after all. He had forgotten that his four-year-old nephew was ill, sorry information of which his mother had apprised him in her last letter: 'Poor little Henri,' she had written, 'has been stricken with a terrible fever. The doctor has been here, and we keep the boy wrapped in cool cloths which heat up immediately and are changed at once; but his fever seems inexhaustible. All depends on the next day or two and the will of God. To lose a firstborn son is a tragedy, as I know all too well. Yves and his wife worry and cannot sleep; we are all praying, and I know that you, too, pray with us.'

But then he reflected that there was nobody in Paris to bear news of a faraway death, had there been one. Aside from his classmates – who never sent messages through the post – he knew few people in the city.

The elaborate script was unfamiliar. Glancing at the signature he did not realize, initially, that it was his sister's: Estelle was a name so long unpronounced in the LaBasse household that he had come to think of her as dead. Only when he returned to the salutation – '*Mon cher frère*' – did it strike him; whereupon he took up the letter and sank, backwards, onto the edge of his bed. Afterwards he could not say whether he emitted the sound of his shock, or simply covered his mouth as a precaution.

'My dear brother,' the frothy hand implored, 'How long has it been? What memories can you have of me? I see you only as a boy in short pants. But fate has brought us both to Paris, and so, I hope, we will meet again. I am not here for long. Having only recently arrived from Nice, I will be departing Monday for London on my way to America. Little brother, there isn't much time. Please come, this evening at eight, to my hotel. Room 426, the Ritz, Place Vendôme. You see that life has not treated me so badly. There is much to tell, and so little time. Do not disappoint me. Your loving sister, Estelle.'

3

Jacques had not seen her in almost eleven years. Shortly after their father's death, when Jacques was nine, and when his academic precocity had only just begun to announce itself, Estelle had taken flight. Seven years older than he, she was their parents' second surviving child, as unlike their eldest brother Yves in temperament as Jacques was himself. Paulette, thirteen at the time, midway between Estelle and Jacques, adored her sister, and had refused to disown her. Estelle was everything Paulette was not, which might have caused resentment in the younger, plainer girl, but instead had inspired fierce loyalty, even pride. Paulette was not particularly intelligent, but she was convinced of Estelle's genius. Like all of the LaBasse family, devout, she did not on that account condemn Estelle's lapses: she simply prayed for her sister, and lit candles for her, and savoured her infrequent letters, a delicious secret between Paulette and the local postmistress.

Jacques had known about these letters, and in adolescent arguments with Paulette had more than once threatened to reveal them to their mother. But he had never read one, and thus had no idea of what Estelle had been doing these many years, nor of where she had been living. As he dressed to leave, it seemed suddenly remarkable to him that he had nurtured so little curiosity about this sister, that after she had vanished from their lives, and after their mother's copious weeping had trickled to a halt, he had accepted her loss, like that of his father, as irrevocable fate.

Now, examining his face in the bureau's speckled mirror, he wondered. He was dark, but remembered his elder sister's curls as fair, the colour of the seashore. He recalled her sudden laugh, the way she used to swing him in the air when he was small, the lacy edges of her two front teeth.

Although tall for a girl, Estelle, like Jacques, had inherited their grandmother's small bones, and she would stand in the kitchen, chopping knife or wooden spoon held aloft, and examine her extended wrists or ankles. 'You wouldn't know me for a peasant, would you?' she'd ask, with mock extravagance. To which Paulette, solid in every joint as their father had been solid, smiled indulgently and replied, 'You're like a queen, *chérie*. A queen. Born for palaces and gentlemen.'

Little Jacques buzzed in and out of these exchanges, caught up in his games of knights and war. Estelle sometimes grabbed him as he passed, a slender brown arm flung around his waist, or a hand upon his shoulder. She would spin him around to face Paulette saying, 'He's like me. We're the changelings, don't you see?'

Then, as sudden as her laughter, she was gone. After school – it was early summer, and already fiercely hot – he had gone to play with his friend Didier. They ventured to the glade of mulberries and olive trees, not far from the shrine of the marabout, where they were not supposed to go, and passed the afternoon digging trenches in a patch of open ground, constructing elaborate fortresses for their imaginary armies and tracing in the dirt, with sticks, the invasion strategies of Arab hordes. This work smeared their skin and shoes and hands with filth; but it was only after the boys decided to enact their battle, and had taken up the sticks as swords, that Jacques – either snagged by one of the silvery thornbushes among which they played, or felled by a shrewd parry from Didier – discovered a rent in the seat of his shorts, a large, two-sided tear that left a flap of fabric dangling like a dog's tongue, revealing his white underpants. He trailed home, at dusk, to disgrace: his *maman* spanked his stripped behind with the flat of her calloused hand, denied him his share of the evening meal, and banished him to the attic room he shared with Yves. There Jacques cried himself to an early, and hungry, sleep.

In the commotion of Jacques's wrongdoing, he did not notice that Estelle was not there. Still overstuffed – at that time their Tata Christine lived with them, a crinkled creature of over eighty who shared *maman*'s marriage bed – the house did not feel emptier without her. And he attributed the raised voices he heard from beneath the covers to his mother's, and brother's, frustration with his naughtiness. But waking the next morning before dawn, he noticed that Yves, who snored ferociously, was not in his narrow bed under the window, and that the rooms beneath him were peculiarly still. A chill took him, a childish terror of abandonment: he ran naked down the narrow stairs, two at a time, moaning, imagining that in the night his family had escaped to another life without him. His father's recent disappearance had, after all, been as sudden: a broad, squat bear of a man, Monsieur LaBasse had sauntered down the street at sunrise one morning, the same as every day but Sunday, his apron over his arm, only to come home in a box, on a cart, his stubby hands crossed on his breast and his features fixed for ever in a stony glare.

Yves was slumped in a chair by the kitchen hearth, his whiskered skin as grey as the dead embers at his feet, his eyes stuck shut. He did not snore. The little boy shook his brother without speaking, afraid to break the odd silence, and it seemed a long time before the older boy started, kicking out a foot in reflex along the tiled floor.

'Is she here?' is what he said.

'Maman? Where's Maman? Where is everyone? What?'

Yves rubbed his filmy eyes and squinted at little Jacques, who hopped and shivered in his nakedness. 'You're up,' he said.

'It's morning. Can't you see? Where is everyone? What's wrong?'

'What isn't, *mon petit*?'

'Is Maman sick? Has she died, like Papa? Where is she?'

'She's sleeping now. Don't worry.'

'But – we must wake her, we must—' Jacques stuttered. Even when his father had died, there had not been this overwhelming air of disorder: the next day had gone ahead, the coffee made, Jacques's hair combed by his mother, if anything more tenderly. 'Why are you sleeping here?'

Yves was standing now, hiking up his sleeves, adjusting his trousers, turning into himself. 'It was a long night, *petit*. I didn't get home until a couple of hours ago. We were hoping there'd be some news, at least.'

'News? Of what?'

Yves put his hands on his little brother's shoulders. 'Estelle has gone away,' he said quietly, fixing Jacques full in the face.

'You mean she has died?'

'No . . . I mean she has gone away. But she'll be back. Soon, I promise.'

'Where has she gone?' Jacques's tone was truculent. He felt annoyed, although he was not sure at what, or at whom: his world was not a game to be trifled with in this way.

'We don't know.'

'What do you mean you don't know? Where has she gone?'

'She'll be back soon, I promise.'

That was all his brother said to him, except to tell him not to speak of it to their *maman*. Paulette emerged from the girls' room not long after, her cheeks puffed by tears, her lips swollen, and she prepared their breakfast in silence. His *maman* Jacques did not see until after school that day, when he clattered into the kitchen, swinging his bookbag, to find her squarely planted in the stiff chair by the hearth, in her widow's black, her eyes strangely small and expressionless. She wept, over the next weeks, at odd times: not just at mass, but in the market, at the sight of oranges, and once when she stood watching the neighbourhood children play soccer in the street. She did not speak her daughter's name again, or not in front of Jacques: she referred to Estelle only once within his hearing: 'The girl is dead,' she said. 'To this life, she is dead, and I grieve as if she had died.'

Departure and death became forever mixed up in little Jacques's mind. Just as he forgot the smoky sweat smell of his father's shirts, he forgot his sister's elegant wrists and ankles, and the way she pinned him on his bed and tickled him till he wept with laughter. He had Didier to play with, and discoveries to make: he did not brood over what was gone.

From Paulette he gathered a little: he knew that Estelle had not run away alone, and that therein, for some reason, lay the greater shame for his mother. She had followed a soldier, a brush-haired youth from the *métropole*. They paused, for a time, in Algiers: it was from there that Paulette received her first, thin letter. It struck Jacques only all those years later, in Paris, that Estelle had discovered Algiers as he had, in the early-summer flurry of love, that she had tripped along the Rue Michelet and drunk wine in the cafés just as he had, and that she had probably, like him, felt she and her *jules* were the first to do so. She had doubtless strolled with her lover along the beaches, swum at the Bains Padovani and danced at night in the casino on the clifftop (an indulgence which he, in his time, never attempted), and had chased after trams, giggling breathlessly, as he had, more recently, with his beloved. Some months later – he did not know how many – she had followed her lover to France, and there, in a country then unimaginable to her younger brother, she had been truly lost.

4

At eight o'clock precisely, Jacques presented himself at the entrance to the hotel. He had never been in so grand a lobby (perhaps he had never been in any hotel lobby; and it changed his life for ever). The light from its chandeliers spilled out onto the square, where women in furs and men in evening dress milled about and long black cars pulled up on the shimmering cobbles. A uniformed brotherhood guarded the doors, unsmiling, their hands encased in leather gloves that Jacques – his fingers raw from the long walk – coveted silently. He felt awkward, his hat soggy, its shape distorted from the earlier rain, his shoes squelching. He kept his eyes down, and slipped in behind three mink-wrapped ladies, whose trailing cloud of scent seemed to offer some protection. When he stood at the marbled reception desk and waited to be spoken to, the wall of room keys in front of him appeared like treasures in themselves, weighty and bright. The oriental carpet beneath his feet, the rich waft of cigar smoke from his neighbour, the stern glance of the fastidious clerk, all announced to Jacques that he was not worthy of this place. He had never felt this way, was accustomed to the pride of intellect and hard work rewarded: humbly born perhaps, he had nevertheless believed that his origins had fallen away in the face of his brilliant future. He wished, for the first time, that he had a visible value in the moneyed world.

But after phoning through to room 426, the clerk smiled, or almost, as he directed him to the elevator. Jacques took the smile to be friendly, not considering until much later that it might have been maliciously offered, a comment upon his sister's virtue. The elevator operator swung the cage shut with his monkey arm and called Jacques 'm'sieur.' On the fourth floor, a chambermaid in a pristine pinafore bobbed at him in hasty approximation of a curtsey.

How wide the door was, on which the number 426 was painted in delicate scrolls. How wide all the doors were, along the broad and quiet corridor. The paint was the colour of fresh cream, its borders gold. Gold borders. How could their *maman* shun such deliciousness? How could Jacques not give in to it, even before the door to his sister's life – on which he knocked, three times, with a mixture of hesitation and willed authority – had opened?

The woman who greeted him was, at first, unfamiliar: she looked like any one of the hotel guests, tall, slender and expensive, her body swayed in the stoop that was considered fashionable at the time. Her throat was laced with emeralds, her blond curls were oiled against her brow, her heart-shaped face powdered and rouged. Her lips were a glistening crimson, her green eyes cold as glass. But when she smiled, Jacques knew her by her teeth.

She took his hand, her smooth, ringless fingers cool upon his wrist, and led him into the room. 'Let me look at you, my darling boy.' She turned dramatically, the yellow gauze of her dress billowing, its intricate beading glittering in the light. 'I'd know you anywhere.'

'Would you?'

She held his chin, turned his face this way and that. 'Certainly. You look like Grand'-mère. You look – like me. Dark, of course; but we are twins. Would you not have recognized me?'

'I'm not sure. Perhaps.'

Estelle laughed. 'Well,' she said, twirling again, 'what do you think? Not bad for a runaway from Blida?'

'Born for palaces and gentlemen. And this.'

'And this.'

The room was indeed magnificent, a salon of robin's-egg sofas and bowlegged antique dressers, lit by soft lamps. Through a half-open door he could glimpse her bed, a plump, shadowy mushroom of eiderdowns and pillows. The air was drenched in the smell of hothouse lilies – they clustered, in profusion, in a vase atop the marble mantelpiece, yellow pistils peering wetly from their lolling white heads.

'Champagne?' She took his coat. 'Will you sit?'

Jacques perched on one of the sofas, and looked around him. At anything but his sister, whose chattering beauty unsettled him. He had not known women like this, women of grace but not of breeding, elegant but somehow not entirely genuine. The slight flutter of her lashes, the abrupt sentences, he took for nerves at his presence; she had a way of fingering the emeralds in the dip of her collarbone, and even that charmed him. He was afraid that if he looked too long at her, he might fall in love.

'So, you are well.' He could not think where else to begin, and Estelle, still standing in the middle of the room, seemed content merely to eye him, coquettishly, then to part her lips in a knowing titter.

'Need you ask? Can't you see?' She broke into a graceful little dance, her flute of golden champagne her partner, and she sang in English as she swirled around the sofas. 'I'm sitting on top of ze world, just rolling along, just rolling along . . .' She stopped, and laughed, and drank. Jacques observed her long, pale neck surreptitiously. 'That's how I am. You can tell them all. I'm going to America. I'm going to marry an American.'

She emptied her glass and came to sit beside him. She took his tingling hands in hers, and leaned close to him: like the room, she smelled of lilies. 'But how are you?' she asked. 'And Paulette? Is she in love? How does she wear her hair? Does she still work in the dress shop – it's been how long? Three years? and Yves – he's married, yes? Is he fat, like Papa? And his wife? He has a child? And how – ' she looked at his ruined shoes ' – and Maman?'

Jacques stayed an hour: Estelle had only an hour before her fiancé – the American – was to return and take her to dinner. As the time for Jacques's departure drew nearer, Estelle grew agitated, pacing the room and pausing in front of the mirror to adjust her hair, the neckline of her dress. When the clock on the mantel struck nine, she held out his coat, and kissed him, and when recounting the event, the word he used to describe her smile was 'brave'.

Jacques slipped out of the hotel and into the chill November air, and walked back to his rooms without supper, tipsy on the taste of champagne and his sister's perfume. By the time he came home from mass the next morning, that evening had already taken on the quality of the imagined. Later he would not remember what they talked about, what he learned then and what he learned afterwards of how her life had been and would be. He would remember only that she moved in beauty, that her melodious, nervous voice was still given to sudden laughter, and that her lacy teeth still gave her the look of an elfin child when she smiled. He would recall always the delicate wave of her wrists – practised in youth in the kitchen in Blida, but perfected in the elegant suite at the Ritz – and her insistent, almost desperate joy at the prospect of America.

He did not guess that her eager eye on the future measured the difficulty of her past, or that the nervousness he attributed to his presence was born of the effort, the constant effort, simply to be what she had become. He did not picture her in any place other than room 426 at the Ritz on the Place Vendôme, a beautiful, gilded creature buffed and cossetted, beaded and bejewelled: he pictured her always dancing her graceful waltz. For years hers was the only English song he knew, and he reserved it for moments of greatest happiness: 'I'm sitting on top of the world, just rolling along . . .'

'And, in truth,' said my grandmother, 'for months afterwards, I believe it was not me but Estelle who walked with him hand in hand in his dreams of Algiers, whose wide eyes gazed at him in amused adoration, whose voice whispered "for ever" in his sleeping ear. He would think of me and hear Estelle, feel her cool fingers on his wrist, leading him to the places of utmost contentment.

'He did not ever see his sister again,' my grandmother concluded. 'She went to America, and she disappeared. His long-lost. So when your mother came into our lives, he was not as taken aback as I was. To him, it seemed like justice. He is a patient man, your grandfather, in spite of what you may think, and a man with a long memory. He has held the memory of that evening his whole life, like a jewel in his hand.'

5

The story seemed to me the stuff of films, and I pictured my vanished great-aunt as Greta Garbo, my grandfather stepping up to the Ritz and entering, from grainy black-and-white to a world of Technicolor, and then slipping back again, when the fantastic evening was over.

I entered my own brightly tinted afternoon full of these images, intrigued at the prospect of unknown American cousins (I was then only moderately familiar with the known ones, my mother's sister's children), but reluctant to share their possible existence with my friends. My grandfather could never be conjured young and handsome to Marie-José or Cécile: they would only have scoffed.

So I waited, and told my mother, expecting her delight to mirror mine: more Americans among us, more of us among the Americans – something like that. A past branching like a rabbit warren along unexplored corridors, which might yield anything.

My mother listened, but she was not entranced. When I finished, she took her hand from Etienne's wrist and laid it idly in her lap. We were on the patio, in the early evening shade, and the cicadas were screaming over the whirr of distant traffic.

'That's where she ended it? That's all she told you?' My mother's voice was rich with scorn. 'Believe it if you like. Told that way, it makes a lovely story.'

'What do you mean?'

'Nothing.' She stood to fuss with Etienne's straps and, from behind, tickled him under the arms. He chortled, his mouth wide with glee, his arms reaching out in lazy spasms. She brushed a fly from his face. 'This young man will need his dinner soon,' she said, flicking with her foot at the chair's brakes in an expert, unconscious manoeuvre.

I extracted my mother's version only through badgering and pleas. Negotiations were interrupted by my father's return, and by supper: only as we tidied up afterwards, while the dishwasher pursued its drugged rhythms and my father sprawled in his armchair in the living room listening to *Aïda* at thunderous volume, did my mother capitulate.

'If you must know,' she said at last – as if her contempt for my starlet great-aunt had not made not knowing impossible.

According to my mother, who knew it, she claimed, from my father, my grandfather had seen Estelle one more time, much later, in the 1950s, when she was dead. The American who took her to New York had abandoned her there. No longer sitting on top of the world, her beauty fading and her visa on the verge of expiry, while the war in Europe heaved towards its beginning, Estelle cast around in desperation for someone to marry. She found him in a modest widower, a clerk or insurance salesman from the gloomier reaches of New Jersey. After a hasty and unfestive ceremony, she moved into his clapboard house in a suburban town and tended the handker-chief lawn, dressed and fed his three children who, as they grew older, made it clear that they liked her as little as she liked them. She didn't care for the widower, although he may not have been a bad man, and she didn't care for the callouses and chilblains that marked her delicate hands and feet. Eventually, said my mother, when the war had stormed and ebbed in Europe, Estelle scraped together what little money she could, and fled. Not to Paris – which was, *après guerre*, famously bleak – and not to Blida, or even Algiers, where her sister Paulette, still (and ever) unmarried, manager, by then, of an elegant shoe shop downtown, urged her to come. She skirted that city because her unforgiving mother presided there, over the LaBasse family, and it was too late to make amends – and set her sights instead on Tangier.

What she did to earn a living in Morocco, in the short years still allotted her, my mother wasn't sure. But that she ended her days mired in poverty, unvisited by her family, unloved and alone – of that my mother was certain. It was a cancer that killed her, but presumably her spirit – the fey dancing spirit that twirled the floors of grand hotels and restaurants in the thirties – was long dead.

'Your grandfather knew, from 1948 onwards,' my mother told me, 'exactly where she was, and in exactly what a sorry state she was. And did he do a single thing? Did he lift a finger?'

I waited.

'Hah. You know he didn't. They were too afraid – such

good Christians – that this pathetic, divorced, fallen woman might corrupt the morals of their precious children.'

'Of Papa?'

'Precisely. You would've thought the poor woman had leprosy, the berth they gave her.'

'But Grand-père saw her again, you said.'

'For the funeral. The funeral! She was dead. The LaBasse funds may or may not have run to a tombstone, I don't know. You'd have to ask your father. They may not even have bought her plot in perpetuity, for heaven's sake. Not that it matters now, but there she is, or her bones are, all alone in the cemetery in Tangier. Or dug up and thrown in the sea to make room for someone else. Nobody ever went to put so much as a flower on her grave.'

'I get the point.'

'It's not – it's not that. Not in the end. It's that they did nothing when she was alive. They pretended she didn't exist.'

'How do you know?'

'Your father told me. The first he heard of her was the funeral – he must have been a little younger than you are, maybe nine or so, and his father hops off to Morocco. "I never realized travel was so efficient," he said when he came back. "It's not far at all. We should go on holiday." Or something like that. He said something like that.'

We had long finished cleaning and were talking by the stove, she with her back pressed to the fridge. We heard my father's footsteps cross the hall, the dining room.

'You won't speak about it, will you, to him? It only upsets him. Maybe when you're older, or when – I don't know.'

'What are you two up to?' asked my father from the doorway. 'Listen, *chérie*, I think I'd better run back to the hotel – just a few papers to look over – you don't mind, do you?'

'Of course. Whatever. Of course.' But my mother's features were set anew in a glazed panic, and her fingers fluttered over the pristine countertop in pursuit of imaginary crumbs. I kissed them both and, as my father didn't offer a ride, set off on foot to join my friends.

6

I could not decide whether my grandfather was sentimental or heartless. I could not determine whose version was true. I could picture the romantic young Jacques in Paris, and Jacques the righteous Catholic and father protecting his family, and I could even see the little boy, careless, frolicking in the streets of Blida: but I could not connect these images into a single person, into my grandfather. And by the same token, a short month later, I couldn't tell what I felt in the days following the shooting. Must I hate him – his was a vicious crime of rage and indifference, the surest sign of a cold heart – or must I love and pity him, a broken and sick man whose soul had been momentarily gripped by self-destructive madness? I was washed, alternately, by these extreme opinions; that both might be simultaneously possible I never considered. It was a matter of choosing a side and of taking it.

My family and my friends made the decision for me. In the initial aftermath of the 'Bellevue incident', as the local paper termed it (with a blurred ten-year-old snapshot of my grandfather on the front page, in late-seventies gear, his lapels stretching to the edges of the frame and his striped tie fat as a fish), I found my routines ruptured. The Bellevue did too, which was perhaps more serious.

Released from hospital within twenty-four hours, her back an intricate map of stitches and plasters, still pocked in places by splinters that the medics had not had the patience to remove, Cécile was gathered up by her irate parents and returned to Paris; but not before they paused at the *préfecture* to press charges, thus ensuring their return, and a trial. The bullet, lodged in the wooden balustrade at the poolside, was prised out by expert policemen, an exercise that interrupted swimming for a day and, because of the fluttering plastic tape demarcating the scene, made of my usual playground a pilgrimage for inquisitive locals. Laure, too, departed unceremoniously, her father paying the bill only after delivering an enraged lecture to the front-desk clerk.

Thierry's father – torn, it seemed, between horror at his employer's act and amusement that his odious offspring, shaken but essentially unhurt, should have been disciplined into silence for the first time in years – teetered on the brink of resigning, until my own father sat him down with a bottle of scotch and some blunt talk about the changes in store, and possibly with an open chequebook too. Thierry's father, and Thierry too, stayed put.

None of the staff, in fact, quit: it was too late in the season to scout for other work, and my father, visited by an authoritative demeanour none had known he could possess, gathered them together the very morning after and reassured them, speaking of his own father with respectful regret, as if the old man had been the wounded party, a brave general forced into retirement by an unforeseeable and tragic injury. My mother, contrary to my expectations, did not gloat, but cleaved instead to her adopted parents and spent long hours sequestered in our living room with my dry-eyed grandmother and Tante Marie, who flew in from Geneva, discussing strategy, how best to staunch the flow of malicious gossip and redeem the family name. Even Etienne seemed to sense the heightened tension in the air, although it elicited from him not sober grimaces but gales of spooky laughter at peculiar moments – when he was being bathed, or when the sun set and my mother, smoking furiously, paced the hallways of the house they had built for him.

The Bellevue, though, had sprung a leak. At this, the busiest of seasons, the guests trickled away. Not all, but enough to furrow brows and lighten the load of the chambermaids. My father, against his own father's wishes, battled cancellations by accepting, for the first time in the hotel's history, a German package tour, a crowd of identical, rowdy couples in their forties and early fifties, whose wan and unfriendly offspring would take over the grounds, and above all the pool, for their Teutonic games, hurling gutturals at one another and making – as I suppose we always had too – a general nuisance of themselves. They didn't swim at night, though: my father ordered that the bulbs be removed from the underwater lamps, and he posted an unsightly plaque at every entrance to the deck limiting the pool hours from dawn to 8 p.m.

7

Not that all these changes mattered much to me. From my first awakening after the deed, I developed a phobia about the scene of the crime. I could not bring myself to follow my father up to the hotel; and when, after my grandfather had been formally arrested and released on bail and had come to 'rest', for an indefinite time, in one of the spare bedrooms down the hall from mine (it was feared that his presence at the Bellevue, like that of a ghost, would be bad for business), I found myself all the more weighted with guilt.

On the first day, I waited – naively, I would later feel – for Marie-José to call or to come by. She was my best friend. She did not know that I had lain beneath her feet and listened to the drama unfolding overhead; she would, I reasoned, want to be the first to tell me how it really was, what they had all thought and felt. She would laugh about it. We would laugh – appalled, greedy laughter. She would want to bring me over to her side, the swimmers' side, Cécile's side, where I belonged.

She did not call.

That night as I failed to sleep, it came to me that Marie-Jo was not sure of me; that precisely because she didn't know that I had been there and thought that I might therefore believe the LaBasse version of events, she must be waiting for me to call. I sprang from bed early the next morning eager to clarify, to make amends. I dialled – not without trepidation – no later than eight-thirty, imagining my beautiful friend stretching, cat-like, among her sheets and reaching for the pink phone by her bed. But it rang only once, and Marie-Jo's mother's voice came on the line.

'Oh Sagesse. Of course. She's out, I'm afraid.'

'Out?'

'An early tennis match with her father. Yes, out. I'll tell her you called.'

I knew it at once for a lie. And when I called at dusk, the hour at which our gang always dispersed for home, the same tinny grown-up's tone informed me, with no effort at conviction, 'I don't know where she is. Sorry.'

I waited, again, a day and a half – during which time I succumbed, my need for the sea like a drug, and took the bus to the public beach. I swam there alone among the noisy groups of kids and hid when I thought I saw people from school, then trailed home feeling worse – and tried, once more, near noon. Marie-Jo herself picked up.

'Oh, it's you.'

'I've called – maybe your mom didn't tell you – several times.'

'I know.'

'Are you okay?'

'I suppose. Yeah, okay.'

'I can't really face the hotel, but I feel as though – well, we've got so much to talk about. My grandfather, you know – it's crazy.'

'Yeah.'

'What's it like over there?'

'You know. Look, Sagesse, I'm really busy right now. Lunch, yeah? I'll call you back, okay?'

Which she did not. I eventually learned – from Thibaud, of all people – that Marie-Jo was to be a prosecution witness at my grandfather's trial. And so she and her mother had decided it would be best if she didn't speak to me about the event, if she didn't speak to me at all.

To describe it now, it seems a small matter. But to my fourteen-year-old self it was a first loss, an unimagined betrayal, a radical skewing of my everyday world. Marie-Jo had not, after all, moved away; she had merely moved away from me. I knew that her diversions described an arc only minutely different from before; but that infinitesimal alteration separated our steps, one from another, with brutal absoluteness. I missed the glow of her skin, her laugh, her lewd asides, the musty smell of the rug in her bedroom. I would have publicly denounced my grandfather – so quiet, with his sedatives, reading and praying in the room down the hall, deprived of his view of the sea, quieter than Etienne, as quiet as an absence – to get my life, and Marie-Jo, back. But between them, he (simply by being there) and she (simply by not) had chosen my side for me.

For a long time I was literally hungry for her company: I could feel my longing burning calories, hollowing out my stomach and scratching at its walls. But such deprivation has its limits: we are not made for constant and precipitate pain, just as we cannot sustain surprise or even disappointment. Being human, we cicatrize. And Marie-Jo would come to seem as distant, as unknowable as anyone. When, much later, she sought to mend our friendship, I could muster no emotion for her. This was an abiding lesson in my fickleness, in my aloneness. In time I would come to see it merely as a question of refining the movement from one state to another, of rendering it more efficient, less painful.

Thibaud, it turned out, was my unlikely saviour. He telephoned that same afternoon, after lunch, his the only hand, or voice, extended to me from our former circle. Our grappling beneath the pool united us, perhaps, in some way bigger than itself. Or maybe, for him, it was simply the force of an adolescent boy's lust.

Luncheons in my parents' house had suddenly become infinitely more dreadful than those I had loathed at the hotel. My grandmother and my mother shovelled silently, casting occasional meaningful glances at the ceiling; beyond which, somewhere, my grandfather consumed his meal from a tray; and my plumply fatuous Tante Marie, her second and third chins quivering, her cheeks winter-rosy, offered comments worse than silence between her bites. 'Etienne is such a big boy now,' she might say, smiling falsely at my emaciated, heavy-headed brother. 'How tall – or long – or whatever, is he? You do keep track, I imagine?' Or: 'I spoke to the boys – ' her rapacious sons, Marc, Jean-Paul and Pierre, three, five and six years my junior, who had remained at home with their father ' – and Jean-Paul is very concerned that I should tell you about his firefly collection, Maman. He adds to it daily. He wanted to send you a jarful, but I told him the bugs would probably die in the mail.'

'Yes. They would.' My grandmother was at her stiffest with her daughter. Marie was my grandfather's favourite, but my grandmother preferred Alexandre.

Above, behind, throughout the meal, my grandfather hovered, mentioned only in undertones or after a stammer or a nervous pause. Except for Marie who, bless her, behaved as though nothing were amiss and regularly included 'Papa' in her random prattle. My own father did not partake in these lunches: all bluster, he might have made them more tolerable. Whereas 'the incident' weighed upon everyone else, so that our very movements seemed a trick of time-lapse photography, it infused my father with a zeal, almost an exuberance, that whirled his solid form through the days and nights, in meetings, surveying and patrolling, into town and out again, his sleek BMW scattering the gravel of our driveway often only when the rest of us were in bed. He had come into his inheritance – who knew for how long, but still – and his gestures, always large, were at last purposefully so. In an obscure and unspoken part of himself, he was grateful, for the first time, to his own father. Gunshot or no, it was about time.

This enthusiasm was not, however, infectious, and had to be masked from the clutch of grieving womenfolk, who saw only the LaBasse reputation in jeopardy and the glory of the Bellevue under threat, not to mention the spectre of my grandfather, who refused to rise above his humiliation. My grandmother had to bully him, in those early days, into dressing and shaving. After he fired the gun he simply stopped, the way animals in freezing water will shut down long before they die, their vital signs a faint and intermittent murmur that can be nurtured and reinvigorated, or else allowed to lapse altogether.

None of us – not even my formerly rebellious mother – would let my grandfather simply lapse. Deprived of his defining presence, we could not imagine our lives, which had been but atoms spinning around his. Ours was a vortex of complex emotion, to be sure, but even if one's energies are devoted entirely to hatred, it is a tragedy to lose their object. And not even my mother hated him purely.

8

In that first week, each luncheon, each afternoon, proved slower and more agonizing than the last, and I seized upon Thibaud's phone call in spite of my confusion about our tryst, and about him. He thought we might meet at the hotel, but I declined, suggesting instead a café in town behind the central post office, next to the porn cinema, where nobody I knew would ever go.

'Like criminals on the lam?' he joked.

'Just like that,' I said. 'You don't know what it's been like.'

We met at four o'clock, when the city was still calm, the workers in their offices and the summer people at the beach. In the café, among the few furtive single men and tarty, thickening women, Thibaud shone, his black curls lustrous. He seemed, like my father, healthier and more cheerful for our trouble.

'Your grandfather's really done it this time,' he said, bending a tiny espresso spoon around his thumb. 'This one won't go away.'

'I guess it won't. Glad you think it's so funny.'

'What's it like at your house, then?'

I told him, as succinctly as I could because I didn't want to talk – or think – about it. 'My brother finds it hilarious,' I said. 'Like you. He's taken it better than anyone else.'

'It is hilarious, in a way.'

'Not for Cécile. Not for the hotel. Or my grandfather.'

'He'll go to jail, you think?'

I shrugged. 'But you tell me. I'm the one in quarantine.

What are people saying? Do you all still hang out? Did your parents say anything?'

'My mother was appalled, of course. She thought we should leave at once. But then she felt a bit better when I told her I hadn't been there.'

'Hah.'

'Yeah, well, it suddenly made it someone else's problem. And she loves her room and her routine here, and her masseuse, and all that, and I guess my dad won her over. Said he didn't know if we could find another place at such short notice, and certainly not for the price, so maybe we should just go home if she felt that strongly about it. And she found she didn't. She even called Cécile "that rude girl whose mother cheats at bridge". So we're staying the next ten days.'

'Your dad didn't care?'

'He said he thought it was about time. Couldn't understand why we hadn't been stopped from hogging the pool before now. That was the failure of management, he said, and this was just the inevitable result. He went on about how many times we've spoiled his afternoon swim, and said, you know, as a joke, that he might've done the same if he'd ever had a gun handy. He was pretty funny about it. He doesn't really give a shit, to be honest.'

'Thank God somebody doesn't.'

'But he did ask about you. He said it must be hard on you.'

'How does he even know I exist? Did you tell him about . . .?'

'No, no. But he's not a fool.'

'And everybody else?'

'Half the people are gone. Boom. Just like that. The hotel's weirdly quiet, except that your dad is all over the place the whole time, pressing flesh, generating goodwill. It's bizarre.'

'You're telling me. But Thierry, say, or Marie-Jo – what about them?'

'It's strange, you know. I think they're all still meeting up somewhere, but they don't invite me. Guess I'm not part of the target practice club. I ran into Thierry yesterday, and he has this bandage on his arm – it's nothing, really – and he was friendly enough, but secretive, or something. He said he couldn't swim till his arm healed, and he can't play tennis, and that he's taking advantage of the time to do his summer school work. But he was in a hurry to go somewhere, and when I said "Will you be at the tree tonight?" he looked at me like I was crazy. I haven't seen the others from your crowd, the year-rounders. The rest of us, the guests who are left, we all swim like adults, on our own, now, and then head off to our separate corners. It's a different place. I don't mind it so much. They're mostly jerks anyway. But I wanted to see you.'

'And Marie-Jo?'

'Not a trace. But I get the feeling she's militant, from what Thierry said.'

'Meaning what, exactly?'

'Something about a petition. She wants to keep your grand-father from running the hotel.'

'But he's not running the hotel. I doubt he'll ever run it again. And he's probably going to prison anyhow. That's crazy.'

'Keeps her busy. I wouldn't worry about it. You haven't spoken to her?'

'She basically hung up on me. I haven't seen anybody since that night.'

'Just me, eh?'

I tried to look happy about it. 'About that night?' I said.

Thibaud frowned. 'Yeah?'

'Nothing.'

'Want to walk? This place is creepy.'

We ambled down to the port, through the dusty streets. He put his arm around me, tucking his fingers into the waistband of my jeans, rumpling the bottom of my T-shirt until he found my skin, which he stroked, slightly, as we walked. A feat of coordination, like patting his head and rubbing his belly at the same time. I was too hot, pressed up against him, and I found each step, forcibly in unison, an effort, but I didn't withdraw.

On the quay, the ferries and tour boats were disgorging and

absorbing people in great numbers: old women with sun hats and straw baskets, families in shorts and sunglasses, a few businesspeople looking creased and harried, heading home early. The boats at their moorings clacked in the swell, and gulls strutted the pavement, pausing to poke their beaks at crumbs and abandoned *frites*. It was breezy, and the wind was just another noise in the hubbub, fluttering the racks of T-shirts and the tiny animal-shaped buoys on sale outside the stores. Some marines paraded by in uniform. The garçons in the cafés leaned at identical angles, their arms folded, and eyed the proceedings with a jaded air. The children's carousel at the end of the pier threw out a fearful tinkling melody as it rolled its few tiny clients around in gentle circles – on horseback, in cars, or in miniature airplanes that rose and descended and rose again, a whirring foot or two, in time to the music – while the parents, mothers mostly, looked on and waved. The sky was a very bright blue, and the oily port water a murky black, edged with foam and garbage.

We strolled, like other summer couples, just as we had that evening on the beach not long before. Then I had marvelled to think how like them we were; now I was beset by our difference. I was the grandchild of an almost-assassin. If not all, then most of these people around us had seen his picture in the paper and read about his crime. I imagined them turning and pointing at me, calling out, chasing me, the great, disparate crowd united in animus. But when I turned to squint at Thibaud, he was smiling, his teeth bare to the sun, and he bent and kissed me on the lips as if I were anyone else.

9

For ten days I pretended, with Thibaud, that I was anyone else. Not a child of the LaBasse family, not trapped in the whispering unease of my parents' house. My parents, it seemed, were too busy trying to keep our lives from capsizing altogether to want to worry about me. My grandmother and my aunt – who stayed only five days before returning to her bug-enthralled offspring and their tedious father in Geneva – spent all their time attempting to coax my grandfather out of his gloom, and even my brother was shunted to the sidelines, fully into the care of his nurse, which he did not like at all: he raised his voice in protest, waking in the night to wail, mournful, vulpine, in the room next to mine, where I held him and sang to him until he went back to sleep, with little sucking noises and his hair damp on his forehead.

Thibaud and I sat in the all but abandoned air-conditioned cinemas in the afternoons, inhaling the stale air, clasping our clammy hands and kissing; or we took the ferry across the bay and walked along the shore, pretending we were in another country. One day we rented a little sailboat at the beach, and set off to cruise the coast's inlets and bays, but our boat took on water almost faster than I could bail it, and early on I caught a powerful swipe in the back of the head from the unruly boom, and our picnic sandwiches foundered and disintegrated in the salt water at our feet. On the way home the wind came up, and we found ourselves in ever increasing intimacy with a stationary aircraft carrier, whose gunwales leaked urinous waterfalls and whose sailors beetled about, tiny, upon its decks. Thibaud was amused, and I terrified, until finally I renounced my frantic bailing and huddled in the stern of our little craft to cry while he guided us – not without difficulty – back to the marina.

Once on the beach, I gave in entirely to my misery, at which Thibaud initially registered astonishment and then vague embarrassment and irritation.

'We're home safe,' he said. 'It was funny. I'm starving, though. Aren't you?'

'But it's everything. Just everything. This day, it's like everything else. It's all bad.'

I hid my head between my knees, sand and salt all over me, and shed salty, sandy tears for a while, waiting for his arm to snake around my shoulders as it so often did, proprietorial, sweaty, not entirely pleasant, and yet I wanted it. But the touch didn't come, and when I looked up, blinking in the afternoon light, Thibaud was gone.

I stopped crying at once, partly out of anger, and partly because I knew that nothing looked more foolish than a girl alone in a public place in broad daylight with her face a sodden mash. I didn't know what to do, and didn't have the energy to move, and although I was furious, it also seemed logical that Thibaud, too, would leave me, unsightly, Medusa-haired pariah that I was – until he reappeared along the shore, shining as ever, his maw crammed with a *chantilly*-slathered waffle and another, wrapped in wax paper, for me.

Thibaud was stealthy and committed, and I compliant, and we managed to arrange several evening meetings, too, in the shadow of the fort between the hotel and my house, an hour or two snatched from my distracted family on flimsy pretexts. We climbed the fences into villa gardens whose owners were away, and lay among the trees there, nightly re-entwined, I ever vigilant that my jeans not come down off my waist, no matter how often his fingers reached inside to prise me open. It was always I who eventually grabbed Thibaud's wrist and turned the luminous face of his watch skywards, only to gasp, with exaggerated horror, at the hour. He could have prolonged these stolen embraces for ever. I, too, noticed that in the rhythm of our kissing the time seemed to trickle away at unearthly speed. I never asked myself if I enjoyed it: it was my gift to Thibaud, the price I paid for his company. But I did enjoy it. I craved it even as it frightened and sometimes bored me, just as I craved the oppressive pressure of his arm around me; and each night when we parted, it felt like falling, like falling away from myself and back into a place where I didn't exist. Walking home, I counted the days left to us, and as they dwindled, I became aware of a sensation like vertigo, a sound in my head like the whipping wind. I did not know what I would do when he left, with five blank weeks of summer still ahead.

In those days, tinged as they were with desperation, etched as precisely as a picture in a frame because we knew – I knew – that they would so soon come to an end, that it was a story, not real life; in those days, I pushed my family to the edge of my sight, so they were but blurry images wafting inconclusively there; and I imagined that they did the same to me. But they were parents, and I a child, and although their outward selves had made no sign, they were all along plotting a path for me.

IO

On the Sunday before Thibaud's departure, my family, having forgone them the week before, returned to its rituals of religious devotion: we went to mass. My mother even convinced my father to go, and we took my grandmother with us. My grandfather remained in his room in our house, to watch the service on his private television (his only connection, at that time, with the world), and he suffered Etienne to be wheeled in alongside him.

I dreaded the outing: the brave smiles, the guarded curiosity and malice of the other parishioners, the tender concern of the priest, who clasped my grandmother's hand between his fleshy palms and kissed her forehead, whispering, 'The Lord tests us. He tests our faith.'

I, who usually enjoyed church – a year or two before, for a whole winter, I had seriously thought that I might have a vocation – hated every second of that Sunday. It did not worry me that God – whom I imagined as benevolent – knew of our troubles, or that the priest – whom I disliked for his gluey baldness – did also; but that he spoke of them there, on the church steps, that everyone else around us knew (yes, there was Thierry, at the front, skipping out the side door so he wouldn't have to speak to me), that they discussed us over their three-course lunches or on the telephone ('They all came but *him*. Well, he wouldn't dare, would he?'), that they scrutinized us slyly from under their sympathy-creased brows ('Haughty as ever, the old bitch. You'd think this'd bring her down a peg or two – but no!'). My mother hated it too, I could tell: her face was fixed in a mask of terror that looked, alas, more like disgust. Her forehead and chin perspired through the makeup, and she daubed at them repeatedly with a lace-edged hanky.

We got through it, though, and we escaped (at so leisurely and sociable a pace that no one would have guessed it was an escape) to the air-conditioned isolation of my father's car.

'Wasn't so bad, was it?' cajoled my father, reaching across to pat his mother's hand.

'Awful,' hissed my mother, under her breath, to me in the back seat.

'Next week I'll make Jacques come,' my grandmother said. 'We have to put this behind us. He must be seen. He's not a criminal, after all.'

Isn't he? my look asked my mother. She frowned.

'Only if Papa is ready,' said my father with his newfound authority, backing the car smoothly up the lane and pausing to nod and smile at a couple from the church. 'It'll all be fine. Things will settle down.'

'It's your father I'm concerned about. Not them,' my grandmother sneered. 'Those people – with a few exceptions – have never done a thing for us. He has to realize that they don't matter.'

'Surely he knows that,' said my mother, brushing invisible smut from her blouse. 'What's troubling him isn't other people, surely. It's that he's done something he never thought he could do. It's facing himself that's the problem. Surely?'

Neither my grandmother nor my father said anything for a moment, and then my father said, as if it were a joke, 'But that's what all of life is, isn't it? Being tripped up by unpleasant truths? Just got to get back on the horse.'

'He was not in the wrong,' my grandmother interjected. 'He was very tired. Overworked. That's all.'

'Lunch?' said my father.

Over the meal – we travelled twenty miles inland to a castellated village on a hill, where the restaurant tables, beneath

85

their crimson parasols, were occupied by foreigners: we had had enough of the familiar for a while – my parents divulged their plan for me.

'There are still five weeks before school starts,' my father said, toying with his cutlery.

'I know.'

'And our lives are . . . disrupted. Yours too. You don't play with your friends, just now—'

'We don't "play". I'm not five years old.'

'You don't go to the hotel,' said my father, looking at me. 'You trail around town. And that fellow you're so fond of is leaving soon.'

'Thank God,' said my mother. My grandmother, her mouth a moue of distaste, focused on her melon.

'What I mean is—' My mother was struggling, suddenly, to keep me on their side. 'You're too young for – attachments. I know that this has been hard on you, but—'

'No harder than for you.'

'What your mother is trying to say is that we thought it might be good for you to get away for a while. Till things settle down.'

I grimaced. 'Summer camp, Maman? Are you going to do what you've always wanted and send me to summer camp?'

'How about the States?' said my father. 'Wouldn't that be fun?'

'Would it?'

'I spoke to your Aunt Eleanor,' said my mother, 'and she suggested it, actually.'

'Aunt Eleanor? Jesus.'

'Sagesse.' (My father.)

'Sorry. It's just . . . it's not her, so much. It's Becky and Rachel, that's all.'

'You haven't seen them in five years.' (My mother.)

'I've seen them enough to know I don't like them.'

'People change,' said my mother.

'Quite,' said my grandmother, who hadn't thus far spoken. 'Your parents think it would be good for you. For a few weeks.

And then life will be back to normal, and everything will be fine.' She sliced decisively at a wedge of cantaloupe, speared it along with some prosciutto, and ingested the mouthful with her unique precision. And it seemed there was no more to be said.

II

I could have struggled. Like my father when barely older than I, with his own father, in Algiers, I could have planted myself and roared and said no. But I did not see the point. I was being offered an escape. And when I returned – they promised – everything would be back to normal.

The morning Thibaud was to leave, we met at the fort and walked around its lower ramparts. We could hear the recruits drilling in formation, behind us, up above. We leaned against the rib-high stone wall and looked out at the sea. The fateful aircraft carrier – American, of course – still idled at the entrance to the harbour, its tiny seamen invisible in the morning haze. Thibaud put his arms around me, and I felt as though I floated overhead, among the exercising soldiers, watching the couple that we made. A tricolour snapped erratically. Our words seemed like lines, memorized.

'You'll come visit, in Paris, in the fall,' he said. I smiled. 'And we'll be back next summer.' I didn't believe, at that juncture, in next summer. 'Maybe I can get my parents to come down at Christmas. Maybe I can come alone.'

I fingered the buttons of his cornflower-blue shirt. He was incongruously dressed up for the highway, the drive home.

'Will you write to me from the States?'

'Of course I will.'

'I love you, you know.'

I looked at him, unable to believe he had said it. I felt an overwhelming urge to snicker. I knew an answer was expected, and also that I couldn't bring myself to form those words. 'Me too,' I said.

He kissed me: I loved his smell, I loved the line of his back under his clothes, I loved the slight, soft roughness of his adolescent skin. But I could not have said with any certainty that I loved *him*.

'I'll miss you.'

'Me too.'

We kissed again, our tongues dancing in the tunnel of our joined mouths. Somebody above us whistled appreciation.

'I'd better go,' Thibaud said. He looked at his watch, holding his wrist with his other hand. My gesture.

'Yeah. You'd better.'

'Everything will be okay, you know.'

'Sure.'

As we parted, he handed me an envelope, my name written on it in his spiky script, and underlined.

'Don't open it till you're on the plane.'

'That's days from now.'

'Oh. Well, whatever. But not till later. Much later.'

'It's a letter?'

'What else would it be?'

'I'll wait.'

12

I placed the envelope with my ticket and passport and the travellers' cheques my father gave me, in the sacred pile of absolute necessities. I imagined its contents many times in the dwindling days at home. I filled Etienne, as I pushed his chair down the drive and out into the world for walks (I had used to do this more often; I did it in off-seasons, still, when the call of outside society was less enticing), with all the truths I imagined Thibaud might have set down on paper. I had never received a love letter before. Perhaps, I told my captive brother, these lines would hymn my limbs, the sheen of my hair, the curve of my lips. Perhaps Thibaud was confessing the duration of his passion, its stretch either into the past ('I have loved you, from afar, since first I stepped into the Bellevue years ago') or into the future ('We will marry. Can you wait for me? Are you as certain as I am? You must be!'). Certain of nothing, I desired, I demanded, Thibaud's reassuring certainty. With it – although its substance was still only imagined – I could be proud: I had a boyfriend who loved me in spite of, or because of, or alongside my terrible family.

I did not want Etienne to be jealous (I could not promise him that 'love', like an airplane, would ever transport *him* beyond the reach of our history) but I didn't care enough not to tell him. Or else, for all my protestations, I did not believe strongly enough in the existence of his cloistered mind; and, like everyone else, assumed he didn't understand.

Whatever I willed into Thibaud's sealed envelope, it was to the end of self-disclosure. My reaction to his serenade – my reaction would reveal to me who I was, or where, and how I felt about Thibaud (I missed him, a great deal; but I missed Marie-Jo also, possibly more), and this was why I fingered the creamy stock nightly, and kissed it before going to bed, so that by the time I set off on my own journey, the envelope in my new handbag was no longer crisp, its ink smudged slightly by my moist caresses.

13

I was, officially, an unaccompanied minor, but old enough to protest about the humiliating plastic placard announcing the fact. I flew from the airport at Nice to Paris, jittery about flying and about the miles opening between me and everything I knew. I watched the sea and then the mountains recede beneath us as the plane circled back over the land and headed north-wards. The stewardess, as promised, took special care of me, her painted smile particularly broad as she offered me orange juice, a tiny sack of nuts. I felt like my brother, incompetent to the world, and resisted by refusing to smile. I pretended to read, feigned sleep.

Waiting in one of Roissy's chime-filled satellite pods for the flight to Boston, my fingers greasy with newsprint and potato chips, the rubberized, stale smell of airplanes already in my skin and clothes, I toyed with Thibaud's envelope. I toyed, too, with the thought of calling him (he was there, in Paris!) and fished for a coin and his number and then, at the thought of his eggplant-haired mother (who else would be home, at three in the afternoon?), I shuffled back to my seat.

Only in the broad anonymity of the 747, a mother and infant struggling in the seat beside me, the plane swooping up between the bumpy puffs of cloud – only then, before the grinning stewardess (a new one, of course) and her trolley of drinks could bear down on me again in pained solicitude, before my legs cramped from disuse and before my clothed annoyance at the baby, the mother, the stewardess, the terrible film soon to air, the plastic tray of plastic food, my parents, my spoiled American cousins and their horridly cheerful mother, my aunt, at all that was behind me and to come and at my symbolically uncomfortable present in the bargain, broke free and tainted Thibaud's letter completely – only then did it seem the right moment, at last, to open it.

My index finger insinuated itself into the gummed triangle, the pad of my flesh seeking the path of Thibaud's tongue, breaking the seal stuck by his saliva. It was easy. The envelope, stiff, did not tear. Inside, the single folded square of graph paper was flimsy and unworn. It seemed less substantial even than the envelope's fussy lining. The infant next to me, attracted by the rustling, extended a sticky fist, and I pulled away, pulled my body and Thibaud's fluttering page to the corner of my seat next to the aisle. The stewardess bumped my elbow with her buttock: she was hauling her infernal trolley to the front of the cabin. I was at the front of the cabin. I should have known better than to read Thibaud's letter then. The moment, the possible moment, had passed. But I, resolute, unfolded my momentously awaited page.

Three words. '*Je t'aime, Sagesse.*' That was all it said. I turned the paper over. I was looking for more ink, but there was none. He hadn't even signed it. I had been expecting answers: I was to get none. I stuffed the page back into its casing, unaware till too late that I was speaking aloud. 'Fucking useless,' I said. The stewardess, the mother, the infant recoiled aghast.

'Orange juice, please,' said I.

Three

My grandfather's great-aunt by marriage, Tata Christine, was a solo traveller. Not a glamorous adventuress, trailing chiffon scarves to far-flung palaces, but a small, stout woman like an apple doll, with veiny forearms and bowlegs kept hidden beneath a voluminous black dress, always the same black dress, which she wore until it rusted and the seams pulled through. Then she would count out precisely the coins in her purse and buy the exact yardage necessary of the same black cloth, and make the dress anew.

In the two photographs I know of her, her hands are clasped against her ribs, holding herself in, and her hair, knotted in an invisible bun, is parted with military precision down the centre of her scalp. By the time the pictures were taken, when my grandfather was a boy, she didn't have much hair, and its steely strands are separated by a wide gulf of parting, like a pipeline along her head. She doesn't smile, but the paucity of teeth left to her in age is evident from the puckering of her mouth. The effect is cheerful, as if she were smiling in spite of herself.

She must once have been young, lithe in billowing muslin and curls, winking and giggling with the labourers and barrel makers in her native Brittany village. She had a girlhood like any other, and a young-womanhood. But she was old and alone, resolutely old and alone, for so much of her long life that it is impossible for me to imagine her any other way.

Algeria was claimed by the French in 1830 and settled by *colons* from 1845 or so onwards – the year of Tata Christine's birth – but it was, throughout her youth, a wilderness of wild animals and violent fevers, a mythical dark shore, where the odds of a speedy demise all but outweighed any prospects. Had I been Tata Christine, I would simply have said no when my new husband – Charles, a policeman, perfectly well employed – proposed emigration. Or perhaps not: perhaps there was no muslin, there were no curls and no flirtations. Perhaps the indistinct outline of North Africa, for all its terrors, was a brighter form than the familiar trees and valleys and pathways of her childhood.

My great-great-grandfather, Auguste, was the man with the idea. He was Charles's older brother, a swarthy barrel-maker whose Breton future was laid out in the rolls of iron and the stacks of planks to be soaked and hammered into shape. When he heard that land was being given away – a plot for every willing farmer – he dropped his tools and flung off his leather apron and proselytized, like an evangelical, until his own bemused wife Anne and his brother and young Christine, barely twenty, agreed to come with him.

Their journey was not, like mine, a matter of seven hours, mere grizzling infants and malfunctioning headsets. The four adults, with Auguste and Anne's first two children, one still at the breast, set off on foot for Marseilles, their pots and blankets and salvaged treasures of home stacked onto a pair of sad-faced donkeys. The party slept in the open air, or in the shelter of generous farmers' barns. They ate poorly, they blistered, they pressed on. They piled aboard a rotten ship at Marseilles, pressed up against the mass of hopeful travellers, and vomited throughout the crossing.

Then they were born into the pitiless light of Africa. Their allotments were swamp in winter, dust in summer, the terrain long the home of vindictive creatures – from the mosquito to the jackal – that did not want to relinquish it. The native population too, elusive in their drapery, passing by at gawking distance, eyed the newcomers with disdain and rage. There was still war, then, between the French army and Algeria's insurgent tribes, a sowing of brutality and ill will that would yield its most bitter fruit only much later. The *colons* clustered in compounds and bolted their doors against the land, dreading the dawn of the new day.

I imagine that this is when Tata Christine ceased to be young. But perhaps not. After all, with the exception of Anne's infant, they all survived the first year. They learned to farm by farming, to shoot by shooting. They made mistakes. If they had prayed before, they prayed far more frequently, their conversations with God colloquial, constant, indispensable. They built a life of sorts. My great-grandfather was born, and two sisters, the last taking Anne's life in exchange for her own. Christine brought them all into the world, although God granted her none of her own, and in this way she found her calling: a midwife, a *sage-femme*.

Charles died at forty-two. He might have died anyway, patrolling the streets and bars of his native town, but it was malaria, a specifically African ailment, that claimed him. Christine, all of thirty-eight, sewed her first black dress, slipped into it (now, surely, she was old) and away from their farm, leaving the land to Auguste, his second wife, and their clutch of skinny children.

It was 1883, and Christine began her travels. Back, back on foot and horseback, to the boats. Back, on an emptier ship, to Marseilles, and back, up the winding of time and the roads of her youth, to the place whence she had set out. Was France changed, or was she? Both, doubtless. The winters were too cold. She missed the shine of dark skin, the smells of fragrant spices. She lacked her sense of embattled mission. She quarrelled with her brother, in whose house she was forced to live. Not enough babies were being born to busy her, and those that were fell into the waiting palms of older, more known midwives. When her own sister-in-law called for another woman to deliver her child, Christine – a grey wool shawl around her black dress (still her first) – turned heel and set off back, back again. She was in France for all of a year and a half.

She settled in a cottage in a village not far – a day's travel – from her first, near enough to visit Auguste and his family, but far enough to elude the patriarch's tyrannical reach. She revelled in the rediscovered odours of Africa, in the colours of the sky and earth. She practised the guttural twitches of the local language. She loved the light. In colonial terms she was an old hand, her wisdom desirable as it could never be in France: Christine soothed mysterious fevers, calmed rebellious stomachs; she knew how to ward off the *schkoumoun* and how to encourage the birth of sons.

A mother, a grandmother to the young women newly arrived from France, she was also in demand for the births in the hills, among the nomads and the mountain tribes. A swaddled man would beat on her door in the night, his bare feet cracked from the journey, and carry her back with him on his donkey to a settlement uncharted by the French, where an Arab or a Berber woman – sprawled, all belly, in a hut or tent, or on a blanket in a cave – puffed and screamed in the back of her throat, awaiting Tata Christine and deliverance. Two days, sometimes three at a time, Christine disappeared into the brush: she did not discuss these travels with her fellow Frenchmen, but they knew. Sometimes they heard the banging at her door, or the saddling of the animals at dawn. They certainly saw the food which appeared, afterwards, upon her shelves: the honeyed cakes and jars of olives that kept Tata Christine almost stout. During the war (the First), food, like men, was scarce; but the people in the hills did not forget her. Even when there were no babies to bring, my great-great-great-aunt's larder was stocked with gifts, bundles that appeared like orphans on her doorstep while she slept: a jug of oil, a basket of eggs, a trio of fat oranges.

When at last she moved into my grandfather's house – his own father, whom Christine had brought into the world, having but recently left it for eternity – she came ostensibly to help her nephew's wife. But the journey to Blida was her last: with a small trunk and her rusted black dress (she was truly ancient then), she came to their house to die. That was something, the one thing, to be undertaken within the embrace of the family. She whose sons and daughters numbered in the hundreds, if not the thousands, their colours and fates as scattered and various as the landscape, shuffled into the LaBasse house and withered there. She was buried next to her nephew, rosary beads between her fingers and her hands clasped – as in the photographs – to her ribs, holding herself in.

2

I did not, of course, go to Aunt Eleanor's to die. My life was just beginning, a fact I could never forget because it was so often repeated to me by Aunt Eleanor herself, given as she was to vigorous, impromptu hugs: 'Lambkin, it'll all be okay. Don't be down. Your life is just beginning and it's gonna be great.' She was as solid as my mother was fragile, an athletic woman in her mid-forties with a muscled jaw and a corona of auburn hair. Her traits were not unlike my mother's, but they sat differently, moulded into an American form. Her eyes blinked more nakedly in their sockets. She favoured denim or shorts at weekends. She came home from work with pink sneakers and sweat socks below her tailored skirt – an almost parodic indignity to my European, teenaged eye. She bleached, rather than waxed, her downy moustache, robustly unafraid of imperfection.

From the moment my plane landed at Logan Airport, America ceased to be mine. It had been, for me, 'a shining thing in the mind', the imaginary place of my future, the way Algeria was the imaginary place of my past. But Algeria would shimmer intransigent, forever untouchable; while America, what I saw of it that summer, assaulted me and was itself.

They were all waiting outside the smoked glass doors, the four of them, peering and waving and baring their orthodontic excellence (little Rachel's was still in progress, her mouth a glittering fiesta of tracks). They encircled me and seized my luggage: I clung to my handbag as Rachel tried, almost violently, to claim it. Ron, Eleanor's husband, kissed me on both cheeks ('You are French, after all,' he joked in his nasal, high-pitched voice) and I got a mouthful of his beard, twice. He was a big man, and hairy, like my father, but sloppy somehow.

It was evening, but still hot, and the station wagon thumped on potholes as we wound out to the highway. The furnace breeze blew in the half-open windows and I turned my nose to it, breathing still the airplane smell, taking in the scrub and wreckage, the endless necklace of car lamps stretching into the dusk. I stared at the world beyond the car for miles; Becky and Rachel stared, surreptitiously, at me. I felt like crying.

'It's such a treat for us, isn't it, girls? It would've been great if your mom and dad could've come too, but this is a busy time for them, so . . . next time, right girls?'

Becky punched her sister's thigh for the hell of it, although she was in principle too old for such tormenting.

'Mom,' Rachel wailed.

Once off the highway, Ron pulled into a gas station. Here at least the smell was familiar, and the coil of the pump. The road beyond looked big. There was nothing that wasn't man-made between us and the horizon: a strip of shops, asphalt, neon.

'It's a long way to come by yourself, isn't it? We were afraid we'd miss you, or that we wouldn't recognize you, but you look just the same. Doesn't she?'

'I don't remember,' said Rachel. Becky didn't say anything. She just eyed me, my clothes and my hair and the goose bumps up my arms from the breeze.

'Isn't that so, Ron?' Eleanor asked as he swung himself back into his seat and wiped his hands on his jeans. My father never wore jeans. 'Doesn't Sagesse look just the same?'

'You look like your mother. Just the same,' he agreed, and laughed, although I didn't know why.

They were referring to my nine-year-old self. We had come to visit in the spring, that year, after a trip to Washington, D.C. and New York, without my brother. Eleanor hadn't seen Etienne since she had come to France, when he was three. The cousins had never seen him, not old enough to remember. Becky was looking at me, I thought, to see if my retarded, crippled brother and his wheelchair were discernible in my person. Or maybe my almost-assassin grandfather. I didn't know whether she knew about 'the incident', why I was there at all. Perhaps she was just looking. I felt uncomfortably young among these people, and tired at the sound of their voices; but older than Becky, although she was older than I was.

I remembered the last, the only, visit. I had had a chocolate brown suede jacket then, bought in New York. I had worn it the entire time, aware that Becky coveted it. She played tapes of Bruce Springsteen and Tears for Fears, wanting to impress. She insisted that the French couldn't make rock music, and I told her she just couldn't understand it. She made fun of my accent, when I didn't believe that I had one. She was just trying to get back at me, my mother said, because she was insecure. Her room was decorated with Laura Ashley wallpaper, a mass of little pink flowers. I had been forced to sleep in there with her, stretched out under a quilted coverlet that matched her own, in a bed the twin of hers, suffocated by her music and her stuffed animal collection. I had hated her. But she looked different now: reassuringly sullen. I, more subtly than she, looked her up and down. She was almost sixteen. She had three studs in her left ear. I could smell patchouli and cigarettes on her clothes.

I was old enough, or considered distressed enough, to merit a room of my own. The Robertsons lived in a picture-book white frame house set back from the road in a suburb south of Boston. It was a large house, but not as large as its neighbours', which were closer in on either side than others along the street.

'Ours is the original,' Eleanor explained. 'They sold off the land later, and built the others. I like to picture it alone, surrounded by trees, the way it was in the beginning.'

It was still surrounded by trees. Everywhere was green, rampantly green, and growing. The sky was all but invisible for the verdant canopy. I missed the reluctant, thirsty trees of home, with their twisty trunks and scrabbling limbs. The fertility around the Robertsons seemed obscene.

My room, though, was wonderful. I had a high, old double

bed with ringed posts at the corners, and taut white sheets. There was an armoire and a chest of drawers — a highboy, I learned it was called — to match ('Your grandmother's bedroom suite,' Eleanor volunteered; I sometimes forgot that my mother had had parents too, and that they had died). The floor was glossy, and creaked, and the wing chair in the corner seemed to sit gingerly upon it. The big window — which gave onto a cluster of trees, through which, when the branches moved, blinked a light from the house next door — rattled in its frame. Eleanor had put a bunch of daisies in a glass and a copy of *Seventeen* magazine by my bed, next to the fringed lamp.

'I hope you'll feel at home in here,' she said. 'We want you to feel right at home. We only have a few rules: consideration for others, help when asked, and keep your sense of humour.'

Becky appeared in the doorway behind her mother and rolled her eyes at Eleanor's humanist litany. 'Mom,' she said, 'get real.' She took her hands off her hips. 'Dad says, does Sagesse want dinner or is she too tired?'

'I'm okay,' I said.

'Which means?' Becky crossed her arms over her breasts. She was impressively sullen.

'Yes, please. I'd like to join you for dinner.'

Becky turned and went. Her mother sighed. 'I'm sure you're not like that with your mother. We all go through it, but it can be hard to bear. C'mon, I'll show you the bathroom. You share it with the girls.'

That first night, I woke before dawn to the sound of Etienne's crying, a hollow, keening sound. It was in fact a cat in heat, somewhere outside the window. At first, I didn't know where I was, and the bulbed bedposts menaced in the gloom. Aside from the wailing, the silence was absolute. I got out of bed and tiptoed down the hall to the bathroom. All the doors were shut. I peed, and the trickle resounded, embarrassing. I was afraid that the flush would waken everybody, and stood peering into the bowl for some time before I found the courage to flick the handle. I felt as though the house itself were listening with me. Back in bed, I didn't fall asleep for a long time. My insides were gassy. I lay waiting for intruders. Only when I heard the first stirrings of my aunt and uncle did I allow myself to let go, my vigil kept. I dreamed of the safe, pale shapes of my bedroom.

3

Life at the Robertsons' was backwards: Aunt Eleanor left for her office (she worked as a family lawyer in a glass tower in the city, uncoiling bitter divorces and bickering over custody cases) before I got up in the morning; Uncle Ron, a professor at one of the local colleges, a small, un-famous one where he lectured on the history of sport, a subject I had not hitherto known to exist, was on vacation for the summer, and it was he, with his broad, lazy gestures and thin, persistent laugh, who kept the rhythms of the household. He drove Rachel every morning to her tennis camp, where she spent the day's hottest hours lined up among other sparky children of privilege, practising ground strokes with balletic aplomb; and he picked her up at four each afternoon. He packed her lunches, too – tuna salad or salami and cheese piled between hearty slabs of brown bread, a waxy piece of fruit, a pair of cookies in a plastic sack – meals which she scorned and smuggled home again as often as not to slip untouched (except the cookies) into the trash. Sometimes, fearful of being caught and forced to choke down the limp but formidable sandwiches, she stuffed them under her bed for a day or two, awaiting the biweekly garbage truck. There they festered and perfumed her room as surely and offensively as the air fresheners that lent the Robertsons' bathrooms their antiseptic twang.

But Rachel, at eleven, was at an age where she could do no wrong, and her malodorous hoarding passed unnoticed. Rather, Ron and Eleanor focused their concern (it was a family in which discontent was manifested as loving concern) on Becky – who refused, often, to eat at all; who flounced; who circled around her family with a terrified haughtiness and spent several

CLAIRE MESSUD

days trying to gauge whether I was of it (and hence to be despised) or not, like a dog sniffing at a stranger's pant leg.

Becky had had, at the outset of the summer, the prize my mother had always hoped for for me: a summer job. As she was on the threshold of her junior year in high school, this prize was professionally necessary. Eleanor explained this to me on my second evening there, as she darted around the flower beds after work in her suit and sneakers, yanking weeds, while I trailed behind holding open a plastic garbage bag for their remains. (We had a garden too, of course, but my mother let one of the gardeners from the hotel tend to it. 'Dirt,' she used to say, 'does not interest me.') If Becky was to secure a place at a decent university, as they hoped (and tacitly demanded) she would, it was necessary to be able to prove that her summers had not been wasted, that she had either been earning or learning, and preferably both.

Becky had had the ideal job for a girl her age, Eleanor said. Eleanor had helped her to find it. She had been the assistant to a woman named Laetitia, a lady of independent means and a daughter of the sixties, whose mission (she had trained as a doctor) was to bring food and medical care, without judgement, to the downtrodden of Boston's Combat Zone. Laetitia was a self-starter: she didn't go in for government programmes. She made up and delivered over a hundred packed meals a day to the homeless and diseased (so many salami sandwiches – I pictured them stacked up, an inedible mountain), and once a week she drove her van to a specific corner where she tended the coughs and cuts of the same, and – 'Don't tell,' cautioned Eleanor – passed out free needles to the junkies, although it was then against the law to do so.

'She is such an impressive woman,' Eleanor said, fiddling with the garden hose. 'She does remarkable work. But try telling that to Becky. Becky – ' she wrinkled her nose, officially disappointed ' – only lasted two weeks. To each her own, I suppose. But I don't know how she expects to get into college at this rate.'

Becky would later confide that she had found the work

alternately dull and frightening. She was either slathering entire
loaves of supermarket bread with Hellmann's mayonnaise, milky
goo which got under her nails and into her hair, or steeling
herself to approach the twitching, dead-eyed bundles of rags to
whom Laetitia ministered, to press the food upon them. I could
not, myself, have done such work; I didn't understand how
Eleanor and Ron could expect Becky to do it either. Becky
told me, too, that Laetitia was herself alarming: bony, with wild
hair that smelled of seaweed (her own diet was macrobiotic),
she seemed, always, to be shedding skin, in amoebic patches, on
her arms and neck. She would fall asleep at odd moments – in
the van, in the Zone – leaving Becky to wonder if her employer
was dead, or succumbing to a coma, and uncertain whether to
waken her or to send away the jittery crowd strung along the
sidewalk outside. And most of all, Becky said, she couldn't stand
the needles. They gave her the creeps.

Becky had quit without telling her parents. For several days
afterwards she left each morning as if going to Laetitia's house
in Back Bay, only to stop at the Common and sit there, like a
homeless person herself, waiting for the day to pass. Of the
revelation, when it came, Eleanor said: 'We were sad only that
she didn't feel she could confide in us. We're on her side, you
know.' And Becky: 'They were mad as hell. Mom especially.'

4

It dawned on me in those early days that I was, in this place,
remarkably, a cipher. I didn't speak much. The tidal wave of
American English was tiring for me, and it took all my energy
to keep up, and anyway I felt that my personality didn't
translate. I couldn't make jokes in English, or not without
planning them out before I spoke, by which time they ceased
to be funny and I couldn't be bothered to voice them. It was
that way with most statements of more than a sentence or
two: I passionately did not want to make mistakes, because my

identity as an American was at stake. So I confined myself to questions, and encouraging echoes, their idiom easy to mimic: 'Cool' and 'Awesome' and 'You're kidding!'

But because they didn't know me, my cousins didn't notice. They thought me reserved, perhaps, or pensive, or homesick (which I often was, but they didn't ask about my home), and each projected onto me the character she wanted or needed me to have. I suddenly looked different from every angle, and was free. They didn't seem to remember, even, about Etienne, or else they thought him better not discussed, and for the first time I felt that part of myself cut away. I was absolved of all responsibility, and I liked it.

For Eleanor, I was cast as the enviable adolescent daughter, the placid girl that Becky ought to have been and that Rachel would, with luck, become: old enough for proper conversation, and yet obedient. Clearly my mother had not mentioned that I, too, was difficult. The sisters were not close. Eleanor did imagine in me a complacency, the complacency of her own and my mother's middle-class childhood, with which she felt my mother had never broken.

'I don't see how she can stand not to work,' she said once, looking hard at me as though I should have an answer. 'But I guess she's in a different culture now. I guess it suits her.' She paused. 'It wasn't easy for me. But I'm a little older, and I had the sixties on my side. Your mother was just never interested. I was the weirdo in the family. Mom and Dad were thrilled when she went to France the first time. Less thrilled, of course, that she fell in love with the place and then with your father. She was a French major. A real twin-set-and-pearls girl. She liked being at a women's college. I didn't have the choice, but a few years later, she did. Things were changing that fast, back then. We're just very different, dear, that's all. I've always been one for a fight. You've got to be, in life, Sagesse.'

For Ron, my silence was coy and flirtatious: 'There she goes again, speaking with her eyes,' he'd say. 'Louder than a thousand words.' He was bluff, but not convincingly so, a gentle soul in a footballer's body who masked his fear of being laughed at only by laughing constantly himself, at things that weren't remotely amusing. I came to this conclusion only long afterwards: at the time he merely made me nervous, and I did all I could to avoid being left alone with him. But I think he, too, who deferred to his wife in all things, absorbed an impression that I was a 'good' girl, more conservative and reliable than their Becky, more withdrawn than the exuberant Rachel. And, in my troubles, to be left alone as much as I wanted.

Rachel thought me exotic. At the beginning she was forever wanting to show me things, to include me with her friends. She marvelled over my clothes and my little bag of makeup ('Your lipstick's by Chanel? Wow! Can I try it?'), wanting me to be an older sister still close enough to care about, rather than dismiss, her preoccupations. She called me 'Gesso', and then 'Gesso the Gecko', and because I could not trust myself to express my annoyance lightheartedly, I let her, which allowed her to believe I was the sort who could be played with, and trusted, and which kept me in her favour.

Becky wasn't so sure. We became friends, in the end, over a misunderstanding. I'd been there three or four days, and although the family was welcoming enough, I was lonely and bored. Becky, jobless now for some weeks, was too, but she kept her comings and goings secret from me. She had friends, with whom she disappeared for hours. I slept a lot, and spent afternoons on a blanket under one of the immense trees, reading *Jane Eyre* in English and writing imaginary letters to Marie-Jo and to Thibaud, communiqués which my pride would keep me from ever setting out on paper, let alone sending. Once I tried to sketch the house from the yard and abandoned the project in disgust.

5

I was pretending to read about Jane's miserable experience at the Lowood School, my eyes skating over the paragraphs as if they were so many squiggles, when Becky ambled across the lawn, her long, reddish hair fluttering loose, catching the sun. She wore a tank top, and her throat and shoulders were smattered with freckles. Her breasts, smaller than mine, hardly moved as she walked. She flopped down onto the grass a few feet away from me and tipped her face to the afternoon light. It was around four, and Ron had gone out to pick up Rachel and buy food for supper. ('Wanna come? See the thrills of Star Market?' he'd asked from the kitchen door, nasal and laughing. 'I didn't think so. Must be a good book!')

When she spoke, her words were directed away from me, at the blobs of cloud.

'I'm sorry?'

'I said, "Do you smoke up?" '

It was not an expression I had heard before, and I took it to be a colloquial reference to smoking, period, which would have been a sufficiently illicit thrill in the Robertsons' anti-tobacco world.

'All the time, at home,' I said, then clarified: 'Not at home, I mean, but with my friends.'

'Good.' She whipped out a little plastic bag and a stone sliver, which I didn't immediately recognize as a pipe, from the back pocket of her cutoffs. 'Dad won't be back for at least an hour. There's plenty of time.'

With exaggerated concentration she proceeded to select a seedless thumbful of the contents of her bag, and to jam it into the bowl of the tiny pipe. She had a lighter, too, although I didn't see which pocket it emerged from.

'This is great stuff. Doesn't take much to work.'

As with Thibaud's question under the swimming pool, I knew there was an appropriate response that had nothing to do with the truth. This time, mercifully, I could guess what that response should be. 'Cool,' I said.

I still had two and a half weeks to spend there, and in that moment I had my choice: I could spend them with Jane Eyre or with Becky. Becky, at least, was alive.

I watched her draw in the smoke and hold it in her lungs like a diver, and when it was my turn I copied her. I didn't choke, or cough, and I forbore from complaining about the burning in my throat, which was, after all, no worse than that caused by an unfiltered Gitane. Three or four times we repeated the little ceremony, passing the pipe back and forth, our cheeks ballooning, our eyes watering. It didn't seem to have much effect on me, or not that I could tell. I felt readier to laugh, maybe; but that readiness may also have been an expectation that laughter was the effect of marijuana. Becky, though, was transformed – not into some intoxicated monster, but into a possible friend, indulgent, beatific.

'God,' she said. 'This stuff is great. Around here you really need it, y'know? I don't know what your family's like, but mine – arrggh!' She made a show of tearing her hair and slid back, flat on the grass. 'Isn't the sky incredible? Aren't you so bored? Isn't my dad ridiculous?'

I laughed. I lay back too, and could hear the tiny tickings of the grass blades. The earth smelled like pennies. 'The sky is incredible,' I agreed. There was no breeze, but high above the clouds were chasing across the ether, their shapes erratic and amusing.

'Sometimes I just want to fall in,' she said. 'You wonder if it'll ever get any better, y'know? I tell myself I'll give it till college – till I'm away from these guys – and if it doesn't get any better then, then *bam.*'

'Bam?'

'Then I'll kill myself, of course. I mean, it can't be any worse to be dead, and maybe it's really cool, y'know?'

'If it's awful, you're stuck there. You can't come back.'

'Maybe. I'm thinking about reincarnation, whether I believe in it or not.'

'Do you?'

'I haven't decided. It wouldn't be so bad to be a plant or a horse or a shark or something. It's being human that sucks. We're responsible for all the bad shit. Our parents' generation has poisoned the planet, and we'll all probably die soon anyway.'

'Things like Chernobyl.'

'Oh my God, and pesticides and all that. I saw a show on TV about what they do to the fruit and vegetables and stuff. And then we eat it. I'm never having kids.'

After a minute, she said, 'Will you?'

'I don't know. I never thought about it.'

'With all the shit around, they'd probably be born deformed or something.'

'Maybe.' I sat up. I was thinking of Etienne. She suddenly was too.

'Oh Jeez. I'm sorry. I never meant – I didn't think.'

'It's okay. He'll never have kids, anyway.'

'No.'

'It happened at birth, you know. He wasn't made that way.'

She was sitting, too. 'What's it like?'

I plucked at the grass, not looking at her. 'How do you mean?'

'Well, he doesn't talk, right? That's what Mom said. So, I mean, how do you—'

'I don't know. He's always been there. I don't, I mean, he's not – he's just a part of me, or of us, y'know?'

She considered this in silence.

'And he's happy. He's always happy to see me. He laughs a lot.'

'Right.' She stood up. 'Maybe it wouldn't be so bad to be reincarnated like him. Happy, and, well, he can't do anything wrong, right?'

'I'd rather not be reincarnated at all. I'd rather go to heaven.'

'Yeah. Wouldn't we all?'

We heard the car pulling up, and the doors slamming.

'Shit. Shit!' Becky was stuffing the bag and the pipe into her shorts. She started running clumsily across the lawn with the tail of the bag still flapping behind her. 'Quick, let's get upstairs before they come in. Can't you just hear Rachel – "You guys smell funny." Jesus! We'll go in your room, then they won't make us come down.'

I left Jane Eyre rustling her pages under the tree.

Once we were in my room, the door shut, we laughed so hard that I had to sit down on the floor.

'Stop,' Becky gasped. 'Stop or I'll pee in my pants.' And then: 'Oh my God, I can't, I'm gonna—'

She flung open the door and disappeared down the hall.

'Hello?' Ron's voice curled up the stairs. 'Are you gals up there?'

'We'll be down in a bit.'

'No need. I just wanted to be sure. Do whatever you're doing.'

When Becky came back, she smelled of soap. She lay down on my bed, backwards, with her feet on my pillow. She was dreamy now. I wanted to play with her hair, which was fanned out across the sheet, but I didn't know her well enough. I missed Marie-Jo, but our friendship seemed far away, like a novel I had read long ago.

'Do you have a boyfriend at home?' Becky's eyes were shut.

'I don't know. Sort of.'

'Do you love him?'

I thought of Thibaud's letter, now crumpled in the bottom of my bag. Several times, in spite of myself, I had taken it out and read it again, always hoping there would be more, hoping his handwriting wouldn't look so childish.

'I think I'm too young to be in love,' I said, realizing as I spoke that I was echoing my mother.

'Juliet was your age. You know, Romeo and Juliet.'

'Yeah, well . . . do you? Are you in love?'

'Nope. My plan – ' she folded her hands behind her head and raised her face a little to look at me ' – is to have lots of mad affairs with guys who love me far more than I love them.' She lay down again. 'I plan to be adored. In the meantime, I'm trying to get over the hurdles.'

'Meaning?'

'I figure it's time I lost my virginity. I mean, have you?'

'No.'

'I didn't think so. I'm pretty good at telling. But what's cool about you is that you're foreign, so it's harder to know. You don't scream "virgin", or anything.'

'How can you tell?'

'Just can. I don't seem like a virgin, I don't think. I try not to. But maybe guys can tell anyway. The thing is, guys don't want to do it with a virgin, not unless it's a serious relationship. So seeing as I don't want a boyfriend, I just want to lose it, I've got to behave as though I've already done it.'

'So how do you do that?'

She shrugged. 'Act like it's no big deal.'

'But can't they, I mean, won't they be able to tell?'

'Not necessarily. I don't think necessarily. And if they can, then not till it's too late, so it doesn't matter.'

'I guess.'

'Don't you want to?'

'I don't know.'

'I bet your boyfriend wants to.'

'I guess.'

'You could do it here, you know, in America, and then it'd be a lot less scary there, with him.'

This logic seemed somehow flawed. I must have looked sceptical, because Becky grew annoyed and retreated into her old brusqueness. 'Think about it, anyway,' she said. 'I'm going to take a shower.'

After she had gone, I lay on the bed with my head where her feet had been, over her imprint. I thought about it. I was afraid of sex, but maybe she was right, it was just something that needed to be done. I was intrigued by what she had said about me, about it being hard to tell. Nothing mattered, there, in that three-week space: I wasn't anybody in particular, so I could be anybody I wanted. I could, if I felt like it, have sex. Or I could pretend that I had when I hadn't. I wished I hadn't told her that Thibaud and I hadn't done it: but even so, I might have been lying. I could tell her I'd been lying and she would never know for sure. My self seemed like a fistful of puzzle pieces thrown in the air: I was free to rearrange them into any design I chose, adding in new bits, leaving old ones out, and if I didn't like the result I could simply re-jig it. I pictured my limbs and torso and head floating, detached, through a sky of floating limbs and torsos and heads, and then falling to earth in different combinations, forming different girls who were all me. It was thrilling, and my heart sped up at the thought, hammering inside my heavy chest.

'Whatcha doing?'

It was Rachel, still in her tennis outfit, her dark hair struggling to escape its ponytail. 'I thought Becky was in here, too.'

'She was.'

'Are you and she going to be friends now?' Rachel stepped cautiously around my room, picking things up and putting them down again: a T-shirt, a French mystery novel, my hairbrush. She stood plucking my hair in wads from the brush. 'Are you?'

'What?'

'Going to be friends.'

'Maybe.'

'But you're still the Gecko, right?'

'Right.'

'You lose a lot of hair. Y'know, in the brush.'

'I guess.'

'Does that mean you don't want to come to the séance tomorrow after all?'

Rachel had invited me to a séance at her friend Elsa's house, five doors down, the next evening. In the basement, after supper. A horde of giggling eleven-year-old tennis players.

'Of course I'll come. I don't really believe in that stuff, though.'

'That doesn't matter. As long as you come. We're going to call up the ghost of Elsa's grandmother. It'll be way cool.'

'Great.'

'You can call up a French ghost, if you want.'

'Maybe.' I didn't have any to call up. The ghost of a country is harder to summon. I was too old for séances, and I thought Rachel probably was too, but she was very keen.

'I think I'm going to have a nap before dinner,' I said. 'Wake me up?'

'You bet.'

6

During the evening meal, a purposefully civilized affair at the dining room table, in the course of which Rachel was called upon to detail the progress of her tennis game, a duty in which she revelled as it gave her a chance to display her not negligible anecdotal gifts, my mother telephoned. It was after seven in Boston, so past one in the morning at home.

'Is everything okay?'

'Fine, sweetie, fine. I was just missing you, that's all.' Suddenly, now, French was our language, our way of being private. I was on the phone in the Robertsons' kitchen, and they moved in and out around me, clearing the table, clattering at the sink.

'How are you? Is everything okay there? Your cousins aren't so bad, are they?'

'They're all right. Why are you up so late? Where's Papa?'

'Oh, he's so busy nowadays. He'll be home soon, I'm sure. He might sleep at the hotel. I was reading, and I thought, why not?'

'And everyone else?'

'Everybody's fine. Your brother's asleep, of course. He misses you, too. I catch him looking at doors. To see if you'll come in. He doesn't understand.'

I wondered if Etienne had really noticed that I was gone. I hoped he couldn't tell how long time took to pass: I'd been told that dogs couldn't tell, so maybe he couldn't either.

'And your grandfather has gone home, so that's a good sign. Your grandmother took him back yesterday. I think he's coming out of it. The antidepressants take a while to work, but now it's all going to be fine.'

'Are you lonely?'

'A little, maybe. We miss you. But you're having a good time?'

'Fine.' I couldn't think of anything to say. 'We're going to Cape Cod, sometime. Everyone's very kind. Do you want to speak to Aunt Eleanor?'

'It's okay. We spoke already.'

'It's dinnertime, is all.'

'You'd better go then. I just wanted to see how you were. Be good, sweetie. We love you.'

Later, upstairs, I worried about my mother. I could not imagine what she was doing all alone at one in the morning, nor why my father was not home. I wondered what she did – besides take care of Etienne; but the nurse was there for that – when I wasn't there. Her life seemed suddenly implausible, a great, empty mistake. This place, practical and vast and so American, was where she was from: it had been home to her. What did she feel, now, there? As though she'd thrown up the jigsaw pieces of her life, for a lark, and when they toppled towards the earth they didn't fit together at all any more. And then she was stuck with them (with me, with Etienne), and there were no more tosses, no more chances. I tried to imagine how I'd feel if someone told me that was it, I had to stay with the Robertsons for ever. I'd have to behave as if it made sense, day after day, and then hope that by force of habit I would simply forget that it didn't. But I would always be lonely, the way my mother was lonely. I'd always be pretending.

Then I thought about my father and my grandparents. About the Bellevue Hotel, which was their way of forcing reality, their bulwark against absurdity. Maybe my grandfather had simply got tired of pretending. Maybe it was as simple as that.

Many years later, I learned a little about scientific ideas. I learned that in the eighteenth century, in a burst of rigour, scientists deemed it necessary to study, for the first time, the structure of the female skeleton. They had been examining men's bones for years, but it occurred to them that the peculiar afflictions of women required special attention, that their secrets lay in the osteal geography of the fairer sex. Their conclusions revolutionized not only medical but social understanding. Woman, the scientists explained to scores of German medical students, all eyes on the female skeleton dangling cheerily at the lectern, Woman has a smaller brain, and wider hips. Her constitution is lower to the ground, and that great, gaping cavity in her abdomen is the centre of her soul. Woman is mother, a separate creature from man, with a distinct and scientifically proven role. She is the Angel in the House, they said, or others said after them: it's bred in the bone.

What the scientists did not mention, perhaps forgot themselves, was that the woman on whom this analysis of Woman was based wasn't one. Her hands and head and hips and ribs were not born together. They were the bones of different women, wired together. The scientists threw the pieces into the air, and this is what came down. And there were no more tosses, no more chances. Women were stuck with Her, even though she didn't really exist. It made me wonder, how much is pretending?

7

The séance was a pretence, one in which Rachel and her friends delighted. Becky couldn't believe I'd agreed to go.

'You must be joking! Don't you want to come into town with me instead? A bunch of us are going to the movies.'

'To see what?'

'Dunno yet. Does it matter? Anything would be better than a séance with a bunch of little kids.'

But I had promised, and so I went. Rachel held my hand as we strolled down the road to Elsa's house. Her feet itched to break into a skip; her ponytail jiggled. It was a golden summer evening, and we glided through the buttery air while Becky stalked off downhill, in the opposite direction, to meet her friends at the trolley that would take them to the subway that would carry them into town.

Elsa was a twelve-year-old anorexic with blue veins bulging

through her skin. Her face was flushed, and when she spoke or laughed or even breathed I could detail the workings of her joints and muscles beneath her taut cheeks. She had a furious, spooky energy. Elsa's parents waved benignly from the living room as we passed: they were apparently unfazed by their daughter, although she looked like a spectre one of her own séances might have conjured.

We were not the first to arrive, nor the last. All of us – about six girls besides me, some of whom I'd seen playing with Rachel in the street, and one lone, gentle boy named Sam – were ushered into the basement, into a capacious but tattered playroom. The furniture – a sagging brown plaid sofa, a few straight-backed chairs, a menacing black TV set mounted on a cart – had been pushed back against the walls. Elsa flitted about, drawing the curtains across the high slivers of window to create the requisite gloom, and she hung a red scarf over the shade of the standing lamp in the corner.

'Doesn't it have to be totally dark for the spirits to come?' asked a plump girl whose T-shirt fit like a sausage-casing, and who seemed inclined to bossiness.

'My mom said no way.'

'But it's not going to work otherwise.'

A flurry of debate broke out, and the girls seemed automatically to divide behind thin Elsa or her fat rival, whose name was Nan. The boy, Sam, sat on one of the wooden chairs, humming to himself, looking at the dark TV screen. I sat beside him, leaving Rachel in the fray. I thought enviously of Becky's crowd, rattling along the subway lines, headed away from the suburbs and their basements.

'You're the French girl, right?' Sam asked. He had very large, dark eyes and a sparrow's brittle body. 'Rachel's cousin?'

'That's right.'

'Cool.' He thought for a moment. 'How come you're here?'

'I promised Rachel.' I rolled my eyes.

'I know. I promised Elsa. But this stuff is so dumb. They've been doing it all summer and it's just crap. Elsa thinks it's really grown up.'

'You're the only boy.'

'So?'

'Don't you mind?'

'Naw. I mean, I mind this, it's so dumb—' he gestured at the squabbling girls. 'But I'm used to girls. It's easier to be with them.'

We lapsed again into silence and watched the vacant TV.

Eventually we all settled into a circle, cross-legged, holding hands. Elsa intoned, her voice raspy for one so young: 'Everybody, con-cen-trate. Close your eyes. We're going deeper, together. Deeper . . . deeper. O spirits, we ask you to join us in our meeting, to speak to us and show us you are here.'

Somebody giggled. Elsa's voice changed back to its normal pitch. 'Who was that? If you're not serious, go home. Just leave. Because it only takes one person to spoil the whole thing.'

'Come on, Elsa, lighten up.'

'Why should I? You wanted to come. Do you want to speak to ghosts or not? I want to speak to my grandmother, who died last year. I want to find out how she is. This is serious.'

Rachel, on my right, squeezed my hand. 'You okay?'

I nodded.

Elsa began again in her deep singsong. I peered around at the group, their faces bathed in red light. Their eyes were shut, except for Sam's. I thought he winked at me. Becky, I thought, would be at the cinema by now. My parents, at home, were in bed. I couldn't imagine where Thibaud might be, or what he could be doing. I considered excusing myself, but left my hands where they were, damply linked on either side.

Elsa was baying to her grandmother: Anna, she called her. If there was a spirit world, I thought, it must be overrun with Annas. How would the right one know to come forward? I could hear Elsa's parents moving around overhead. I didn't know if I missed my own parents. I wasn't sure how I felt about anything: any life before the Robertsons seemed dim and far away, images laced around the edges by blackness. I felt as though I'd fallen into a chasm and I clung there, on a ledge in the wall, with no way back and only bottomlessness in front of me. I felt as though I was listening, and waiting, to be saved, just as the girls around me were listening and waiting for ghosts. I didn't know whom I could call: any spirit that could save me would have to be unknown. Tata Christine, perhaps, in her black dress? Or my great-aunt Estelle? But their spirits, if they existed, were in Africa, not in any Boston basement. Elsa's grandmother Anna was conveniently located in the local cemetery; she didn't have far to come.

Elsa claimed to have been visited by her, and Rachel obligingly uttered a few words of endearment in a croaky old-woman voice ('I'm at peace. I love you, Elsa. Be good to your mother'), which she later insisted had not been affected but had welled up within her, unsought. But Elsa's grandmother had been German, and had carried her accent, apparently, to the grave, and the voice that spoke through Rachel was decidedly American. The little girls – with the stout exception of Nan – wanted so much to believe. Certainly Rachel would not admit doubt for a second. But I knew that if there had been ghosts in the room, one would surely have spoken to me. Even Elsa's grandmother would have told Elsa to eat more.

After 'Anna', there were two more attempts, with different girls leading. But patience was wearing thin, and whispers and titters kept erupting mid-séance.

'I'm going home,' said Nan, defiant. 'This is stupid.'

'Wait,' cried Rachel. 'Don't you want to do levitation?'

Maybe, I thought afterwards, this was why she had invited me along. I was bigger than any of them, a greater weight than any except Nan, whose forthright fatness made her a dodgy prospect for lifting. I was made to lie on my back in the middle of the floor with all the girls and Sam huddled over me on their knees, each with two fingers from either hand wedged under my body. Like Gulliver at the mercy of the Lilliputians, I tried briefly and unsuccessfully to survey my captors without raising my head. I am, I thought, a dead weight: it was rather pleasant. Becky, I thought, might be right about death.

There was a low humming, like bees, and I realized they were chanting, very rapidly, in their little-girl voices (even Sam had a little-girl voice), 'light as a feather and stiff as a board, light as a feather and stiff as a board, light as a feather and stiff as a board'. Slowly, unevenly, I felt myself rising. I shut my eyes. They were lifting me, it's true, but so lightly I could hardly feel their fingers. I was rocked slightly, and straightened, as one side caught up with the other, but nobody poked or prodded me. I could feel air slip into the space beneath my back, and my spine began to tingle, the way it did when I stood, awed, beneath the massive vaults of Chartres or Notre Dame. It was the physical feeling of relief and excitement that I had always associated with God.

It didn't last long. They let me down with a walloping thump. But in those seconds, with the buzz of voices resonating like a hive, I soared. I wasn't sorry, after all, to have been there. Their hands had carried me, not a ghost's; but that, at least, didn't feel like pretending.

8

By the time we left for Cape Cod, I was growing used to the Robertsons. I couldn't compare their life to home, but I tried. I made a list:

1. Ron cooks.
2. No maids.
3. No rules.
4. No God.
5. Eleanor never cries.
6. The trees.
7. I am invisible.

I didn't put Etienne on the list, or rather, his absence, but I grew accusatory: it seemed to me that he accounted for a lot. My grandparents did too. Etienne and my grandfather were the reasons that we had maids, and rules, and — for all I knew — God. Between them they were the source of many of my mother's tears, although just about anything could make her cry. (There was, of course, the additional difficulty that my parents didn't get along, but I would not, then, have seen it that way and hence did not consider it.) As for my undesirable visibility at home: partly, I recognized, it occurred because it was home, but also because in seeking to avoid the blot that was my brother, all eyes trained on me.

I decided that I loved America. I told myself that I had always known I would. I loved that it was all future, that the furniture of my past (of my present) couldn't follow me there. (What did Algeria mean to the Robertsons? Or the Bellevue, even?) As I grew closer to Becky, the idea that American life was imaginary receded.

Eleanor and Ron were ambivalent about my bond with their eldest, but I was – to them – a good girl, and they trusted my influence would prevail. Moreover, they could see that I was unfurling.

'It's great to hear you laugh,' Eleanor said to me one evening, after she had stopped, while pruning the hedge along the porch in her business suit, to watch Becky, Rachel and me chasing a Day-Glo frisbee and falling about on the lawn among the clouds of midges. 'You were such a quiet thing when you arrived. I haven't seen Becky and Rachel play together for ages.' She gave me one of her spontaneous hugs, brisk and vigorous.

Smoking marijuana was essential to my friendship with Becky. That and drinking, which I had only done in a modest, civilized way at my parents' dinner table. But Becky and her friends drank under porches or in bedrooms or in the cemetery after dark, crouching behind headstones or in the shadows of minor mausolea to evade the probing lamps of patrolling police cars. They drank quietly, purposefully, anything they could get their hands on, in sickly combinations – Vermouth and 7UP, scotch and orange juice, cheap gin and soda water – or they guzzled potent, sweet liqueurs from squat bottles: peppermint schnapps, Bailey's Irish Cream, a foul, sticky green drink purportedly melon-flavoured.

I took to it, this clandestine consumption, proud to be able to imbibe impressively and yet seem sober, to drift into the Robertsons' kitchen without visibly weaving and to carry on a plausible conversation with Ron and Eleanor. I hid my fumed breath by rummaging at once in the fridge, or by standing at the sink and drinking glass upon glass of water from the tap. Becky deemed me 'incredibly cool'.

Even she was excited at the prospect of a long weekend on Cape Cod. This was their annual event, their Bellevue, four days by the grumpy Atlantic shore, paddling in its chilly waves, guests of another family, the Spongs, the Mrs., Amity, a friend of Eleanor's since college. Amity, herself of Mayflower stock, had married well: Chuck Spong was an investment banker, son of an investment banker, son, in turn, of the founder of the bank, a lineage endowed with brains as well as breeding, or at least with a keen eye for the markets, so that when I first met them they floated like a hovercraft upon a plump cushion of financial security which would only billow further with the years and carry them noiselessly into the realm of the stupendously (but discreetly) rich.

Amity, unlike Eleanor, was never called upon to don a suit and trail off into the hurly-burly of town, a freedom which she shared with my mother but which sat in her like happiness, a languorous delight in being alive. She painted, and upon occasion sold her paintings, scenes of comfortable lives which hung in almost every room of their summer house: a bowl of lilies by an open window, with the sea rippling in the distance; a broadstroked couple, faceless, in polo shirts and sunhats, seated on an evening lawn, pearly cocktail glasses in hand; a nest of sailboats bucking alongside a little girl on a pier, her bathing suit and pail the same exuberant cherry colour. Amity did not have a dark side; Eleanor struggled to suppress her own; in this they were joined.

Amity had four bright children, ranging in age from twenty-one to ten. Three of them clustered together in age and the fourth, Isaac, was a beloved afterthought. Of the older three, our interest lay not so much with Lily and Charlotte, at twenty-one and nineteen too far gone into the clutches of adulthood, but with seventeen-year-old Chad, a calm boy with sleepy eyes and tangled dirty-blond hair, who was indulgent of his little brother as Becky almost never was of Rachel.

Their house, all wood and glass, hid just behind the mile-long strip of pure sand that was the beach, cloistered by trees which, toughened by the salt wind, reminded me at last of home. Salt and sand were everywhere within it, too, in the cracks between the floorboards, in the window linings, in the furrows of the scattered rugs. There was nothing fastidious about the Spongs, for all their wealth: they seemed, if anything, more relaxed even than Ron and Eleanor. Peace wafted through their rooms like the moment after a long sigh. This was, of course, only when they were empty.

The evening we arrived, spilled out of the steamy station wagon that had carried us, through Becky and Rachel's bickering and Ron's weird laughter and Eleanor's chirpy commentary, all the way from Boston, the house was bubbling with anticipatory busy-ness. Isaac and Chad were setting the long table on the deck (from which the long-lost ocean was visible, in pieces, through the trees); Amity and her daughters were waltzing evenly through the dinner preparations, their faces unblushed by the hot stove. Chuck greeted us at the door, and with him Anchor, their black Labrador, whose powerful tail thwacked each of us in turn as he spun in excited circles around our wilted group.

Chuck, like Ron, was bluff; but unlike him, was somehow believable, trim in his short-sleeved madras shirt, conservatively handsome, his blond hair not unlike his sons', but groomed and trimmed into agreeable submission.

'They're here!' cried Isaac, with unaccountable glee, running, bare-breasted in his swimsuit, across the living room, navigating the low, peach-toned clumps of furniture, to stop abruptly at his father's elbow and grow suddenly shy. We were immediately surrounded, and embraced, and flattered. I was introduced, all smiles ('What a treat, Sagesse, we've heard so much about you. And what a lovely name! And what a pretty dress!'), my mouth sore at the corners and my teenage self acutely conscious of the film of car sweat on my nose and chin.

We were shown to our rooms, Becky, Rachel and I to one broad square downstairs, a wall of windows, with twin beds and a truckle, all made up for us. Isaac and Chad were in the next room, and our windows and theirs opened onto a shared patio, from which steps led down to a dirt path to the beach. Lily and Charlotte shared a bigger room across the hall. Next to that was a playroom, graveyard of discarded toys, a tangle of bats and nets and life jackets. The grown-ups resided two floors up, on the far side of the house, out of the way.

'You're on the little bed,' Becky said to Rachel, 'because you're the littlest.'

Rachel didn't complain. She opened the door to the patio and went to knock on the boys' window.

'Ike,' she was saying, 'open up. Let's take Anchor down to the beach for frisbee!'

'It's almost dinnertime,' Becky called.

Rachel stuck her head back in. 'Buzz off, you. If they say we can, then it's okay. You can't boss me here.'

'Whaddaya think?' Becky asked me, bouncing on the edge of her bed. 'Cool, huh?'

I concurred.

'We can come and go and they don't care. It's great.' She sighed. 'I wish we had a house like this.'

'At home, in France, we live by the sea,' I said. 'Not quite so close as this, but close.'

Becky didn't seem interested. She rummaged in her suitcase and pulled out a bathing suit. 'I wish I'd made Mom buy me a new one,' she said. 'I look like the Hindenburg in this.'

'I'm sure you don't.' The suit was light blue, with little yellow flowers on it. 'I bet the colour really suits you.'

'I want a bikini, y'know? Something that gets you noticed, that's sexy. Or even a different colour. Mom wouldn't let me have black.'

I had two suits in my case: a flowered bikini and a black tank. 'You can borrow one of mine if you like.'

'As if,' Becky snorted. 'Like it would fit me.'

'I'm sure it would.'

She sighed again. 'What do you think of them? Really?'

'They seem nice.'

'The parents, yeah. They make Mom nicer, too. She's so busy trying to prove that we're as well-adjusted as they are that she stops being a freak. More or less. But what about, y'know, them?'

'I didn't get much of a sense yet. They all seem very friendly. And the blond girl – which one is she?'

'Lily.'

'She's beautiful, like a model.'

Becky made a noise in her nose. 'I guess. They're in college, those two. They treat me like I'm about twelve. Most of the time. But, y'know, Chad?'

'He seems nice too.'

'So, do you think he's cute?'

'Yeah, sure. I guess so.'

'Maybe you should sleep with him, don't you think?'

'What?'

'For the first time. Like we talked about, remember? He has really nice arms, and great hair, don't you think? And he wouldn't, y'know, make fun of you or anything.'

'Why don't you sleep with him? I don't even know him. And you're the one who's so eager to do it.'

'Yeah, well.' She turned back to her bathing suit. 'This suit is gross. I hate it.'

9

I should have guessed that Chad was Becky's Thibaud. That she had pined for him for years, played games hoping he would notice. I'm sure that if I saw us all now, today, from afar, I would recognize it at once. At the beach, at meals, the afternoon we spent wandering the streets of the nearest town (along, it seemed, with a full half of America's well-heeled youth and many of their parents), Becky joked and pressed Chad on my attention, and me on his. It was her way of allowing herself conversation with him, and her way of forcing his value upon me; but I took her at her word, and flirted as best I could with this dappled representative of American boy-manhood, on his way to his final year at St. Paul's, and thence to the impressive college (Princeton, as it happened) that the Spongs did not, like Ron and Eleanor, hope, but rather knew, their child would attend. From there the steps into freedom were actually steps into the same good-natured imprisonment as his father: the coveted MBA, the family firm, a premature enrobement in grey suiting and suspenders, the Apollonian locks shorn sufficiently to suggest a touch of the madcap behind the reassuring veneer of fiscal responsibility. But all that was in the future, a future so unquestioned and unexamined that Chad, at seventeen, was wholly without anxiety, his sleepy movements so ripe with entitlement that he could afford to be generous, and patient, with everyone around him, from his father to little Ike, to the Robertsons and me.

For Chad, I was novel in ways Becky simply could not be. He, like me, could feel the liberating irrelevance of my presence (I didn't have to be borne, lived with; I was there but soon wouldn't be; I was something different), and, I suppose, without flattering myself, that he found me attractive. On Saturday night, the third night, when we barbecued en masse on the beach and sat (exactly like something out of an American film; I could not have planned it better), after our gritty pork chops and black- ened corn cobs had been discarded, young and old alike around the fire with a guitar, he offered me, not Becky, his sweatshirt against the night breeze, and he wanted to show me, further along the sand at a point of total darkness, the configuration of the stars: Orion's Belt; the Dippers, big and little; reclining Cassiopeia; the Pleiades, in their tiny clustered twinkle.

We strayed for only a few minutes from the fireside, and never more than a hundred feet, but it was enough for even Rachel to assume that something was up.

'Do you really like him?' she asked later, in bed, her knees to her chest and her eyes alight. 'Will you go with him?'

'We leave on Monday, silly,' I said. 'He was just showing me the stars.'

'Yeah, right,' said Becky, from her bed against the far wall. 'Sure. You're such a tease, Sagesse.'

'A what?'

'A cock-tease. You lead guys on.'

'I do not.'

'Puh-lease. You make out you couldn't care less, and then you're all over him.' She batted her eyelashes in sarcastic imitation and put on a strong French accent. 'Oh *oui*, Chad. Yes please, Chad, take me avay and show me ze starrs.'

Rachel hooted.

'That's just mean. You know that's not fair.'

'Oh, ze French darling iz not 'appy. Poor leetle zing.'

'Come on, Becky. Don't be so . . . don't.'

Becky's smile was not entirely friendly. Her freckles looked like spots.

'Well,' she said, 'I just think you should know, if you're doing that innocent French girl act, that this is America, and here you either put up or shut up. You can't go around leading guys on and then not, y'know, deliver.'

'You're making a big fuss about nothing. What was I supposed to do, say I didn't want to see the stars?'

'I wanted to see them too,' said Rachel.

'There,' Becky said, 'you could've asked if anyone else wanted to come along. So he wouldn't get the wrong idea. And you didn't need to take his sweatshirt.'

'I was cold. I gave it back.'

'Ze leetle zing vas cold. Poor leetle zing.'

'I don't get what you're so angry about. It doesn't matter. Surely it doesn't matter?'

'Well, Shirley, it does. Because Chad's a really nice guy.'

'I know that.'

'And I can tell he has a crush on you.'

'He does, Sagesse,' Rachel said. 'It's totally obvious.'

'And I don't want him to get hurt. That's all.'

'You guys, we leave the day after tomorrow.'

'Tomorrow, actually,' said Rachel. 'It's after midnight.'

'Whatever. But it doesn't matter, is my point.'

'What about the party tomorrow night?' Becky said.

'Tonight,' Rachel corrected.

'What about it?'

'Yeah, well.' Becky slid under the sheets and turned to face the wall.

'You're not really mad at me, are you?'

'Of course she's not,' said Rachel, getting up to turn out the light. 'I wish we could sleep with Anchor in here.'

'Gross,' said Becky, into her pillow but loudly. 'You're totally gross, Rach. Anchor stinks. And he's always trying to lick your face.'

'I love him.'

'You're totally gross.'

I laughed at them both and thought myself forgiven.

10

The party the next evening was, like the Robertsons' visit, an annual event. At once cookout and cocktail party, it gathered the summer residents (or at least those of a certain stature) and sprinkled them on the shore and in the house and on the various decks. It was a party for all ages, their hair still wet from the sea, their summer cottons mysteriously crisp. According to Eleanor, we were mingling with senators and policy makers and even a writer or two, although none of the names she mentioned meant anything to me. Ron, I could tell, was nervous about the party: his laughter was almost constant, almost frightening, and then in the moments when he stood alone, his face lapsed into the slackness of utter desolation, and he even neglected to pluck at his beard in the delicate manner he usually affected to evoke thoughtfulness.

There were white-haired and hairless men, and women weathered and not, made-up and not, all laughing earnestly and reaching out to brush Amity Spong's mandarin gauze arm as she slipped among them, the consummate hostess, to rescue the fallen: the husbands and wives abandoned only to each other, or the bespectacled, academic-looking men whose very demeanour flashed 'conversational death' as surely as if it had been spelled in neon over their heads. There were young couples, too, in their late twenties or thirties, whose central preoccupation was with their children – so many of these latter fair, all of them under seven or so. The women of this set contrived to appear both glamorous and exhausted, their crows' feet a badge of maternal loveliness, their tolerance for the clutching and pummelling and wailing of their toddlers infinite.

There were, for me, further revelations of the Spongs' floated world. I spent some time in conversation with a robust, freckled young woman named Abby who, while stoking her square frame with canapés from a tray that she had all but sequestered to ensure private consumption, and in between licking her fingers and quaffing her gin and tonics as if they were water, assured me that her whole life had changed since, the previous winter, at just sixteen, she had finagled her way into the circuit of adult cocktail parties in Boston, on the Cape and, upon occasion, as far afield as the Hamptons. I did not know what or where the Hamptons were, and long afterwards imagined them to be a supremely elegant couple living in rural Massachusetts, and an invitation to their home the very acme of Boston society.

I suffered Abby for as long as I was able, my proximity to the punch bowl a soothing compensation for her company, and by the time I escaped to search for Becky the party and its guests had taken on a roseate glow, a benevolent softness attributable not solely to the twilight but also to the ease of my drink-warmed limbs.

I wandered smilingly, glass in hand, from scene to scene, past Ron, who had not seen either of his daughters in some time, past Amity Spong, who directed me down to the shore. I was then briefly waylaid by Eleanor, eager to introduce me to the Harvard French professor with whom she was conversing, but she released me almost immediately when it became clear that neither he – who saw a virtual child before him – nor I – who saw a schoolteacher – could muster the will to discuss France, that bloated, vague myth of France which meant too much but different things to both of us; and that, this aside, we had nothing in common.

Becky I found some way along the sand, at the edge of the trees, sitting cross-legged with her blue cotton dress hiked up into a small pond around her. She was surrounded by several teenagers I did not know, and as I approached I caught the now familiar acrid-sweet waft of marijuana smoke. Only as I dropped down beside her did I realize that I had taken up a place between her and Chad: his back had been to me, and I hadn't recognized his dark blazered form.

'Hey.' He put his arm around my back and passed a pilfered bourbon bottle, half empty already, into my lap. 'We wondered where you'd got to. I told Becky to go find you, 'cause you were missing all the fun—'

'And I told him to go find you himself.' Becky's cheeks were flushed, and her ringlets trailed confusedly at the edges of her face. Her lips were moist. She emanated disarray.

'Had a few?' I asked. 'I'll need to catch up.'

'Go on then.' Chad's hand, still on the bottle and in my lap, jiggled it back and forth. 'Drink up.'

Conversation in the group was idle. Several strands, all involving escapades of illicit alcohol or drug consumption and ensuing run-ins with parents or the law, seemed to weave in and out around me, overlapping and too effortful to follow. I took a swig from the bottle and moved to pass it on to Becky.

'Again. You've gotta catch up. Drink double.'

I drank again. 'What about the parents?' I asked.

'They don't care,' Chad said, his attention on the joint that was following the bottle around the circle. 'They're doing their thing and we're doing ours. Relax.'

'Yeah, Sagesse. Relax.' Becky, passing the bottle, had the bitter tone of the night before. 'They aren't even your parents. So chill. "I ahm so vorreed, ze parents might puneesh moi." You can't do anything wrong, so just have fun. Let Chad here show you a good time.' She winked, grotesquely.

What followed I still consider an American initiation. It could never have been part of my familiar – my former – circle by the pool at the Bellevue. Given the choice I would have cleaved to Becky, rather than lose her friendship over Chad, in whom my fancy was only passingly, and passively, engaged; but I could not make this clear, in the seaside huddle, and still remain the girl Becky had decided I was, who I wanted to be: cool, indifferent and selfish. Chad put his hand on my knee to attract my attention (the bottle coming round again); Becky was jealous. I turned initially towards her, not him, and saw her features distorted by a narrowed glare.

I should perhaps have stood and ambled off, back to Eleanor and her French professor, or even to the odious Abby. I might have found Rachel and Isaac, the safe shore of childhood. But it wasn't possible. I still hoped to prove my friendship for Becky, to show that I wasn't a tease or a drip. So I stayed, planted on the edge of the gathering, half-smiling, attuned only to the rhythm of the circling bottle (when it was empty, another appeared miraculously in its stead, and travelled, albeit more slowly, around and around again), and its minion, the glowing ember of marijuana, which, likewise, replenished itself and kept circulating.

Night fell. No adults strayed to our end of the beach. The sounds of the small children melted and disappeared. The party was shrinking, but we didn't notice. One youth stood up and left, his steps singing softly in the sand as he strode away. Someone thought they saw a bat in the trees. Much laughter. I believed I heard three people on the far side of the circle speaking Spanish.

'Why Spanish?' I asked Chad, but he didn't answer, or appear to understand. He put his arm around my shoulder: 'Cold? Want my jacket?'

I shook my head. He did not remove his arm. I couldn't – it was all so fuzzy now – figure out how to make it lift, and thought of it, obscurely, as Thibaud's protective embrace. Becky, by then, had turned her back to me. Later, when I looked again, it seemed that she had gone, until I realized that her outline had merely altered: she was shrouded in some other boy's blazer, some other arm around her. Two others drifted away. By then we were only five, Chad, me, Becky and her admirer, and a small, swarthy boy who seemed to be called 'Pop' and from whose personal cache the bottles and cigarettes seemed to flow. I was blurred, and very heavy, and anxiety roiled and spun within my leaden frame. The others had grown as unintelligible to me as the chorus of tree frogs.

'I think I'd better go to bed,' I said. 'I don't feel very good.' In France, I thought, at home, this never would have happened. 'I want to go home,' I said. I was trying to shake the weight of Chad's arm across my back, but even when he retrieved his limb the weight was still there. I stood, and heard the waves, so gentle a moment before, thundering in my ears.

'I'll take you.' Chad was at my elbow.

'Yeah, you take her,' I heard Becky say, although I couldn't really see Becky anywhere. There were no adults left along the beach to witness my stumbling. The sand filled my sandals, clawing at my feet with each unsteady step. The evening was cool, but I sweated anyway, unpleasantly moist in every crevice.

'It's not far,' urged Chad's disembodied voice near my ear. His hand supported my elbow – as if, I considered in my spinning, mole-blind world, so courtly a gesture could possibly keep me upright.

'I'm okay,' I lied.

'I don't think so.'

'No, really.'

'Let me help. We'll get you some water. We're almost there.'

Between the pines the air was fragrant. It should have been pleasant. We were near the house now: I could hear the late-stayers' muted voices, interrupted occasionally by a blaring laugh (Ron's?). I could see shadows moving and the flicker of the odd cigarette, heads silhouetted against the Prussian sky, the deck where they all stood rising above like a ship's prow.

Like a ship's prow on a high sea. They tossed. I gasped. I looked down again, steps now from the open window of my room. But it was too late: the bucking of my head had triggered the outraged bucking of my insides.

'I think—'

'Oh shit, Sagesse—'

'I can't help it.'

'Can't you make it to the bathroom?' Chad's voice was very small, but insistent.

'I don't think—'

The high seas loosed themselves within me. Or rather from within me, onto the patio steps, and onto Chad's trousers, and onto the pine-needle bed of the path, a roaring, victorious vomiting which signalled my utter defeat.

Upstairs, they could not fail to hear it. Those who were 'responsible' – the parents – could not, even as they might have liked, pretend not to have heard it.

I could feel Chad wavering in his spattered chinos, contemplating flight, as the bourbon and the dregs of punch jolted their way back up my oesophagus in tough little spurts. But he was a Spong, and he stayed put. His hand was barely a moment away from my elbow, and when I had straightened, and closed my mouth, and swallowed on my burning throat, he led me up the steps and through my room to the bathroom, with its wicked, sallow light, and there he daubed and doused me, and his own soiled legs, and plied me with glasses of water.

II

There Amity Spong and Eleanor discovered us, their own tipsy faces grimacing in disapproval and worry, then in horror at the sight of the little foreign guest, tile-white, soaked in cold water, shivering on her knees beside the toilet bowl in case there was anything still left to come.

It was Eleanor, nostrils flared, who stripped me and bathed me, who fetched my nightgown and stood behind me while I brushed my teeth; who relented slightly at the sight of my tears and enveloped my shuddering body in one of her stonier embraces before leading me, chastened, to bed. Ron – poor

Ron – I later learned, was dispatched along the beach to retrieve Becky from the arms of her new beau, while Chad, being a boy, and not having fled, was summarily dismissed and told that he – and we – would be dealt with in the morning, in order that Amity Spong, with the ever affable Chuck at her side, might ride the last crest of her annual fête with typical aplomb.

Pop was gone by the time Ron found his daughter: a mixed blessing, because with him went all trace of drugs, the cloud of pot smoke having long since subsided into the seaside breeze; but in Pop's absence the other boy, Becky's boy, had succeeded in unbuttoning the bodice of her blue dress, and Ron, poor Ron, came upon the youth clamped like a suckling infant to her tiny breast, Becky, his firstborn, lolling like a corpse alongside three empty Maker's Mark bottles with her hair in her mouth and her right nipple in someone else's. It came as a shock to her father, a shock for which his inevitable response – that nervous laughter – proved inappropriate and curiously troubling: 'I thought,' said Becky later, in the morning, before the thundercloud unleashed and she again turned her back on me, 'from the way he laughed, that maybe he was going to kill me, to kill us both.'

Which he did not. The youth, not nearly so gallant as Chad, or perhaps merely less identifiable, turned heel and sped along the beach away from the house, leaving Becky, barely more sober than I, to button her modesty and stagger back in the wake of her father's enraged bulk.

Rachel, meanwhile, who had been playing Monopoly with Isaac in the boys' bedroom, came through to gawk at me, huddled as I was in my bed and miserable, and eventually at Becky, too, to whom she muttered, in Cassandra-like litany, 'You've really done it this time. You're really gonna get it. Boy, you're in big trouble,' until finally Becky threw her pillow at her sister with a sharp 'Shut THE FUCK up', and turned to face the wall.

12

When you are fourteen – or fifteen, or sixteen – none of it, on such a morning after, seems at all possible. Such moments of disbelief, so integral to adolescence, are reserved in later life for incidents of awesome import: murder, say, or abandonment, or birth. But the true, roaring, abysmal, jubilant wave of absurdity, the cry of 'How can it be?' is not the less powerful, at fourteen, for exploding on the heels of the trivial. Then, to have vomited on the steps at the Spongs' country house seemed as grave as to have driven drunk and hit a child, or to have fired a weapon from on high into a giggling crowd.

Blithely to say it seems unreal is not to capture the complexity of the state: what has come before hovers like a dream, and what is yet to come is unimaginable. The future stretches far to the horizon, but between now and it a chasm has opened, for which no possible bridge can be seen. This was my second encounter with such rupture, and already I was learning that such times, when all that was fixed is suddenly inchoate, are perhaps more real than any other: the passage of time inflicts itself in each ticking of the clock, the light is brighter, the outlines of objects painfully distinct. And mixed with fear and dismay lies an undeniable, glittering anticipation, a detached curiosity: something must happen that I cannot foresee; noon will come, and evening, and tomorrow; that bridge from here to there must be built and must be crossed, and when I turn back from the other side, the very chasm will have closed up as if it had never been.

Our 'trials', or, more accurately, our sentencing, occurred severally, in private. This process, which took place after a breakfast of ominous silences, was hasty: our group was to leave immediately after lunch, and none of the adults wanted their last meal together sullied by our crimes. I did not know what Chuck Spong said to Chad, nor what Chad suffered. When Becky asked him, sobered up and glum, what price he had to pay for his part in our disgrace, Chad merely shrugged and said, 'Don't worry about it. I'll live.'

As for Becky, and for me: I fared much the better. Through-out my interview, Eleanor paced the length of our girls' bedroom, from the window to the door, her trajectory forked by the truckle bed at the room's centre, so that, in effect, she described an almond oval, the shape, I thought at the time, of an enormous, all-seeing eye.

'I am extremely disappointed in your behaviour, Sagesse,' she began, as I had known she would. 'And frankly, concerned. It is always more difficult to discipline a child that is not your own. I've been thinking a lot about this.' She paused and raised an eyebrow, in order to peer at me from beneath it, through her blinking, hooded eye. 'I've lost sleep. I have some choices. You could say that it's not up to me to punish you. I could call your parents, and explain the situation, and leave it up to them.' She paused again, observing with utter calm the deleterious effect her words were having on my complexion and my breathing. 'Which I would essentially prefer.'

'Aunt Eleanor, I—'

'Grant me the respect, Sagesse, of allowing me to say what I have to say. Respect, as you know, is a key tenet of our household.'

'Yes, Aunt Eleanor.'

'I would prefer it. But I also know that your parents are in the midst of some very trying times. I'm forced to wonder – because I know you are a good person, and because we're friends, aren't we? – whether the problems at home, and your inability just now to confront them, didn't contribute – well, whether we aren't obliged to consider that there are extenuating circumstances. Tell me, Sagesse, do you do this at home?'

'Do what?'

'Drink. Get drunk.'

'I've never – I didn't – no.'

'I didn't think so.' Eleanor seemed genuinely wistful. She stopped pacing, and flattened the pleats of her shorts with her forefingers as if contemplating her belly. 'I can't just let this go. But mostly, I'm disappointed. That you didn't feel you could talk to me. That you didn't have the strength or the sense of security to admit what you were feeling. That this was the only way you could find an escape from your problems.' She sat beside me on the bed, encased me with her muscular arm. 'In some ways, I can't help feeling we're at fault, Ron and I. I've tried to create a secure, healthy environment these past weeks, and it clearly hasn't been enough. And now it's only a few days till you go home. So, I'm sorry. And I want you to know you can talk to me, about anything. At any time.' She smiled, revealing, closest to my eye, a pointed, yellowing bicuspid.

Baffled, I could not follow the abrupt volte-face of her lecture, which seemed to have mutated into an apology. 'I'm sorry,' I said. 'So sorry. I didn't mean to spoil this weekend. You've been wonderful to me, so kind, and I behaved very badly. I don't know how it happened. I—'

'If Becky hadn't—'

'It's not Becky's fault. Really, it's not. It's mine, it's my own—'

Eleanor clicked exasperation. 'I'll be speaking to Becky in a minute or two. She and I will discuss her situation. This is about you. I'm glad that you're sorry. I knew you would be.' She stopped by the window and looked down to the beach. 'We both agree that there has to be some punishment, don't we?'

'Of course.'

'So. You'll have dishes and bathroom duty, at home, until you go. Dinner dishes, every night.' I waited; there had to be more. 'Okay? Are we agreed?'

I nodded.

'That's all. Now you can go. Send Becky in. And tell Rachel to stop listening at the door.'

'Yes, of course. Aunt Eleanor – so you won't – I'm sorry – my parents?'

'There's no need for them to be further upset just now, don't you agree?'

'Thank you, Aunt Eleanor.'

She closed her eyes, as if exhausted. 'I'd like to help you

through all this,' she said. 'Ron and I would like to try. Okay?'

According to Rachel, who eavesdropped, Becky encountered no such patient understanding in her mother. Eleanor raged and sobbed and sulked and meted out arbitrary, vicious punishments: no outings, no desserts, no friends to the house. Becky, Rachel informed me, was 'way pissed'. Perhaps inevitably, she blamed me; to Rachel, she called me 'a cunt', and said she would no longer speak to me.

'Don't worry too much about it,' Rachel said, throwing herself at my midsection in unconscious imitation of her mother. 'You're still the Gecko to me.'

13

I had not thought I would be eager to go home. I had thought to have found, in my shape-shifting American self, a power unexplored: but my form was, alas, dependent upon other people's vision. Becky did not forgive readily. In my remaining Boston days, she skulked and shirked and resumed her paths of secrecy, as if I were a fat-backed spider or her parents' two-faced flunky, only faultily disguised as her peer. There were no more cemetery nights, no giggling conversations between the trees or on my bed. Rachel invited me to a final séance, but I declined.

Nor was I relieved by my aunt's concern: all along, I realized, when I had believed that I appeared to her a model girl, she had seen in me some wound, had thought me a voiceless jelly of neuroses and repressions that she, with her psychobabble, sought to reshape into something more robust. She had seen me as my brother. I was sickened, and in doubt. Perhaps I did not, as Becky had assured me, 'scream virgin'; but did I instead transmit, as clear as sonar to those who could detect it, waves of sorrow and damage? If so, how could I staunch them? And if not, how could I measure my new-found hatred for Aunt Eleanor, who in imagining them had all but created them?

The Bellevue, of a sudden, and the certainty of my family's gaze, beckoned. Those last five nights, I dreamed repeatedly of home. It was perhaps inevitable – the rhythm of any such foray into freedom, its intensity and its falling away – but I was also washed in sadness to have lost, in coming there, my dream of America; to have lost virginity, if not of the technical kind, then of another. Did I know, then, that I would return, begin again, forge a self anew, as I have done? I do not think so. Then, a week was still long, a year unimaginable, the stretch of my future invisible. I did not know what I already carried with me, nor what I would have yet to bear.

14

Now, almost a decade later, with so many American years behind me, I still see this place like any immigrant: here in my tiny apartment on Riverside Drive, or in the library at my studies, or downtown in the cafés and nightclubs, I am invented and reinvented. I meet people who ask about my trace of an accent, or the way I halt, upon occasion, in my speech, and they are satisfied by my answer, whatever it is. I can appear foreign or native, exotic or invisible, depending on my whim. I am, to different friends, American or French, or a plausible mid-Atlantic hybrid, and for most of them my background conjures only their misty adolescent visits with schoolteachers or parents to the parapets of Notre-Dame, or sweltering August afternoons in cars or minivans, touring the Loire Valley. There is nothing real about my history, and most of it I do not tell. Even the Robertsons lurk in shadow, an unknown corner of my life, to all but Chad Spong (his hair now groomed exactly like his father's), with whom I dine irregularly, lunch or supper in expensive linen and silver restaurants for which his discreet fortune foots the bill.

I still wake up at dawn, with the eastern shaft of light casting its momentary eye upon my studio floor (the rest of the day the room is dark, the seasons themselves obscured by the apartments opposite), and think eagerly of home, only to remember, as I blink into awareness, that like so many other homes, it exists, as it was then, only and unreachably to me.

Four

I

My father loved his homeland. Of this I am certain. When, in those last, crazed weeks of June 1962, fuming buses and flatbed trucks poured into Algiers from the mountains and beyond, overflowing with white refugees and the tokens of generations, and juddered their honking, diesel-drenched way to the wild bazaar that the port had become, he stayed shuttered at home and pretended, for as long as he could, that all would be well. A boy of seventeen, he clung to his world: his parents had crossed the sea to France and a new beginning a year before, leaving their obstinate adolescent in the care of his grandmother. He had not wanted to leave; nor had she. They still did not want to.

Towards the end, young Alexandre scrabbled for any portents of stability, however fragile. Had de Gaulle not once promised, that famous day in Mostaganem, that Algeria was part of France and would forever remain so? And would the country's French inhabitants not hold him to that promise somehow, in spite of everything? Had the downstairs neighbours not, but eight months before, opened a restaurant in the Rue Bab Azoun, and did it not spill its dance of shadows and conversation nightly onto the plaza?

These, at least, were the phrases with which he soothed the old woman. She, bedridden and in the final stages of her cancer, insisted that the very breeze and the bougainvillea were French and would remain so, unable to concede that the deed was done and the country lost. He monitored the radio broadcasts and filtered out the reports of slaughter that punctuated the news. He played instead the swollen 78s of Debussy or

Mendelssohn to which his grandmother was, even at the last, partial. The apartment was cloistered from the piercing sun, its heavy nineteenth-century furnishings (the shape of his own mother's girlhood) filmed with dust that last month when the *bonne*, Widad, no longer came, having excused herself tearfully after eight years of service on the grounds that it was, for her and her family, no longer safe: the bodies of too many Muslims lay fly-bitten in the streets.

An odd normality did persist: neatly suited, the doctor rapped on the door morning and night to check on his deteriorating patient, measuring blood pressure and dosing morphine. And a nurse, a quiet young nun in starchy white, padded about the apartment in the afternoons, leaving Alexandre free, when he chose, to go out. Twice a week, Sundays and Thursdays, his parents telephoned from their new home, their anxiety and the crackling line one and the same, blurring them. His mother offered to come, and wanted to (it was her mother, after all, who was dying), but Alexandre put her off, and off, with the hollow assurances he would use again later in life. She, afraid and wanting to believe him, believed.

At night, in the cavernous darkness, he lay awake, awaiting only death and departure, both of which seemed so impossible that they shaped themselves instead as fear. He listened until the street noises started up again near dawn, jolted from near-sleep by the rumble of vehicles in the small hours, or the irregular patter of footsteps on the pavement outside. He envisioned attack and pillage, flashing knives and walls of flame, mental pyrotechnics all the more extreme for the dulled quiet in which he, and his husk of an ancestor, spent their hours.

He read to her and cooked for her, although she consumed little more than clear broth and the occasional mouthful of bread. Alexandre sipped his morning coffee alone, cross-legged on the terrace, watching the movements of the city, its jerky rushes to departure, its veneer of familiar calm. Daily, Algiers held fewer friends to reassure him that life would go on, and although they drifted to France, these people were, to his purposes, as good as dead. Walking the streets, he could hardly believe that just that spring he had strolled these same paths with his comrades, that they had batted at each other with their briefcases; that in spite of the *plastiquages* and the ubiquitous smell of burning he had been preoccupied, above all, with playing off one pretty girl against another, with going as far, sexually speaking, as was feasible without courting disaster. Everyone had been aware of what would have to be (the peace accords with the FLN had been signed in March, and that after so many long years of battle), but they had thought – no, more than thought, insisted – that they could continue in the familiar round of their days.

Granted, that familiar round differed for some. My father had a cousin who had joined the OAS, a boy of twenty-one, his childhood playmate, now a terrorist flickering on the fringes, in order, as Alexandre and his friends saw it, to whip up hysteria and make matters worse. The OAS was responsible for the corpses, brown and white, or for most of them. Many secretly supported them, blasting the tattoo of '*Al-gé-rie fran-çaise*' on their car horns, or on their pots and pans; but in the flesh, their members were outlaws, and unwelcome.

As late as early June, this cousin, Jean, had appeared at the apartment unannounced, after dark. His knock alarmed my father, convinced that Arab murderers were beating at last upon the door, but the sight of Jean was hardly preferable. Ostensibly, the young man came to pay his respects to the dying, but in the kitchen, in a whispered hiss, he exhorted my father once more to join him, to fight to the last man, with the last bomb.

'And Grand'-mère?' asked Alexandre. 'How could I leave her?'

'And her grave?' countered his cousin. 'Will you just leave that, and this – ' he gestured ' – your life, as if it were nothing? Come on, man, look at the choices.'

Failing there, Jean tried another tack: 'And the *métropole*? You think they want us there, any more than you want to go?'

Alexandre hesitated. But he said 'no' a final time, and, after allowing the young man to kiss his slumbering grandmother, hurried him out the door and back to his desperate cell.

Inevitably, change bore down upon my father. His suspended quiet – the life of a man in his third age, not his first – crumbled. The university library burned to the ground, and with it his final hopes. Then, the following Monday, his grandmother forsook consciousness, a development that prompted young Alexandre to the highly unusual step of calling his parents. His mother sobbed into the ocean of air between them, while his father suggested the names of friends who might help – all of them, Alexandre knew, already gone.

That evening, on his round, the doctor drew my father aside. 'It's a matter of days,' he told him. 'Two, maybe three. I'll try to come by, when I can. But my wife and children are leaving on Wednesday, and I myself am due to fly out before the weekend. I've got a lot to see to before then. I can't do anything now but bear witness, and that is as well done, or better done, by the sister. She'll get the priest. You need to be making your own plans. There isn't much time left.'

'I can't leave her.'

'Do you plan to bury her here, or take her to France with you?'

The choice had not struck my father clearly before that moment: he was young, unaccustomed to the rituals of death. He had forgotten there would be a body. But the answer seemed evident: 'She'll come with me, of course. For my mother, for the funeral.'

The doctor clicked his pen several times. 'Are you sure that's what you want?'

'Absolutely.' It occurred to my father that his grandmother, having made Algeria her home, would be loath to leave it even in a coffin; but he knew, too, that she was French above all, and that an Algeria no longer French, no longer Catholic, was no resting place for her.

'It might be easier, given the circumstances—'

'It is my family's wish.'

'Have you been to the port? Have you seen?'

Alexandre waved his hands in dismissal.

'Have you booked passage on a ship?'

'I'll take care of it. I will.'

'Is there nobody to help you?'

'I'll manage.'

The doctor shrugged. 'I'll try to come by. I'll see what I can do.'

That night, the nurse stayed. She sat beside the old woman's bed in the puddle of light cast by the lamp, knitting, her prayer book open upon her lap. Alexandre perched opposite, in shadow. He held his grandmother's hand, running his fingertips back and forth over her ridged nails: two months before, those stubby digits had peeled potatoes and tousled his hair, had written out shopping lists in the crabbed remnants of a once elegant hand. Eventually my father slept, in his hard-backed chair, soothed by the nun's clacking needles and the knowledge that the wait was almost over. He slept better than he had in weeks. His grandmother, too, seemed more peaceful, her breath a shallow snore.

In the morning, instead of the doctor the priest came by, a tall man with the mournful face of an El Greco portrait. He delivered the last rites. All bone, his hairy toes unseemly in sandals, he embraced Alexandre, then spoke in hushed tones to the nurse, and departed.

The nun stayed on, and by this Alexandre knew his grandmother might die at any time. The younger woman rested for an hour on the sofa in the sitting room, her shoes neatly paired beneath her, and when she awoke, unwrinkled, she deftly plumped the cushions as though she had never lain there. Alexandre brought her coffee.

'Do you have somewhere else to be?' he asked.

'No.'

'And no plans? Aren't you planning, like the doctor, to go?'

'God doesn't care who governs this country,' she said. 'I'm not going anywhere. But you need to get home now, to your family in France. Go this morning, and arrange for it.'

'This is home,' said my father.

The nun shook her head, with a small smile.

2

Alexandre set off for the port. As he drew nearer, the streets grew crammed with traffic. The paved expanse by the water, inside the gates, was thick with people, milling and shouting among their packages and the abandoned furniture of the already departed. He passed beside a refrigerator, a stack of studded trunks, a battered armoire. Some families had clearly been there for days, their shirts and blouses grimed, the men's chins whiskery, the women's hair greasy and unkempt. They gave off the sour stench of travel, in heat, which mingled everywhere with the fetid drift of sewage. Others, newer to the vigil, arranged their belongings into tidy pyramids and fed their children cold sausages and bread from string bags. One young mother suckled her baby, her mottled breast bursting from her modest sprigged shirtwaist. A few feet away a fat man swayed uneasily, fanning himself with a newspaper, a limp handkerchief on his naked crown, sleeves rolled up to reveal his butcher's forearms an angry crimson from the sun. The elderly sat blank and tear-stained upon their cases, clutching at incongruous objects: a frying pan, a mantel clock. An abandoned canary twittered in its ornate cage, alone on a bollard. The children, to whom the scene was an adventure, marauded in small packs, taunting the infants and bullying the leashed dogs, so that mingled with the calls and cries of people came the variegated, desperate barks of canines big and small.

Several red-faced sailors, sloppily uniformed, pushed through the fray, their destination an office on one side of a pier. Alexandre pushed behind them, sliding in their wake. He envied them their size and their nonchalance. From the mainland, they had no attachment to the crowd. Their task was to man the ship that would ferry the refugees away; then, perhaps, they would stay in Marseilles, perhaps return for more, again and again until all the white flotsam along the shores of Algeria had been cleared. It might as well have been cattle they were transporting. They did not, as did Alexandre, see toil and marriage and death in the fraying sacks and rope-bound boxes, or in the creviced features of the peasants and housewives; they saw only cargo. And they knew, unlike the haranguing, paper-waving mob that clustered around the harbourmaster's office, that when the ship pulled out of port, they would be on it.

They strode easily into the office, but at the restraining hand of a sailor more gross even than they, the door was barred to all others, my father among them. Jostled, he stood incredulous.

'But I want to book passage,' he said loudly to the vast chest of the man in front of him.

'Don't we all, sonny. Wait your turn,' said a woman at his shoulder. 'I've watched three boats go without me, and I'm not going to miss the fourth.'

'My grandmother is dying.'

'She won't need a place then, will she?'

My father turned away from the woman's shrill voice. He pushed against the swell of bodies, like everyone else.

A stout official emerged from the building, fingering a list. He stepped onto an overturned bucket; he cleared his throat. 'This afternoon's departure is fully booked. Only those with tickets purchased through the central office, for this ship specifi-cally, will be permitted to board. If, at 3 p.m., any berths have not been filled, then they will be open to those first in line. We will take nothing more than what you can carry when you board. We cannot accommodate furniture of any kind. Please remain orderly. There will be two departures tomorrow, but be advised that they, too, are fully booked.'

The crowd broke into rowdy protest.

'My grandmother – a coffin—'

The official was close enough to look my father in the eye. 'A coffin would be considered furniture. No coffins allowed.'

How amusing, in other circumstances, such a veto might seem: 'No coffins allowed – can you imagine?' said my mother to me, with a guilty titter. 'It's ridiculous.' But my father was never able to make light of it.

'And me?' he asked.

'Have you a ticket?'

'No.'

'Then I suggest that either you stay here, like everybody else, and wait for standing room – which could take several days – or else go to the booking office in town and purchase a ticket.'

'For when?

'How would I know? You can see how many people there are.' He looked at my father's crisp shirt, his neatly combed hair. 'Don't you know somebody who could help you? That would be the best way.'

Alexandre walked back through the city. His cousins, Jean excepted, were not in Algiers. His closest friends were gone, and had been for a month or more. His last girlfriend had left for a three-month English course in Kent and now, he knew, she would never return. He was reluctant to call his father and ask for help, but this he resolved – on seeing the queue, two blocks long, outside the ticket office in town – to do. He made a detour to pass in front of his neighbour's restaurant: its open windows and bustle, he decided, would reassure him.

It could not. An array of envelopes blanketed the mat inside the door. A notice on the glass, handwritten, hasty, announced that the establishment would be closed until further notice. The tables were set, the napkins folded in their flowery cones at every plate, already wilted and forlorn. His nose pressed to the glass, Alexandre could see, on the bar at the rear of the restaurant, bottles standing in disarray: liquor, wine, empties, jumbled up together. My father sat on the curb, stared at his shoes, and started to cry.

Monsieur Gambetta, the neighbour in front of whose business my father crouched despondent, appeared, a shiny, bulbous man in his late forties, jangling a great ring of keys. Theirs was, for my father, a serendipitous meeting: Gambetta was expecting a cheque and thought it just might have been delivered to his restaurant. He recognized young Alexandre, and when he learned of the boy's troubles, offered a solution. Well connected as they were, he and his wife had secured not merely tickets, but an entire cabin for the crossing, forty-eight hours thence.

There was no reason, he said, if Alexandre didn't mind sleeping on the floor, why he couldn't share the space with them.

'It's very hard,' he said, a sympathetic arm around the boy's shoulders, 'to be suffering from the death of your grandmother at such a time. We're happy to do what we can, in the face of our tragedies.'

'But Monsieur,' said Alexandre, 'my grandmother isn't dead yet. It's true, she's dying – they say it could be any moment – but she's still alive.'

'You wouldn't leave her?'

'I can't imagine – No. I think, from what the doctor has said—'

'Let's wait and see.'

'The priest came this morning.'

Both men were awkward. Alexandre did not feel he could broach the subject of the coffin. He thought about it, though: it occurred to him that perhaps it could lie in the cabin's floor space, and that he could sleep on top of his grandmother. But he didn't mention it.

'I'm so grateful,' he said.

'Think nothing of it. We can arrange, on the morning of, when to meet. We could go to the port together, depending . . .'

'I'm so grateful. Perhaps, when we get there, my parents—'

'Think nothing of it.'

From that moment on, my father spent the hours praying for his grandmother's demise. He sat in the hard chair in the gloom, the knitting sister impassive across the sheet, and listened eagerly for the death rattle. The old woman was unlikely to open her eyes again: all she needed to do was to let go. He whispered in her ear, when the nun left the room: 'It's okay, Grand'-mère. God is waiting for you. Grand-père, too, and your sisters, and paradise. Let go, Grand'-mère.'

But his grandmother, like her fellow colonials, braved adversity tough and recalcitrant. Her tense was the present continuous, and she clung to it with all the blind will of a mole. 'I am dying', 'she is dying', 'our country is dying': the tense lingers in a defiance incomprehensible to those who are resigned, simply, to adopting the past.

Twenty-four hours passed, in which Alexandre did not sleep; nor did he eat, even when the nurse brought him soup. He was trapped, with the old woman, in the ongoing, in that chasm between past and future.

The nurse, who knew of the Gambettas' offer, reassured him: 'She will die. She will die in time. God wills it. Have faith.' But he could not believe her. He could not remember what faith might mean. Had he not had faith in de Gaulle's promise? Had he not had faith in Gambetta's restaurant?

On the evening of the next day, the nun, ever practical, sent an unwilling Alexandre to do the unthinkable: she dispatched him to the undertaker's to order his grandmother's coffin. She advised him to spare no expense: 'If you pay, they'll have it ready by morning. Pay enough and they'll work through the night.'

'She's dying, but she isn't – How can I, when she isn't?'

'Because you must. Because she will be.'

When he returned, however, well after dark (minus his grandfather's gold watch, with which he had had to bribe the swarthy carpenter; and all the more firmly set in his plan to take the coffin to France, as the undertaker had informed him that burials were very backed up and bodies were putrefying in the morgue), his grandmother was breathing still. She had barely stirred. The nun was unravelling a new skein of yarn: other than that, nothing had changed.

They sat with her, again, through the night, although several times my father, depleted, gave in to sleep, his head lolling to his chest. Each wakening start was accompanied by the hope – but no, she lived on.

At nine, on a morning fiercely hot and airless, Monsieur Gambetta came to the door. 'We're going now,' he said. 'Because of the crowd at the port. Surely you've seen them?'

'Of course.'

'Not yet?' Gambetta made an embarrassed nod towards the bedroom.

'Not yet.'

'By two, my son. You have until two, at the very latest. After that we'll be boarding, and they won't let you on without us. Did you hear that the widow Turot's throat was cut last night? In her apartment. Not three streets from here. Hard to know who to blame. It's time, my boy. At the port, before two. We'll be as near to the gangway as we can get, in the ticket holders' section. Courage.'

My father then pretended to pack. He paced the apartment, removing silver from drawers and pictures from walls. He took the sepia photograph of his grandparents on their wedding day from its frame and folded it in four, so that it would fit in his trouser pocket. He took his shirts from the dresser and laid them on his bed, only to put them back again. He placed three silver coffee spoons in each sock, where they were initially cool against his ankles. He removed a cushion cover needlepointed by his grandmother from its cushion, and stuffed it, along with a single pair of underwear, into a canvas sack. To these items he added a small framed watercolour of the Bay of Algiers which had hung, for as long as he could recall, on his grandmother's wall, a light-filled, buoyant picture painted early in the century, in happier times, a tableau in which the water winked in the foreground, the city's residents strolled the seafront and, up the hillside, the buildings gleamed, pristine, unmarred by dust or blood.

He took down his grandmother's photograph album, weighed it, and left it on the sofa; then returned to pluck from it an assortment of memories, trying to guess what his parents would most want, tearing the edges of some, until he had a handful to go into the bag. Every so often he slid into his grandmother's room: the nun would look up and shake her head, and Alexandre would begin again his restless perambulations of the flat.

At ten-thirty there came a hammering at the door. The coffin maker sweated on the landing, Alexandre's watch shiny on his wrist.

'It's downstairs, on the truck. Help me carry it up – I'm by myself. Can't do it alone.'

It took the better part of half an hour to hoist the unwieldy box up three flights. Alexandre was drenched in sweat, and had to rest at every storey. He knew little about coffins, but could tell that this one was enormous, long enough for a man of six feet, and wide.

'It's huge,' he panted, halfway up. 'So heavy.'

'You didn't tell me how tall she was. Couldn't take any chances. And the wood I had handy was thick. There's no help for it. Better too big than too small, you know. She's got to rest in it a long time. She might as well be comfortable.'

When at last they reached the apartment, they laid the coffin, its door swung wide, on the living room floor, alongside the sofa.

'Where's the dead then?' asked the carpenter, wiping his slick, hairless brow with his slick and hairy arm.

'She isn't – just a minute.'

My father went to the door of his grandmother's room. Her knitting to one side, the nun leaned over the old woman, cradling her head with one hand and beating at the pillow behind her with the other. As Alexandre came into the room, the nun let his grandmother's skull slip gently back into the newly blooming down. The nun, so long unruffled, seemed flushed, her smooth face pink and beaded.

'I wanted her to lie nicely. She's gone, poor dear. While you were on the stairs. She's ready to come with you now.'

'But when?'

'As I say, a minute or two ago, when you were in the stairwell. She didn't suffer. The Lord is merciful.'

There wasn't time for my father to cry, or to wonder at his elder's impeccable timing. For the promise of a standard lamp, a soup tureen and a silver candelabra, the man from the carpenter's was persuaded to shuttle Alexandre and his grandmother to the port. From the sheet beneath her they made a sling, and lifted her, still warm and in her nightgown, into the living room and into the box. She lay marooned there, tiny in the space. The nun shadowed them, praying quietly.

'She'll shift around. She's not stiff enough,' said the man. 'Got anything to hold her still?'

It was Alexandre's idea to use the sofa cushions, their faded green velvet of no other use to him by then. The men stuffed them in around the body, one squashed at her feet and two flattened along her sides. Beneath her head they laid the pillow from her bed, which gave off the sickly scents of illness and her perfume.

'That'll do.'

The man let Alexandre bend to kiss the old lady one final time, allowed him to rearrange her hands (those ridged finger-nails!) across her chest, and then he swung the hinged lid and fastened the shiny bolts in place.

Full, the coffin was even heavier, but to Alexandre, precious. He was careful on the descent. He didn't quite believe that his grandmother would not flinch at the bumps, and so took great pains not to scrape the box in the turns, or to let it fall. Once she was safe in the truck, the two men returned one last time to the apartment. The nun had packed her things, was ready to make her way back to the hospital. Alexandre took his canvas sack and threw into it, at the last, a cardigan of his grand-mother's, and the little cedar crucifix from above her bed. The man shouldered his lamp, crooked the tureen under his arm, and asked the nun to wield the candlestick. The three of them left together, without bothering to lock the door.

The nun declined a ride, preferring to stroll the stifling streets for the first time in days. She embraced my father, and blessed him. 'You've done well,' she said. 'Your parents will be proud.'

3

It was almost one by the time they reached the port. The truck could not advance even to the gates, so thickly massed was the ramp down to the pier. A few vendors with more interest in money than in politics had installed themselves along the sea-front to cater to the departing, and they hawked fruit and ice creams and french fries in waxed cones at inflated prices.

Unloading my great-grandmother was one thing; proceeding to the far edge of the pier reserved for ticket holders proved another. People crushed up against them; some banged on the box; children scurried underneath it. The older men and women stepped back to let them pass, and one or two crossed themselves furtively. The carpenter's man smoked while he hauled, puffing out of the corner of his mouth, allowing the cigarette to droop and rise with his breathing. When he was done, he spat the glowing butt into the fray with an upward flick of his chin.

The sailor at the barrier was mercifully young, and evidently had not been apprised of the decree against coffins: he lifted the gate for them without question when Alexandre caught sight of Monsieur Gambetta and the latter, waving, called out, 'He's with us. Let him through.'

The ticket holders were calm, their end of the pier compara-tively uncluttered. They waited in the heat-shimmered shadow of the sleek ship, the *El Djezair*, a vessel whose canvas-covered lifeboats dangled like baubles above its deck. The air was saltier at this end, less choked with the fumes of decay. Alexandre, the coffin maker and their load advanced without obstruction to the Gambettas' pile of suitcases. No sooner were they unbur-dened than the man gave a small salute. 'Best of luck. See you over there, maybe,' he said, and was gone.

The Gambettas stood beyond surprise. Madame Gambetta's cherry mouth fell agape, and her fingers fluttered to her hair as if its bun might unravel from the shock.

'What's this, what's this?' sputtered Gambetta.

'My family – a funeral – she must come with me to France.'

'Quite. Oh, quite, but my boy, I don't see how—'

'I thought we could put her on the floor. I'll sleep on top of her. She won't really be in your way. It's not so far. I'm sorry, but you must understand—'

'Quite. Oh yes, of course, but I don't – well, no. I see.' Monsieur Gambetta sat back on his suitcase, his features crumpling in defeat. 'No, you're right. Naturally. We'll manage. She is, uh, properly – I mean, the box is—' He pulled at the fleshy lobe of his ear. 'It's just, it's very hot weather, you know?'

'It's a proper coffin. Very solid.'

'Yes, I can see that. It seems extremely – big.'

'He didn't have her measurements.'

'No. I see.'

Madame Gambetta stepped forward and spoke in a whisper from behind her linen handkerchief. 'You're absolutely sure she won't smell? I'm very sensitive, I can't help it. I should be sick.'

'There's been no time. She's only just gone. And the coffin is very solid.'

'As long as she doesn't smell.'

How I pity the poor Gambettas, whose kindness was repaid with a corpse. But they were not going to abandon the boy there – how could they? – and he too young to be mixed up in such a business. He should have been flirting on the esplanade, as handsome as he was, not standing hunched and crushed before them with the burden of the dead on his shoulders.

'We're all on a hard road,' said Gambetta. 'But we're on it together.'

'And Our Saviour will guide us,' said Madame, crossing herself. A moment later, when she thought my father's attention elsewhere, she rolled her eyes at her husband and hissed, '*Quel cauchemar!*' What a nightmare.

But the Lord showed mercy upon the Gambettas. When the moment came to board, Monsieur was called upon to fight for my great-grandmother, and he did. 'I paid for the cabin and I can put in it anything that I choose. I could transport a horse or a washing machine if I wanted to. The space is mine. Now give this boy a hand and show some respect for the dead.'

Madame stood to one side, all sombre dignity, and shook her head. 'Imagine,' she murmured to a cluster of fellow passengers. 'The boy is bereaved and they want to rob him of a proper funeral. As if selling out our homeland weren't disgrace enough.'

A minor uproar ensued – had these people not lost everything? Could they countenance a further theft? – as a result of which the coffin was hoisted up the gangplank by two sailors, on whose impressive musculature the great weight appeared to float. The Gambettas followed, and Alexandre, all of them laden with the *bibelots* of the Gambettas' apartment in bulging leather cases.

The party crossed the deck and stood, arrested for a time, while the deceased and her casing were manoeuvred down the narrow well to the floor below, where the Gambettas' cabin was located. There, the grey corridor was very narrow, and the coffin could only advance on its side.

'Be careful,' urged Alexandre, picturing his grandmother pressed between the velvet cushions.

'Show some respect,' admonished Gambetta again.

But when they reached the cabin door, it immediately became clear that there was not sufficient space to turn the coffin.

'We won't be able to get it in,' said the sailor in front. 'There's no room. The angle is too sharp. The corridor's too narrow. Won't go round.'

'Try, man. You haven't even tried,' said Gambetta. Madame shook her head, whether in agreement with the sailor or her husband it was not clear.

They tried. For a quarter of an hour they tried. They tipped the coffin on its end, they pushed and scraped it; they pulled and grappled with it, their breaths spuming in the heat. Even the strong men wearied at the box's terrible weight. And the sailor was right: my great-grandmother would not, could not, share the Gambettas' cabin.

'What now?' asked my father, his limbs jellying from the prolonged emotion.

'What indeed?' asked Gambetta.

The first mate was summoned, and then the captain. The corridor, so full of people, grew stuffy, and Madame, tightly corseted, threatened to faint. Alexandre fanned her busily with the packet of family photos from his bag, which made only a little breeze.

The captain, a slight man with a prissy moustache and crooked teeth, stood silent for some minutes, his arms folded across his brass-buttoned breast.

'I have a proposal,' he said at length to Monsieur Gambetta, leaning forward on his toes as if sharing a secret.

'This young man is the next of kin,' said Gambetta. 'Put your proposal to him.'

'In principle,' said the captain, turning to lean towards Alexandre, 'coffins aren't allowed. Not at this time, when we need every square foot for passengers. They count as furniture, you see.'

'But my grandmother—'

The captain raised a hand to silence my father. 'Hear me out, young man. I appreciate your difficulty. I was going to suggest, for the dignity of all concerned, a burial at sea.'

'Well – indeed,' said Gambetta.

'How perfect,' breathed Madame, her colour returning. 'A solution.'

'I suppose – I guess – what choice do I have?' asked my father, who by now felt so unwell that he had turned his improvised fan on himself, and was beating furiously.

'None,' said the captain. 'If you wish to sail today.'

And so my great-grandmother came to rest in the mouth of the Bay of Algiers. No sooner was the ship under way (its decks a writhe of passengers, their waving arms like an infestation of worms) than the captain stood up at the stern, the coffin held aloft beside him by four solemn-faced sailors (one of them all but chinless, so that his mouth seemed inadvertently to fall open) and read through a silvery megaphone the prayers for the dead. My father stood there also, by the railing, and when he bent to kiss the coffin, his tears fell in splotches onto the rough wood.

The crowd on shore could see the funeral too, or so my father believed, because they seemed to grow still, and a hush fell over the bay in the brilliant afternoon sun. When the coffin slipped, with a muted splash, into the oily Mediterranean, and was swallowed, the ship's human cargo stood motionless and wide-eyed: mourning this reminder of the dead they left behind, and their own deaths to come, and the glinting white glory of their city, lost to them like Atlantis, wavering there on the hillside, so near, but gone for ever.

4

So I, who then still could, went home. It was, as my father took my bag from the BMW boot and set it on the white gravel, and Etienne swayed in his chair in the front doorway with such force that his straps squeaked, and my mother, poised to push him down the ramp towards me, paused to hop, a little, and throw her dainty hand over her open mouth in a gesture of girlish pleasure; as the hairs on my skin rose to the dry salt breeze, which carried upon it an edge of burning and the end of summer – it was as if, with my father's arm around my shoulder, and our steps on the shimmering stones as crisp as those on Arctic snow, closing the gap between us and my mother and brother until there was none, and the insects seemed to quiet their whirring and the very air to pause – as if I had come home to utter reassurance, and to rest. But that sun-sprinkled reunion on our drive was only an apparent amnesty.

My grandfather had returned to the Bellevue, of course, and to his wife, whose brisk solicitude and defiance would drag him, combed and jacketed, through the next day and the next; and so our house – my house, the one in which we had lived since I was five or so, built in readiness for the wheelchair my brother did not then yet have; and so, perhaps, more his house than mine – was ours, or mine, or his again. But the shadows of that first week and of the trial yet to come flitted in the corridors as present as ghosts or mice, scrabbling in the walls, or in our minds, intermittent but never wholly gone.

In my absence, my mother, who had no extra flesh to lose, had nonetheless shrunk, so that her stylish blouses hung with breezy awkwardness from her shoulders and her tendons bulged. My father, as if he had fed upon his wife, had billowed, his neck like a toad's in full song, itching, slickly shaven, at his collar. The living room looked whiter, the light more harsh, and my footsteps on the marble rang more loudly than I recalled, like footsteps in a hospital. Only Etienne was the same, grasping – or trying to – for my hair, my T-shirt, my biscuity airplane smell.

'You've grown,' my mother said.

'I don't think so.'

'You've lost weight, then.'

'In America? No chance. You're the one—'

'Don't be silly.'

'She's like a bird, your mother. I'm waiting for her to fly away.'

'Oh Alexandre!'

He put his arms around us both. 'I'm just glad to have both my beautiful women with me, where you belong.'

We squirmed, wife and daughter. It shames me to remember it, but we did.

'You're so hot,' my mother complained, wriggling free. 'You emanate heat.'

'One kiss?' he called after her, as she headed for the kitchen.

'Not now.'

'Why not?'

Her voice was faint, around corners and through doors now; but audible. 'I don't want to.'

'You won't reject your poor father, will you?'

I said nothing, submitted to his moist embrace. It was my first night home, and I saw no reason to spoil it.

5

That moment in front of the house blooms so clearly in my memory, as if it had lasted for hours, and yet the weeks that followed, the months even, surface in an ill-assorted jumble. Through them all moves the smell of wet earth, the dulled roar of rain. The weather that autumn was bad for morale, bad for the Bellevue's revenues, as the British and other northerners opted to stay home with their own damp rather than to pay for the privilege of ours. Even in the cocoon of my almost-childhood, I caught whispers of global economic disaster: words like 'recession' and 'downturn' and 'belt-tightening' sifted into playground conversation. In those months before Christmas the Berlin Wall would crumble, and the television would echo the Germans' carousing through our living room. The newspapers suggested that all wars might be drawing to a close, that our century's long-abandoned notions of progress – towards a better world, inhabited by better men – should perhaps be dusted off and re-examined. In the same breath, it was proposed that the recession upon us might now be permanent, just punishment for a prolonged era of excess.

But in our lives these momentous happenings and their attendant prophecies tinkled like distant bells. Our days, as they grew smaller and darker, alongside a slate-coloured sea, were fashioned around my grandfather's imminent trial. It loomed among us, unspoken, unenvisioned, and we bumped against it only to shy away:

'Christmas? Well, it all depends. We'll see.' My mother, to me.

'A dinner party for our anniversary? Not before. I think we'd better wait.' Papa, to my mother.

'Not in November. No houseguests in November. You know we can't.' One to the other, I don't know which.

In the last days before school started, I didn't go to the hotel once. I have no memory of seeing my grandparents, although I must have: I felt ashamed of my grandfather, and certain that he, too, must be ashamed in front of me. It was my life, after all, that had been most gravely affected by his error, or so I thought, as I began again to miss Marie-José and to dread the lycée. Nobody mentioned that he, too, had lost friends and reputation; or that my parents had; or that he might actually go to jail.

I know that I was denied the shopping spree that usually preceded the return to classes. My mother allowed me one sweater – a charcoal angora turtleneck, which I chose for myself and stroked and held against my cheek in the bluish light of the department store, and again in the privacy of my bedroom; and which, after that hideous autumn, I never wore again, believing somehow that it had soaked up the ugliness and that it rendered me ugly; or uglier, because it was a time in which my looks became extravagantly important to me, when each glance in the mirror disappointed my vanity – and that was all. We couldn't afford more, she explained, in those uncertain times. Maybe later, she said, when the cost of 'all this' was clearer.

'Remember, chickadee,' my mother whispered in English one night by my bedside, 'it's not that your life is so hard, it's just a little harder, for a while. Up till now, we've been lucky, that's all. You'll be lucky again.'

I decided, in my anger, that they liked it, that adversity strengthened them: my mother whittled to pure bone, my father sinking into flesh, but both of them emerging purer, more utterly themselves. In those months, they seemed to draw together. The murmur of their voices in the night was rare, but that murmur almost never rose or broke in the waves of ire to which I had long been accustomed. I took this, at least, as a good sign (how curiously we read the runes of everyday life): I deemed the portents of our household, like those of the wider world, mixed.

Fourteen, the Stoics believed, is the age at which reason pullulates, as natural as the spring, in the young mind; but as it mingles with the breast's instinct, or as the two did in me, surely they give birth to unlikely forms. What, after all, is reason, but a means to lead us along the paths of our own desire? We find hope where we can, and where we cannot, invent it.

6

I went, of course, to school; but school, for me, had changed. I took the same bus, to the same mournful grey brick building. The school was still protected from the street by its forbidding wall and iron gate; its forecourt was still cobbled and rang with adolescent clatter in the breaks; the hallways still smelled of must and disinfectant, and the same wall-eyed Arab mopped them, endlessly, through the afternoons. I was entering the *troisième*, my schoolbag bloated with a panoply of subjects as it would not be again – geography and Latin, philosophy, physics and literature. Soon I would choose, and focus my studies, but there were exams to pass first, at the end of that year.

I had always anticipated them, just as I knew that Marie-José would be in another classroom on another hall, and that if I was careful our paths need not cross. What, then, was different? I was. Or they were – the other students, my friends. Either they passed notes and whispered about me, or else I imagined that they did: the difference matters little. I cut my conversations short; I manufactured activities and engagements; I slithered past smoky knots of chatter in the lobby, at the bus stop. I'm not sure whether I declined invitations until they stopped coming, or whether there were, from the start, none to decline. I assumed, at the time, the latter. Even the friends who tried to stick by me, perhaps them most of all, I found repulsive, fearing that they wanted only to gawk, to cadge invitations to my house and spy upon us there, or to lure me back to the Bellevue and to ask 'Was it here? Was he standing there?' Or worse: 'Is your grandfather at home? Could we go see him? Does he look different?'

These fears recalled those I had suffered as a small girl, new

to school and its brutal society. Innocent then, I was taught to
be afraid. At five or six I had, as other children did, invited little
girls for games and *goûter* in our back garden, only to discover,
one balmy afternoon early on, that my playmates had little
interest in tag, or in my rows of fluffily attired dolls. They
circled instead around my inert brother – it was his first
appearance in their time – who lounged in a madras-lined,
specially designed basket on the patio slate, at three or four
immobile as an infant, blinking peaceably at the swaying
branches and the sky's inviting blue.

'What's wrong with him? Why doesn't he move?'

'He's so big. He's not a baby.'

'Didn't you know, he's like an animal, my mother said. She
said Sagesse has got a brother who's no more than a dog.'

'What does he eat? Can we feed him?'

'He's like a doll.'

'But horrible. All spitty.'

'Will he never talk?'

'What's wrong with him? It's gross.'

'He farted!' The gaggle started back in fits of artificial gasping,
plugging their noses.

'Will he eat dirt?'

'I don't know,' I said, in agonies, twisting my frock in my
fingers, looking, like my brother, at the sky.

'Let's see. Let's try.' She was a chubby girl with amber
ringlets, the leader. Delphine. At recess I had seen her clamp
her bulk upon another girl's chest and yank her victim's hair,
her knees digging into the other girl's ribs. I feared her,
wondered that I had – willingly, no less – invited her to play at
my house, so that now here she was.

The other girls, three of them, followed her commands with
chirrups and squeals, their little fists balled around matted clumps
of grass, grey soil and pebbles. They were descending upon my
brother, who burbled oblivious at the sparrows, and all I could
do was stand by, my dress twisted up above my underpants,
twisting it further in my alarm. No sound would come out of
me – as though my mouth were crammed with grit and ash –

and I was even uncertain if I was breathing because everything in me stuck. I didn't know whether I should save him, or even if I could.

My grandmother (why was she there?), God-like, scattered them like chickens: suddenly among us, she batted them back and brushed my brother's grimy face, and stuck her fingers, diamond ring and all, into his mouth to scoop out any stones. She hoisted him, as if he were an ordinary child, upon her hip, his silken hair splayed against her bosom, and retreated, leaving me alone with my guests, who cowered and shed crocodile tears, but only for a moment. Delphine suggested that we play dress-up next, and so we did: I duly traipsed upstairs to fetch the dress-up box, and we festooned the garden and our bodies with my mother's garish mini-dresses until the other mothers, one by charming one, came to take their daughters away.

But I, I moved through the afternoon as if through ice, aware, like a child in a fairy tale, that I had let evil into my house and could not control it; and obscurely unsure of whether my brother was me, whether all my promises to him had made us one being; or whether I was no different from the others, my hands full of dirt. I had not stopped them, after all.

My parents didn't punish me for the afternoon's events; nor did my grandmother. But for many years I didn't invite children to my house. I went to theirs, or else we played in the grounds of the Bellevue, on the pretext that there we had more space for our games. Zohra fixed our afternoon tea in my grandmother's kitchen, which, safe but for the occasional dancing wasp, held no disclosable secrets.

As I grew older, I bestowed rare invitations the way I would later give my nakedness: the sight of my brother I reserved for those I loved most, as a test, and over time more than one had failed it. Only when my girlfriend had taken on Etienne as she had taken me would I allow a titter, or a joke, at the expense of his flailing arms or spasmed tongue: those jokes — and I had shared many with Marie-Jo — were at the heart of me, the place where I was both like my brother and like everyone else, conjoined.

7

A peek at my criminal grandfather was not, however, a gift I wanted to give; and I thought myself old enough to keep anyone from asking. My American forays with my cousin had taught me that there were people, my age or slightly older, who would, by force of their own immediate interests, accept me without questions, as long as I could make my interests mimic theirs. That is to say, I knew to seek out the very pot-smokers whom I had, with others from my school, readily disparaged little over a month before. Our small town was not Boston: the clique to which I turned was smaller and, to parental eyes, still less savoury than Becky's friends, not least because its leader, a lanky, shaven-headed youth a year ahead of me, was an Arab, the son of Algerian immigrants who kept a North African sweet shop – piles of fly-kissed lurid orange cakes and greasy sugar-soaked doughnuts behind smeared glass; the sort of place my mother hurried past with her chin up, holding her breath – in a shabby side street off the market. Sami – whose name I had long thought was an American affectation, not realizing it to be, to a Muslim, as common as John or Peter – had a reputation as a dealer of hashish. He worked on it, too: his movements were jerky and surreptitious, and he carried his bookbag as if it were contraband. His jeans, like an American rapper's, hung in folds from his scrawny hips and marked him as a rebel. His girlfriend, a soft-fleshed girl named, unwieldily, Lahouria, but called simply 'Lahou', was in my history class. Cocoa-skinned and curvaceous, she worked at slackening her features into an aggressive pout, but was by nature as frothy as her inundating chevelure, a mass of curls so carefully oiled that it recalled running water without actually moving at all.

Their intimates included a pointy-faced, spotted boy we all called Jacquot, known for sliding his fingers along girls' thighs during science films or on the bus; and Frédéric, who had dabbled in my own – my erstwhile – social set the year before, when Marie-Jo had favoured him briefly with her attentions.

He was the son of a prominent pharmacist, a woman and a widow, and so had teetered on the verge of Bellevue acceptability. Now, though, it was said, he pilfered pills from his mother's vault and sold them, repackaged in sandwich baggies, in the schoolyard after class.

He was the one I approached, in the early weeks of term. It was lunch hour, and he had taken shelter from a sudden downpour under a bookstore awning, three blocks from school. I had been sliding among the stationery shelves inside the window, feigning interest in binders and envelopes, willing the hour to pass, when I glimpsed his shivering back.

'Long time,' I said at his elbow, loudly enough to be heard above the rain and the swishing traffic.

'Hey.' It took a minute. 'Sagesse, right?'

'Yeah.'

'Marie-Jo's friend?'

'Well. I was.'

'She doesn't speak to you either? She is one prize bitch. Bet I know why.'

I shrugged. I didn't want him to bring it up. He didn't.

'You in Lahou's class?'

'Yep.'

'Ponty's a dragon, I hear.' He was the history teacher.

'He's okay, if you know how to deal with him.'

'She doesn't, then. He gives her a lot of grief, yeah?'

'I guess.'

'You going back?'

'Got to. I've got philosophy in ten minutes.' We looked at the curtain of rain; I eyed the dark down on his lip.

'Shall we make a run for it?'

I giggled. 'Unless you've got a better idea.'

Back at school, our clothes stuck to our skin and our shoes squelching on the linoleum, we loitered a moment by the stairs.

'We should have coffee sometime,' he said, reaching for a soggy cigarette from his jacket pocket.

'If you promise not to talk about Marie-Jo.'

'No problem. With Lahou, maybe?'

'Why not?'

'You look like you could use a laugh or two.'

'Or a smoke or two.'

'You?'

'Why not?' I called this from the stairs, over my shoulder. I made it seem casual, or tried to. I made it seem as though I wouldn't otherwise be on my own. But that was the thing about Sami's crowd: they were all involved in the same deception, and without each other, would each have been alone. I doubt Frédéric was fooled; but he didn't mind, either. In this way, and swiftly, I insinuated myself into their group. It seemed, at the time, that I was choosing a new place for myself. I entered their circle, of course, thanks to Frédéric. He was the link; he could vouch for me. At that first lunch, in a burger joint with mucky floors, Lahou was suspicious of me, and of my goodwill.

'How would you know what it's like?' she asked, licking ketchup off a plum-varnished finger. 'Ponty's not up your butt. You're his pet, for God's sake.'

'He's easy, if you get on his good side.'

'Like how? Be reborn white and rich?'

'I'll show you, if you want.'

'Sure.' She shook her head, and snorted. 'I'll believe it when it happens.'

Lahou, far more even than Marie-Jo, was a man's woman. She was surrounded not just by Sami but by Jacquot and Frédéric, and they treated her not like one of them but like an orchid. Like sex, indeed, which is what she represented to them, her cleavage enhanced by underwire and Lycra, her snub features perfected with paint. She and I had nothing but Ponty in common, and now Frédéric, and eventually marijuana, which would ease the way somewhat; but that was all, and sitting on the orange plastic moulded seats in the Flunch, sizing each other up, we knew it.

She was the child, I would learn, of a French mother and a Tunisian father. The latter was elusive and the former a shrew. Lahou's older brother had become an observant Muslim, and he was known to slap his sister and call her a whore. She had three younger sisters, and defended them fiercely. I never went to her apartment, and she never told me any of these things: they seeped somehow into my consciousness, probably through Frédéric, and knowing them made me obscurely proud of her, although she did not know that I knew them and we still had nothing to discuss but the boys and their behaviour.

Sami was moody, his murky home life the cause of unforesee-able swings from rowdiness to black silence. He was vain, and thought his hawkish features alluring: he made a great effort to grow sideburns, and removed them; then fashioned a wispy goatee which proved a source of friction between him and his girlfriend ('It's pubic! It's totally pubic!' Lahou insisted), and, as testament of his love for her, dispensed with that in time. He had tapering fingers of astounding mobility, which reminded me of spiders' legs, and a pronounced, sweet smell, of cinnamon and smoke. He was an actor, his role part American gangster, part raffish Frenchman. It led him to shoplift an expensive watch for Lahou's birthday – a gesture that moved and appalled me in equal measure – and to believe (or purport to) that not doing homework was a revolutionary stance, rather than simple foolishness. He was fond of money, and liked to whip the pile of notes from his deep pocket and count it, openly and again, while his friends talked around him. Once, in a particularly gaudy temper, he rolled a spliff with a five-hundred-franc note, and none of his cohorts had the courage to tell him that they thought the act preposterous. I only saw him break out of his persona twice, and the self beneath seemed shabby and afraid.

Jacquot was Sami's foil, his fool. Always funny-looking, he had adopted early on the role of clown, and by the time I knew him it had become an ill-fitting garment in which he was trapped. He did not want, I would discover, to paw the girls: he wanted hopelessly, doglike, to be loved by them, touched by them, and he knew no other means but that one, a monstrous self-parody and guaranteed to fail. He smoked to forget his awkwardness and would often grow intent afterwards, his scabby cheeks aglow as he devised schemes to end world hunger or bring down the government, or discoursed upon friendship or fate, brushing ever more fervently at the lock of oily hair upon his forehead, and pausing only to suck his incongruously white teeth.

'And another thing – ' he would cry, with an ill-timed parry at Sami or Frédéric ' – I've just thought of this . . .'

They did not appreciate Jacquot the philosopher, and Sami was apt to grapple his friend around the neck or cuff him, with a menace only half indulgent, and hiss, 'Shut it. Do you hear me? Shut . . . up.'

But I liked him, and he me, and as was perhaps inevitable, given the narrowness of his acquaintance, he took to following me with little gifts (a candy bar, a fountain pen) and showed all the signs of childish infatuation – doomed, as ever.

In this company, among whom I moved unbelieving, Frédéric was the closest thing I had to a friend. The others were so far from my world and possibilities that their carryings-on, like Becky's, seemed neither to contain nor to implicate me. Their interactions were like a television programme that I watched, albeit religiously, and I felt for them the detached fondness that one reserves for fictional characters. I was aware that our lives were overlapping only briefly and thought this certainty would keep me safe. It was the same for Frédéric as for me, although we never spoke of it. He, like me and unlike them, went home to a large house overlooking the water and altered his posture and the cadence of his voice as he walked in the door. He knew that he would pass his exams and go on to university – he planned to study law – and that his forays into the 'culture' were but a form of adolescent rebellion, acceptable to himself if not to his thin-lipped mother.

She, whom I met more than once and found harried, but in a pleasing way, like a worn blanket, was politically liberal – of the generation of '68, as my father was also, although he only chronologically and in no other sense – and so had few social dealings with my parents; but in a town of that size, they had, naturally, met, and the distance between them was purely theoretical. Frédéric and I were, to put it bluntly, of the same social class, with the same manners and similar discontents; and as I got to know him, I realized that his reputation as a dealer stemmed from a single incident in which, on a dare, he had stolen from his mother a quantity of temazepam; and from his association with Sami and Lahou and Jacquot, which my former friends could not explain to themselves in any other way.

Doubtless, rumours began to circulate about me, too: I could not fail to note the glances that followed me in my new circle. With Lahou or Frédéric at my side, I passed Marie-Jo every so often and saw her stop talking and stare and then take up her chatter all the more heatedly, jigging her head in my direction and casting a furtive, telltale eye my way. She would have been talking about me regardless, I told myself; at least now she had something else to say; at least I didn't have to imagine that the night by the swimming pool was always on her lips.

She may have thought I was going out with Frédéric – had I been observing myself from afar it would have seemed plausible. He was tall, and not unattractive, although his ears stuck out too far. He had a low laugh, the sound of which evidently pleased him, as he would prolong it by seconds beyond its natural end. He was clever, if not as clever as he assumed, and appealingly reckless, and bored with the town and its people.

'I chose my friends,' he said once, as he walked me to the bus stop after an afternoon spent dropping coins in a video arcade, 'because all the others are cretins. They're so fucking boring, and they think everything's just fine. They'll settle in their little lives and become just like their parents, and go to Paris once a year and think it's so cool and impressive. Fuck that.'

'And Sami's different? Or Lahou?'

'You don't have any idea, do you? They're on the move, girl. They've already asked so many questions and taken so many beatings for it that whatever happens from here on, they come out ahead.'

'Not if they don't finish school.'

'You think a university education is everything? You think

it'd change their lives? There's no work for anybody, sweetheart. Who needs it?'

'Who are you kidding?'

'You're so bourgeois, Sagesse. No different from the rest.'

'And you?'

He shrugged.

'So you'll ride a motorcycle to your law classes. That'll make you special?'

'I won't rot in this town. Nor will Sami.'

I was quiet, wondering whether he believed what he said.

'Only two more years,' he went on, 'and I'm out of here.'

'Lucky you.'

I wasn't going out with him. I can't say it hadn't occurred to me (dear Thibaud, to whom I had never written, no longer seemed a consideration; I shuddered to think what he would have made of my life as it was), but Frédéric wasn't interested. He claimed to fancy only older women, and dark-skinned ones, which I took to be an affectation. I suspected him of being in love with Lahou, at least a little, a devotion which would consign him to celibacy for some while to come.

8

It was around the time of that conversation, in November, that Marie-Jo was caught in bed with a young soldier from the barracks. I heard this news from my parents, at supper.

'What about your friend, then?' asked my father, piling his plate with dollops of creamed spinach.

'Who?' I had not mentioned the new gang at home, fearful of my parents' displeasure, and certain, somehow, that they were only temporary company.

'Marie-José.'

'Oh, her.' I wrinkled my nose.

'Well you might. Can't say I'm sorry you've drifted apart under the circumstances.'

I thought he meant the trial, although it seemed to me odd that he would refer to it so cheerfully, and I concentrated on cutting my meat.

'Extraordinary behaviour.'

'What?'

'This business with the soldier.'

My father was as much amused as anything – his sense of humour was always bawdy – but my mother shifted in her chair, and when he was explaining the facts only slightly more explicitly, she interrupted him – 'Alexandre, don't!' – in a way that made him stop. But he continued chuckling to himself as he ate, a man undauntable, as he was in those strange months of zeal and mania. Later, when it had passed, I would marvel at my father's hummingbird speed, at the fluttering ubiquity of his thick-bodied self; and still later, we would come to see it as a kind of madness, and a foreshadowing. I have no photographs from that autumn, but if I did, my father would be smiling hugely in all of them, his lips stretched apart, the glimpsed cavern of his mouth the only darkness, the hint that his grin was too broad to last.

The details of Marie-Jo's transgression I gleaned at school: 'He was inside her, on top of her'; 'she'd only just met him'; 'her mother stood there until he was dressed and then marched him out'. I was intensely pleased by Marie-Jo's misfortune, and even forgave my mother the stiff little sex talk that she subsequently felt prompted to foist on me.

My mother, at that time, had been much alone. When my father was tending to his grand new responsibilities, she moved in mysterious paths. She frequently went out, but I did not know where to: she was not shopping, because we strove to save money; nor carousing, because her temperament and the temper of the time did not allow it. Sometimes, I knew, she was at my grandparents', and sometimes plunged into her charity work (she sat on the board of a homeless shelter, and took, in those days, even greater solace in those less fortunate than we). I knew, too, that she prayed, in church, alone, as regularly as she had her hair done or her nails manicured. This was a habit of long standing, and often, finding her away from home, I pictured her in her pew, her eyes on the Virgin and her nostrils full of incense.

On the afternoons when my huddle disbanded early, or when I couldn't bear to idle alongside them yet again, I drifted back to an empty house, empty but for Etienne and his nurse, Magda, who lounged, feet up, on the white sofa, and passed the hours leafing through romance magazines (*True Love*, *Wild Passions*), picking at her fingernails and keeping only the most desultory eye on my snoozing brother. By myself, I roamed the corridors, disturbing the still air, sampling perfumes in my parents' bathroom, testing the mattresses in the spare bedrooms, slipping, shiftless, and coming to settle in my own room, lying on my bed with the door shut. I came to feel secure in the quiet, which was, as it turned out, unfortunate.

But as for my mother: she did not turn to me, as she always had before, for confidences. As she whittled her bony self, she ate her words rather than her meals. She spoke to Etienne, who could not understand, in whispers; and to me, hardly at all. Although I pretended otherwise, I missed her perfumed confabulations in the kitchen or at my bedside, precious as they grew rare. When she came to see me, already in bed, in the wake of Marie-Jo's exposure, the sex talk seemed an occasion, a reaching out.

'I don't have to tell you about the risks,' said Maman, smoothing my duvet with her manicured hand. The diamonds of her ring sent sparkling shafts along the wall.

'No.'

'It's so different from when I was a girl. It's a dangerous thing. In so many ways. Not just physically, but emotionally too. That, at least, hasn't changed. You have to be ready for it. And you can't be, not so young. Your friend—'

'She's not my friend.' I stuck my chin under the sheet. I was lying down. Only my nose and eyes were exposed.

'Whatever. She risks her life before it's begun. I hope we've raised you not to be so foolish.'

I sat up again. 'Don't worry, Maman.'

'You're all still children. And morally—'

'I know.'

'Faith is so important. You're old enough to realize that.'

I didn't answer. Faith, from what I could see, played very little part in any of our lives then, in spite of our weekly pilgrimage to mass.

'I trust you,' she said. 'I know you wouldn't disappoint me.'

She gave me a look, as she said this, that let me know she didn't trust me at all. Or perhaps that was merely the interpretation of my guilty conscience. I was spending my time learning how to be invisible in familiar territory – a homespun version of my American lessons – and had grown unaccustomed to scrutiny.

In a corner of myself, I actually envied Marie-José's humiliation. Caught, she was released from the efforts of extremity. I knew that she was under curfew, that she could no longer go out at night, that her mother organized family weekends and trips to the theatre to keep her daughter in check; and while, at school, we concurred that this was cruel punishment indeed (what teenager spends time, happily, with her parents?), I secretly longed similarly to let go, to be told, to be saved as my brother, in spite of everything, was saved.

9

What – can I be truthful, I wonder? – was my brother to me, in all this confusion? A sack, a pod, a thief, myself, sagacity, bridge of life's terrible isolation and its most hideous emblem. He alone was resolutely himself, fast against the swirling current in that time, and yet he alone knew what that self was, if knowing was part of him. And only he was protected from that current, by our efforts, and that only for a while. He disgusted me (if this is the time to be truthful, then I will concede he always had): his spittle and the redness of his mouth; his translucent skin, the fingers like fronds, the buckling spine that snaked its semi-solid way beneath his surface. And the smells: his odours, those we spend our lives couching and disguising, of piss and shit and sweat; and then, too, the sweet, milky baby scent right up against his neck, which was the scent of home. I raged and hid my rage; he was nothing and all things. He was, I sometimes told myself, what was left over from the past, whereas I was what would be. But we were the same, and he was inescapable, and how could I not love him for that? He alone kept every secret; he alone holds them still.

And when I came home to that house and thought it empty although he was there, it was because – how to describe it? – it was as if when I stood alongside him only I were in the room. But this is not correct: it was as if I, and more than I, a superfluity that was yet not superfluous, shared the space. Words cannot hold what he was, and is; chimerical, they cannot give him shape. He wavers beyond them, but always *there*: if 'home' had for me a name, it was his. And now that we are no longer under the same roof, now that his scent is with me only occasionally, in the back of my throat, in the moments between sleep and wakefulness (or at those rare times when I visit him, in his ice-green room across the ocean; and then only in whiffs behind the sticky pink assault of disinfectant), he is still home to me, in all its lost possibility.

What I have here, around me, in my books and in the jumbled roaring wonder of the crumbling city, is not that. I could not live and be myself with my brother; I was, inevitably, only too eager to escape him when the time came (as, it transpired, were we all in our ways). But when I die, I want to be buried beside Etienne.

10

I may say, and it may have seemed, that faith played only a small role in our lives, then: but that, too, is disingenuous. Even at fourteen, I was well aware – as I stretched my unbreakable leash and ventured into faithlessness – that the bonds of faith, religious and otherwise, governed the tiniest movements of our household. I might have mocked confession or communion, or my mother's quiet meditations with the saints; any one of the wayward and declining LaBasses might have indulged our darkest impulses; and yet we knew ourselves to be bound to our faith, cement-bound, blood-bound, in a proximity shared only by a few hundred thousand, those who were, like us, exiles of French Algeria.

I didn't question such matters. Even when I stamped my tiny foot in teenage rebellion, it was a gesture accompanied by the whimper of the already defeated. The logic of my upbringing was indisputable: we were Catholics, we were French, we were Algerian. Ours, as a personal heritage, a gift indeed, most particularly for us, the Europeans of North Africa, was the doctrine of Original Sin.

St. Augustine is Algeria's first child, her most celebrated offspring. He is all of us, and his is our abiding legacy. Born in fourth century Bône (*bled el-Aneb*: in Arabic, the 'land of the jujubes'), half Berber, a boy who caught nightingales and stole fruit from the pear trees for his pleasure, he grew hard and fearsome in his Christian age. But he remained human: he revealed his faults – he confessed – for their redemption. He cast the harsh light of Africa upon his religion, upon the here and now, a present reality of guilt and punition; but he lived for a corresponding beyond, a perfection hereafter; and my family's dreamed perfection, always past, or beyond possible, was but a mirror of his.

Some would contend that Albert Camus, godless in this godless century, provides the errant confessor with an Algerian rival, but Camus's stoic philosophies of humanism and justice, of a moral stance in the face of our mortal futility; his hopeful search for peace among men – they are but a naive and timorous flicker in comparison, everywhere overshadowed by Augustine's imperious, outraged, all-seeing Divine, able to weed out even the dissemblers. (Who else would consider the falsely faithful a tribe that merited address? St. Augustine was nothing if not a cynic.) Augustine's gimlet eye is always on the gates to his City of God, that gilded metropolis which shimmers forever in an impossible tense, like my brother, like an Algeria forever French.

And St. Augustine, for all his humanity, his youth of pleasurable sin, his reassuring comprehension of our lapses and his inspiring and familiar devotion to his mother (a cultural characteristic of the *pieds-noirs*, if you believe our historians, right up there with *soubressade* and siestas), in spite of all this which draws him into our hearts, his most abiding contribution, his primary offering is, of course, the doctrine that binds and condemns us, the one that orders our species to pay for Adam and Eve's indulgence. And for St. Augustine's, for that matter. Chez LaBasse, we all knew it from the cradle – all except Etienne, I suppose, who might have been considered to embody it instead – and as the time drew near for my grandfather's trial, it was the premise behind our prayers, and the unspoken dread in our conversations. All of us, generation upon generation, living – no, wallowing – in Original Sin, endlessly punishable for it, shaky in our mistrust of grace.

We looked around and saw only occasions for repentance and torment, even where others were rejoicing. For the first time my eyes were drawn, at table, to the frames behind my father's head: there, on the dining room wall, couched in gilt, writhed Burmese depictions of hellfire that my parents had acquired in happier days. Colourful and superficially pleasing, they were also the stuff of nightmares: pallid, frog-faced men and women stirred and bobbed in vats of boiling oil, jabbed by flaming pokers. One woman was made to fornicate with a livid spike while demons danced behind her. And the demons themselves: empurpled and engorged, fanged, with looping tongues and spidery scarlet wings at their backs. All around them surged a burning sea, molten, gold and red, and rather beautiful. How had I seen only the gilt for years? And how could I not see it all, glaring down at me, as an omen?

In November, the Berlin Wall came down, a televised fiesta of torch-bearing, seething, ecstatic youth. In the screen's darkness, in the flames, in the pallor of the young faces, the images were not, alas, unlike those before which I had been lately and unhappily dining. And my father but glanced at the set as he walked through the room, and said, 'There'll be a price to pay for that, too.'

My mother, who had had a letter from Eleanor, announced that Becky was being threatened with the public high school for her final year if she failed to improve her grades, and added, in doleful tones, with an unfamiliar brutality, 'Well, that's her future shot. Eleanor might as well cut off the girl's legs.' I, at the time, was more concerned with Becky's crimes: 'What did she do, exactly?' 'Eleanor doesn't say. I told you. She's always had trouble with Becky. I've always thought she didn't really *want* to be a mother. Not then, anyway, and that was why.' But looking back, I am struck by the menacing gloom that my parents cast in concentrated beams onto the wider world, surely hoping that thereby my grandfather's guilt – his own, particular sin, which was theirs also – would remain obscured.

II

The trial crept up on me. I was, of course, trying very hard to ignore its coming: that had preoccupied me for months. For that I was prepared to lounge in alleys and arcades with friends whose company, already by December, had grown dull to me, and to feign interest in their petty diversions. (Although perhaps this disenchantment is in some measure retrospective: at the time, Machiavellian though I thought myself, I would never have considered that I could simply walk away, that I was using them, like an undercover cop, for my own purposes. From an American perspective, I see myself in those months like a member of the Witness Protection Program, surrounded by an odd human assortment chosen only for the efficiency of disguise; but somehow, nevertheless, inescapable.)

Had I been observing more closely, I would have noted the

preparations taking place under our own roof. For a start, there was the resumption of family supper. My father resurfaced at the table one night, and then night after night: hence the conversation about Marie-José; hence my sudden involvement with the pictures behind his head. For a time that autumn, my father, like my grandfather before him, had been the unpredictable, the ghost of suppers – long a tendency, it had become a pattern: a place always, or usually, set, often unoccupied, cleared away after a hasty phone call once my brother, mother and I were already tucked in front of our soup. What with my mother's lack of interest in food and the fact that my brother had usually been fed by Magda beforehand, I loathed those fatherless evenings; the only eater, I felt as if I were a guzzling panda or sleek pot-bellied pig supping for display.

So I noticed my father's return, and was grateful, and pleased, too, to have him stay in upon occasion after dinner, with a scotch and a book, in his study upstairs, or even, once or twice, in the living room with my mother. But it didn't occur to me that this togetherness was anything other than spontaneous. In fact, my parents were steeling themselves. My father – who, given his elation, must have wanted more than ever to be out of our family mausoleum, fluttering and humming and ferociously alive – sacrificed his desires for my mother's benefit, to pacify and reassure her that their life would continue, by recreating antique rhythms, for even a month, and pretending that nothing had changed.

My brother's outings in the car were stopped, his walks confined to a few short blocks around the house, because my mother – she told me later – woke up one morning convinced that the press, in seeking further to defame the House of LaBasse, would seize upon poor googly-eyed Etienne, innocent and indefensible, as the emblem of our distress (the way Zohra, because of him, saw me, metonymically, as tainted and pitiable), and would plaster his photograph on the front page, or at the very least, in colour on the back. (In fact, during the trial, not a single paparazzo plagued us, although a snapshot of my grandparents entering the courthouse on the first day did appear on the local page three, a picture in which my grandmother, scowling so that her brows met above her fearsome nose, and with her torso billowed beneath its loden coat, cut far manlier and more robust a figure than her slight husband, my grand-father, whose white horseshoe of hair was fluffed like a chick's, and whose eyes sagged wet and mournful above his milky jowls.)

They – my parents – anticipated press attention, and stress, and anxiety even in their idiot son, and in their anticipation doubtless created all these things except the first; but such fretting was unusual, because the trial's verdict was never in doubt. Nothing if not honourable, even in depression, my grandfather was to plead guilty to his crime.

This was not at all to my grandmother's liking. She sat on the sofa in our living room one Saturday afternoon days before the event, wrapped in a scarlet sweater that made her look like a large bloodstain blotted on the white damask, and she wept. I cast an eye from my corner, my fascination masked by the geography text in front of me.

My mother, as I have said, was prone to tears, and their formation and course along her cheeks were familiar to me; but my grandmother had never cried openly in my presence.

'Ah, Carol,' she muttered several times, twisting her tea napkin back and forth, 'the shame of it. I thought I could persuade him not to; he's never listened. It may be the drugs he's been given, or someone else – that lawyer, Rom – I've disliked him from the first. He seems to think – and Jacques seems to believe him – that this is the only way.'

'Explain to me again?'

'The only defence, apparently, is incompetence, insanity, whatever. To plead not guilty, that is. Given all those horrid kids, all ready to stand up and point the finger. We have to see them, too. That boy, that smarmy one who never grows, the accountant's son – he practically spits on us when we pass him. He was such a well-brought-up little boy, too. I don't under-stand why Alexandre hasn't sacked their parents, I really don't.'

'But not a one of them is sixteen, are they? They can speak, but they aren't witnesses – isn't that what you told me, months ago?'

'The little slut, that Marie-José Derain – she's had a birthday now. She's sixteen. And the one from Paris, the girl who was hit. Her too.'

My mother stood to pour more tea. She was using the silver service, a present from my grandparents. Etienne tried to reach for the bevelled pot, which shone in the lamplight.

'Calm, my sweet, calm,' said my grandmother, patting at her grandson's dry brow with her crumpled serviette.

'He's finding it all a strain, poor love,' said my mother.

I allowed myself an exasperated snort – how could she know? – but not loudly enough for them to hear.

'Aren't we all?' My grandmother sighed. 'You see, we've got the mitigating circumstances, which Rom says will emerge regardless, and to better effect if Jacques is straightforwardly conceding his wrong.'

'But—'

'If it weren't for the little Parisian howling for blood . . .'

'So you've said.'

'But my dear, the worst of it is – what I can't stand is—' Here my grandmother's voice wavered like a warped record, and I abandoned all pretence of reading. 'They might – he might have to go – to prison.'

The last word emerged in a prolonged wail, and it was as if the tears erupted in a single burst all across her face. Slicked with them, her features, like the teapot, reflected the lamplight.

'I know, my dear, I know.' My mother – could it be? – perched beside her formidable parent-in-law and embraced her, burying her face in the older woman's powdery neck, muttering soothing platitudes. 'Sh, sh, sh,' it sounded like. Etienne found this sight exciting and started to bob back and forth.

'It might kill him,' said my grandmother in a raspy voice. 'It could.'

'Well it won't. And it won't happen, so don't worry. It'll be a fine. A man like him? They'll just fine him. It's the not knowing that we find so difficult.' My mother said this with her torso still clamped against my grandmother's, but her head drawn back. She resembled both an ardent suitor and a cobra preparing to strike.

'He's guilty as sin. He should go to jail,' I mumbled from my chair. I thought myself inaudible, but my mother arched further and glowered over at me.

'What did you say?'

'Nothing. Really. Nothing.'

Features rigid, fists clenched, she pulled herself upright, knocking my grandmother's teacup and splashing a buoyant brown stripe along the sofa's white arm. Etienne rocked in a frenzy and started to crow.

'Here,' I offered, on my feet at once, 'I'll take him to the kitchen. And I'll bring a sponge.'

By the time the excitement had subsided, the sofa was wet and my grandmother's face dry; and my treachery, by mutual, if tacit, agreement, overlooked.

I retreated to my bedroom to allow them to lament in private. Sprawled across my single bed on my belly, my head dangling over the side so that the blood pooled in my skull and made it feel ready to burst, I longed for a friend I could telephone who would make the whole thing seem like a joke.

Instead, I wrote at last to Thibaud: a long, rambling letter in which I lied about how things were and how I was and what I had been doing. I noted that I thought of him constantly and didn't understand why he had never replied to my letter from America, months ago. The next day, a Sunday, I posted the envelope before I had time to think more about it. In truth, I couldn't believe that he still existed, so unreal did all of it – my whole life before – seem to me by then. The letter seemed, at the time, like an entry in my diary, and nothing more.

12

The trial began on a Wednesday, the Wednesday after that upsetting Saturday afternoon. I had only a half day of classes, but it was not suggested that I accompany my parents and grandparents to the courthouse. I was too young; insofar as was possible I was, like Etienne, to be spared.

My parents were to pick up Grand'-mère and Grand-père, and so were ready early, when it was still dark, the bloody spill of dawn just washing over the black sea. My mother wore a navy suit, an Hermès scarf with peacocks on it, and carried a little handbag with a large, gilded clasp. She looked more like an actress in a 1940s film than the real daughter-in-law of a genuine felon. I noticed a little ladder in her dark stocking, poking down the back of her left thigh from beneath her skirt; but I didn't tell her. Perfume billowed around her in expensive waves. My father looked less dramatic, but equally spruce: he hovered behind his wife, broad in his pressed grey wool, a glittering pin through his tie and his still-tan cheeks smooth in their fleshiness, his greying curls pomaded and combed. At the door, as I loitered, still in my nightgown, my hair in knotty strings, he made a joke and stuck his tongue out at me: I was struck by its deep pink healthfulness. A trial, it seemed, was like a cocktail party: providing you were sufficiently well dressed, you didn't need to worry about what you would say.

I was to stay home, miss class, spend the day on my homework: that was their plan, and mine also. The house was by no means empty: in addition to Etienne and his nurse, Fadéla, the housekeeper, was at work, already on her knees on the foyer floor.

I had, at my desk, in my room, a pile of library books about Camus and Sartre for my philosophy project. All I had gleaned from my studies thus far was that Camus and Sartre had initially been friends, and then were no longer; that neither considered themselves philosophical allies; and that Camus, a *pied-noir* like my father and my grandparents and, by extension, like me, too, had been mired and unfriended by the problems of his – of our – country. I had grasped that he was on the Left, politically, unlike my relatives and unlike most Algérois, who were proud of him but suspicious. But just as he disappointed his compatriots in this way, in the matter of Algeria he could never please his allies, could never be sufficiently liberal, because his fundamental aim had been to hold on to the land of his heart and his childhood – to keep his home; while the aim of the Left had been decolonization, justice and the future. Or, as my grandfather saw it, and doubtless my father too, although he never said, the Left's programme – and de Gaulle's – had been a wholesale betrayal of France's finer principles, and a betrayal of us, her people, and of the *harkis* in the bargain, who were her people, too. And of Algeria, for that matter. 'And who,' the old man would say today, if he could, the paper open to that nation's latest atrocities, with a rueful smile on his lips and his eyebrows fanning over his eyes like a madman's, 'who is surprised? Not I!' Regardless, Camus was lucky, my family had long believed, to have met his end before his homeland did.

I wanted, really, to write an essay about what it was like to be penned into a corner where every choice was wrong, where nobody would trust you and where the truth could not be told because it didn't exist. Camus knew it, and in my little way I knew it too. We all knew it, in my house, but we didn't talk about it. I wouldn't write about it, either: the assignment was to compare the existentialism of Sartre with that of Camus. My teacher wasn't interested in their lives, or in my relatives' notions about their lives. I had before me *Nausea* and *The Stranger*, and at my feet other books by the two men that I found difficult to read and impossible to understand.

I don't know whether I thought that by attending the trial I could influence its outcome – the way, as a child, I had believed that my simple presence could somehow keep my family safe, and so had tagged along on countless tedious walks and errands purely to ensure my mother's, or brother's, or father's continued well-being. Or whether I simply could not bear any longer the empty grey light at my window (the sun, after its spectacular

awakening, retreated fast behind the too-familiar veil), and the
soporific sentences of France's great men.

I rang Frédéric, who was still in bed, and suggested that we
go to watch my grandfather being prosecuted. I had forborne,
all those weeks, from ever mentioning this event, but Frédéric
registered no surprise at my changed heart.

'It's happening right now?'

'Well, it's beginning now, this morning. It's already begun.'

'We could just walk in?'

'I'm not sure. But I'm family, right?'

'But a kid.'

'I don't know who I hate more in all this, my grandfather or
Marie-José.'

'The bitch, for sure.'

'Why's that?'

'The old guy's old. And he's family.'

'So?'

'Yeah, well.'

There was a moment's silence.

'You want me to go with you, is that it?'

'Aren't you curious?'

'Sure, but . . . is there a jury? The whole works?'

'I don't think so. There was a lot of talk, y'know, with my
parents, a while back, about which court it would be. But
Cécile wasn't hurt, not really, so it's not that serious.'

'And you say he's pleading guilty?'

'Yep. My grandma doesn't like it.'

'So what's to see?'

'How do you mean?'

'There's no freak show, no surprises, nothing fun . . . the
judges will ask a few questions and . . .'

'Marie-José is testifying.'

'I know. The whole school knows. She's been acting like it
makes her into some major movie star or something.'

I sniffed. I had not known that everybody knew, and Frédéric
had not been friend enough to tell me.

'Look, wouldn't it be more fun to hook up with Sami and

Lahou and catch a movie downtown this afternoon? You could
get some work done by lunch, and then—'

'Yeah. Thanks, Fred. Never mind.'

13

I decided I would go alone. In conscious imitation of my
parents, I dressed up. I braided my hair in a single fat plait, and
put on a grey skirt and one of my mother's blouses, a butter-
coloured one. I wanted to look as grown-up as possible. I wore
a raincoat of my mother's, but as I was taller than she, it barely
reached my knees. I added, like her, a silk scarf. I considered
a pair of her sunglasses, the better to disguise my youth, but
figured that on so gloomy a day they would only attract
attention.

After slipping out with merely a shout to Fadéla – who toiled
in some invisible region of the house – I caught the bus into
town, and spent the journey trying to gauge whether the other
passengers were staring at me.

Walking to the courts, I marvelled that I had ambled the
same streets with Thibaud when the asphalt shimmered in the
heat and the city dozed; that I had scuffed the same curbs at the
heels of my gang in later, danker days; and that here I was again,
as if in disguise. What made these three girls – so unlike in
demeanour and purpose, so remote, emotionally, one from the
other – what made us one and the same? How was I the same
girl I had been just the summer before, in Boston, or on Cape
Cod? How did I know I was; but more seriously, how could
anyone else be sure? What if Eleanor had been sent a counterfeit
niece – how would she ever have known?

As I climbed the steps of the courthouse and passed through
its forbidding portals, leaving outside the sooty curlicues and
arabesques of French bureaucratic architecture for an internal
renovation all fluorescence and efficiency, linoleum floors and

black vinyl benches upon which to wait – indeed, as I moved from the grand eighteenth-century exterior to such contemporary bleakness, I thought, in passing: who would even identify this, photographed in and out, as the same building – I wondered about the guilty who had walked here: the frauds and the thieves and the murderers. The trio of summer bombers, had they survived to injure others, would have walked these steps, the sweet-tempered eighteen-year-old checkout girl along with the two boys, a stranger to her mother. But I wondered, above all, about the Nazi War Criminals, that scattering of men my grandfather's age and older, being brought, so late, to justice. Paul Touvier, first in line, had been arrested and charged earlier that year; but there had been, for as long as I could recall, national grumblings and fussings about these few, our truest emblems of evil, who appeared in the newspapers as cruel-lipped young thugs and again, alongside those photos, as freck-led, bespectacled old men in tweed jackets or patterned pullovers, with a tremor of fear in their faces, their features spread and reapportioned and so wasted as to look completely other. I wondered how anybody could be sure enough to condemn them. Their victims, the survivors, pointed their fingers and shouted 'Him, it's him!'; but how could they be certain – the outside so altered, the skin flaccid and puckering, the hair gone, the voice quavering, the stance curled into a question mark; and the inside, the dark soul, untouchable and unknown? Like Colonel Chabert, or Martin Guerre – one had to choose, from so few clues (a glance, a trembling chin), to believe or disbelieve, to throw one's faith behind one identity or the other, true or false, villain or victim. I wondered whether it was, in the end, just a choice.

And did this mean, I wondered as I scanned the trial sheets for my grandfather's courtroom (as inconspicuously as possible, my back to the hennaed receptionist, so that all she could see was my plait and my raincoat: I didn't want to be revealed as a child, as his grandchild, for one, and as a minor summarily to be sent home, for another), that in carefully selected circumstances, far from this town where the web of my life was commonly known, I might successfully be reinvented, pretend to be anyone, from anywhere, and be believed? That I might not have to live forever as Sagesse, the daughter in the youngest generation of the LaBasse family, older sister of a drooling mutant, grandchild of a criminal, seemed delicious.

This was a simple realization, to be sure, and a common one – in New York, surrounded by the like-minded, I have come to consider it an American realization – but although in Boston it had hovered in my consciousness, it had never touched me with such clarity as it did in the sandwich-scented corridor of the Palais de Justice. If I decided that the three Sagesses who had walked in front of this building in the past months were not the same girl, then who was to quibble?

If that were so, I countered to myself, if one was many different people, each distinct, then my grandfather could not possibly be prosecuted: the passive, delicate fellow he had become, his brow drawn up in permanent anxiety, bore no relation to the raging blusterer who had pulled the trigger. But the later self had always lived within the earlier, and the two, though separate, were inseparable. And while we, his kin, might not recognize him, it was society – Cécile and Marie-Jo and even the lawyer, Rom – who stood outside my grandfather and concurred that he was the same man, that he owned the same clothes and had the same wife and the same dentures, and remained, indisputably, one and the same, however altered he might appear in manner or in temperament.

But what, I wondered, if he had forgotten? Could an amnesiac be responsible for what had been done in his earlier incarnation? What linked us all our lives, I thought, was memory, fluted and flawed though it might be. Without that – if we, his family, claimed him but he did not know us – would my grandfather still be guilty? Where were the limits of sameness? When could we stop, at last and in relief, being the same person, the person we did not choose or want to be? Or was it, I wondered, adjusting my mother's scarf at my neck and pulling back the heavy swing door to my grandfather's courtroom, feeling the hollowing sensation that my clever thoughts had been circular and for nought, a crude and ineluctable matter of the flesh?

The room was bright and sallow, large, but not as cavernous as I had imagined it. It had no windows, and sat on a scrubby mud-brown carpet. At the far end, slightly raised at a panelled counter, two men and a woman presided, the judges, solemn but unremarkable people no older than my parents. A court reporter typed to the left, a young man with bristly fair hair and an elongated head. I scanned the backs between me and those officials and picked out the trio that was my family, grateful that they did not turn around. Cécile did, however; she craned her neck and frowned, and returned to face the voices, her own parents' smooth crania slightly cocked on either side of her.

The first voice belonged to the woman judge. She had been asking a question, although I did not hear it. There was a brief and reverberating silence, followed by a voice I knew, smaller than usual, but deliberate and clear: my grandfather's voice. I turned to find him, at the right of my line of sight, far across the room, and caught him by the characteristic swoop of his arm as it reached to smooth back his hair.

I looked at him, and heard his voice, but not what he said, and felt, just then, a hand on my upper arm. A police officer, in uniform, whispered something in my ear. He did not try to move me. I took in his ovoid shiny face and the bluish swathe of his jaw. I was as if struck deaf; I didn't know whether he wanted me to sit, or to leave, or to identify myself.

'It's my grandfather,' I whispered back. I tried to be very quiet, not wanting my parents to sense any commotion or to notice me. The officer said something else. All the while my grandfather's voice was rising and falling, with the drowsy persistence of an August wasp against a window pane. I looked back at him, and he glanced, as if telepathically, at the door and at me, and our eyes met. His eyes, sad as a basset-hound's, locked onto mine across all the room's bright distance, and his voice faltered in its rhythms; and I was struck, like a shaft, a physical pain, by the sorrow and the awfulness of it, by the

loneliness of the diminished figure in his dark suit, alone on the
ocean of brown carpet; and aware that the look that passed
between us was one of agonizing recognition: we saw, and
knew, each other. Our blood was the same blood, and this, this
instant of dreadful mutuality, was the reason that one could
never escape one's self. He was my grandfather and would
always be, and I felt a terrible pity for him that was love. And
as the officer began to tug at my arm, I smiled, a brittle and
doubtless tearful smile, but one designed to communicate to my
grandfather that after all these months I had forgiven him, and
that I understood and accepted what had just passed between
us.

I don't know if he saw me smile, because then I blinked, on
account of my welling tears, and the officer opened the door (it
seemed, after all, that he wanted me to leave), and I slipped out
of his grasp and back into the hallway where, suddenly, I could
hear properly again – the telephone at the reception and the
hennaed woman's nasal greeting; the shuffle and clack of steps
in the nearby stairwell; snatches of conversation between a
lawyer and her client as they brushed past me ('I really don't
think you should say that. And above all, keep calm') – and
where I hunched my shoulders and headed for the street.

Five

I

The trial lasted another day and a half. My grandfather didn't mention to my parents that he had seen me; nor did he broach the subject with me. It made me wonder about that summer night, the night of the crime; and I became convinced that my grandfather, with some inner sense, had seen me then, too. That secret night, with its cool smell of greenery and the lemon scent of Thibaud, the spit of gravel on my back and the soughing sea – I felt as though my grandfather had recognized me there, and that in some way we shared that night's guilt and treachery. If I could forgive him his sin, perhaps he could absolve me of mine. It would be our shared secret.

Thinking this, I felt the warmth between us again like a current, and I allowed myself to worry about him and his fate. I, who had come home, skipped lunch and changed my clothes, had lain on my bed to read my philosophy books until dinner-time, dozing over them because they were too difficult, almost wondered whether the morning's outing had been only a vivid daydream. My mother returned alone at around six, saying that my father had gone on to the Bellevue, with his parents, to see about some business.

'How'd it go?'

'Fine – I think. Who knows? Your father thought it went well. Your grandfather gave his account, you know, and what with procedure, that took up a lot of time. Then they started with the witnesses – the girl from Paris first, and then her parents—'

'They weren't even there. What do they know?'

My mother looked surprised. 'It's standard. They spoke about the hotel, and your group of friends, the way you kids all hang together—'

'They're not my friends.'

My mother shrugged. 'More tomorrow. Marie-José tomorrow, I expect.'

'Hm.'

'Your poor grandfather. I know I've had my ups and downs with him, but if you could've seen him up there—'

'I know.'

'You don't, though. You can't imagine. This has broken him. And when you think about it, the life he's had and all he's been through, and still, all he's accomplished . . . and now this . . .' She sighed. 'It's no way for a man to be, at his age.'

'You don't think they'll send him to prison?'

'What do I know, *poupette*? I hope not.'

'Grand'-mère thinks it could kill him.'

'Let's hope they don't. I really hope they don't. The strange thing is . . .'

'What?'

'Nothing.'

'What's strange?'

'Nothing. It's just your father.'

'What about him?'

'It doesn't matter.'

'Maman—'

'I just get the impression – it's very odd – that he'd prefer it.'

'Prefer what?'

'Prison.'

I thought about this for a moment. 'That's ridiculous.'

'Oh, I don't mean he would admit it. He might not even know it. And maybe I'm just wrong.'

'Maybe you are.'

'It's just that he talks about all this as if prison were a certainty. Not to your grandparents – I don't mean with them. But when we talk, the two of us.'

'He's probably trying to prepare for the worst, don't you

think? I do that – like I imagine that I've failed a test, even when I'm pretty sure I haven't, so that—'

'I don't think so. He talks about being free, free to run the hotel as he wishes, that kind of thing. Free, when it's over.'

'Don't you think we'll all feel free when it's over?'

'But when it's over and his father is in prison. Don't you see the difference?'

'You're imagining it, Maman. I've got a grudge against the guy – he's made me into a social leper and I lost my best friend – and I don't want him to go to jail.'

'Don't you?'

'Maybe I did. But I don't any more. I swear.'

My mother patted my cheek, in an oddly paternal gesture. 'Glad to hear it. Now, what have you and Etienne been up to today?'

2

Perhaps my mother, I have since thought, was right about my father's wishes, and perhaps my father had found some convincing means to convey those wishes to the powers of the law. Because at the beginning of the following week, when everyone reconvened for sentencing, my grandfather was condemned to seven months in a minimum security prison. My grandmother made a show of swooning in the courtroom, so that my father had to hold her up, but my grandfather just hung his head and folded his hands together and waited to be led away. I learned these details from the newspaper, not at home but at school, where Lahou slipped me a copy before math class, with a sisterly hug. Now that I so clearly needed to be protected, she was full of smiles for me, her last doubts quelled by my public disgrace.

The newspaper had used again the photo of my grandfather taken on the courthouse steps, but they had cropped out my grandmother altogether. He hunched and squinted, as I had seen him in the dock, small, frail and alone.

'What will happen now?' I asked my father that evening. Our house was imbued with a strange tenderness, our regard for my grandfather manifest in our lowered voices and in our eagerness to please and appease one another.

He put his arms out towards me, spread wide as if to envelop. He said, as they had been saying for months, and as I had learned not to believe, 'Don't worry, my angel. Everything will be fine.'

'Grand'-mère says it might kill him.'

'Nonsense. I've seen the place. It's like a rest home, almost. He'll be away, as if he were on a trip, for such a little time you'll hardly notice he was gone. He'll be home before school is out.'

'But the hotel—'

'I'm running the Bellevue, and have been for months. I would've been running it regardless. He's getting on, your grandfather – he's over seventy, you know. About time he retired. He deserves a rest. None of this would've happened if he'd learned a little sooner to take it easy. He was just overtired. Think of it as a cure.'

'Prison isn't a rest. Is it, Maman?'

My mother tried to smile. 'It doesn't help anything or anybody to wish things were different,' she said. 'We have to ask what to do next, what God would want.'

'And what's that?'

'We must try to help your grandmother, for one thing. This is hardest for her.'

'She's a strong woman. A remarkable woman,' said my father. 'She'll be fine. You'll probably find she's busy helping us. She's always been the one who keeps everyone together.'

My mother gave my father a strange look, as if he were telling a secret I wasn't meant to hear. I thought about it, later, in my room, and remembered that it was my grandmother who told the stories, who wove a narrative out of the lives of the LaBasses, and that in this sense, at least, my father was right. And it was my mother who had more often than not unravelled those stories at her leisure, and put them together again another way, with a different, darker meaning. It seemed, though, that in these months between crime and punishment, my mother had changed, had joined forces with her mother-in-law, and that she would now be engaged in weaving my grandmother's stories even tighter. In this way the women would strive, together, extra hard, to keep the family whole.

The fulcrum, though, around which our little family revolved, was shifting. My grandfather had long been made mythic – in his brilliance, his difficulty, his determination – and now, with this final judgment, had evaporated into myth. (To my father, seven months might have seemed the blink of an eye, but to me, then, they were still an interminable round of days, not least because I had been made to understand that I was not to visit my grandfather during this time: he did not wish me to see him in prison. This was not a memory of him that he ever wanted me to have.) There remained, in his stead, the fleshy, flawed presence of my father, around whom the women's spinning would have to begin. Like a caterpillar encased in its pupa, he, too, would disappear beneath their silky threads, to emerge transformed: no longer my hapless, infuriating father, he would become the scion and patriarch of the House of LaBasse, master of its tiny clifftop kingdom, the Bellevue. His sleek fattening, in this light, made sense: he had been preparing for the transition, so long awaited, and although he would assist in it only passively, he had had to will its onset. What is a hero if not a man about whom stories are told? Till now, my father had not known heroism; but my grandmother and mother would change that. Stories are made up, after all, as much of what is left out.

Later that night, I heard my parents talking in the front hall downstairs. Their voices resonated against the marble. My mother was telling my father that he should fire Marie-Jo's mother, and Thierry's father in the bargain.

'You can't imagine what it's like for your mother. And now – they'll be positively gloating. Honestly, Alex—'

My father would have none of it. 'This is a business, Carol. A business, not a popularity contest.' He was parroting his own father. 'Maman will get over it. She trusts my judgments – why can't you?'

'Maybe because I live with you. I know you too well.'

My father's voice got deeper and quieter, the voice he used when he was angry and trying not to show it; the voice they both used when they were arguing and didn't want the substance of their altercation to reach their children's ears. (Who knew, after all, what Etienne could understand? Displays of rage made him shriek – when they didn't make him laugh instead.) They moved back towards the living room, so that all I could catch were their alternating rhythms. I returned to my bed, where I lay on my stomach and put my head under the pillow.

3

Christmas, a few weeks later, was subdued. My grandmother spent it with us, staying overnight in the room my grandfather had used. We watched the Pope on television, rather than going to mass, and the service seemed to last for ever. My mother sat forward on her chair as though the television's rays could grant salvation; but my father, like Etienne, fell asleep with his mouth open and emitted little bubbling snores.

Etienne's *fête*, too, the following day, was hushed and private, although it was an event usually celebrated with particular verve, so that my brother, if he could indeed reason in some secret part of himself (we lived our lives as if he could, a sort of Pascalian gamble), would not think himself stinted. His presents – which we took turns opening for him – were modest and practical: a couple of shirts, a new plaid rug for his knees. Only my grandmother, who gave him a fine felt hat with a blue and green feather in it ('he's a young man, after all') and an Italian glass lamp that lit up like a swirling mauve jewel ('to go to sleep with, for pleasant dreams'), tried to counter the austerity of the day. And my father, switching the little lamp on and off, said, in an attempt at lightheartedness, 'I always think it's better not to dream at all. I imagine that's Etienne's privilege.'

As for the new year – ringing in a new decade, which ought, I thought, to have been filled with fireworks and dancing – my parents, having declined all invitations, remained at home, watching the clock as if it were doomsday, and, after pouring each of us (including Etienne) a thimbleful of Veuve Cliquot in honour of the coming hour, sent both son and daughter to bed. I saw in the new year on my window ledge, observing the distant twinkle of lights in town and imagining that I could distinguish the whoops of crowds at the edge of my hearing.

The year before there had been a party at the Bellevue, in the restaurant (such festivities were my father's province), and Marie-Jo and I had waltzed together, she in a grown-up sequinned dress and I in girlish velvet, and we had run streamers around Etienne until he was bound by strings of gay colour, which he loved. Days later we were still plucking odd snatches of ribbon from the spokes and seams of his chair.

'Next year,' Marie-Jo had said, 'we'll get my brother to invite us to a bash at the Fac – ' her brother was five years older and away studying economics in Marseilles ' – it'll be wild.' I wondered if that was where she was, in a dress even shorter and skimpier than last year's, or whether she was in her pink bedroom, all alone like me. I wondered whether she remembered her promise, and was sorry.

4

Far away in Paris, Thibaud, at least, was thinking of me: a letter arrived, in his jagged handwriting, enclosed in a card. The card unfolded into three panels, each displaying a set of obscenely full air-brushed lips. In the centre panel, a lewd pink tongue protruded, and rested, pointed and shiny as if actually wet, upon the lower bulb of flesh. Thibaud's letter was not correspondingly intimate; indeed, it was almost formal, somehow old-fashioned.

He had been glad to hear from me, he often thought of me, he was pleased that I was doing so well in spite of my grandfather's trouble.

'After all,' he wrote, 'it's not as though you did anything wrong. We weren't even there (haha). But seriously, his problems aren't your problem, and I'm glad you've understood that. I'm sorry that we haven't been in touch sooner. I don't know what can have happened to your American letter (maybe their postal system is as bad as Italy's?) – but now we are.' He didn't say whether he still felt the same about me, but he said he couldn't wait for the summer, that he was working hard ('Only one more year to the *bac*!') and that he was considering preparing for a *grande école* if all went well, and possibly aiming, in the long term, for *l'ENA*. He wanted to hear about the trial, he said. I sniffed the letter to see if I could smell him, but it smelled of nothing except, perhaps, a faint trace of ink.

I wrote back at once, and lied some more, saying that my grandfather's sentence was basically like a cure, and that we all felt fine about it. I pressed for confessions of desire, not knowing whether I felt it for him but knowing that I wanted him to feel it for me. I wrote that I missed his fingertips on my stomach ('et cetera'), that I could still taste his kisses, and that I wondered what he might remember of me – 'of my body', I wrote, which seemed explicit enough. I no longer worried about his eggplant-haired mother, or even about Thibaud himself, and whether he might laugh at my nakedness. I was playing a role – vixen, vamp – and he, like a convict (in the States, many women write love letters to convicts, I have since learned; an impulse which makes perfect sense to me, as long as the convicts' sentences are lifelong), was safely distant, as distant as if he existed only in my imagination.

5

In mid-January, Sami was suspended from school for a week. His crime was not drug dealing, although it might have been; it was insubordination. He had menaced a math teacher – a woman teacher – with his fists, and had threatened to find her house and 'straighten her out', after she announced to him after class one day that unless he changed his attitude he would not only fail but be in serious trouble with the principal. This threat, in the wake of his, was immediately borne out, and although he claimed not to care, I could see – even his beloved Lahou could see – that he was afraid. The principal, a burly, bearded man, had rolled up his sleeves and had propped his bulk upon his desk, so that he loomed over scrawny Sami in his pink plastic chair, and had said, 'Get this, you little jerk: any trouble you think you can make in this school is not a fraction of the trouble we can make for you. Hell, I, all by myself, can make enough trouble for you that you'll be mired in shit for years to come. Don't think we don't know you, because we do. And don't think I won't act on my word, because I will.'

Sami was apparently unaware that threatening a woman teacher might have been construed as cowardice. I said this later to Lahou, who tossed her chevelure and snorted haughtily that, 'Sami is not a coward.'

'I didn't say he was,' I said, although I thought so. 'I just said that's what it could look like.'

'He's right, you know. What happened to him is racism, pure and simple.' She glared at me. 'And don't say anything. Because you don't know the first thing about it.'

'I guess I don't,' I said, which was true. But I kept seeing in my mind the twitching of Sami's jaw when he had told us, in the café, what had happened, and the twitching of his knee in its denim folds. It seemed like cowardice to me. 'Is he going to stop dealing, then?'

'I don't know. He'll cool it for a while.'

'What about you guys?'

'What do you mean?'

'Well, if your mother finds out that Sami's been suspended—'

'Which she probably will.'

'Won't there be problems?'

'Maybe. I don't know. Yeah, probably.' Lahou seemed to shrink, to stop shining. Even her hair seemed to droop. 'You don't know the first thing about it.'

And although this was not a reason or an excuse, it was the reason that I found, later, when I tried to understand my mistake, the reason why they came to my house. Lahou, if not Sami, had been kind to me, and was my friend; and I thought I might compensate for the gulf between us, for my inability to understand, by revealing myself.

It was a Thursday, a couple of days into Sami's suspension. At lunchtime, he hovered outside the café, looking suspicious and hollow-cheeked in the unsparing winter sun. Jacquot hopped up and down in his shadow, a skanky little jester, hands in pockets. Frédéric, Lahou and I came out of the schoolyard together: Frédéric was busy being solicitous of Lahou, cracking jokes, repeatedly reaching out as if to touch her arm, or her shoulder, then thinking better of it, and withdrawing. Lahou flirted back, cautiously, with her body and her eyes but not her voice, and less as we approached the other two, her light turning, heliotropic, to her lover.

Settled, five around a little table, we waited for Sami's lead. He had noted the dance between my companions, and glowered at Frédéric. Lahou took his hand, and smoothed it between her own. 'Everything okay?'

'Like you fucking care.'

'Oh come on, Sami—' I began. The scowling waiter slammed a clean ashtray between us and took our order. He knew us, knew that we ordered little, tipped not at all, and stayed a long time.

'What is this?' Jacquot said, worried but smiling. 'The glums meet for coffee?'

'That's us,' said Fred, offering cigarettes around. 'Bravo. At last we've got a name.'

There was a silence. We could all see Lahou's fingers tracing the bones and veins of Sami's hand, back and forth, like soothing a cat.

'How's home?' asked Frédéric. 'How're they taking it?'

'Don't be an ass. Didn't tell them.'

'What did you do this morning?' Lahou asked.

'Hung out.'

'Where?'

'Around.' I could not imagine what this meant.

'Outside, though. Right?'

'Maybe.'

'I knew it. Your hands are so cold. As cold as if you'd been out all night besides.'

'And this afternoon?' asked Frédéric, who had poured the contents of his matchbox onto the table and was arranging the little wooden sticks into geometrical shapes. 'What's on?'

'You're not,' said Sami, with a narrow-eyed flash at his rival. 'You're definitely not on.'

'No. I'll be in history class. So I guess you're right.'

'Seems like the master needs a laugh,' said Jacquot. 'A quick round of shoplifting, maybe? Crack a few cars?'

'Shut up.'

Our coffees arrived and Sami stared down at his. I felt pity for him.

'We could go to my house,' I offered.

'What?' Fred looked at me as though I were insane.

'It's Thursday, right? My mother's out on Thursday after-noons. Guaranteed.' This was a recent certainty: she went with my grandmother twice a week to see my grandfather, on Tuesdays and Thursdays.

'You live up the hill, don't you?' Sami asked.

'She's Little Miss Rich Bitch. Of course she does.' Jacquot said this with a smile in my direction, but it made me nervous.

'Well, I don't know about you guys, but I've got a test. Sagesse's house isn't worth a zero in history.' Frédéric started putting the matches, one by one, back in their box. 'Who's suspended here, anyway? Just one of us, right?'

'Do you mean it?' Lahou's eyes were wide, her pouting mouth an O.

'Sure – I mean – I—' I was already worrying, wanting to retract. 'My mom will be home by five, so I don't know . . .'

'That's hours from now.'

'A few.'

'It'd take a while to get there,' said Frédéric. 'You guys should think about that.'

'Yes, it does, on the bus—' He was trying to help me out of it, and I clung to his buoy. 'Maybe it's not such a good idea for today.'

Sami checked his watch. 'It's not one thirty yet. There's loads of time. A view from the heights, a tour of the house. An educational afternoon.'

'Warmer than wandering around outside,' said Jacquot. 'It's nippy.'

'Great. Let's go.' Sami summoned the waiter to pay.

'This week, it's hard for us to find anywhere private,' Lahou whispered to me as we walked out. 'I'm really grateful.'

Frédéric put his arm around Sami's shoulder in a bluff, artificial gesture. 'No stealing, my man,' he said, in a silly Corsican accent, as if that would make the comment acceptable. 'Don't get our Sagesse here in any trouble.'

'Fuck you.' Sami twitched out of his friend's grasp. Frédéric drifted away with a vague wave.

6

The other three were cheerful now, restored at the prospect of an escapade. But I was in a panic. What had I done? What would we find? Did they know about Etienne (how could they not)? Would his nurse turn me in to my parents? Would Fadéla still be there – how embarrassing for everyone – or might she, by the time we arrived, have left? Could Magda, could Fadéla, somehow be bribed into silence? Would my brother find some sly way to reveal to my mother what had occurred? And what would occur? What if Sami or Jacquot decided, overwhelmed by my parents' comparative wealth, to pilfer a trinket, certain that it would never be missed? No, I was thinking like my mother, who counted the silver spoons every time a replacement nurse or babysitter had been to the house.

I was certain that the bus driver spied on us in his rearview mirror, memorizing our faces, the dark-skinned faces especially, of teenagers who should not have been riding the bus up the hill at that hour of the afternoon. What cause, I imagined him to be thinking, did brown-skinned youth dressed *like that* have to be riding up the hill at any time? There was nothing there, I imagined him saying later, cap in hand before the sergeant at the police station, for them. And what if, I thought as we got off the bus and the three of them, so unpresentable, jeered and jostled each other and proceeded, like oblivious goslings in my anxious wake, along the broad avenue and into my quiet street, where there were no sidewalks, and we fanned down the middle of the asphalt, what if my mother's car had broken down, or my grandmother had felt ill, or the visit had been made earlier in the day; what if I opened the door to find the two women at tea, the bevelled silver service between them on the coffee table? What if, what if . . .

But to my relief, my mother's car was not in the drive. I made the others wait, and went to check the garage.

'Wow.' Jacquot, after prancing around the front garden, sniffing at the mimosa in mock delight, planted his feet wide on the gravel and threw back his head. 'This is quite a pile. Can't wait to see inside.'

'Jacquot—' Lahou frowned.

'Will you marry me, my dainty cabbage? Will you, my doe?' He made a great show of kissing the back of my neck, under the collar. His spitty lips left cold snail tracks on my skin.

'Gross. You're gross.'

'Jacquot—' Sami, this time. The other boy sprang like a dog to heel.

I stood on the doorstep, fumbling for my key. I did not want to find it. I pictured myself turning to this trio with my pockets inside out: 'I'm so sorry – I've lost my key – we can't—' But it slipped into my palm, and instead I began, 'You guys. I just want to say, you know, um, I've got a brother, and he – do you know about my brother?'

Jacquot mimed a spastic.

'Jacquot!' Lahou shook her head in disgust. She smiled at me. 'It's okay, yeah.'

'Well, and he's got a nurse, too, and she'll probably be around, so – well, if you guys come in quietly, I'll check it out. I don't want to scare her or anything.'

'Sure.' Lahou was nodding earnestly. 'Whatever you need to do.'

Sami grunted. Jacquot put a finger to his lips.

'Stop being a dickhead,' Lahou said to him. 'Or get lost.'

The front door, weightily resistant to my touch, creaked as it opened. The air inside was still and quiet. With a modicum of scuffling, the three followed me into the marble hall. Jacquot tiptoed across to the sculpted Venus on her pedestal, and kissed her exaggeratedly on the lips, his hand rubbing her stone crotch. He mimed ecstasy. I indicated that they should stay put, and strode into the living room, where silence hung, a drapery, over everything but the mildly complaining radiator along the wall. The blinds over the French windows were half down, their midday position, to keep the red oriental from fading. I wandered into the dining room, and through the swing door to the kitchen, where the oven clock blinked green at me, insistent, showing the wrong time.

'Hello?' I called softly. The nurse's rooms were beyond, and no sound came through her door. 'Etienne? Magda? It's me.' I waited. I knocked gently.

'Everyone's out,' I said, in an almost normal voice, not quite believing the house was ours. 'Magda must have taken Etienne somewhere. Out, you know.'

'It's nippy, out,' said Jacquot. 'Hope they bundled up.'

I led them into the living room. Lahou flopped down in an armchair, her schoolbag at her feet.

'It's gorgeous here,' she breathed. 'I love it.'

'Wouldn't we all?' said Sami. He roamed along the walls, his fingers skittering in their spidery way, not touching anything. He landed at the window. 'Can I?' he asked, uncharacteristically polite, pointing at the blind.

'Sure.'

Jacquot whistled as the garden came into view, its gentle manicured slope.

'We can go outside,' I said. 'The view is from the garden or upstairs, not here.'

I unlocked the doors and walked them to the place from which the port, the town, a snatch of sea were visible. The water glittered between the trees. It reminded me, all of a sudden, of America. 'It's nothing compared to the hotel. That's where the view is really beautiful.'

'Views are for old people,' Jacquot sneered. 'You don't have a pool.'

'At the hotel.'

'I think Frédéric's got a pool.'

'I don't think so. They're by the beach.'

'Have you been?'

I had, but lied, shaking my head.

'Well, then.'

I didn't persist. I was starting to relax. It was almost two-thirty and if Magda and Etienne came home I would simply say we'd been let out early. It would be fine. 'Want something to drink?'

'You got whisky?'

'Orangina or Coke. Christ, Jacquot, you just don't know when to stop.'

Sami remained in the garden when we headed for the kitchen.

'Probably better if we don't smoke inside, right?' he offered. I was touched by his thoughtfulness. He whispered something to Lahou.

'WC?' Jacquot asked. I directed him to the flowery powder room in the corridor, and hoped he wouldn't piss on the floor. I made a mental note to check that the seat was down after he was through.

Lahou helped me put glasses, and little bottles of Coke, on a tray. My mother always bought the individual size so that the soda, half empty, wouldn't go flat. I made sure to take the mustard glasses, so it wouldn't matter if they got broken.

'We need something to eat,' I said. 'What do you feel like? Chocolate? Bread and jam?'

'Doesn't matter,' said Lahou. 'I'm not really hungry.'

'But we didn't eat at lunch.'

She waved, vaguely, as if this were commonplace.

'I feel really odd if I miss a meal,' I confided. 'Excited, kind of lightheaded, but like I might pass out. You know?'

'Huh.'

I rummaged in the cupboard for jam. 'There's some Nutella here too.'

'Sagesse—'

I stopped. 'What?'

'I know this seems bizarre, but what I said to you in the café?'

'Yeah?'

'Well, I just wondered, you know, if Sami and I could – if there was somewhere we could go to be private. Just for a little while.' She was embarrassed, twirling a lock of her hair in her finger. This was the first moment it dawned on me (I had wondered what would occur; now I knew) that Sami and Lahou were hoping to have sex in my parents' house in the middle of the afternoon. I settled the tray on the counter, fussed with the glasses, didn't look at her.

'I don't know – I mean, I'm not sure it's, uh, cool, exactly.'

'It's not like we'd make a mess or anything. I mean, you must have a spare bedroom, in a house this big?'

'Of course we do. But—'

'You don't know what it's like, Sagesse.'

I thought of Thibaud, and the abandoned villa gardens by the fort, with the singing branches and stars overhead and the dewy dirt beneath. 'I do too.'

'You can't. Because you wouldn't say no if you knew.'

'It seems wrong, here. You know?'

'How come?'

'I don't know.' We faced each other in the kitchen. 'Plus I'll have to hang out with Jacquot, right? No thanks.'

'Sami will have spoken to him. He won't bug you, I promise. Aren't we friends?'

'Sure, but—'

'Do this for me, okay? Just say yes?'

'All right.'

Lahou jumped a little, and kissed me on both cheeks. She smelled of vanilla. 'We'll do something for you. I'll pay you back. Thank you so much.'

'Promise you won't turn back the bedspread.'

'Promise.'

'And you'll put a towel down, or something. I'll give you a towel.'

'Whatever.'

'I guess it'll be okay.'

'It'll be fine. I promise. You know you can trust me.'

'Not Sami, though.'

'He'll do what I tell him. He's a lamb.'

I picked up the tray and headed for the door.

'One other thing?'

'Yeah?'

'Would it be okay if I took a shower first?'

'A shower?'

'To get clean.'

'I guess so.' I put the tray down again.

'You could just show me where to go, and then Sami could come up in, like, a few minutes.'

There seemed little point in protesting; Lahou had clearly planned it all, on the bus, or in the café even, as soon as the invitation had sprung from my mouth. 'Come on, then.'

Upstairs on the first floor all the doors along the corridor were shut, a sign that Fadéla had cleaned each room.

'That's my room,' I pointed. 'And that's Etienne's. Don't go down the end. That's my parents'.' I spoke in a whisper because I was conscious of colluding in something very wrong, and I didn't want even the walls to know it. 'You can go in there.' I pointed at the door to the room lately occupied by my grandfather; the irony was not lost on me. I took a plush purple towel from the linen closet, beach-sized. It wouldn't show hairs or spots, I figured, and it was considered mine, at least in the summer.

'Here's the bathroom.'

'What's that way?' Lahou looked to the other end of the hall.

'Another bedroom. My dad's study. I don't even go in unless I'm asked. Promise you won't?'

'Of course not. Nice bathroom.' She bounced across to the mirror above the sink and bared her teeth at herself. 'I'd love to live here.'

'Yeah. I'm the only one who uses this one, so don't worry about making a mess or anything.'

'Thanks. Really.'

I shut the door on her. All the doors were shut. I went back downstairs to take the drinks and snacks to the boys.

Sami and Jacquot were in the living room, Jacquot bent over the stereo.

'Leave that alone, hey? It's my dad's.'

'Bang and Olufsen. Amazing.' He ran a hand over one of the freestanding speakers. 'These are incredible. The sound must be incredible. And so thin!'

'Leave it alone, Jacquot.' Sami didn't turn around. He was squashed between the rose velvet love seat and the wall, in a little space that forced him to lean back, precariously, almost at the angle of the speakers. His attention was focused on the watercolour of the Bay of Algiers, the one my father had salvaged from his grandmother's apartment.

The painting wasn't big, about thirty centimetres square, and it sat, in shadow, in its narrow dark blue frame. Surrounded on the wall by etchings and prints, overwhelmed by large, gold-framed oils – powerful abstracts, gaudy spurts of paint to which my father was partial – it waited, rarely noticed, like a half-closed eye. But Sami had been drawn to it at once, to its unobtrusive placement, and then, up close, to its apron of azure sea, erratically white-capped, broken by the sandstone finger of the port and three rollicking, ridged-hulled ships, tricolours aloft, at anchor. Behind the bay stretched the white rise of the city, a thousand precise terraces and roofs climbing into the sunlit sky, the European curlicues and the higgledy-piggledy casbah, all their outlines drawn as if with a single hair, interspersed with delicate little palms and cypresses and other trees of variegated greens, and with broad, brown avenues like branches. A statue on horseback could be made out near the sea, in a plaza lined by fig trees, to the right of the picture: the Duc d'Orléans in the Place du Gouvernement, facing, as French national pride demanded, the conquerable interior. Tiny people in djellabas and Victorian suits dotted the waterfront in groups and pairs, too small to have faces, too small to have hands, but joyful in their attitudes – they could not be otherwise, bathed in this cerulean paradise, from which a warm, salty breeze seemed to emanate, and on it, the imaginary drift of jasmine and bougainvillea.

'Your folks from there?'

'Huh.' I felt embarrassed, as if I were confessing to a set of sins against Sami and his kin. 'It was a long time ago.'

'I thought you were American, really,' Jacquot put in. 'That's the word at school.'

'Just my mom. My dad's family was from there.' I gestured at the picture.

Sami extricated himself from the little space. 'I never knew that.' His features, hawkish, betrayed nothing.

'Guess you don't read the papers, then. It was all in the papers about my grandfather. With the trial, you know.'

'So does your old man vote for the National Front?'

'What?'

'Does he vote for Le Pen?'

'Don't be ridiculous.' I could feel my cheeks burning. My grandfather had said that he didn't, but he had said, too, that he understood it. He believed in the Algeria that had been – not in the one Camus yearned for, that utopian, impossible City of Man; nor, indeed, in Augustine's transcendent City of God; but in the earthly city that he had left behind, where people, and races, knew their place. Where, indeed, he saw the placid paradise of the watercolour before us: an Algeria that had no more existed than did the dream, the might-have-been, in my own imagination, where Sami and I might have strolled the African streets as friends. My grandmother said things like, 'There are Arabs, and then there are Arabs.' As a child I had wondered what she meant; standing then in my living room, I knew that she meant there were Zohra and Fadéla, and then there was Sami. She had also been known to say, 'They didn't want us in their country, and we don't want them in ours.' So much for utopias. I was embarrassed, and afraid.

'It's not a ridiculous question,' Sami said. 'That bombing, in the summer, remember? It shows it's still important now. Everybody knows that it's people like your family who—'

'Not my family.'

'People like your family, then, who—'

There was a noise, a cry, from upstairs.

'Hang on.' I ran out into the hall. 'Everything okay?'

'Lahou was halfway down the stairs, naked but for the purple towel which made her skin shine like a queen's, or like that of the marble Venus. Her hair, wet at the ends, fell over her shoulders in loose springs. Her mouth was open. She clasped the towel at her bosom with one hand, while the other flailed in spoonlike gestures.

'There's a man. Upstairs, a man.'

'Where?'

'In the hall – in the bathroom. He came in the bathroom.'

'Sagesse?' It was my father. 'Is that you, Sagesse?'

'Shit. Oh shit. My dad. Get in here.' I opened the door to Etienne's elevator, and saw, to my surprise, Etienne inside. He appeared to have been sleeping, but his head snapped up and he made a happy burble at the sight of me. 'Get in here.'

Lahou, cringing and atremble, goose bumps rising on her velvety arms, scuttled into the tiny box.

'You guys,' I hissed into the living room, 'go in the garden or something. Hide. It's my dad.'

'Why would he mind?' asked Sami.

'Just do it. Please?' I ran for the stairs. 'Papa? Is that you? Papa?'

My father loomed, bullish, in the hallway. His hair was matted on one side of his head and his eyes bulged in their sockets. The pulse at his neck ticked furiously. His shirt sagged, half unbuttoned, and the curls of his chest glistened. He was barefoot, and his feet, covered with black hairs, were very white. His belt was unbuckled.

'What are you doing here?' he asked, the sound from his throat tight, as if the air were being squeezed out. 'And who was that little Arab girl?'

'A friend. Just a friend.' A shaft of light caught my eye from behind my father's creased shoulder. A door was open in the hallway. It was the door to the spare room I had offered to Lahou, the room where my grandfather had slept.

'You should be at school.'

'It's out early.'

'No it's not. Take that girl and go back to school.'

'Papa, why is Etienne in the elevator?'

My father took a very deep breath. He was holding himself in. He looked the way I looked when I knew I was in trouble: not guilty, exactly; more defiant.

'Just get out of here. Just take that girl and go.'

'She'll have to get dressed first.'

My father slapped at the air and made a *pfft* sound. I darted into the bathroom to retrieve Lahou's clothes. The T-shirt gave off her cheap, sweet scent. My father did not move when I passed him. As I walked down, step by resounding step, I could hear him cracking his knuckles on both hands.

Lahou dressed in the elevator, in front of Etienne, while I held the door partway open for light. She had to twist away to keep his fingers from her stomach. Etienne loved skin, and Lahou's was particularly enticing. She tried not to grimace, but he and I both saw her, and she, afraid and embarrassed as I myself had been minutes before, knew it.

I thought of wheeling my brother out into the living room

before we left, but didn't know how he had come to be in the elevator. I didn't want to get into any more trouble. So I shut the door and left him. All afternoon I kept picturing my brother boxed in, in the unbroken blackness. Was he afraid? Maybe he liked it. He hadn't made a sound.

The boys had hopped the garden wall early on; we ran into them at the bus stop.

'I'm sorry,' I said. 'That was really weird.'

None of them said anything. They didn't brood on the incident, or refer to it. I had the impression that such unforeseen and surreal moments were not uncommon in their lives, and that they tolerated them without ever realizing that they were doing so. Sami was far more interested in the revelation of my *pied-noir* background, and I thought that might prove the day's most damaging event.

7

In the short term I was right. Sami and, at his behest, Jacquot, cooled towards me. Sami, at least, had revolutionary aspirations, and if I was not prepared more loudly to repudiate my heritage and its implications, I had no place alongside him. Not that I was an outright foe; I was too evidently ashamed for that. I simply could not be a friend. It was like failing to get security clearance for a government post. Lahou was more forgiving: she saw our bond as a matter of feminine trust, on which the broader world's politics had no bearing; and she had seen and been repelled by my brother, and felt guilty for her repulsion in a manner manifested, endearingly, as loyalty, one-on-one. Even so, she saw me less and less with her male retinue in tow, which meant less and less altogether.

Frédéric didn't care. He had known all along of what stripe the LaBasse family was, culturally if not politically. Ours were comparable societies. But he was a young man much concerned with appearances, and he played to both sides – Sami's and mine – while giving in to neither. In my way, even I was useful to Fred in some of his various guises; it was just that I no longer stood any chance of being truly cool, in his particular set, once I had been dismissed, thumbs down, by Sami.

These repercussions from the afternoon's events at least made sense to me, in the ever-shifting tectonics of the schoolyard. I could bend to them, behave accordingly, because their rules, although arcane and unwritten, had been instilled in me over many years in the company of my peers. Besides which, in the wake of the Marie-Jo cataclysm, this falling away seemed gentle, almost fond: these were my pretend-friends; now we would pretend less energetically; in time we might simply cease to pretend at all, without rancour. It would be fine.

Home was another matter. When I returned home that evening, after sunset, Magda was feeding Etienne in the kitchen, and my mother, in an apron, was talking on the telephone while stirring some winy stew on the stove. My father was not in, and for the first time in a long while, he did not surface for supper. Somebody had put away the glasses and the unopened Coke bottles, and had stowed the tray.

When we sat down, my mother's bright – too bright – and hungry chatter filled the dining room: 'And your grandfather has asked us to get him the works of Balzac – he's always loved Balzac, and wants to read them all over again. And it turns out he can receive magazines, so we thought we'd get some subscriptions . . .'

Odder still, later, while we were stacking the dishes in the dishwasher, my father's humour, easy, bluff, rolled into our evening like a soothing breeze. I waited for the awkwardness, the acknowledgement, however slight: a glance held, a forced joke, the sharp smell of fear or of anger. I tried to insinuate ('How was *your* day, Papa?'), but wide-eyed and cheerful, fine actor that he was, my father gave away nothing.

My grandfather and my father both looked my secrets in the face when I was fourteen, and kept them hidden. How adult I felt, to be entered into the family's rolling conspiracy of silence: who could be sure what anyone else knew or did not know?

But whereas in my heart I believed, if perhaps incorrectly, that I had recognized my grandfather, and our bond, in the courtroom's lonely figure, I knew that in seeing my father that afternoon, as if for the first time, I did not know what I had seen. Too many shards rattled spiny and unconnected: the man's disarray; the strangled tones; the light behind him on the carpet; and my brother, resting in the corner of his cold, infinitely dark, purpose-built cage.

A single shard more might have organized the rest for me, and did, later, so that now I remember the incident as if I had seen her. It may well have been Magda herself, with her lush Slavic lips and almond eyes; she didn't last long with Etienne afterwards. Or my father may simply have dispatched Magda to the cinema or the department store and smuggled in a woman, a girl, anyone, anyone's. It could even have been Marie-Jo. I never saw her, but in my memory now I walk past my father to the bar of sunlight and trace, with my tender eye, which might be his, the alabaster rise of her shoulder and the outline of her buttocks under the sheet. She, of herself – her features or the quality of her soul – matters not at all; she merely orders the narrative, and so can't be left out.

Far more important to my understanding of my father, or to its failure, are Etienne and his hours in the elevator. How many hours? How many times? But this must of necessity be overlooked, because there is no one to tell it and nothing to say. And to my understanding of myself, the fact that I left Etienne there, and shut the door again upon him.

Six

I

The Algerians, of all eras and all hues, might be presumed to love life. A third-century Roman inscription at Timgad, in the south, exhorts: 'The hunt, the baths, play and laughter: that's the life for me!' It is certainly a myth among the *pieds-noirs*, that the culture, sun-drenched and sparkling, dwelt in joy. But across the centuries, their voices – those resonating voices of Augustine and Camus – tell a different truth.

Both men asked, one before God and the other a man alone on his darkling plain, whether life was worth living; and both answered 'yes' with a desperation and a defiance that can have been born only of 'no'. Catholicism's strict prohibition of suicide is, in fact, Augustine's. It was he who first threatened that eternal reward would be denied those dead by their own hands: 'Christians have no authority to commit suicide in any circumstance.' But his logic, so carefully worked, a subtle synthesis of commandments about self and neighbour, could only have been necessary if he saw the temptation. He, whose early laughter and revelry led, on his return to Algeria from Milan, to years of loss and tumult, who learned how much of earthly life was sheer endurance, wrote, in old age, that 'from the evidence of this life itself, a life so full of so many and such various evils that it can hardly be called living, we must conclude that the whole human race is being punished.' Hence his belief in Original Sin: we must be punished, at least, for a cause. Life, that punishment, must be suffered to its natural end for only one reason: for God.

To Camus, whose footsteps followed so belatedly along Africa's northern coast, Augustine's evils became absurdity; the teetering flail of the void gaped where God's safe shore had loomed. Alongside the futile Sisyphean trials of his fellow men, the song of suicide could only beckon. But again, he said no. Not for God, but for man. He preached revolt, and passion, over the soothing melody of escape.

Both stood fast, shouted louder against it than almost any others, surely because its siren-song played so loudly, so buoyantly, in their ears. It plays in my own. It played louder still in the ears of my father, born with Africa in his blood from both sides, and left to live, without revolt, in a dispassionate and alien border. And if Augustine and Camus, with their different signs as weapons, could stand fast against the lure, it was because they confronted it, looked straight into its sweet face, and spat. My father did not acknowledge the music, until doubtless he did not know even that he heard it. Eyes shut he sang along: 'By pining, we are already there; we have already cast our hope, like an anchor, on that coast. I sing of somewhere else, not of here: for I sing with my heart, not my flesh.'

2

My parents met in April 1971, at a crowded table at the Café des Deux Garçons on the Cours Mirabeau in Aix-en-Provence, on an evening of unfurling leaves when the light fell dappled through the plane trees. My mother, shy Carol, wore a crimson cashmere twinset that set off her clear, freckled skin and the dark lustre of her hair distinguished her from the other girls, three fellow American students, blondes, Amazonian by local proportions, with fine little noses and large teeth. My father – the friend of Guy, a boyfriend of one of these girls, Lili, both girl and boy now lost and all but faceless in our familial lore – was the interloper, a day-tripper from real life along the coast, arrived in a car of his own, who had apparently merely stumbled upon the collegiate grouping as upon fairies in their bower. His dun mackintosh was British, the collar upturned; his shoes

gleamed. His chin, at the end of the day, sprouted a shiny
stubble that only enhanced his Latin charm. My young parents-
to-be did not look – but for the brevity of my mother's tartan
skirt, at which she tugged periodically, although seated, for
modesty's sake – of their era. They were untouched by the
revolutionary, unbuttoned spirit of that moment, a bond each
recognized in the other.

'I thought you must be French,' was the first full sentence
my father uttered to my mother, a compliment, as she took it,
after months of attempting that very deception, which caused
her to smirk and glance coyly at the ground.

She had been in Aix since September, on a nominal, overpriced programme sponsored by her Catholic women's college,
and, although enamoured of all things Gallic (upon her return
home, according to Eleanor, young Carol insisted on slurping
her coffee – with hot milk, if you please – from a cereal bowl,
in the absence of an oversized *tasse*), she had spent most of her
days in the company of her compatriots, cushioned by gaggles
of girls from other American institutions, many wealthier and
almost all worldlier than she.

Carol was the quiet girl, the confidante of her intrepid
fellows; the others – girls with names like Coco and Sally and
Lili – recounted their exploits to her, congratulating her even as
they did for being unshockable, although they knew that she
was, silently, aghast, and in this lay at least part of their pleasure.
'Pillow talk,' Coco or Sally or Lili would say, 'is the best way
to learn a language.' My mother would smile. 'You should try
it, Carol,' they would add; and she would blush. She was,
by her own account, a diligent student, but unremarkable.
She considered herself plain and fat, because her station in
the sorority's hierarchy seemed to demand it. In fact, she was
neither. She just felt safer classified that way.

Invisibility has always been vital to my mother; it is her cloak,
her security. Was it Flaubert who said that 'Not to be like one's
neighbour – that is everything'? For Carol the inverse was true.
I'm sure that part of my father's appeal – so darkly handsome,
such lovely, liquid eyes, not a hint of the stoutness to follow –

was the quintessential Frenchness of his demeanour: the way he moved his hands, the confidence with which he flicked his lighter for her friends; the fact that he carried a lighter at all, although he did not smoke.

Carol, in an instant, was smitten. Being Carol, she did not think to probe her friend, or Guy, the now-lost boyfriend, too deeply about Alexandre LaBasse's present, let alone his past. Instead, she fretted over what he thought of her. A relentless and familiar litany, traded countless times by nightgowned near-adolescents in the dormitory past midnight, it was now at last hers to utter, and her turn to be reassured. 'Did you think he noticed me? Really? I thought, maybe, when he made that joke? He's single, you're quite sure? And how old? Gosh. What does Guy say about him? Maybe he prefers blondes? Did I look fat? Are you sure? My rear end, in that skirt – if I'd known I'd meet him I would never have worn it. Do you think I stand a chance?' She failed, then and later, to ask 'Who is he?' thinking simply, and wrongly, that he was France incarnate, a sort of male Marianne. But who would have been able to tell her otherwise?

As for my father, he appears on that mote- and blossom-streaked boulevard, at Guy's shoulder, running his hand through his hair and smiling his sleepy half-smile, blocking the girls' view of the street and the evening light with it, a mystery *contre-jour* – and I cannot say, to this day, how he comes to be there.

As a child, one accepts one's parents' stories as the truth, each gleaming bead nestled, in an unbroken strand, between the others: their meeting, their courtship, their marriage are all but a hasty prelude to the crucial event of one's own birth. Their lives exist only as a tidying explanation of one's own. It does not seem possible, certainly not plausible, that I was myself unimagined, or that their existences held any meaning independent of one another, or of their future offspring. I have marvelled that Carol or Alexandre could ever have believed themselves the protagonists in any narrative, when their manifest destinies were but supporting roles in my own. Not till later does it dawn that the anecdotes and their rhythms, familiar as any bedtime story and as unreal, are a careful condensation of years, of morning after morning in which they awoke, separately and then together, into days as freighted with anticipation or wonder or despair as my own. Once they exist, even as a wish, these days, so unknowable, beckon, and with them comes the knowledge that they can only ever be glimpsed obliquely, inaccurately (although I know that the Deux Garçons remained 'their café' and the sauntering prima donna with her poodle their private joke): that they belong to others – to Carol, to Alexandre – and will never be mine. Yet they are my stories too, my blood, and their weight, known or unknown, is my burden.

So, my father, on the boulevard, beloved already of the shy American whom, he will say, he claimed in his heart from the first (theirs, in spite of all that followed, was a fiction of love at first sight; and he more than she, for whom it was quite possibly true, would insist upon it): he was twenty-six, nearing twenty-seven, old beside the American girls, old as a rock in the coursing river of undergraduates that flowed in the streets of Aix. He had a car – a sputtering Renault 4, and secondhand, but a car – and a job of exaggerable importance in his father's hotel.

After university he had started, sober-suited, at the reception desk, so that Jacques could see his son duly humiliated, or so that Alexandre would know the business inside out – depending on whether you listened to my mother or my grandmother – and, with the interruption of his unremarkable military service, had proceeded to a desk in a glass-enclosed enclave of the hotel's management office, where he shared with several others Mademoiselle Marceau, the secretary who then, in the days of my parents' meeting, must have been attractive in a rounded way, but who by the time I knew her had grown owlish and feather-fat, always apparently scowling beneath the angry shelf of her brow.

In the beginning, my father was not an ideal employee: he felt entitled to respect, as his father's son, and grew peevish that it was not granted. He read the newspapers in the morning, and shirked in the afternoons. There were young ladies to dine with, with whom to picnic inland in the spring breezes, or to whisk along the coast roads to restaurants by the sea. The outing to Aix must have been such a truancy and, as love bloomed, his absences can only have grown more frequent and more apparent to his obsessive father. During that period, it was his mother (not yet fully imposing then, a woman still handsome and slender, without the permanent crevice of displeasure between her brows that so frightened me as a little girl) who stood in his defence. Only her interventions kept Jacques from supplanting his heir and replacing him with some avid young turk.

My father, having defied his own father as a boy in his wish to remain Algerian, and lost, did not defy him again, or not openly. It must have seemed important to follow a path that looked, to the world, like a choice; but in my grandfather's dominion there was no such thing. Jacques had built the Bellevue for a dynasty; in retrospect, it must have seemed that he had fathered his unruly son for the same purpose. My aunt, 'La Bête', had no head for business, only a fine Catholic desire for family and a fear of her father's mercurial temper (this although she was his pet, and could do no wrong in his eyes). At nineteen, she married, followed her *bon bourgeois* husband to Geneva, and there sank into a bliss or a misery of which her own relations remained cheerfully ignorant. This, too, was the fate my grandfather had envisaged for his daughter: she was dealt with, her house was large and pleasantly appointed, her sons healthy and her husband profitably employed.

But of my father, Alexandre: when I was small, the scanty facts that followed his sea crossing seemed sufficient to me. University, the military, the Bellevue, formed a clear, inevitable line that easily bulked to fill the nine years before which, in the amorous halo of my imagining, he became relevant again to my story. They seemed, or must have, sufficient to Carol as well, because she never wondered at his decisions, at the clamp that kept her love, then her lover, then her spouse, in his glass office in the Bellevue on the clifftop overlooking the Mediterranean.

In subsequent years she learned to rail against Jacques LaBasse, but always with the grimace with which one rails against Fate, or God, the immovable. For all her complaints, she never truly believed they would leave – for somewhere, or something, else. And then, with my birth, and more absolutely with Etienne's, the argument became pure sham.

My father, and his parents, had their reasons. My grandmother, initially, could not see the point of Carol, although she was thankful, at least, for my mother's religion. But Alexandre, when he stood before the table of Amazons and plucked my diminutive mother from among them, may at first have seen the grand challenge of seduction, a lure already long familiar to him: he would have known that Carol, quietly preening and hoping, had none of her friends' wiles; in Becky's terms, my mother 'screamed virgin': even I can detect it, in her glance, in the pictures of the time. It might, knowing young men, have begun as a wager between Guy and his friend: 'Can you bed the unbeddable, wear down her resistance? Even you, seasoned as you are, can't crack this one!' And my father, sure of this as of nothing else: 'Watch me.'

To be fair, I will concede that theirs may have been a more innocent coming-together, that my father, jaded as he was, may have faltered at the charm of wary young Carol, and strained to find an unexpected future in her hesitant smiles. Regardless of his initial impulses, he swiftly determined – perhaps the first time they sat together over *diabolo menthe*, watching the passersby, their poodle lady among them; or the afternoon he drove her to Marseilles for her first bouillabaisse, and she ended up buying a pair of frivolous, shell-covered sandals that tinkled when she walked; and certainly by the time he brought her to the Bellevue for Sunday lunch, and they spent the afternoon wandering the *chemins de la plage*, redolent of cedar and dust and the sea, that later, always, I would consider my own – that she was his salvation. She was, to him, all that America was to me before I went there: a shining idea, without history, without context. She did not, like all the girls along the local corniche, know of his dalliances and suspect his easy smile.

More importantly, she had no interest in politics; she appeared only dimly aware of her homeland's then-current controversy, and voiced only pity for both the young draftees to Vietnam and their rebellious counterparts at home – 'It all just seems so sad,' she would say, with great earnestness, a soft, dark lock falling over her welling eye. As for Algeria, and the scars it had scored across France, she was as unversed as if the conflict had been buried for centuries. She not only did not take sides, she did not know what the sides had been; as a consequence of which, by the time she married my father, her side (like mine, later) was chosen for her. When, back in Boston, she heard Eleanor screech at the mention of 'that filthy war of torture', Carol was affianced, and indifferent. Alexandre was French, Eleanor was not: Carol announced to her sister, as Lahou had to me, 'You don't know the first thing about it.'

My mother was not so much incurious as naive: what my father chose to tell her, she believed. It was always enough; it had no reason to be untrue. His mother, and even his father – who seemed, if not tyrannical, at least straightforward – lent credence to Alexandre's autobiography. Carol was far more concerned about making herself – not French enough, not able to cook and with, her future mother-in-law informed her, no sense of style – acceptable to her prospective family. They were haughty about all things American (even her Catholicism was deemed low and lax); she would never have dared to question their world, and its infallible rhythms.

My grandmother explained, simply, after it was all over, that my mother had never been told because she had never asked.

'My dear girl,' she said to Carol, in front of me, 'it just never seemed relevant. It was in the past. Alexandre had "turned the page", we were all turning pages then. By the time you appeared on the scene, it was so long ago.' She went on. 'Your parents, you see, we might have expected them to enquire. But they never did.'

3

There had been time, but never opportunity. My mother's parents – whom I know only from photographs: my grandfather Merlin, a rangy, bespectacled bank manager with hair pasted across his scalp as shiny as paint, a man who loved to work with his hands, who built tile coffee tables on weekends and staked his vegetable garden in ordered rows, felled not by his cancer but by the first, toxic dose of chemotherapy; and his sharp-eyed wife Vi, plump as a loaf and, I have always imagined, yeast-smelling, with rippling arms like pastry dough and an assortment of stiff hats for Sunday church, who outlived her husband by only a year and died of a broken neck after falling down her basement stairs, according to Aunt Eleanor too frugal to turn on the light when venturing to retrieve a jar of her famed tomato pickle as recompense for a neighbour's help in Merlin's weed-filled zucchini patch – were ambitious for both their daughters, having lost their firstborn and only son to meningitis when he was only three. But their ambitions stretched only as far as Boston, a couple of hours' drive away. Their world was small. (How curious, and typical, that their antagonistic Eleanor should have chosen the life they wanted for her, while Carol, the spit of her mother in youth, was to drift out of their ken into a country they could hardly imagine.)

When Carol returned from France, for the summer and her senior year of college, Vi trembled in her corsetry at the child's announcement – love, an engagement, a Frenchman – and pressed affable Merlin to give the girl a talking-to.

'It's puppy love, Vi,' her husband assured her. 'I fancied a girl I met in Florida, when I was about Carol's age. But she loved that swampy heat, while it made me break out in hives. Could never have worked. I came home, my mind settled, and I met you. The one for me.'

'Merlin, this is France we're talking about, not Florida.'

'Shush, Bubbles – ' this was his nickname for her, although neither my mother nor Eleanor recalls her as particularly effervescent ' – Carol's home now. She's got a year of college to go. It's a long time. It'll pass.'

'Look at Eleanor and her craziness, Merlin. Has that passed?'

'It will, sweetie. It's all God's will.'

God did not see eye to eye with Merlin and Vi on Carol's future, and nor did my mother. They had not known that her reserve overlay such stubbornness, and Vi, unfamiliar with pop psychology, never imagined that her own solid intransigence served only to sharpen her daughter's will.

By September, Merlin, at his wife's request, had written to Jacques LaBasse (in English, his only language) to ask where Alexandre's family stood on the union. Jacques wrote back (in English also, a stilted letter, written with a dictionary to hand), explaining the family circumstances, the Bellevue and Alexandre's fine prospects. He commented that fate was unpredictable and youth headstrong – a flight of bombast for which Merlin rather liked him, but which reduced Vi to tears of fury.

'*He*'s no help. My God, is there nothing we can do?'

'Looks that way,' said Merlin. 'As long as she's happy. We've raised her right.'

Not right enough, it seemed. At Thanksgiving, Carol set off for a weeklong visit to France and her fiancé, with a shell-pink shantung suit in her luggage and every intention of marrying. The plans had been under way all autumn. The reception, small but elegant, took place in the hotel restaurant, spilling out onto the terrace because the weather was unseasonably warm. Carol told Jacques and Monique that her parents could not afford to come but sent their blessing; and told her parents of the deed only when it was done. She came home, as planned, but only to collect her things; and to try, in a few weeks, to console her distraught mother ('They're Catholic, Mom. It's so beautiful there. You'll come and see.').

Merlin was grateful, at least, that Carol had withdrawn in time to save him the cost of spring tuition. 'As long as you're happy,' he told her; and to his wife remarked, 'She's got a glow on her she never had before. It must be right. Wouldn't want her to end up a mousy thing, stuck at home.'

'You'll regret it,' was Vi's final word. 'It's not your world. Life isn't make-believe, you know. You'll come home crying before it's all over.'

'Different strokes, eh?' said Eleanor, home for the weekend. 'How are they on women's lib? Lousy, I bet, like all Catholics.'

Merlin and Vi never made it to France. Merlin's cancer was diagnosed in the late spring, and he was dead by June. Vi had no desire to travel on her own. 'Who'd look after the cats?' was her persistent excuse, to which Carol had no suitable answer.

4

Upon arrival at the Bellevue, installed in a small flat on the ground floor of the residence block, my mother initially was entranced – by the varying colours of the sea, of the sky, by the aura of history and the glamour of the Parisian guests in the restaurant. She did not care that she had not graduated from college, and hardly noticed that, as Eleanor had pointed out, she had merely traded one patriarch's roof for another's. She found Jacques aloof, apparently indifferent to her, too preoccupied with his little empire to do more than smile occasionally at the top of her head, or ask her practical questions in the simplified, formal French he used with the Portuguese labourers. Monique was more demanding: she sat my mother down at her polished dining table for long afternoons of tutoring, not only in the language but also in the mores of her new home. 'We do not put our hands in our laps during meals. We keep them in clear sight. It is far more respectable. We do not tip our soup bowls away – how curious it looks when you do, as though you were fishing! Far better to spill soup on one's own clothes than on the hostess's tablecloth. Consider that she may have embroidered it herself! It may have been part of her trousseau!'

My young mother attempted improvements upon her three-room apartment, only to fall foul of Monique's – or rather, Madame LaBasse's: Carol was not, then or ever, invited to call her in-laws by their given names, and was grateful, after my birth, to be able to resort to '*Grand'-mère*', along with me. '*Maman*' simply could not form itself in her mouth – notions of tradition, which extended even within the newlyweds' four walls: 'You can't put carpet in a bathroom, dear girl – whatever are you thinking? It's positively unsanitary. And I thought you might prefer this bedspread, really, to the florals that you've been looking at. So much more tasteful. It's a gift, you must accept it.'

How Carol tried. She wanted, very much, to belong to this new, old world. She had her hair cut by my grandmother's coiffeur, and piled her bathroom shelves with the creams the older woman recommended. She learned to cook my father's favourite meals at his mother's elbow, drenching vegetables in unaccustomed salt and trying to appreciate the virtues of bloody meat. She was taught to choose the skinniest and most withered beans in the market, rather than the crisp, robust stalks that appealed to the eye; it was impressed upon her that Alexandre preferred his tomatoes almost still green, his grapes peeled. She could never develop a taste for the grass-flavoured milk, and so stopped drinking it. LaBasse women, my mother was told, did not wear earrings; it was vulgar. They wore no rings other than their engagement diamonds. Carol learned to read quietly during the siesta time, or else to slip out for a walk; but she could not bring herself to sleep in the heat of the day.

She could not tell whether she loved or despised her mother-in-law, the imperial creature, and, having no one to discuss it with – Lili, Sally and Coco having long since vanished, their foreign memories packed away with their textbooks and souvenir Provençal tablecloths – did not dwell on the matter: she depended on the older woman, her only hope of becoming French. Not till too late did she realize that the recipes and expressions she had so studiously mimicked, until they inseparably constituted her French self, were the antiquated trivia of an Algerian life no longer extant, or rather, existing only in such households as her own, and as a result of virtuosic mimicry all round.

Sometimes, even in the early days, she marvelled at what she had so rashly decided, craved the chattering twang of her native language and the slack afternoons she had long ago spent with Eleanor, bare legs dangling, flipping through *Mademoiselle* on the porch of her parents' house, or racing down the asphalt to wade in the weedy creek at the end of their road. She longed for television, as she had known it, and hummed outdated advertising jingles to herself, or sang the words, alone in her living room. She missed the easiness, above all, but told herself there was merit in difficult pleasures, and when, salty with sweat, she tumbled delightedly in the wedding sheets with my father, she reassured herself that the sacrifices were worth it. Besides, she could still hear her mother's squeaky voice prophesying doom ('You'll come home crying'), and resolved to try the harder to prove small-minded Vi wrong.

When Vi died, the quality of my mother's nostalgia shifted: the clapboard house, and with it the creakings of her youth, was sold (by efficient Eleanor) along with most of its contents, and there was nothing to go back to. That was when Carol began to be unhappy, when she started to rail against her father-in-law, her mother-in-law, France — tentatively at first. The apartment, its bathroom floor chilly in winter and its faucets spitting, seemed to close in upon her. Alexandre's parents resided three floors up, on the other side of the building, but when she heard footsteps overhead she imagined that they were theirs. She noticed that the Bellevue gate was locked at midnight, and compared their lives to those of animals in the zoo. She tried, as a mark of initiative, to befriend the hotel guests — young women, like herself, some still travelling with their parents; a middle-aged English couple who came to paint watercolours side by side on the patio; a trio of Italian youths who flattered her and excited her husband's ire — but they only stayed a while, and left again, for lives that seemed much more real than her own.

My father, in these early times, was not oblivious to his young wife's confusion, but he had been raised to believe that a woman would bend, easily, gratefully, to her husband's life, and that this was love; and he observed, and tasted, and admired all that Carol was learning from Monique ('The *gratin* was delicious – just like Maman's,' he would say, in highest praise), considering it his part of the contract. He made love to her, ardently, often. He figured she would settle, in time.

It was a relief, then, for Carol to be pregnant with me. It was, unquestionably, the right thing for her to do, and it made her belong, for a while without reservations, and in any event, forever, in a way that she had not before. My grandfather took notice: he held out chairs and opened doors for her, declared her radiant, reserved for her the smiles that illuminated his otherwise mournful face, his brows almost airborne in their quivering abundance. My grandmother's tone softened, from critique to advice, and her 'my dear', for a time, meant precisely that. Alexandre was tender, and overjoyed. He stroked her belly and massaged the small of her back, brought her treats from the hotel kitchens at noontime, like a diligent sparrow. He threw himself into his work, wanting his pleasure to spill over the Bellevue grounds: he ordered a vast bed of lavender planted in my honour, eager to hear the bees swarming over it, and a pair of orange trees to mark his fruitful union with his wife. The gardens so flourished under his oversight that my grandfather granted him care of the hotel's catering as well: Alexandre planned other people's weddings as enthusiastically as if they were his own, and undertook, of his own accord, the promotion of the hotel in the region and, in time, in the nation at large. The time of lectures and suppers and committees was begun. He wanted everyone to share in his surfeit of beneficence, to know that the future would be glorious. It was an early, short-lived expression of the exuberance manifested much later, much longer, at my grandfather's incarceration, the first – or my mother's first experience – in the cycle of zeal and inanition that marked out my father's life, the great sine curves of his soul.

Which is why she should have known then, or thought to ask. But Carol, too, was absorbed in her pregnancy, in the new scents and sensations, in her fear about the delivery (not least because it would be conducted in French) and in the prepara-

tions for my impending life. The bedding and the tiny garments
ribbed in blue or yellow seemed to her infinitely dear, so
French, and she scoured books and magazines for elegant French
names, exclaiming over obscure saints and pursuing their histories, only, too often, to find their martyrdoms sinister and
bloody. (Marie, which is my first name, taken from my aunt
and from the Madonna herself, was not hard to find; but Sagesse,
a fantasy, they came to on their own, finding it euphonious and
thinking, perhaps, and wrongly, that I was the child of their
wisdom.) She took my father's enthusiasm to be her due, the
reward for her suffering. She asked no questions, even when she
woke before dawn to find him pacing the flat, naked as a bear;
or standing over her, smiling softly in the gloom. Once he sat
all night at the speckled Formica table in the kitchen, scribbling
plans for their future – for our future – which he would not
divulge. She came to him, bleary with sleep, her stomach a
giant, gleaming marble beneath her filmy gown.

'What in God's name are you doing?' she asked. He looked
up only for a moment, and reached out a hand to caress me:
'Saving our lives, my dear. I'm saving our lives.' And he winked.
'Back to bed, to sleep. You need it.' She did, and she went, and
in the morning, finding him ruddy and fresh, she imagined it
had all been a dream.

And then there was me – after whom, what could there have
been to ask? Carol's days – and nights – were full to overflowing, as her swollen breasts were with milk, and my every tooth,
my every step, my every mumble was committed to record.
Their needs retreated in the face of mine. I had become the
protagonist. Then again, not so very long after, there was
Etienne: he, gasping, raised a multitude of questions, but the
course of my father's late adolescence was not among them.
The future, for both my parents, slipped away as stealthily as a
smuggler's skiff from the cove below their window, and my
father's torpor before his little boy seemed only a mirror of my
mother's own. Now, truly, they were stuck. But in time
Alexandre raised his head from his chest, and with Jacques's
permission and his money, began to build the villa, which was

to be a monument to Etienne's imperfect (more than perfect) future, forever entwined with theirs (this little boy would not grow up and move away – ever) and our family home.

In this way, the question was endlessly avoided. Carol knew – it was a bead in the family history repeatedly burnished – about Alexandre's hasty departure from Algiers, about his grandmother's burial at sea, about the lost apartment (for which small restitution was made only when I was fourteen, in the very months I have described, almost thirty years after the event) and the lost heirlooms, which rendered the few bent photographs, the scattering of spoons, so precious. But what of his arrival in Marseilles?

5

His parents and sister met Alexandre at the port, and tried to reimburse the Gambettas for his passage, but the couple, ever honourable, refused. All my grandfather could offer them was a lift to the train station (a small gift, but one which, given their luggage, required Monique and her daughter and bleary Alexandre to remain an extra hour at the docks, seedy even then, an hour during which my usually reticent grandmother would not let go of her son, her nose buried in his stale shirt as though he were every reminder of the world, and the mother, she had lost), and a wave good-bye as they boarded for the long ride to Toulouse and Madame Gambetta's nephew. And then? Then the LaBasse family drove home to the Bellevue along the winding crests of the coast, in silence, Alexandre asleep behind his father, who spied on him occasionally in the rearview mirror and shook his head in baffled dismay.

Alexandre was, in that spring and early summer so rudely interrupted, to have prepared his baccalaureate. Once in France, the summer before him, he acknowledged himself unready and enrolled, for the autumn, to repeat his final year of school. But there were months before September – months in which he might study, or hike the Alps with friends (his younger sister was to go, in August, to Switzerland – already, although she had not yet met her future husband, her inclinations drew her there); or even comb the beach for girls (his former hobby, the way a budding naturalist tracks beetles, or fossils) with whom to watch the sunset. But he claimed tersely that he had grown unused to companionship, and spent the mornings sleeping and the sultry afternoons in his bedroom, not reading, not even piecing jigsaw puzzles, merely sitting on the edge of his bed – alert, as if awaiting a call – his head cocked vaguely to the wash of the surf.

His father grew impatient, assigned him tasks around the grounds. The hotel was still new, and there was much to be done: walkways to be paved and lanterns to be installed, scrub to be cleared of rocks and speckled with flower seeds. Alexandre proved an unhelpful recruit: he would either lie and say he had gone to work when he had instead strolled down to the headland and the fishermen's village below; or else turn up late, when the sun was already scorching, and manoeuvre clumsily among the paid labourers, more a hindrance than a help.

'He's bone idle. It's pure laziness. We've raised a bloodsucking monster,' fumed Jacques, in front of his son. 'Look at him. Too stunned even to blink. Blink, you idiot. Blink!'

His mother said nothing while her husband browbeat the boy, but later, after bedtime, she would slip into his room with a steaming cup of verbena ('So soothing – drink!') and sit with him, the soul of patience, waiting for explanations, until he turned his face to the wall, the tisane untouched and cold, and said only, 'Goodnight, Maman.'

Alexandre did not cry (which was just as well; his father would have slapped him), nor did he speak. Obdurate, he volunteered nothing. He could not even be bothered to tease his sister, who needled him constantly to no avail and finally confided to their mother, 'He must be in a very bad way. He's positively moronic. It's frightening, almost.'

'He's homesick,' Monique informed Jacques. 'We can't imagine the disintegration he has witnessed. He needs time.'

'Crap. He's homesick, fine. He needs to work. His future is here. This is his home now. Why isn't he studying? He doesn't even read, for heaven's sake. This is France; he is French. He's got to move on.'

'You know it's not as simple as that.' Monique herself missed the routines of her Algiers life, the afternoons with friends now dispersed from Normandy to the Pyrénées. She felt she understood her son. 'Starting again isn't always easy.'

'Of course not. It takes work. And that slug of a boy doesn't know the meaning of the word.'

Monique did not argue with her husband. She never had; it was a matter of education and principle. She said, quietly, 'I think you judge him harshly, my love.'

'And I think you spoil him. Rotten.'

Alexandre, in part, did not know what to do with this new life before him. Growing up in Algiers, chafing at his father's yoke, he had imagined himself a popular local entrepreneur, perhaps a restaurant owner like Gambetta. He had foreseen a life of boisterous inclusion and not-too-much work, cosseted by the city's fountains of delight: an elegant wife, a dark-skinned concubine or two, leisurely weekend retreats to the cooler air of the mountains, dusk beneath the almond and jujube trees while little children – his own, or other people's – scampered in the dust. He had not thought practically; he had not been ambitious beyond the city of his birth. When his parents and sister had left for France, he had seen their departure above all as a liberation from his father's nagging, a release from lectures about the importance of a practical, mathematical education and enforced hours bent over calculus problems as little interesting to him and as unintelligible as Sanskrit runes.

In France, both literally and metaphorically, Alexandre was dépaysé: only the Mediterranean and the gnarled pines were familiar. Here, his father had built a gated enclosure to stand for the family and its home. Jacques's ambitions for his son had crystallized just as Alexandre's own, always murkier, evaporated; my father, in whom initiative had never been encouraged, felt stymied, and stifled. Beyond the hotel gates might as well have been Zanzibar, or Miami: he did not want to know. But he could not breathe in his father's house either. He began to suffer, in that summer, from asthma attacks. ('Allergies,' his mother concluded. 'Is it jasmine? Is it lavender? Is it milk?') Speaking little, he felt, by August, that he had lost the ability to form most words: he simply could not speak. Eating, too, became an obstacle. His Adam's apple seemed a fat, fibrous pith in his craw, around which only the occasional jug of water might slither.

In his dreams – bright, hot dreams to which he clung for as long as he was able, as they were so much more vivid than his waking hours – he walked the familiar route from his grand-mother's apartment to the port, empty of life, empty. He sucked the bitter taste of soot in his throat, walking faster each time, his steps echoing, his skittering eyes scanning the alleys and win-dows for snipers, and his heart boomed like a gong. In the dreams he knew that the last boat had gone, that he had been left behind, but that something vital awaited him, if only he could make it to the port in time, and alive. Sometimes shots rang out and he ducked, trembling, into a doorway, or threw himself under a car; sometimes he made it to the Place du Gouvernement with its fig trees and stalwart equestrian Duc d'Orléans (almost there!), only to find the square seething with Muslim youths who cried out and pointed and set upon him, tearing at his clothes; sometimes he came across a bicycle or a car to speed his journey, only to discover that its tyres were flat or its engine was out of order. Never, no matter how he forged on, no matter how his semi-conscious mind insisted on prolong-ing the dream, never did he make it to the port and its mysterious promise.

Alexandre didn't think to run away; he had nowhere to go. Mostly, he didn't want to wake up to the tangle of sheets and his father's haranguing. He didn't want to be at all.

In September, dressed, like a doll, by his mother, Alexandre followed his sister down to town, to the lycée – the very one, with its cobbled forecourt, and doubtless with the same wall-eyed janitor who mopped the floors in my day. He was growing gaunt (hard for me to imagine, but it is true); he fumbled with his cuffs. He skulked in the back of the classroom, his face turning, involuntarily, to the window's light. The teacher's French babbled foreign in his ear; his pen, slippery, would not stick between his fingers; he took no notes.

Had he not been handsome, he might have escaped the scrutiny of his fellow students, if not of his teachers. But the girls flirted with him, and the boys found, in this, a reason to attack. When he opened his mouth, they mocked his accent; they ridiculed his clothes; they taunted him as a freak, a racist, an African. They cursed his provenance, and his presence. They parroted their parents' politics and argued the Algerian War around him as though he were a bottle of beer. He said nothing, which only enraged them further. He did not tell his parents, or his teachers; and his sister, who witnessed his daily punishment, remained mute as a calf, trying, hidden in her clump of girlfriends, to dissociate herself from this pariah.

'We weren't even living together, until this summer,' she confided to those who would listen, 'and when he arrived, he was someone completely different. It's like I never knew him. He frightens me. He doesn't eat.'

Then, one lunchtime, in the quiet of winter, Alexandre, like a spirit released from stone, rose up in a fury and battered one of his tormentors. He broke the boy's nose and shattered his eardrum, while half the school stood watching in a respectful semi-circle, Marie among them. Before the principal could stumble from his post-prandial nap to the yard, my father had fled, his jacket and satchel in a heap by the gate, his shirtfront streaked with blood.

He vanished. He didn't go home. He hadn't been seen on the bus or in the streets downtown. Night came and there was still no sign. Morning dawned, and his bed lay empty. Jacques raged; Marie cowered; Monique schemed and fretted. A search was begun. The train station was checked, and the naval barracks. A team of policemen winnowed the mountainside behind the town, beating the grasses. Even my grandfather, by the second day, paused in his tempest to pray. My grandmother turned back Alexandre's coverlet, left his bedside lamp alight. She had thought she understood him, but could not will her way into his mind. They were trapped two nights and three days – a short time, comparatively – as Alexandre in his grandmother's apartment had been trapped, in the moment between the past and the rest of their lives.

A fisherman in the hamlet below the Bellevue found him, before nightfall on the third day, huddled, semiconscious and quivering, in an abandoned cottage at the end of the single row of houses closest to the rocks and the buffeting winter waves. The fisherman had been looking, at his wife's behest, not for my father but for his errant cat, a fat marmalade puss whose imminent litter had pushed her out of her home in search of privacy.

At first, the fisherman thought my father was dead. The man's throat prickled from the ripe stink of urine and vomit. He noted the angle at which the boy slumped, and even in the half-light could discern the blood on his white shirt. And then he heard, between the waves, the ragged crackle of my father's breathing, and caught sight of the bottles upturned around him on the musty floor.

Somehow, from somewhere, my father had procured both sleeping pills and brandy (was this planned? Had they been hoarded for months? Were the pills so old as to be his grand-mother's, slipped among the treasures in his canvas sack in case of need? And the brandy: neither then nor later did any shopkeeper admit to having seen him, a wild-eyed, bloodied boy, let alone to having offered him the cup of oblivion) and had attempted his own end. Incompetently, as it transpired, but with greater conviction than his own father might have expected. Never in danger of actually expiring from his toxins, Alexandre in those seventy-two hours had nevertheless con-tracted an impressive case of pneumonia, in part because of his weakened state, in part because of his undress and the force of the cold sea air. Sweat-sogged and burning, he was lugged like a carcass up to the road, and an ambulance. He almost died, not directly by his own hand, but certainly by his own intention.

The recovery was slow: my father had a new, and further

place to travel from. When he arrived, he was a different young man, closer to but not exactly like the boy he had been before his troubles began, the boy he had been growing up in his parents' house in Algiers. With this difference: he did as he was told. He seemed to welcome his father's tyrannical guidance, and if it was only a semblance of welcoming, then he hid his true feelings well. It was as if the brandy, or the bilgewater, had leached him completely of his desires, so that he might be filled, and fulfilled, by other people's. No, this is not entirely true: he retrieved his desire for girls, his Don Juan nature. Which could also be seen as a willingness to become any girl's desire. Protean, quicksilver, he impersonated an earnest student for the young librarian; a flattering cad for the cynical waitress; a male Marianne for my mother.

Alexandre waited out the next summer and returned to the same lycée the following autumn, beginning his final school year for a third time. Students who remembered the incident of the winter before could not reconcile the easy, muscled lad with his sullen predecessor, and somehow came to accept that this Alexandre LaBasse, gadabout charmer, was quite literally a new student. So his life resumed its course: he studied, although not hard; he dated; he made jokes and played pranks; he passed his exams, and went on to the local university for several more years of the same. His trough was never again mentioned by his parents, except to each other. Carol didn't ask, and wasn't told, until too late.

6

In the spring of 1991, a scant month before my sixteenth birthday and not long after Easter, twenty years into my parents' communal life, on a pristine late April morning when the burgeoning lime-coloured foliage waltzed on its boughs and a submarine bubbled up for air in the harbour before breakfast (I remember it clearly: my father on the lawn, in dew-soaked espadrilles, with binoculars, counting the seamen as they sprang from its hatch, grateful for the sight of land), my father, in his starched striped shirt, kissed us one by one, more wetly than was usual, so that I wiped a daub of spittle from my cheek, and he shut the front door behind him with a delicate click. It was early, especially as his enthusiasm for the Bellevue had waned by then, and he often lingered over breakfast – toast, and more toast, buried under jam – until after I had left for school.

'So early?' I asked my mother.

She, distracted, in her housecoat, stood by the sink fingering the fronds of her belt. 'Says he has a lot of meetings.' She scowled. 'Says.'

'Then he probably does.'

'No doubt.'

'Bridge today?' It was a Tuesday, the day on which, in that year, my mother and grandmother joined a third Samaritan and visited the sick Titine, a newly housebound friend of almost sixty with a severe and chronic respiratory ailment, who trembled and wheezed her way through a gallant rubber once a week before rewarding her guests with iced port and her housekeeper's famous cheese straws.

'Naturally. Now hurry up, or you'll be late.'

The day was like any other for me. I was, like my father before me, a rehabilitated student; but unlike him I worked hard, and wanted to go far. My friendships of the year before had eroded without enmity to civil hellos (except for Frédéric, with whom I still chatted, and who sometimes ran me home on the back of his scooter), and I had found myself an earnest set of twins, recently arrived in town, gangly, bespectacled, with whom to linger on the quiet periphery of my school's society. That April day, I traipsed with Aline and Ariane to the library after school – as I did daily; as eighteen months before I had speciously assured my mother I was doing – and sank into the French Revolution until after six. I would like to claim a premonition, a flash of understanding or even an unheeded spasm in my chest; but to do so would be a lie. The day, my day, was unremarkable but for the glimpsed submarine and the

235

recurrence of a flaky rash on the twins' forearms, their unified dermatological protest at the strain of an impending test.

I missed the police car, which had come at five, stealthily, with no sirens, and gone again, with promises to return and fetch my mother. But my grandparents were with her and my brother in the living room, and I knew from the hunch of my grandfather's back, from the ominous quiet as I entered, that something was amiss: something grave. The way they all turned, at my brother's burbled indication, and gaped at me as though I were a phantom; that they hadn't heard my step in the hall, although not one of them was speaking; that nobody had thought to turn on a light, although the inner reaches of the room loomed powdery grey; that my mother tried to call out, and seemed unable to, and darted clumsily to my side, where she attempted (with such curious force – it's the pressure of her arms I remember, their pent will), although I was taller than she, to fold my face to her bosom, to make herself bigger, big enough to fit the occasion.

There were no hysterics. It was the black silence that spoke the moment, the absence of expression. There were no words, no tears, no rage sufficient for this. Besides, we were confused. Had I not, and had my mother not, cursed my father in the preceding months and uttered, more than once, those irretrievable words 'I wish you were dead'? You have to be careful what you wish for; my first thought (and again and again, afterwards, and sometimes even now) was that my will had killed him, that it was my fault (and my mother's no less than mine: our fault, like the mother and daughter in Strindberg's *The Father*). Or perhaps it was my grandfather's doing, or even my grandmother's, drowning him in her distilled love, as cold as pickling alcohol. Or shall we blame it, as we could blame everything (and he takes the blame; he couldn't refuse it; and he smiles nonetheless), on Etienne?

What does it tell you – about what we knew without speaking, about who he was and who we were – that not one among us, when informed that Alexandre LaBasse had taken his life (another gun, a different, smaller one; and whence, mystery like the brandy and the pills of years before, had he procured that?) cried 'No, it's not possible. Not him!'?

7

My father had had no early meetings. He had had no meetings at all that day. He had left a memo the night before for Mademoiselle Marceau, who had always colluded in his deceptions, asking her to cancel his lunch with the director of the local tourist board, and reminding her to delegate the interviews of potential restaurant chefs to the catering manager ('She'll do, for the preliminary round,' he'd written). Mademoiselle Marceau assumed, as she always did, that 'something had come up', meaning some young chippy with a yen to see St. Tropez before the season was in full swing. Like Cerberus, she guarded my father's empty office and deflected enquiries, so that nobody knew he wasn't where he ought to have been. My mother had rung at noontime, only to be told that my father had 'stepped out'; and my grandmother, who had stopped by his office in the afternoon with a vase of lilacs from her penthouse garden, was informed that Monsieur LaBasse had been detained longer than expected on the far side of town.

He left us around seven-thirty; within the hour, according to the coroner, he was dead. From our house, he drove away from town, past the Bellevue gates, and kept going, the window down and the roof open to the warm wind, its chittering like full sails, the sun doubtless reaching, tentacular, to kiss his forehead and the back of his skull. He drove through the morning snarl of the outlying villages, past the rows of greenhouses where the winter flowers are forced. He drove. There was a cassette of Debussy piano music in the tape player, although it was not playing when he was found. I imagine his last ride was smoothed by its undulating ripples, the music that his grandmother so loved.

He pulled onto the narrow track that led out to the pine

grove at the third headland from town, a spot where we had picnicked in past years. He had picnicked there, no doubt, on many other occasions, and more recently; it was a lovers' idyll. He shut off the engine, his prized black BMW pointed towards the sea, its nose between two mighty, bleached trunks, its wheels on a soft bed of last year's dried needles. He got out of the car: he walked to the top of the rocks and sat – there was dust on the seat of his trousers when he was examined – watching the swirling water eddy and nip at the boulders below, perhaps even catching its spray on his hands, or on the white exposed flesh between his socks and the cuffs of his worsted wool. He had, in his pocket, a rosary: he took it out, and rolled its beads, the beads of his life's story, catching with his thumbnail the spaces between them, feeling them, trying to stretch those interstices wide enough for a finger to fit; and failing. He did not sit there long (he couldn't have, if the coroner was right); he was not, any longer, in the yawning gap of contemplation. He knew what he was doing. But he wanted his last view to be that of his beloved sea, and the scent in his nostrils to be the sweet, dry fragrance of the pine trees; and he wanted to remember the salt on his cheeks, the way the sea breeze crept under his clothes to tickle his hairy skin.

He returned to the car. He was fastidious, my father: he shut the door behind him. He unlocked the glove compartment, withdrew the gun, locked it again, and replaced the key in the ignition. He glanced once more at the water, heard its whispering and the murmur of the canopy over his head. He caught the faint hum of a motorboat chugging far away, drawing nearer. He checked the rearview, to ensure the grove was empty but for him. His jacket lay neatly folded on the back seat. He did not loosen his tie; he did pull up his socks, so that they would not be bunched up on his corpse's ankles. He took up the gun, a .38: silver, it hovered between him and the vista, between him and his invisible home on the far side of the ocean, directly southward, the home that breathed only in the pluperfect, in the tense where there had been a future. And he pulled the trigger.

Seven

I

But that was later. Over a year later. And it was neither imagined nor possible in the first months of the new decade, early in 1990, when my grandfather was in prison and my father soaring, full of hope and the brief thrill of a real life, in the here and now.

After that day with Lahou, Sami and Jacquot, and the peculiar encounter with my father which I did not at first fully understand, the configuration of my life (of our lives) altered again, like a kaleidoscope turned with the gentle twist of a divine hand. I found myself alone once more, sustained by my correspondence with Thibaud, in which I described non-existent friends and parties. Thibaud applauded my courage and insisted that I make time in all this gaiety for my schoolwork: he himself, he assured me, did little more than study (more than one person can make up stories: I later learned that from October or so onwards, he had been embroiled in a passionate romance with the Danish au pair who cared for his cousin's children. She was nineteen, an older woman, with hair as fair and fine as strands of silk. Upon hearing which I pictured her scalp teeming with grubby silkworms, busily spinning), and had his heart set on *Sciences Po*, which might take an extra year or two of preparation but was worth it. His own father was a *polytechnicien*, but Thibaud couldn't abide the sciences, mostly because he couldn't seem to do well in them. All this he confided (and the girlfriend, eventually, but only when he finally revealed that he would not be travelling with his parents in the summer, and so would not see me, because he was headed for Norway and Denmark, and not alone), encouraged me to raise my eyes beyond the walls around my little life; for which I was, and remain, grateful. Far away in Paris, he held my hand through the months that followed, and although our exchanges were sequinned with lies, they brought me a courage, and a patience, that was true friendship.

Bereft, however, of immediate companions, I grew sluggish. I felt as though my body wavered like a beached jellyfish, its limits indistinct, incapable of locomotion. I dragged myself to school and home again; I cried, little salty rivulets, at television advertisements for yoghurt and sunblock. I began reading the newspaper – not the local one, tainted, for me, by its portrayal of my family, but *Le Figaro*, and, sometimes, as an intellectual exercise, *Le Monde* (it was a strain to confront such streams of uninterrupted type), which I perused at my desk during lunchtime and left for the janitor when I went home.

Home: the January afternoon had further sullied that place for me, too. I was learning from my reading that not only Sami but great numbers of the populace found my grandfather's politics heinous; but also, which I felt somehow I had known, that they found our history ghastly too, an insidious pollutant in the aquarium of French honour. France's error made flesh, the *pieds-noirs*, and with them, the *harkis*, were guilty simply for existing. In the national narrative, my father's family was a distasteful emblem, linked, by circumstance, not only to the vicious undeclared war of their homeland, but in dark historical shame to the collaborationists of Vichy and, further back still, to the ugliest excesses of the Dreyfus affair.

St. Augustine and Camus might have been Algeria's most celebrated offspring, but the former colonials' most vocal champion, at that late date, was no Algerian at all, was Jean-Marie Le Pen, whose porcine eyes and thread-thin mouth glowered regularly at the world from the pages of the press. This was the political voice of my grandfather's people – and inevitably, of my father's too – the bitter grizzling of those who fought for Catholicism and a nostalgic ideal of France, a pure France that would, and did, label me 'foreign' for my American mother (my *pied-noir* father, on the other hand, was foreign only to the great majority). My family believed in a country that could want no part of them, would rather they had been gloriously martyred in Algeria, memorialized in a curly arch or two at metropolitan intersections, and conveniently forgotten.

Wary of my father's clan, I tried to ask my mother about it, about what had happened and where my family stood.

'It's so complicated, dear,' she said. 'And so sad, for all concerned. Most people − like your grandparents, and your father − were just people, just living their lives. They didn't ask to be born into that mess, and they came here to "turn the page" − that's how your grandfather puts it. They have griev-ances − just ones, if you ask me − about how they were treated. And they lost their homes. But you can't live in the past; you have to play the hand you're dealt. People are just people, in the end.'

'So why do they hate the Arabs? They're just people too.'

'Nonsense. They don't hate Arabs. They love Zohra, and Fadéla too, for starters. Besides, it's complicated. I can't begin to understand, or to explain. They are what they are.'

'But they don't have to be. We all have choices. We can choose to be different.'

'That's your Aunt Eleanor talking. And maybe I used to believe that, too, when I was young. When I came here. But sometimes there isn't a lot of choice in the matter.'

'You can't believe that.'

'Can you choose not to be sulky? Can you choose to be beautiful, or brilliant? Can Etienne choose to walk?'

'You can choose lots of things. I could choose to be a Buddhist, say—'

'You could.'

'Or I could convert to Islam. Or I could be an atheist, and that would be a choice.'

'It would have to be something more than a simple choice, sweetheart, or it wouldn't mean anything at all. It would be like a friend I once had who chose the church she was married in simply because she liked the stained glass windows.'

'What's your point?'

'We don't choose what we believe, or don't believe. That's my point. And if we do, we're fooling ourselves.'

'Well, I don't believe you, then.'

'That's up to you. Now help me with this batter, would you? If you can pour the milk in, a drop or two at a time, while I keep stirring . . .'

2

Perhaps, then, my mother had no choice over her loss of faith in my father. For years she had turned a blind eye to his tardiness, his occasional lapses from sight. Perhaps Magda, on the verge of departure, whispered something in her ear. Perhaps, once my grandfather was hidden away, my parents both believed, at last, that their real lives were beginning; and behaviour which had lurked invisible in the twilight of pretend was suddenly glaringly obvious. Perhaps my giddy father was so careless as to come home with lipstick on his collar, or earrings in his pocket. If she had always believed him before (surely she had chosen to believe?), then something changed. She may have seen him; one of the ladies with whom she socialized may have seen him. It doesn't matter; it wasn't, to her mind, a choice.

One windy March night, late, several months after the incident with Lahou and the boys, when I had slid back into believing that my family, in all its awfulness, was the only certainty I had – an evening in which my father had been absent from the dinner table, and had not surfaced by the time I went to bed – I was wakened by my mother shrieking. It sounded so little like her that at first I thought it must be Etienne, suffering some dreadful attack. I leaped from beneath the covers and into the hall; but Etienne snored in his bed. The sounds that so distressed me wafted up, thready, from the living room below. My next thought was that my mother had been assaulted, as she read, by an intruder – maybe Sami had gathered a gang to rob my parents' house? – and I faltered at the top of the stairs, debating whether to sneak along to my parents' room and summon the police. Then I heard my father's voice, a sonorous rumble: I could picture it, he trying to embrace her, to quiet her outrage, in his arms, to stifled sobs; she, flailing and resisting, like a desperate moth. He sounded imperturbable, but I knew otherwise. His pattern was exactly that of a summer thunderstorm: the slow gathering, the darkening of the sky, the spooky calm, the greening of the landscape and the ominous rustling; and then the explosion, anticipated but still always a surprise, in its steady wrath. And after a time, its passage, an intermittent booming, and then calm again, with no indication that the event had ever taken place.

I sat, after a moment's hesitation, on the top step, and listened, chin forward, sucking the ends of my hair, my nightgown tugged tight over my knees and tucked under my icy toes, again in my confessor's pose of childhood, of nights when they had fought about my grandfather's tyranny or my grandmother's meddling, about my father's indifference and my mother's frustration, about the care of Etienne or how I should spend my holidays – or sometimes about vile dinner parties my father had arranged, or about money for household repairs, or about the inefficacy of the gardener – anything, really, and always something, feints, baiting matches, hedging the fact of their fundamental incompatibility, my mother's terrible loneliness, my father's weakness.

This argument, though, sounded different. My mother's high-pitched laments did not stop, and my father's clap of thunder did not break. My father was not winning; he was not even trying to win. I deciphered peculiar words in my mother's torrent: 'humiliation' and 'lies'; 'the dignity of a jackrabbit'. I was shivering. I listened, as my mother's voice dropped an octave, swelled again, did not abate. I considered pattering down the stairs, forcing tears onto my cheeks as I had when I was little: it had always made them pause, and turn to me, the small, frail creature they had created, and put their differences aside. My father would carry me back up to bed, or my mother would lead me by the hand, and one or other would tuck me in and stroke my hair until I fell asleep, secretly proud of my achievement. I did not think they would welcome me now; I was too old, and too knowing. They might have turned their fury on me, and that, too, would have been preferable to this; but equally, they might just have drawn breath, ordered me away, and resumed quarrelling. I hesitated, warming my toes in my kneading fingers, breathing down the neckline of my nightie to soothe my chilly nipples, then tiptoed back to my cold sheets.

3

The next morning, my father had left the house before I got up. My mother, impressively sullen, squinted at her children from between puffy lids, and barked orders at Etienne's new nurse, an innocuous, stout young woman with cat's-eye glasses and a prominent beak.

'Everything okay, Maman?'

'Just eat your breakfast,' she answered, in English.

'We'll talk about it when I get home, okay?' I didn't know what 'it' was, but sounded as though I did, and my mother winced.

'We'll see,' she said. 'We'll see.'

I don't know whether she did wrong to tell me. I'm sure she didn't want to; but she thought that I had divined the truth, and besides, she had no one else with whom to discuss the matter. Her mother-in-law's allegiance could be surmised; and the older woman had worries enough already. And although my mother had friends, ladies of comparable standing in the town, she didn't want to hear that they already knew, nor risk their indiscretion: 'We've had enough dirty laundry for a lifetime,' she said.

That afternoon she took me with her to the supermarket – the very one where the bomber girl had once worked – and piled the cart with Findus frozen meals and cans of soup (not, in our house, accustomed fare, but chosen, she informed me, so that my father could fix himself something on his own when he came in late) and afterwards directed us to a nearby *salon de thé*, decorated with fake gas lamps and potted fig trees, where she forced a *mille-feuille* upon me and ordered only a camomile tea for herself, peering bleakly at the urinous liquid and sipping with exaggerated daintiness. She must have cried more during the day, as her eyes were still waterlogged – in the market she had kept her sunglasses on – and seemed to seep, involuntarily, at the corners.

'Your father has been entertaining mistresses,' she divulged eventually, her locution antique so as to buffer the fact. 'Regularly.'

I swallowed. 'You mean, he has a mistress?'

'Not exactly. No. Then it would be easier to sort out.'

'Then, what?' I was trying to seem adult, to play the role of confidante. Not wanting to gape, I turned my attention to my pastry, prying it, with my fork, into its thousand layers. An image of Marie-José in bed with her recruit sprang unbidden to my mind.

'His attention span is short. There are a number of them.'

'Since when?'

She blinked. 'We haven't got into that. Since forever, maybe.'

'How do you know?'

'How do I know? What does it matter? Who they are doesn't matter either. I don't want a full accounting. It's just – especially now – when all eyes are on us, what with your grandfather – I don't know – it's so selfish.'

'What are you going to do?'

She looked at me and brushed a dribble from her lashes. She didn't answer.

'Well, are you going to leave him, or what?'

Her face opened, all its features separating in surprise. I could tell that the notion had not crossed her mind.

'Leave him? For what? And you, your brother – I don't think so.'

'But if you can't – will he stop?'

'He denies nothing, he promises nothing. "I am what I am," he says. "It's up to you." Up to me – as if anything in this life were my choice. As if his family hadn't dictated everything from day one. It's a nonsense.'

'Do you love him?' Part of me wanted to laugh, speaking of my father in this way, at the unreality of our exchange, as false as the decor around us.

'What does that even mean? And what does it matter?'

'Does he love you?'

'So he says. Can't live without me. As always.'

'Maman, listen. If nothing matters or means anything, what difference does it make? You have to decide what you think is right.' My pastry lay dismembered on my plate, streaked with yellow custard, inedible.

'There's nothing to decide, sweetheart.'

'Then why tell me?'

'Because I have to tell someone. So I don't wake up wondering if I imagined the whole thing. And I thought you already knew.'

'Because of that afternoon?'

'What afternoon?'

Then I recounted, because it was too late to go back, the events of the January afternoon at the house, which now, suddenly, made sense (I wondered how it could not have dawned on me before). And she, to whom it had apparently not occurred that her husband might be 'entertaining mistresses' in her home, dissolved. The tears that had been lurking inside their bloated sacks gushed forth. She put her sunglasses back on, propped upon the slick of her bony cheeks, but they could not hide the shudder of her shoulders as she cried. I recalled Becky, in Ron and Eleanor's sunlit yard, blithely announcing that if life did not get better she would kill herself; and I was cramped by the sudden fear that were I in my mother's place, after so many years of trying, I might consider it the only solution.

'You won't do anything silly, will you?' I asked, in the car, on the way home.

She kept her fuzzy eyes on the road. 'You know me, dear. Of course I won't.'

4

Thereafter I dreaded my father's return in the evenings, and was sickened by the civilized façade my parents maintained, whether for my benefit or Etienne's it was never clear. They did not touch – but this was not new. They were unfailingly polite; they bounced the conversation along like an india rubber ball, as insubstantial. In subsequent days, my grandfather's morale, his activities in prison, became a favourite topic of discussion, cheerfully neutral. And at night I waited, always, for their distant bursts of anger. Sometimes I took to my perch on the stairs, willing it. But it seemed they had nothing to say to one another, and all that I heard was the faint tinkle of the stereo, its aggravating sonatas and placid chamber music trickling through the quiet house.

In doubt, my father consulted his mother. She, in turn, came to placate my mother, to reassure her that she was not alone. She strove to convince her that this belated knowledge was as much a part of the LaBasse tradition as *aubergines au gratin* and uncarpeted bathrooms.

'Men have needs,' she informed her stricken daughter-in-law, 'that have nothing to do with love. Alexandre worships you, depends utterly on the happiness of you and the children. He takes good care of you. He will always come home to you. And beyond that, there are compromises. We all make compromises.'

Seeing my mother still stony-faced, my grandmother grew more expansive. 'I know exactly how you feel. More exactly than you know. It's a phase, I promise you. Jacques, before we came here, before he had the hotel – a brilliant young man, he was undervalued, insufficiently challenged. In such situations, men seek – what? – consolation, you could call it. Proof of their worth. They're like children, really; insatiable. You should be grateful; it keeps him from pestering you too much, leaves you time for your own pursuits.'

And further: 'My dear girl, it's hardly new. I always assumed you were aware, that you understood how things worked. The power, don't you see, is all yours, just as it has always been? What is different from a year ago, really, except a tiny, irrelevant piece of knowledge which you would do best to forget?'

'Everything is different from a year ago,' my mother replied.

My grandmother tried again: 'It is our job, as wives and mothers, to keep families together. You know that. It's why you've kept Etienne with you, although it hasn't always been easy. What if I told you that I'd been through much worse? And we've survived. And more than survived.'

My mother raised a sceptical eyebrow — pondering my grandmother's idea of survival, when her husband was in jail for assault with a deadly weapon; and wondering, too, what my grandmother could deem worse than my mother's sorry trials. My grandmother sighed, sinking back in the sofa's cushions, and closed her eyes (to see with her mind's eye? to avoid seeing at all?) and told her.

5

In the period immediately after the Second World War, my grandfather was a restless young man. He had drifted into the hotel business not out of any love of service, but rather because, during the last years, '44 and '45, when North Africa had been liberated and France had not, a fellow veteran — his commanding officer, in fact — proved to be, demobbed, the son of the manager of the glamorous Hotel St. Joseph, a Moorish fantasy on the clifftop that had long been host to Algiers' most illustrious visitors. Jacques was ambitious, clever: but the disruptions of the wider world had intervened upon his life, distracted him from the strategic career planning he had imagined he would undertake. Besides, any plans for greatness that he might have made would have involved the powers of metropolitan France, and those powers, during his twenties, were otherwise engaged. The hotel job, when it was offered, recalled his glamorous sister Estelle, his pre-war dreams of glory.

In 1948, at thirty-one, he was, then, in junior management on the staff of the St. Joseph, something of a dandy, physically slight but greying impressively at the temples. His dark hair was receding manfully from his large-featured face, lending his appearance a gravitas it had theretofore lacked. Famously efficient, he was known around the hotel's hushed halls for irascibility at the slightest incompetence: the grubby collar, the undusted side table, the wilting rose in the lobby's vast bouquet – any of these was sufficient to incite a tirade. But he was careful, and thorough: he hunted down the culprit, and chastised only that subaltern. He praised where praise was due, albeit gruffly, and with his superiors he affected an almost painfully respectful demeanour, as if to say, 'I am ready to be chastised in my turn, should I deserve it.' Still, promotion was slow in coming. The ranks of the staff were bloated, he complained to his wife, by codgers in tenure, men with fat bottoms in easy chairs, idly smoking pipes, men who thought nothing of sucking the hotel dry, as if they were themselves guests, and would continue to do so until they retired. He chafed; at home, he ranted; he prayed that his talents might be recognized, that he might be used to his fullest capacities.

And he worried about money: his salary was small, the needs of his young family great. He looked at his son, a sturdy child with dimpled limbs and a surfeit of energy. He surveyed with distaste the mess this boy made – coloured blocks lay strewn around the apartment; at mealtimes, the lad in his high chair spilled his milk daily, as if on purpose, puddling the carpets. He resented the child, born too soon, and the obstacle this greedy toddler represented. He resented, too, the swelling beneath Monique's smock that would be Marie, another mouth to feed, another bundle caterwauling in the night, that already, not yet breathing, deprived him of his wife's attentions and of the privileges of his marital bed.

'Can you imagine,' said my grandmother to my mother, 'such frustration? A man of such promise, with such force of character, hemmed in on all sides?'

My mother was silent.

'Frankly, I could not imagine. I did not know,' my grandmother continued. 'How could I? This was all I'd ever wanted – not money, or luxury, but a husband I loved and respected, who, for all his ascent was slow, was himself respected. He took the collection in church, you know, the youngest member of the congregation to do so. Our apartment was small, to be sure, but we were just beginning, and I had faith in him, as we both had faith in our beautiful country, where it was a blessing in itself to stroll the streets at dusk, in the pink light, hand in hand. Our love was about that place, too, for me, and all that we might make of it, and of ourselves in it. I, pregnant for the second time, with my darling little boy at my side, floated in possibility. I believed in the future, whereas Jacques – he did too, of course, but he also had a sense of time, like a wind, and of the years that had already been lost; and each day he was steeped in the day itself, in its worries and disappointments. It is hard to be great, in constrained circumstances.'

My mother's lips twitched at this familiar assertion of my grandfather's greatness, long a constraint on her own, and her husband's circumstances.

'Besides, I had help. I wasn't alone, the way he was. In that world, even in modest households, we had help. Khalida was a young girl, a Berber from Kabylie, so fair-skinned you wouldn't have known her for a native, freckled, with reddish hair and a broad, lopsided smile. A dead tooth, up front, but pretty nonetheless. Almost still a child herself, no more than nineteen, but looking less than that. She was the eldest in a large family, and very good with children. Alexandre adored her. Some of his first words were Arabic, words she taught him: *jameel*, which means pretty, and *shamsa*, the sun, and the colours, and the numbers. He could count in Arabic first. She was very clean, and a good cook, and it isn't too much to say we were friends. We would talk about our families – I knew all about the brother next to her in age, and his apprenticeship at the tannery, and I knew what hopes she had for the littlest one, who was about seven, and so bright. She hoped he'd get a scholarship, in time, to the Lycée Bugeaud, and I encouraged the hope. People think we were all racist, but it just isn't so. I wanted her to succeed. I bought her schoolbooks for the child.'

My grandmother paused. Her eyes were still closed and her brow furrowed. 'You know how it is, being a young mother. I had friends, many of them, and family, of course; but I was often at home, and in the kitchen, she would cook and I would sit with my mending, or knitting for Marie, and we would talk. We spent a lot of time together. I trusted her. So it was a shock – not long after Marie was born, and I was exhausted, or I would have noticed sooner – but I was forgetful myself, and Khalida's sudden clumsiness seemed part and parcel of what was happening to me, not something separate. She was apologetic when she put salt in the pudding instead of sugar, or when she broke a wing off my lovely china bluebird, but she didn't say anything, merely looked frightened, with those big moon eyes of hers, always rimmed – the way they do, the Orientals – with kohl. But there came a time when she couldn't hide it anymore, even with her drapery, there was a distinct bulge. I confronted her, and she was indeed pregnant. When I asked who the father was – she wasn't married, although many girls, native girls, her age, were – her face shut up like a suitcase. It just closed. Snap. It was none of my business, of course, so I didn't press her, but I was well aware of the shame it brought on her, in her community, and her family, so I kept her on. Who, with a Christian conscience, wouldn't? It was, if I may say so, an act of charity, because in those days – well, many an employer would have shown her the door, because it spoke ill of her morals, didn't it? Not to mention the fact that as the months went on she could do less and less – no window cleaning, no furniture moving, so she couldn't mop the floors properly, and so on.

'It was Jacques who finally said to me – I was absolutely ragged, doing it all myself – that we should pay her off, and replace her, perhaps even with a younger sister, so as to continue to help the family, but . . .' My grandmother peered at my mother: 'You know what's coming,' her expression said, and then she shut her eyes again, as if they hurt. 'I tried. It was a terrible day. Alexandre was in a very naughty phase; he'd tried to choke Marie in her crib during the siesta. And the kitchen sink had clogged, and Khalida just stood there, for a quarter of an hour, staring at the scummy dishwater and saying nothing, doing nothing, and I said – as kindly as I could, mind you – "My dear girl, we both know this can't go on." She gave me such a look: a black look. Terrible. The *schkoumoun*. The evil eye. And I said, "We want to help as much as we can, because you're quite clearly in difficulty, but it makes no sense to keep pretending that you can work here, because you can't. You need to go home to your family, now, and wait until this child is born. And then maybe we can help you find a new situation, somewhere with friends, nice people."

'She planted her feet; she crossed her arms over her belly, which was big, then. She was carrying high, up front, and the rest of her was still scrawny, her limbs like little freckled pipes. A little woman, but such a terrible expression. "You can't let me go," she said. "My dear girl, I understand your worries, and we'll give you some money to tide you over—" "No, no," she said, "You don't understand." Which is when – well, you can imagine.'

'Jacques,' my mother whispered.

My grandmother took a deep breath. 'It was a terrible day. The worst – almost the worst – in my life. My faith was so shaken. But God doesn't abandon us, not even in our darkest hour.'

'What happened to her? Surely, among her people, she would have been an outcast because of the child. Don't they kill women for it?'

'As far as I know, she was spared stoning at least. I don't know how she lived, and I don't care. From my life, she went.

That was what mattered to me: she went. Alexandre cried for a week: "Where's my Khalida? I want my Khalida." And then forgot all about her, as little children do.'

'And you?'

'I let him take care of it. He spoke to her, he paid her. For all I know, he kept on paying her. He's very moral, Jacques; he knows his duty. I didn't want to know about it. I got the slut out of my kitchen, out of our apartment, and that was my job done. I never saw her again and neither, he told me, did he. I believe him. And if he did, I don't want to know. I had my family to protect, and I did. And we survived. More than survived. And so will you.'

'And the child?'

'A boy. That much I know. A healthy baby boy.'

'But this is different,' my mother began, sitting forward in her chair. 'Alexandre is different.'

'He hasn't saddled himself with illegitimate children, so far as we know. For that, at least, we can thank the women's liberation movement, if for nothing else. And he doesn't chase Arab servants. Be grateful, my girl. The rest depends on you.'

'And live as if it didn't matter?'

'Don't be so American. You know better than that. Live as if your family mattered more – your children, your security. Which they do.'

'But how can I ever have faith in him?'

'That's between you and God. It's your problem. Know that in the wider world it matters not a jot. You are my son's wife, and will remain so, in the eyes of the church, until you die.'

6

My mother didn't need my grandmother to tell her this; she believed it anyway, in spite of the times, in spite of the current divorce rate and the stirrings in her heart at the fleeting prospect of freedom. There was me; more intransigent still, there was

Etienne and, much as she loved my brother, she could never be free while he was alive. It was, indeed, a choice of beliefs, although not to Carol's eyes; and if it changed her perception of her marriage, it altered its actual contours only slightly. Now, at last, she had an excuse for her unhappiness – not in the outlying family, or in her blameless son, but in her husband himself. It was almost a relief. She made use of it.

And I? Once again, my side was chosen – in the *salon de thé*, among the potted figs – before I knew there was a choice. Only years later did I wonder what it was to be my father, stoked with self-loathing, to observe the world through the sheen of failure: born of a failed country, a mediocre businessman trailing in his father's footsteps, an unsatisfactory spouse, the father of a son who could never grow up, seeking always and again the moment of conquest when he might escape his history, himself, and soar unburdened for a stolen hour. But at almost fifteen, I could not look him in the eye, knowing what I knew; and, not looking, I could not see the flickering there of his wounded self. To me he was not a person, in all a person's fragile parts; he was my father, who had betrayed my mother, and me, and even Etienne, a malignant presence unconvincingly masked by his cheerful smiles and premeditated caresses.

My mother had done nothing wrong; my mother was alone and unsupported. That was how she saw it, and how, through her eyes, I came to see it also, and if he had been cognizant, Etienne too would have allied himself with us. We were a lonely trio, not living, it seemed, while my father sallied forth and stole a separate life, a life without us, in spite of us, which was unforgivable. The words he spoke meant nothing – my mother and I so little believed them that we hardly heard them, or heard them only to inspect and unpick them, to discard their apparent import like a fistful of broken threads. 'I have to work late', 'I have an early appointment', 'I'll just stop off for a drink with Pierre on the way home' – we accepted none of it, although we nodded, noncommittally. We studied him the way you study a drunk who claims to have reformed, sniffing his neck for cologne, frowning and muttering if he took time over his appearance, daily battling the impulse to rifle his briefcase for clues to his movements.

He, in return, in his full energy, swung wildly from opaque kindness to tight-lipped rage, aware that he was being measured and judged, doomed again to fail. If he chatted after mass with a woman in the congregation, I scrutinized her from head to toe, beaming displeasure, certain she must count among his harem. If he turned to glance at a young girl in town, at the slim line of her back, I deemed it lechery. I did not want him to touch me, and felt sullied in touching him: kissing him good night, I tendered my cold cheek and osculated the air alongside his own. As my mother remained silent with him, and the evenings lay heavy with tension but empty of argument, I began to pick fights of my own, about anything – politics, my attire, homework, privileges (for which I had little use in that lonely spring), the hours I spent watching television – anything but the real thing, the suspicions born of knowledge that he did not know I had.

7

At suppertime, when he was there, I glared at his placid features, swollen with food, and beyond him at the Burmese torments of hell. I tried to will him into the picture, to force upon him the punishments that were his due. Once, in my willing, I screwed my eyes shut, muttering my hex beneath my breath. I must have remained some moments in that histrionic attitude, because my father silenced my mother's vague chat and asked, in a low, slow voice which at the time I took for anger, but which might simply have been concern, 'Sagesse? Are you feeling sick?'

'No sicker than usual.'

'Is it something you've eaten? Is it a migraine? Maybe, like your grandmother, you're susceptible to migraines?'

Eyes open now to a room that shimmered before me, slightly, I hissed, 'I'm not like Grand'-mère. I'm not like the LaBasses. It's not a migraine.'

'Then what is it?' My father put down his knife and fork. 'Something must be wrong, because there is no other excuse for such extraordinary behaviour.'

My mother sighed. She turned to Etienne, who was at her elbow, and stroked his glistening hair.

'It's none of your business,' I said, with a floundering fear of my incipient, as yet uninvented, lie.

'Don't use that tone with me,' he said. 'How much you hate your parents is your own affair, but as long as you live under my roof, you will show us the courtesy of respect.'

'I don't hate my parents,' I replied, looking at my mother and thereby absolving her.

'What's that supposed to mean?'

'Why don't you have to show us any respect, if respect is such a big deal?'

My father drew a deep breath. He seemed to be rising from his chair. 'What is the matter with you? Do you think you can talk to me as if I were one of your little friends?'

'Let her be,' my mother said. 'Just ignore it, Alex.'

'I will not ignore it. Night after night, day after day, this chit of a girl behaves as though we were trash, here only to finance her good times and get out of the way – as though we were nothing—'

'Don't get carried away,' my mother warned.

'Shut up, Carol. I asked her a civil question – she's sitting there with her face contorted as though she's about to puke – and all I ask is why – and this? I'm treated to this?'

'Just tell your father what's wrong, dear. You're not feeling well, right?'

I glanced at her. She had her hand crooked at Etienne's nape, and he, my brother, was opening his eyes very wide. Their whites, like those of fried eggs, reflected the light. He was liable to pull his lips back over his teeth and screech, a piercing sound like an alarm. My mother was pleading with me. If Etienne lost his composure, the evening would catapult into hysteria.

I concocted my lie. It came to me like a gift. 'You wouldn't understand, and you don't want to know.'

'I've asked. So try me.' My father was standing now. He tossed his napkin defiantly onto the table. He rolled his bulk threateningly on his toes. 'Go on. What is it?'

'I'm bleeding,' I hissed. 'I have my period and I'm bleeding like a stuck pig, and it cramps up my insides as though a hundred knives were being jabbed into me. It kills. You have no idea.'

Deflated, my father sat. He would not meet my gaze.

'Are you happy now? Did you really want to know that? Did you have to?'

'That's enough, Sagesse,' murmured my mother, who had taken her hand back into her lap. 'Don't you think you'd feel better if you went and lay down?'

'All right.' I pushed back my chair and lifted my plate to carry it to the kitchen. 'I'm going.'

'I'm sorry, sweetheart.' My father was embarrassed. He did not think of me as bleeding; he thought of me still, as I thought of Etienne, as a child. He hung his head, his supper no longer pleasing to him.

'Never mind. It'll pass.' I felt guilty for lying, although my mother had all but asked me to. I felt sorry for my father's tamed attempts at love. But the accusations that I wanted to make, the bile I held back, lay in a bitter coating on my tongue.

8

Within my skin I suffered, too: that spring of 1990, my back erupted in boils, painful hillocks of pus beneath my shirt, which my mother attributed to adolescence and chocolate, but which I knew were caused by my parents' quivering restraint, the secrecy in the air. As my peers disrobed to skimpy sundresses, I layered myself more fully with cloth, my back sticky with sweat and sore to the touch. I succumbed to panic attacks, a turmoil of pounding blood and breathlessness that washed over me without warning, in shops or on the bus – more than once, I had to get off and walk the remainder of my journey, my hand on my heaving chest, so that I was often late to my destination. I struggled to eat: all food tasted chalky and bland to me. And I could not sleep. I lay awake listening, night after night, hoping to hear my parents arguing, hoping to hear anything, afraid not of the silence but of its interruption, certain that if the worst would come it would at least be better than this, this terrible anticipation.

My birthday, in early June, came and went. I refused all celebration, hid in my room while my mother iced the cake downstairs, and refused to emerge to the pile of presents that seemed like gross hypocrisy, enraging my father – who had cancelled something, ostensibly a business appointment, although his very wrath convinced me otherwise, in order to be at home – so that he stood outside my door, rattling the handle, bellowing, 'There will be no locked doors in my house.' To which I retorted, through snot and tears, 'Except yours, is that it?' and he cried, 'What does that mean? What kind of tone is that? Open this door right now and explain yourself!'

I burrowed beneath my bed like a dog and waited until he strode away. My mother left me milk and a sandwich on a tray, the repast of childhood illness or banishment, and I gnawed at the stale bread which was my birthday supper after everyone had gone to sleep, perched on my windowsill, cursing my imprisonment, staring out at the winking lights of town and the black water, certain that I understood Becky at last and whispering to myself, with conscious theatricality, 'I have nothing to live for. Nothing to live for. I might as well be dead.'

I tried to pray, to rekindle my former confidence in the church, but God failed to provide any sign, and his intermediary, the priest, droned out sermons as hollow to me as my father's excuses. I couldn't listen. Thibaud's letters from Paris, every fortnight or so, were my solace, and in composing my dishonest replies I thought that at least somewhere, to someone, I lived on unbesmirched. Awake, at night, I imagined myself again in Thibaud's embrace, knowing as I did that this was a fruitless yearning. I could find nothing to look forward to; no deus ex machina presented itself even to my imagination; I saw no way for my former life (I could hardly remember what it had been) to be restored.

9

I despised my brother as myself, had to force myself to stroke his gentle head, traced maliciously upon occasion the frail line of his breastbone and contemplated crushing it – without him, my mother could leave my father, take me with her to a new life in America, abandoning this one as easily as if it were a car with its tyres spinning in a ditch. And yet: his shallow sucking for air, his toothy smiles, his resolute joyfulness were what kept us whole, in our ghastly contradiction. As if aware that he alone was responsible, Etienne spurted in size, stretching his rubbery length a full four inches in as many months, bursting out of all his clothes. His legs hunched in their footrests; all his straps had to be loosened. My mother, shocked by this expansion, asked the new nurse what she had fed him to prompt this Alice-in-Wonderland behaviour, while my father seemed not to notice.

Playing doctor as I had in childhood, I palpated my brother's limbs while he lay in bed, to see whether the bones had separated from their joints deep beneath the surface. It was in the course of one such methodical examination – finger bones to wrists, elbows, shoulders, down the spiny torso on which the little nipples lay quiescent and pink – that I encountered my brother's erection, a brave resistance below the sheets; and it dawned on me that in his silent and supposedly safe cocoon, even there, my saintly Etienne had followed me, and fallen into adolescence, this murky pit from which I could plot no extrication. He, too, was human, neither more nor less; and with an emotion akin above all to curiosity, I wrapped my fingers tight around the protrusion, wound in the white cotton – a little Halloween ghost, a tyke in disguise – and rubbed until my brother arched his back, as much as he was able, and the sheet dampened. Only then did I remove my hand, feeling nothing but the faint trill of his relief; and only in my own bed did I wonder if, in this small favour, I had done wrong.

The wrong, as I saw it, was not incestuous in nature – although I knew that the world's morality could not condone such action of a sister upon a brother – but lay in the very awakening of Etienne to possibilities beyond his grasp, in the bitter and futile assertion of his humanness. As a child he was perfection, willing repository of all we could not ourselves accept, but nevertheless untainted, blind to sin; but as a man, he would be consigned to conflict and despair far more profound than any I could know, and alone in a place where no one could hear.

Words, meaningless though they might ring, as wrongly as we may interpret them, are the only missiles with which we are equipped, which we can lob across the uncharted terrain between our souls. Without them, and yet also without knowledge – of the life outside, of the failure of those very words – my brother had known joy. I had seen it, often, on his face. He lived like Friday before Crusoe, alone in his paradise, or in his hell, but not knowing it to be either – and now, with this sigh, with this relief, his body had communicated desire and been heard, and however my brother registered knowledge, he must know that it had, and, most terribly, would know when it remained, henceforth, unattended. Having been, beneath his sheet, unalone for even a moment, he would know for ever more what it meant to be alone; which I was only just learning, to be sure, but against which I had at least the bolster of language. The wrong I had done, I realized, was to make my brother aware of his prison as he had never before been; to corrupt his joy. And I recognized both that I would keep my act a secret (more for the sake of the world's morality than out of my own dismay), and that I would never repeat it, which was the worst admission of all.

At the same time I, for this, felt less alone, certain that my brother would now know loss; that in this, as in everything else, he and I were conjoined (although of everything else I could not know what he knew). Years later, I wonder if this distress, alleviated by a strange pleasure, is what my father felt in seducing his women: a fleeting feeling of beginning again, of not being alone, of sharing sin and in so doing, relieving it. My father's awareness of his Eden and its loss, like Etienne's, like anyone's, were almost simultaneous. The moment's bittersweet fruit is nostalgia, the dangerous fruit of my father's sustenance, and for a long time of my own.

What would the opposite of nostalgia be? That is the kernel for which I groped, and still grope; that is the answer to the question of whether life is worth living. In committing suicide, my father denied any such answer, or certainly, any such answer that he could accept upon this earth. With such an act, the fabric is rent, the stage behind the drop cloth nakedly revealed: we live 'as if', as if we knew why, as if it made sense, as if in living this way we could banish the question and the 'as if-ness' itself, the way we speak and act as if our words could be comprehended; and such a moment as my father's death exposes again the thinness of that curtain, the unreality – although surely sweat and blood and sex are real, as real as death – of the quotidian. Severed from our surroundings, we have to ask, or else to throw ourselves again into pretending, as though nothing were more real than that.

10

But my father wasn't dead yet. In my naive way, I imagined death quite often, that spring and early summer: his, or my mother's, or Etienne's, or mine – each as a way of propelling us forward, out of the place in which we were stuck. I willed my father's death, in fact. In the night silences, that's what I listened for: my mother's screaming assault, perhaps with a kitchen knife aloft; my father's grunt of surprise. I pictured it: his eyes popping in their sockets, his body crumpling, deflating like a balloon. There was in my imagining no blood, no moment after. My father would walk again, after a poor night's rest, but be a changed man, his vibrancy turned upon us, instead of away. I didn't know death: most real, it was not yet so to me. I couldn't shake the fear and the desire of it, though: I developed an aversion to knives and scissors, to pills and cars. I couldn't sleep, in part for worry that I would rise, in my slumber, and slaughter this man, this treacherous father, in his bed. And as if to compensate for this desire I became, in the daytime, terrified for my parents' safety, as worried that my father might fall or be flattened by a van or a heart attack as I was that his excuses were lies. The whole world seemed a maze of shifting mirrors in which I wandered alone, looking always and frenziedly for the exit back into my real life, where people had substance, did as they said they would, and were whole.

But I could not, at first, see where that change was to come from. Neither of my parents seemed prepared to initiate it. In their own ways, they had bent, stoutly, to a life without my grandfather, and now, again, they were inclined simply to go on, to live as if — as if! — the night of their furious row had never taken place. Heeding her mother-in-law's advice, my mother determined to eradicate the information she hadn't wanted to know; and my father, who had lived for so long as though this were possible, slipping between isolate lives and imagining that he controlled them all, was only too keen to go on. Nobody wanted to talk about it, about any of it; nobody's life was altered, it seemed, but mine, and mine only because I could not twist the stories to make myself an actor in any of them. The disposition of our family upon its stage was not my affair; I was merely disposed, as children always are.

Against this inertia, I realized, the puppeteer would soon resurface to take up the strings again. My grandfather's prison term was drawing to a close. He had immersed himself in

Balzac, studied Spanish on tape, reflected upon the future of the European Union and its ramifications for the hotel trade. He was ready, according to my grandmother, to emerge into a healthy retirement. But the LaBasse households quaked and fretted; and I began eagerly to await the day. He was not Lear, he had not willingly renounced his throne; it had been usurped by circumstance and by my father. Surely Jacques would reclaim it, surely – I decided – he would restore order.

Eight

The afternoon before my grandfather's release, the horizon was hazy and the air sluggish. My father was flying to Paris for a two-day travel industry convention. This, he smilingly assured my mother, was a crucial gathering, a fair at which his physical presence, suntanned and boisterous, was essential. He was compelled – for the Bellevue's greater glory – to sacrifice his ardent wish to be with the family.

'But your father—'

'Knows and understands and approves. He'd do the same. Look, I saw him three days ago, and I'll see him again in three days. The only difference is, he'll be at home. He's not precious about it, believe me. He'd rather put the whole thing behind him, and I feel as he does.'

'But couldn't you have sent, I don't know—'

'If you want a job done right, do it yourself, we always say. It's not a big deal. I'm not going off to wallow in some hedonist's playpen, I'm headed for a huge hall that smells of socks, to talk shop with a herd of fat, balding travel agents in cheap suits. Unfortunate, but it's worth it.'

'Whatever you say.'

We drove him to the airport, my mother and I, our faces sagging in the new heat, our skin beading in the first diesel-filled miasma of summer. He leaped to the curb, fresh and full, his blue houndstooth sports jacket a blip of colour on the bleached sidewalk. He almost stepped on a small, beribboned terrier that yapped ferociously at his ankles, and had to interrupt his farewells to apologize to the dog's mistress, a tight-cheeked face-lift maven with a cloud of platinum hair and a cocoa

265

expanse of crêpy cleavage, firmly corseted in dusky rose and heavily ornamented with gold. The stretch outside the terminal was peopled with such women, some with wizened husbands in tow, clutching leather pouches, others commanding surly porters or paid companions, young ladies with pressed lips and waxed eyebrows whose expressions of permanent disdain and surprise their employers were, it seemed, attempting to recapture from the ravages of time.

'Each one a potential client.' My father winked. 'Or the friend of a potential client. I'll see if I can chat one up on the plane.'

'Why don't you see if you can resist the impulse?' I muttered, but my aside was drowned out by a departing jet.

My mother turned the corners of her mouth in a constrained smile. 'Do what's good for the hotel,' she said. 'And remember what's good for the family.'

'You bet.' But my father's tone, infected by his wife's annoyance, was no longer blithe. 'Raise a glass to Papa. I hope he won't be too tired.'

'Tired?' said I. 'He's been resting for six months.' I spoke out of conscious impertinence, but my parents chose to laugh, easily, almost naturally, as if we were a proper family after all.

'Take care of your mother.' My father made a broad wave. Neither she nor I had got out of the car to kiss him goodbye, and only after he had slipped between the old ladies and the sliding doors did I stir, to take his former place in the front seat.

'Well, that's one menace off our minds for a few days,' my mother said.

'Do you think he has some girlfriend in Paris?'

'I've decided not to think about it. He's going for work.'

'Yeah, but you said that—'

'We'll just keep our eyes on what we can see, all right?'

'That's hypocritical.'

'It's realistic. You have to be a realist in this world. Your grandfather comes home tomorrow, and the last thing he needs to worry about is the state of his son's marriage.'

'Is that why you don't leave him?'

'What?'

'Because you're afraid of Grand'-mère and Grand-père?'

'Don't be ridiculous. I don't leave him because—' She pulled out into traffic, and was quiet as she negotiated the exit onto the main road.

'Why then?'

'Don't be a bully, Sagesse. There are a thousand reasons. And I married your father for better or worse—'

'But you won't even kiss him. You haven't for ages. Since long before all this.'

'What do you know about it? Don't talk about things you know nothing about. Honestly, I—'

'Don't, don't, don't. You're as bad as he is. I hate both of you. I hate it all.'

My mother sighed. Her face in profile was like a skeleton, the skin tugged almost to breaking over its hollows. But I could see that although she was gaunt, a dewlap dangled a little below her jaw, and her neck was beginning, ever so slightly, to buckle. 'Please. Enough. This is my life. This is your life, but not for ever. You're young. Soon you'll be free to do as you wish. You'll escape.'

'Not soon enough.'

'You think I don't remember being your age? You forget that time will pass—'

'That's not it. You just wonder if you'll survive long enough.'

'Well, you will. Just tell yourself it's all just a question of time passing.'

'Marie-Jo used to say that.'

'It's true.'

'Not for you.'

'Oh no?'

'I mean, you're not going anywhere. You're already here. Unless you choose to change things.'

'Thanks a lot. That's a fine way to see my life. Over and done with.'

'That's not what I said, Maman. You're young, too. In the world. Lots of people begin again at your age, don't they?'

'I don't know, dear. But this is my life, and I'll deal with it as best I can. Some things you can't walk away from.' I knew she didn't mean me, or my father, or even my grandparents. 'I figure God knows what He's about,' she said.

'I don't. I don't figure that at all.'

2

The next morning, as if in celebration, the haze had lifted and the mistral – that wind so much a part of the region that it is like a household deity, referred to often and fondly by name – gusted, furrowing the water into white caps and buffeting the windows. My mother and grandmother were to fetch my grandfather while I was at school, and after class I was to head not for home, but to the Bellevue, to my grandparents' apartment, where they, and Etienne, would be waiting. In his honour, Titine, their invalid friend (not yet then confined to her house) had had her housekeeper bake a *mouna*, the traditional Algerian Easter cake (although Easter was long past); Zohra was to stay late, to drink a toast to her returned employer. Several other stalwart friends – old people, old enough to be from Algiers – had been invited to come by in the evening, a modest party to cheer my grandfather's return from his enforced cure.

In spite of myself, I passed the day fumbling my present, eyes on the evening, barely able to concentrate. I kept remembering what seemed the last time I had seen him (although it wasn't), in the dock, which had also felt like the first time that I truly saw him, as a man; when we had looked at each other and I had felt *known*, and that I knew him, too. It was the first time I had understood the family myth, or at least had felt included in it. Like my grandmother, and like my mother (although she would never consciously have admitted it), I believed that somehow, even now, my grandfather could save us, could pull our family together and back from the brink. My mother and grandmother had made room, had made myths, for his disciple, my father, willing him to take the old man's place; and still, the power lay with the patriarch.

I hadn't been to the hotel for the better part of a year. It was half a mile from the house, and yet I had turned my back on it as though it didn't exist. I approached its iron gates like a trepidatious guest, my tread heavy and my gorge rising. The palm trees along the gravel drive loomed taller, their pineapple trunks hairier than I remembered. The waxy bushes, too, were overgrown, reaching out to tickle at my elbow. The grounds whittered and rustled – a cat blundered through the underbrush – but I encountered no people. At the driveway's fork, after deliberately crushing a waddling beetle underfoot, I veered to the right, along the narrower road curling around into the wood, to the residence block from behind, rather than venturing up to the hotel itself, and running the risk of encountering Marie-Jo near the tennis courts. I walked quickly, breathless from the incline and my anxiety, grateful for the back stairs that wound up from the employees' parking lot to my grandparents': I didn't have to see the swimming pool, the paved piazza above it, the old plane tree – and yet, I was curious. At the last moment, I scurried along a disused track behind a stand of bamboo, a shortcut from our long-ago games of cops and robbers, and, edging close to the pebbled wall of the staff residence, catching dust along my back and snagging my satchel, here and there, on creepers, I emerged into a familiar hiding place (still used: three foil gum wrappers winked at my feet), a hollow behind a large bank of laurels, whence I could peer out at my former playground without being seen.

A young couple lounged in the cleft of the plane tree, straddling it like a rocket, looking out to sea. I glimpsed only their backs, the woman's swathe of long, black hair, the man's muscular arm stroking the woman's slimmer, paler one. They were not people I recognized; Marie-Jo was nowhere in sight. A flat-capped gardener pruned in the flower bed to their left, at the edge of my sight, whistling erratically through his teeth. Beyond them the water glittered, crisp, to the horizon. This was an alien idyll; it belonged to other people now. I told myself I had nothing to fear from it, from them; they would know neither me nor my relationship to this place. And yet I couldn't bring myself to crash through the bushes onto the open ground, and I could not imagine striding boldly up to the building's front door. Instead I retreated, back through the foliage and radical clutter and slowly (I told my heart, 'Beat slow-ly') up the rest of the stairs to the building's back entrance.

Rather than take the elevator, I climbed to the penthouse, lurking on landings in the dark between each floor to be sure no one was coming or going from any of the other apartments. I heard, through the walls, Thierry's mother calling to someone from her kitchen; I thought I caught the sound of footsteps behind Marie-Jo's double-fronted door, next to which the bell button flickered invitingly in the half-light, and took the next set of steps two at a time to get out of range. By the time I rang the chime at my grandparents', I was perspiring everywhere, my shirt stuck unpleasantly to my back and its spots, and a trickle oozed down the cleft of my buttocks. I just had time to smear the sweat from my upper lip before Zohra opened the door and crowed at the sight of me.

'My big girl,' she cried, throwing her arms around my waist and raising her brown cheek for my embrace. 'How tall! How fat you're getting! This is a day for rejoicing; all the loved ones home again!'

'Everyone's here?'

'Only your dear father is missing. But he has already telephoned. Come in, come in!' She grasped my biceps in her tight little fingers and pulled me across the threshold.

'Can I wash up, do you think? Before I say hello?'

'Bathroom, yes, the bathroom! You want to be nice and clean for your grandfather, my little chickadee. Poor girl, straight from school. Come!' She came with me to the bathroom, and followed me inside. 'The red towel – you'll use the red towel, yes?'

'Sure.'

'And the little soap, the one for guests? The other is your grandfather's – brand-new for his homecoming.'

'You bet.'

She stood watching me as I approached the sink, apparently unwilling to leave. I could hear my grandmother's voice in the living room.

'The friend, Titine, has come already, with an oxygen tank, no less. Your brother is also here – a big boy, now, too.'

'He certainly is. Do you think – would you mind if I shut the door?'

'No, no. I'm going.' Still, she stood. And then whispered, as she pulled the door closed, bowing out like a courtier, her eyes bright with emotion, 'It's so sad, in the living room. Everyone is wounded. I'm glad that you're here now – a strong, healthy girl.'

I took off my shirt, surveyed my clammy torso in the mirror. The bathroom smelled familiar, of breeze and lavender soap. Its little slatted windows, up high, were half open to the afternoon, and an occasional edge of mistral wafted in. I washed at the sink, soaping my back as best I could, and rubbing it hard with the rough towel, an old one, as sharp as a scrubbing brush. As I passed my blind hand over one of my scrubbed spots it started to leak pus; I encouraged it with my fingers until it bled, a liberal leak in my skin. My shirt was white; I could not dress again until I had stanched the seepage. I rifled through the cabinets for a Band-Aid, but found only a packet of gauze and surgical tape, from which I fashioned a bandage. It took several tries, and more than one length of tape, before I could be sure the poultice was properly stuck over the welt. The bandage, lumpy, felt like a little hunch. I thought of Cécile's back, a village of such bandages on the landscape of her shrapnelled skin.

I dressed carefully. It was unpleasant to drape the shirt, still moist in patches, back on my body. I was combing my hair, preparing to rebraid it, when my mother knocked.

'Everything all right?'

'I'm coming.'

'What's taking so long?'

'Nothing.'

'Your grandfather is wondering where you are.'

I felt a surge of irritation at this ritual deference. 'Tell him I'm on the toilet.'

'There's no need to be unpleasant, Sagesse. Don't spend all day in there.'

I made a rucking noise in my throat. 'I'll be right along.'

I heard her click back along the hall, and tried unsuccessfully to gauge the degree of her annoyance. I finished my braid, fiddled with my bangs, waited. I sat on the toilet and dribbled a little urine into the bowl to make true my assertion; flushed, washed my hands again, practising my smile as I did so. I wiped the vanity with the red towel, then folded it and hung it over the bath.

Then I ventured out, down the hall, past the dining room (from which I could see the pool, at last, empty of swimmers but for a little girl in flowered panties, kicking a yellow board, while her mother lounged on the patio – right about where the shot had struck – and watched), and into the crowded living room.

Zohra, who squatted on a pouffe nearest the archway, leaped up and sprang towards me, making an extravagant pantomime of hugging me as though she had not already done so. 'Here she is, the weary schoolchild! Beautiful girl!' She hovered at my elbow, spritelike, emitting a saltatory energy which unnerved not only me but also – I could tell without looking – the others. 'Kiss your grandfather – there he is!' Zohra pushed me towards him as though I might not have known him. She was not wholly unwise to do so: were he not sitting in my grandfather's chair, were he not the only male in the room besides my brother, my eyes might have skated over him.

He had never been a tall man, but now, even seated, he had shrunk. He perched upon the upholstery like a kinglet on an overgrown throne, as though his feet did not quite reach the ground, while his hands clasped the arms of the chair, splayed like little paws, as if they alone held him in place and kept him from sinking. Smaller (at least to my eye), he had also grown fatter – from the prison food, or my grandmother's bi-weekly offerings of cakes and chocolates, or from his anti-depressant medication – and his face, formerly oval, was now round as a coin, a plump, benign face upon which his eyes, in their cushions, sat matt as liquorice jujubes. His downy hair, sparse and formerly grey, was now white, a faint nimbus above his large-lobed ears. He moved to rise, but the effort was considerable – like a small boy scrabbling from a high stool, but without a boy's vigour – and I stepped forward to kiss him. A soaped smell rose up from him. His clothes – ones that had hung in his closet while he was away – tugged at him like someone else's, tight at the collar, slightly twisted over his belly. His belt, I noticed, was buckled at a hole looser than its former, scored and stretched one. I looked into his jujube eyes, wanting again the flash of recognition, the fiery glance. His lids, lizardlike in their slowness, closed once, twice, as if to wash the vagueness from his eyeballs, as if he were trying to resurface but could not. He patted my cheek – 'I've missed you, little one' – and from his mouth strayed a cloud of briny, old-man's breath.

'I've missed you too.'

The only sign that he was he (but who? The man I thought I had seen across a room? The man I had grown up fearing and skirting? The man of the family stories?) came from his papery hand, which he folded over mine when I leaned towards him, and held, almost desperately, when I straightened, so that I turned and crouched alongside his chair to face the room, my fingers still his prisoner.

I smiled (as I had practised) at the assembly. Arrayed along the sofa to my grandfather's right sat my mother, smiling more brightly even than I; and an imposing woman that I did not know, with a beetle brow and large, dark eyes, in her fifties, perhaps, with broad hands folded in her lap, and black, scarablike earrings that reminded me of the unfortunate creature I had lately squashed on the path. Beside her quivered Titine, wispy and prematurely wizened by her ailments, her pointed chin ticking like an unsteady barometer. At her knee, her silver oxygen tank rested on its trolley, festooned with plastic tubing, ready in case of need.

At my left, my grandmother presided in her tapestry chair, her left hand holding Etienne's. Beyond him, almost unseen, squatted Zohra. We were arranged in a U; the armchair directly opposite my grandfather, which would have closed the circle, remained unoccupied, as if awaiting my father. It was where he usually sat.

'Isn't this a precious day?' said my grandmother.

'Indeed,' murmured Titine and the unknown lady – who I deduced must be the widow, Madame Darty, Titine's intimate friend and, later, the ladies' fourth at bridge – in unison.

'We were just telling your grandfather,' said this woman to me in a deep voice, 'that the flowers are all in bloom for his return.'

'And the – mistral blowing,' added Titine in her piccolo tremor, pausing mid–sentence like a feeble breeze herself.

'Eh?' My grandfather strove to lean forward in his chair. ('So,' I thought, 'they've taken his hearing as well.')

'The mistral,' my mother repeated loudly. 'It's blowing for you.'

As if on cue, the wind swept around the building and set the geraniums on the verandah dancing.

'The good wind,' my grandfather said. 'We could do with more of it. I've missed it, these past months.'

'Your apartment is so glorious,' gushed Madame Darty, who, I was aware, spent the moments when attention was elsewhere scanning the room's contents with an appraising air. 'Such a view!'

'You've not been here before?' I asked.

She shook her head. 'But what a special occasion on which to be invited.'

My grandmother smiled. 'We should break the *mouna*, Titine, that you so generously brought.' She nodded at Zohra, who withdrew wordlessly to the kitchen for this prize, and plates, and napkins. 'Yet another treat we miss from the old life.'

The ladies sighed; my grandfather scowled. A silence followed, in which my brother chose to wriggle, and to offer his version of speech. My grandmother and Madame Darty spoke at the same time, the latter with a nervous glance at Etienne and immediately away, as though it were impolite to acknowledge his presence.

'Of course you'll have cake too, *chéri*,' my grandmother said, 'with a nice glass of milk.'

'You're rather a hero of mine,' Madame Darty was blustering to my grandfather. 'I'd have done exactly as you did, I'm sure. The young people today – let me tell you – I was visiting a friend recently, a widow like myself, but without resources. She lives in a part of town where I wouldn't usually go—'

'Ah—' breathed Titine. It was unclear whether she was adding to the conversation or merely gasping for air. Madame Darty chose to ignore her.

'And my car isn't new, but it is a nice car. Well, not a Mercedes, but a nice car. And as I was locking it – parked on the street, in broad daylight – a group of teenagers ambled up. They were – I hate to say it, but of course – they were Arabs.' She said this in a stage whisper, with a glance towards the door to be sure Zohra wasn't there. 'And one youth insulted me, and they circled the car as I walked away. I saw one of them kicking at the tyres. I was afraid to say anything, afraid for my life.'

'And for your car,' said my mother, with exaggerated concern. Madame Darty nodded gravely.

'Was it stolen?' asked my grandmother. 'Or vandalized?'

'Thank heaven, no. But these kids, they get their fun from terrorizing us. It's appalling.'

'No respect,' wheezed Titine. My brother chortled. Madame Darty made a visible effort not to look at him.

'But poor Madame Darty,' said my mother to my grandfather, 'has suffered worse than that. Just last week.'

'Oh yes?'

'Oh yes. I was burgled.' She shook her head. 'I'm often out in the afternoon – anybody who watches our apartment building would know that, and—'

Zohra came in with the cake on a platter in one hand and a pile of plates in the other. She placed them on the coffee table in front of her mistress.

'Perhaps Titine would care to do the honours?'

Titine shook her head more perceptibly than it shook itself. 'Please.'

'Tea, I think, Zohra. And milk for Etienne. And a Coca-Cola?' My grandfather nodded. 'A Coca-Cola for Monsieur.'

My grandmother cut the *mouna* – a glorified brioche, more like bread than cake, with a hard-boiled egg, like an unexploded bomb, in its centre – and I helped to distribute it, seizing the opportunity to claim my father's empty armchair for myself. All the while Madame Darty continued her tale of woe. She had come home and thought nothing of the fact that the door wasn't bolted – 'except, "Silly me", you know, as one does' – and worried only when she felt a draught, and noticed that the door to the balcony was ajar. The living room was fine, just fine; but then she went into the bedroom and '*Mon Dieu!* It gives me a turn even now!': drawers open, clothes all over the floor.

'I'd interrupted the thief, you see, before they could get through the whole place. But my rings! My necklaces!' She called the police; it was determined that the thief had entered from the balcony, after breaking into the uninhabited apartment next door. ('Delicious cake, Titine,' murmured my grandmother, an insubstantial block to Madame Darty's torrent.) 'And my neighbours had only been gone three weeks. But they knew. The thief knew!'

Her greatest revelations she saved for last. 'They think the thief must have been hiding on one of the landings as I went by – can you imagine? In the dark, like a cockroach.' And then, 'The policeman said he thought it must be a woman. And the minute he said it, I thought "Yes, that's right", because she went straight for my bedroom, for the precious, personal things. Not a glance at the living room. No interest in the silver service. No, she went for the jugular, where it would hurt me most.'

Everyone made aggrieved noises, their mouths full of the *mouna*. Only Madame Darty's portion remained untouched. 'Just waiting on the tea, dear,' she said, patting Titine's knee. 'I'm sure it's delicious; it just looks a little dry to me. So

anyway – ' to the broader company ' – that's when the policeman informed me that there is a band – a band – of Nigerian
women on the loose, burgling houses and apartments all over
town.'

'A band?' I asked.

'That's what he said.'

'But if they haven't caught them, how does he know?'

'He said so.'

'But how could he know how many there are, or whether
they're Nigerian or, or Italian, or British or even French? I
mean, if they've not been caught?'

My mother flashed a warning frown.

Madame Darty lowered her dark brow, and spoke sternly.
'We must, I think, trust the police to know their business.'

'Indeed,' said my grandmother who, having put aside her
plate, was feeding crumbly bits to Etienne as discreetly as
possible. Zohra arrived with a tray, and gave my grandfather his
Coca-Cola first. He seemed to have been all but dozing while
Madame Darty narrated, and now sat up again, brushing the
remnants of the *mouna* from his shirt. He slurped his soda
greedily, without waiting for the tea to be poured.

'It's a terrible worry,' my mother offered vaguely. 'Crime.'

'One of so many, nowadays,' my grandmother added.

'And yet they set about arresting the wrong people,' said
Madame Darty, with a broad smile at my grandfather. He was
looking into the bottom of his glass, as if surprised to find it
empty, and did not notice.

'Zohra,' whispered my grandmother, 'Another drink for
Monsieur.'

Zohra leaped up again from her little perch and took his
glass. 'He's very thirsty,' she mouthed at me on her way out.

Tea was drunk, and pleasantries were exchanged. Madame
Darty seemed to have exhausted herself and allowed Titine
to grumble instead about her health ('The spring is very bad,
for my lungs, because of the pollen. But nothing compared
to the summer, with its terrible heat and no wind . . .'). In time,
the larger woman sat up straight, revealing the fullness of her

bosom, and announced, 'I think I should take Titine home now. You'll all be wanting a rest before the other guests come.'

'You're welcome to stay,' offered my grandmother. 'It's just a few old friends.'

Titine, aghast, quivered. 'Oh no, I couldn't. I couldn't breathe. It gets much worse in the evening. Besides, Jeanne will take me, and you want to get home before dark, don't you, dear?'

Madame Darty shuddered. 'It's spooky, the stairwell now. Thinking of the thief, hiding there. I wonder if I'll ever get over it.'

The ladies' leave-taking was laborious. Zohra struggled to lift the oxygen tank. 'It's on wheels, my dear, just roll it, you know – roll it along,' exhorted Madame Darty, as if to a child, her own bulk hovering instead over Titine who, alas, did not have wheels and teetered unsteadily from one item of furniture to the next, clutching with her clawlike fingers at every available support. Zohra was asked to bring a chair onto the landing, so that Titine might sit in wait for the elevator. My grandmother and mother supervised from behind, offering advice and banter as the little convoy progressed.

'Do you need Sagesse to go with you, down to the car? Can she help?' my mother suggested.

Madame Darty looked me up and down. 'I think we can manage. But thank you.'

When they had been bundled into the elevator, we retreated back to the living room, where both my brother and my grandfather appeared to be snoozing.

'Let's clear up these plates, Zohra,' urged my grandmother. 'Quietly.'

'Sweet of Titine to bring the *mouna*,' said my mother.

'Yes, indeed. Perhaps you'd like to take it home? I've never cared for it myself, although it's a lovely memory. When I was a little girl, all the women carried their cakes to the baker, to the ovens. Streams of women parading in the streets on the mornings before Easter or Pentecost, each with a white cloth over her tray. All those lovely white cloths, pristine, so preciously borne. It was very competitive, you know, whose *mouna* was superior. I like the idea of it, rather than the thing itself. And Jacques – well, he'd rather have a rum baba any day.'

'Maybe Zohra would like it?' I suggested.

'Maybe.' My grandmother had evidently not thought of this. 'Although I think they like stickier cakes, as a rule.'

My grandfather opened his eyes, looked startled.

'Sleepy, *chéri*? Want to lie down?' She turned to my mother. 'A lifetime of siestas and we're positively flattened without them.'

My mother smiled. She stood behind Etienne's chair and rocked it slightly, as if to soothe his sleep; but succeeded instead in waking him. His grey eyes rolled, birdlike, in his cocked head, seeking the source of motion. My mother stroked his hair, squeezed his nape between her fingers.

'Graw,' he said. 'Graaaw.'

'Can the next batch not be cancelled?' asked my grandfather, struggling to sit taller in his chair.

'I don't think so – I thought – you see – I'm sorry, *chéri*.' My grandmother looked truly stricken. 'It's a terrible mistake. I don't know what to do—'

'It's all right.' He heaved to his feet, a little man. He ran a hand over his hairless dome, let his palm rest on his cranium like a blanket. 'I'll go to the bedroom and read for a while. I won't sleep – it's too late. But I may or may not feel up to it. I may or may not come out to join the party.'

'As you wish. Of course, as you wish.' My grandmother was turning very red, foreseeing social disaster. 'I never would've invited them – but we talked about it, remember, and you said—'

'I know what I said. But I'm tired.' My grandfather was whining. I had never before known him, or imagined him, to do so. 'I'll hear the doorbell,' he said. 'I might come, but don't count on me. Just say I'm very tired. It's true.'

'But you've been resting for six months,' I thought again to myself; I did not say it. My mother and grandmother, wide-eyed, watched his progress through the hall. Zohra, at my elbow, shook her head. 'Terrible. It's terrible what they've done to him,' she muttered.

'Well. Well. We'd better get this place cleaned up.' My grandmother clattered the plates together and made for the kitchen. 'We'll get through this evening anyway, my dears, now won't we? It's nothing, compared to what's already been.'

3

My grandfather did emerge, just briefly, but spruce, smiling, in a jacket and tie. He waited till the middle of the party, and passed around the brightly illuminated room kissing the women and shaking the men's hands.

'You look very well,' the ladies congratulated him, one after another.

'Ah, I thank you. But appearances are deceptive. In fact, I am very tired. Now, if you'll excuse me . . .' and on to the next. Greetings accomplished, a toast was delivered, an honour at which my grandfather blushed – his ears turned particularly pink – and showed his teeth. He thanked the assembled company, the doughty matrons in their wafty dresses and the men in their natty blazers: 'It is a privilege to see you all, and wonderful to be home. But I am very tired, alas. Now, if you will excuse me—' and he withdrew again.

When the last guests had gone, my grandmother found her husband at her dressing table, his forearms planted among her lipsticks and perfume bottles, perusing a book of Spanish verbs and reciting the foreign words under his breath.

'Not too tired for that, my love?' she asked, as close to reproach as she ever came with him.

'It requires a different sort of energy,' he said. 'The energy of solitude, which I now have in abundance.'

Turning away from him, my grandmother began, very softly, to cry; but he, immersed in the subjunctive, did not know it.

Zohra helped my mother and me with Etienne's chair, helped

to lift him into the front seat. In return, we drove her home, to her salmon-coloured HLM, sandwiched among half a dozen other such buildings, clad in turquoise or canary yellow, on the far side of town. We dropped her at a traffic circle, in a soapy pool of fluorescent street light, and watched her slip into shadow, a little bowlegged elf, rolling from side to side as she walked, disappearing into the black maw of the development, a white plastic bag containing the remains of the *mouna* swinging at her elbow.

4

My father returned from Paris exuberant. A dalliance, I assumed, had buoyed his spirits, although he raved instead about the productivity of the conference, about his conversations with the élite travel agents ('only the most upscale – the Bellevue is upscale, I told them. We'll soon have that fourth star'), and of the prominence of his hostelry among the competition ('Bertrand was there, from Carqueiranne, and positively green with envy, the way the guys were flocking – but *flocking* – to me'), and he brushed aside my mother's concern that his father was much depleted.

'Nonsense,' he said. 'Isn't a man allowed to feel weary? Think of the emotion of it – very taxing. He'll be himself in no time. It's just a little readjustment, that's all. Did he comment on the hotel, on how it was looking? We're already full, in early July – that's good. That's better than last year.'

'I don't recall him saying anything,' said my mother. 'But we didn't really take the time – he didn't stop by the office or anything.'

'No.' My father pursed his lips. 'Of course not. Well, lucky fellow, it's not his worry any more. But I think he'll be pleased – especially given the way the economy's going. It's a bad time, you know. Pariseau, over near Cassis, is shutting up shop, he says. Thinks this time the recession will last for ever. But he's no businessman, that's the trouble. A businessman can't afford to be a pessimist.'

My mother gave my father a look. 'Quite,' she said.

My father was, to a degree, right about my grandfather. More of him – of what we thought of as him – came back with time. He grilled my father about the state of the Bellevue finances; he grew cantankerous with, rather than indifferent to, his wife and servant. He remarked upon and questioned and criticized even minute changes to the hotel that my father had made in his absence. If I had expected him to display a particular concern for my welfare, however, I was mistaken: he seemed to drift between a world of his own imagining and the business world of figures, peddling managerial advice to his son, keeping an eagle eye on market trends, but unable to notice the simplest domestic movements around him, the lacquer bowl of anemones on the dining table, or Etienne's extra inches, or my new haircut. (As soon as school was out, I had my hair lopped to my chin, as a testament to my unhappiness and in a vain hope that it would relieve the problems on my back.) He manifested interest, unsurprisingly, in my report card, which my father took to him like a small trophy, as if it were proof of my father's diligence, rather than my own.

'You can do better,' my grandfather told me that evening, in our garden, clutching my hand as he had the night of his return. 'You are improving – a mind like mine, underneath it all. But still, yes, you can do better. Each generation should do better. That's how it ought to be.' He looked me fully in the eye, and I thought I saw him there, for the first time, again, beneath his crêped lizard lids. And then he let go, and gazed out at the bushes and the paling sky, through which a lone firefly made wavering progress, emitting its Morse code, and he lapsed into silence, apparently oblivious to the adult conversation around him.

I watched him for a time, his motionlessness, his vague and false benignity, as of a statesman or a prophet – or a broken man. I thought he must be pondering his sin, the gunshot and all that it had visited upon us: I projected remorse, and a quiet tide of grief, a recognition that, Cronus-like, he had been engaged heretofore in the voracious consumption of his children, rather than in their nurturing. I projected — not suspecting that it might be otherwise — a new and generous leaf, a silvery flip in his soul that would lead him at once to liberate and to support us: I willed him to be the man I wanted him to be. When he smiled, a subtle curling of his crusty lip, a wrinkling in the round cheek, I was so convinced of the rightness of my apprehension that I asked him: 'What are you thinking about, Papi?'

'Ah,' he said, without turning to look at me, 'I was just remembering.'

'What's that, what were you remembering?'

5

One evening, in the summer of 1955, shortly after his promotion to deputy manager at the St. Joseph on the clifftop in Algiers, as he sat perusing papers at his fine ebony inlaid desk, in his newly private office, his newly personal secretary, Madame Barre, knocked upon his door. She was a very proper young lady, the wife of a military man posted in the city, and she wore, beneath her carefully combed coiffure, an expression of alarm.

'There's a fellow out here,' she said, 'a peasant. Who claims to be your cousin. I — I've told him you won't be free at all, to call for an appointment, but he refuses — he won't go away. He rather frightens me.'

My grandfather was surprised — baffled, indeed — as to the possible identity of this visitor, and, he confessed to me, not a little embarrassed that such a man should come calling in such a hotel — embarrassed before Madame Barre, whom he knew to be, by birth, his social superior, a knowledge he had contrived, up to that point, to keep hidden.

So when the young man was shown in — his sturdy boots

clomping upon the Beluch oriental, his dusty hat in hand, reminding my grandfather, just slightly, of a particular moment in his own youth, at once delicious and painful, in the lobby of the Ritz Hotel in Paris – my grandfather raised an eyebrow, and glared.

'Do I know you?' he thundered, scepticism in his tone, loudly enough for Madame Barre to hear as she shut the door behind the visitor.

'Serge LaBasse.' The younger man feinted a bow, wriggled his broad shoulders as if an eel were down his shirt. 'I'm your cousin. Or technically, I suppose, we're half-cousins. We've never met, but our fathers – our grandfather—'

My grandfather tapped his pen on the table. 'You must be one of Georges's boys?'

'That's right. The elder.' The young man, whose hair was matted and streaked with gold, whose lopsided pugilist's face was lined and stained beyond its years, whose large, spatulate fingers turned the straw hat in nervous circles, looked relieved.

'You've taken on the farm, then? Your father died, what, three years ago?' My grandfather adjusted his tie pin, his cuffs. Georges had been his father's half-brother, the late son of Auguste's second marriage, one of a long-forgotten brood.

'Six.'

'As long as that?'

Serge shrugged. 'May I?' He indicated a reproduction Second Empire chair, scroll-backed, upholstered in mauve silk. My grandfather sniffed, appraising the soot and dust on the younger man's apparel, then nodded. Serge sat.

'Have you a family of your own, then?'

'A wife. Twin daughters, seven. A baby boy.'

'Well, that's well done for the family name.' My grandfather said to me that he could picture them, pin-limbed, jaundiced, in rags. He focused on the desk, rearranged the floating papers. 'And what brings you to Algiers – trade of some kind?' My grandfather couldn't stop fidgeting because he knew – had known from the moment Serge crossed his threshold – that he had come to importune my grandfather for money.

'Have you been following what happens, in the country, now?' asked the visitor, leaning forward so that his hands, too, with their roped muscles and cracked nails, lay like foreign implements on my grandfather's desk.

'By which you mean . . .?'

'Since last year. Since the uprising.'

'Terrible stuff. Yes, as you can imagine, we worry about such things in the hotel business – it wreaks havoc on our bookings. Or has the potential to.'

'I'm sure.'

'Are you much affected, out where you are? I thought the trouble was down in the Aurès, and over near Constantine.'

The young man looked annoyed, his nose more evidently, and literally, out of joint. 'The trouble, sir, is in the country. Like a cancer that has meta – meta—'

'Metastasized?'

'Exactly. The cities, like anything else, are organs in the nation's body. They, too, will be affected.'

'Come now, Serge. No need to dramatize. For this there is the military. Keep in mind that we're in France, as much as if we were in Bordeaux, or Tours.'

Serge averted his gaze and glowered instead at the items on my grandfather's desk. His eyes rested at length on a jade and silver letter opener, my grandfather's recent promotion gift to himself. Serge seemed to be holding his breath.

'So, you are my cousin, and you are here. We may not know each other, but we are blood brothers, truly.' Even as he said this, my grandfather silently enumerated their vast differences, grateful that no external eye could draw a connection; save, now, for Madame Barre. 'And you must tell me why you've come to me. It can hardly be simply to say hello, seeing as we've never met. Seeing as our fathers barely knew each other . . .'

'Your father was a baker,' said Serge, accusingly.

'He was. He died when I was very young. You probably weren't yet born.'

There fell, again, a silence, during which both men listened

to Madame Barre opening and shutting drawers outside. She
knocked, put her head – now prettily hatted – around the door:
'If you don't need anything further?'

'No. Of course not. Good night.'

The silence fell more deeply when they knew that she was
gone. Young Serge, a strapping specimen, unlike Jacques,
seemed to struggle physically to form words. When finally they
rushed forth, they did so in little jets, as if from a disused faucet.

'The farm is – was – the farm was never big. Never much.
But enough. My father, Georges, built it up – from our
grandfather – a little. He built a new house. Two floors, gabled.
A porch. The barn is – the barn was – fine. I grew up there,
you understand, and my brother and sisters. I'm the oldest. You
know that?'

My grandfather waved with his ringed hand, wanting Serge
to get on with it.

'And the workers, the villagers – the Arabs – their fathers
worked for our grandfather and they worked for my father and
for the last six years they've worked for me – but all my life,
they've known me. Always. I've dug alongside them since for
ever, and hoed, and harvested, and—'

'And now?'

'Was it they? I don't know. I saw no faces. We weren't there,
thank the merciful God. One, Larbi, gave a warning. A man of
sixty, at least, a gentle fellow. He used to dandle the girls on his
knee. At dusk, a warning. And the way things are going, the
way things are, we heeded it. We took the truck and fled. Spent
the night at the neighbours' – we managed to take – hardly
anything. A few, small, irreplaceable things. The ladle our
grandfather brought from France – but not the wedding dress.
Not the silver platter.'

'Against what did you remove these valuables?'

'But I'm telling you. They razed it. Everything. The house,
the barn. The livestock inside. That's the worst of it – the
animals burned alive. And they'd rather that than steal them.
That's how much they hate us – hate me. Hate our innocent
babies. And they've known me all my life. You see?'

'But what had you done to them?'

'Nothing. That's my point. That's what I'm telling you. And when I said to Larbi, "But why my farm?" he replied, "The buildings may be yours but the land upon which they stand is ours. Since for ever." The country's going mad. I'm ruined. I have nothing left. But knowing what has happened in other places, we're lucky to have our lives. There are many who've paid with their lives.'

'Paid for what, exactly?'

'I don't know. I don't know.' Serge looked at the letter opener, at his own hands, grimy on the polished wood, at the imitation Watteau on the wall behind my grandfather. Anywhere but at my grandfather.

'And I?' said Jacques LaBasse. 'You come to me . . . why? Because you think I can rebuild your farm?' He was less stern now, knowing that Madame Barre had departed. He did not know his cousin; young Serge had been, perhaps, a brutal employer. But it was true that what was happening in the countryside seemed not to need reasons, nor to respond to them. 'I'm sorry, I have no money. Only a decent job. And a wife and two children to support.' He was thinking, he said to me, how grateful he was for his mother's little pretensions, for her insistence on his education, for his own natural gifts and the rallying of his teachers, for the progress from generation to generation without which he might, so easily, have been sullying the mauve silk chair and seeping rank anxiety into the perfumed air, burdened with this tale of woe. 'Why me?' he asked Serge again. 'Why do you come to me?'

Serge stared at his cousin. 'Where would you have me go?' He clenched his fists. 'My brother, my sisters, have so little more than nothing, although my eldest sister has housed and fed us for two weeks already. We need – I need – to find work. I'm not begging for money, you know. I'm strong, and young still.'

'I don't know any farmers,' said my grandfather. 'Are you willing to move to the city?'

'If I have to. If that's where there's work.'

'I'll see what I can do, Serge.' My grandfather stood at last. 'I'll do my best. Come back in three days.'

My grandfather had been smiling to himself, staring off into the bushes, because he had done, by his lights, the right thing: he had found a job for his cousin.

'What did you get him?' I asked.

'He was essentially illiterate, poor guy – as I suspected, as was evident from his demeanour. He could read and write, but so poorly . . . there weren't too many options. He was strong. I found him work as a bellboy. It was a start. Not at the St. Joseph – that would've been intolerable for all concerned. But at a perfectly respectable hotel, down on the waterfront.'

I pictured the strapping Serge, sun-lined, his farmer's biceps and solid thighs squeezed into a crimson suit knobbled with brass buttons and braided epaulettes, a pillbox rakish on his gold-streaked curls, elastic under his chin.

'He was back to working with the *indigènes*, of course. There wasn't much I could do about that. Not with his level of education.'

'What happened to him?'

My grandfather waved his ringed hand, wrinkled now, its veins blue mole trails pushing up the skin. 'I wish I knew. He'd moved on from that job before the worst of the trouble came. We had nothing in common, and he wasn't the sort to write letters. I imagine he's somewhere in France, or his children are. I heard he lost the job because he fought. With a Muslim colleague, a respected young concierge at the hotel. He didn't want to take orders from an Arab, or some such nonsense. You do what you can for people, but that's all you can do.'

I nodded, trying to decipher the message I felt must be encoded in this anecdote.

My grandfather spoke again: 'It was Serge, though – it was what he said, what happened to him, I realize, in retrospect, that first made me think, made me recognize that we might have to leave. Made me look to metropolitan France, in spite of myself. Because it was like a cancer, he was right in that, a cancer that metastasized through the most beautiful and precious of bodies, that glorious country. And it's still suffering, all these years later.'

'But it was their land first, wasn't it?'

My grandfather rolled his eyes impatiently. 'You concentrate on your schoolwork, my little one, and don't rattle on about things you know nothing about.'

6

Clearly, I reflected later, I knew nothing about it, not least because I could not locate, in my grandfather's story, the source of his lambent smile, however faint, however many years later. The story only raised questions; it did not answer them. My grandfather had behaved as he had seen fit, as blood and faith had dictated, and this in spite of himself – because all he had wanted, upon encountering this lumbering remnant of his humble origins, was to be rid of him. Serge was not a part of the LaBasse story, tailored as it had been for the glory of our own, ever smaller, circle; just as Estelle, the flighty prodigal sister, could not truly fit the narrative. Little bits of them had been chipped, like grindings, from the larger stones of their selves, and pressed into the mosaic of my grandparents' path: it was a way simultaneously to remember and to forget those who fell by the wayside, who were lost on the road to the Bellevue and success.

And if the story said nothing about Serge – as the story of Estelle revealed, ultimately, so little about her – then I was thrown again, as always, back to the teller, in this case to my grandfather himself, and to my own need to make of him something he might not be. His story was in no way shameful; he had done, so far as one knew, a good turn; and yet I felt that in some way, in his telling, my grandfather had fallen short. I couldn't have said, then, what I would have wanted of him; I merely resigned myself to irritability and remained silent for the remainder of the evening.

But in retrospect – a light in which we may not see more

clearly, but at least have the illusion of doing so, as the event has been filtered, by faulty memory, into a shape that is now useful to us, just as my grandfather's encounter with Serge had been, so that whatever he left out I could never retrieve, so that the story was inflexibly his own — I consider that I wanted my grandfather to have been a hero, to have redeemed Serge's broken life and taken the poor man's family to his more prosperous bosom. I wanted, at the least, my grandfather to doubt his achievement, to see that exchange not as a triumph but as a shortcoming, so that I might look upon the story and cull an immediate meaning, an immediate consoling promise: that although my grandfather had failed to save Serge, he would not similarly fail me, fail us; that he would set no limit on what could be done to re-cement his crumbling dynasty; that he would, in his wisdom, give without counting the cost.

'Concentrate on your schoolwork,' I was told, and I did, working even though I was on vacation, because it was the only thing I could think of to do that seemed like doing; but I was aware that I studied not because it was important but rather as if it were important, because any benefits my efforts might later confer on me could not — or certainly not in time — save the life of the LaBasse family. I feared change, and the absence of change. I concentrated on my books and the boils on my back, as if I were in a dream, a nightmare whose end must come, as if, with my eyes sufficiently tightly screwed, I might get by.

When I was a little girl, I had believed that if you looked long and hard enough at a picture you might enter into it, leave behind the faded furniture of everyday and walk in oil-bright fragrant glades among eighteenth-century picnickers, or join the windblown fishermen along some ageless rocky shore. I didn't muse on how one might get back from within the frame, just stood and willed and waited for another story, another life, to begin around me. When, after failing on numerous occasions to make the leap, I asked my mother whether my belief was misguided, she did not want to disillusion me.

'Perhaps,' she said, 'perhaps it's possible, if you look very, very hard.'

At fifteen, I knew which picture I would have chosen: it would have been the watercolour of the Bay of Algiers, that sun-filled, gleaming wonder, painted at a time when everything still seemed possible, when the city might just have become – the impossible future of that pluperfect past – in time, Augustine's City of God or Camus' City of Man. I would have willed myself into that picture, and made that world different with the knowledge I brought – of the loss and hate to be averted. I would have altered the course of history. I would have willed Camus' dream of a paradise on earth, of a Mediterranean culture democratic and polyphonous. I would have sheltered from the sun alongside Moorish fountains and ambled in the casbah greeting Sami's forebears in fluent Arabic; I would have dreamed in the shade of jujube trees in an air drenched by flowering almonds.

But at fifteen, I was no longer a child, and I knew it to be impossible.

7

The summer burst, in full cicada-song, upon us, the roads jammed with cars whose plates spoke of glamour – 75 and 92 for Paris, but others, too, from Milan or London or Munich – and the beaches overflowed again with their human cargo. The hotel filled, although not with the families of Cécile, or Laure, or Thibaud, and ultimately less than in other years. The Iraqis invaded Kuwait, to American outrage, and the adults, at summer cocktails on patios or in villa drawing rooms – parties which my parents and even my grandparents attended as though the months before had never been; but how else could they have behaved? – discussed the role of Europe, and more particularly of France, in battles that were sure to come over that country and its resources. They noted with dismay the halted construction projects along our coast, the soaring unemployment rate. They lamented the oblivious grandiosity of the nation's leader

('He thinks he's an emperor, that's the trouble,' scoffed my grandfather, once again, of Mitterrand, an observation that I thought would only originate in a like mind). There was talk of the further tightening of European ties, the collapsing of internal borders and the cordoning of Europe as a whole, a move of which my father and grandfather approved, as a means of closing out definitively the other worlds, the second and third. 'What is the second world, Maman?' I asked, but she merely shrugged and stroked my arm.

From our enclave, all the world appeared to be in motion, in the face of which the LaBasse family – never in tune with the times – planted itself, and resisted: there would be no divorces, or selling out (although my grandfather harried my father about his plans to upgrade, to reach for the fourth Board of Tourism star, insisting that this recession was a time for consolidation; and my father, or so he told my mother, replied in American fashion, 'You have to spend money to make money, Papa,' prompting only a disgusted sneer), no accommodation to the superficial, temporary aberrations which they took, well, every-thing, on every plane, to be.

I lived, with Etienne, largely within the parameters of house and garden, willing to expose my riddled skin only to his undiscerning eye: I donned my flowered bikini and read, belly down, on a chaise longue on the patio, my books the replace-ment for my former hours of boredom shared with friends, while my brother ogled me from the shade. I hoped the sun would dry my spots, and it did, somewhat, but not enough for me to venture cheerfully to the beach, to be a leper among the unblemished on its shores. Still sleeping poorly at night, I dozed by day, felt myself to be a peculiar nocturnal creature, without moorings. I hoarded glimpses – like pictures – of lives that had once touched mine: Thibaud sent cards from his Nordic travels, cheerful scribblings about the churches and beer gardens, with no mention of his lady. I spotted Marie-Jo, at a distance, in a speeding convertible with a man's arm around her shoulder, and again, laughing, with Thierry, at the poolside, while I cowered in my grandmother's dining room in a long-sleeved, high-collared blouse, and endured Madame Darty's discourse on Virginia Woolf ('*très* Breeteesh'), whom she thought I should read, as my mother shot me sympathetic smiles from the far end of the table. (Madame Darty, thrilled to have been admitted to my grandfather's circle, provoked in him, as I had noted that first evening, a frustrating vagueness: she so readily held forth – an occupation, at his table, which had always been his own – that he lapsed into silence and total concentration upon his food, feigning so perfectly an old man's deafness that Madame suggested, to my grandmother, an ear doctor whose instruments might remedy the problem. 'Today a hearing aid,' she advised, 'can be no bigger than the pit of an apricot!')

Lahou and Sami had faded entirely from view, but from Frédéric, who telephoned on the eve of his departure for a month in London and Edinburgh, I heard that Sami had withdrawn from school and would not resurface in the autumn, or only as the skulking menace outside the gates come to deposit and retrieve his beloved.

There was talk, in July, of Becky coming to visit in August, a prospect that sent me into thrilled confusion. (I was not sure whether we were friends, nor whether she would want to spend her afternoons at the Bellevue and would force me to accompany her there. It struck me that she might recoil at my newly developed physical deformities, or at my brother's, and deem me a virgin for life.) But the flurry of possibility was short-lived. The plan, it seemed, had been Eleanor's (as had my own trip, I recalled), devised to retrieve her wayward daughter from the clutches of an unsuitable young man; and Becky, when informed of it, had wailed and stomped with such distressing conviction – had refused her food, in fact – that Ron had intervened, and soothed his women, and found the girl an internship in the English department of his little college instead, Xeroxing and collating under a secretary's watchful eye, in the comfort of an air-conditioned office. Becky was to enter her final year of high school – not, as had been threatened, in public school – and was, while I lay sombrely sunning, touring the East Coast from Virginia to Maine to view her options. She would eventually, and perfectly appropriately, plump for Sarah Lawrence, a college overflowing with privileged rebels such as herself, whose primary aim was successfully to limn the margins of respectability, to engage in satisfying black–clad bohemianism without straying beyond the pale.

Upon hearing that Becky's arguments with Eleanor now involved a man (whose unsuitability had doubtless been paramount in her choice of him), I concluded that her defloration had been accomplished at last. It meant that she, too, had slipped further away, into the realm of adulthood; and that now, in my virginal set, I could number only myself and Etienne. (Rachel was not mentioned in my mother's conversation, by which I deduced that she still had not become a problem; for problem is what we all become to our parents, as we cease to be children.)

As for my parents, in their continuing: my grandfather, although he resumed no formal role in the running of the Bellevue, was nonetheless, as I have said, proprietary of his creation. He damped and overrode my father's enthusiasms, frowned upon his son's decisions, drummed his fingers with impatience at Alexandre's plans – 'Castles in Spain,' scoffed my grandfather – until he came to the point of Madame Darty-like deafness with regard to his successor, and beetled about the hotel delivering unsolicited and contrary indications to the senior employees my father sought to manage.

Stymied, my father shrank, his energy sapped. He clung to his title and its privileges, while his own father needled him and whittled away beneath him. My father would slowly loosen his grip, give in to the biblical commandment that he honour his parent, and heed the stronger man's wishes: no expansion, no renovation, no fourth star that year, or the year after. But the capitulation came at a cost – in time, we would see, the ultimate cost – and he rose less early, stayed out less late, clapped fewer backs and threw out fewer – far fewer – belly laughs. He turned to my mother (although not to my mother alone) for succour, and he kept eating.

She, ambivalent, railed now against both men, father and son, but never in the one breath. She alternately defended and denounced her husband, and in this dialectic found a way to go on. She wished him dead, his father dead, she wished the Bellevue under the sea. She was not careful what she wished for, but her wishing (and her praying, which she conducted privately; I do not know what she prayed for), for all its stridency, made continuing possible. Her wishing, far more than anything else, I took as the sign that the family would survive: her wishing for difference was something I had always heard, a tune familiar in its hollowness, and in its very insistence it staved off change. The dark day would come, I assured myself, when my mother would cease her wishing; as long as she wished, we were safe.

8

If, in previous years, I had wondered whether September brought an ending or a beginning, in 1990 I had no doubt. The days had slogged, a behemoth each, unsparing, through the summer. I had not known a time so slow (although as I remember it, I have to tell myself it felt that way, those long afternoons in the garden now telescoped into a single dreary day), so very near to stopping altogether, and yet slow not in fullness, as my American summer days had been, but with a weight of emptiness unaccountable. Such interruptions as there had been revolved entirely around my family (a weekend visit, coincident with Bastille Day, from Tante Marie and her two younger sons – the ever-working husband and his nearest offshoot having remained behind in the estival emptiness of Geneva – marked the nadir among these), and so had not served to reshape the passage of hours, as pleasure so readily does.

The one unexpected and confounding delight that marked that summer came, unheralded, from my father, against whom I remained joined with my mother in tacit resistance. He, for all his dismay at his own father's tentacular and undermining reach through the Bellevue's inner workings, was not unaware of my own doldrums, even as he recognized that to my adolescent eye he was the enemy. In a stand I now see as courageous (then, my side already chosen, I was unsure what to make of it, and would have, were it not for my mother's chilly admonition that he was still, and above all, my father, spurned his advance), he suggested – one tedious night at the dinner table when, in response to his query about my day, I had raised a sullen eyebrow and stretched my mouth into a thin, grim line, without speaking – that he and I, father and daughter alone, should have an evening on the town.

'The belle of the ball needs a ball, does she not?' he jested, with a flicker of his fading bonhomie.

'What are you talking about?'

'Well, last summer it seemed as though we couldn't get you to come home; this summer, you're loath to leave it. I know you've had your nose to the grindstone, but all work and no play makes Jill a dull girl.'

I shrugged, spearing a lone green pea only after great effort. When I looked up, it was past my father, at the gilded torment on the wall behind him. 'Suffering breeds character. We learned it at school.'

My father chuckled. 'Good, very good. Why did the man beat his head against the wall?'

It was an old joke in our house. 'Because it felt so good when he stopped.' I kept my tone flat.

'So, what say you give your head a rest?'

'What would you suggest, exactly?'

'A date. Your old dad is asking you out on a date.'

I sniffed. 'As if.'

'Come off it, Sagesse,' my mother interjected, with more animation than was now usual at our dinner table. 'I think it's a great idea. You can't spend every day moping around the house.'

'And why not?'

'Because you know it isn't healthy. Your father's right. You need to get out – and he's a great one for a good time. He'll show you.'

'Because he's already been everywhere without us?'

My mother stiffened. 'Because he's your father, and he has invited you, you little minx.'

My father, during this exchange, had turned almost tenderly back to his food. He was piling his plate with a second helping of slick little roasted potatoes, and the corners of his mouth glistened with a matching oil. He looked as Etienne looked when tucked up in his bed, about to be abandoned, with no recourse. My mother made a face at me, a 'Go on' face, her brows furrowed and her nose narrowed, with a light, ducklike dipping of the head.

'When did you have in mind?' I asked, spotting a stray gleam on my father's chin.

He looked up.

'Your chin,' I said, patting with my napkin at my own.

'So it's a date with my nanny, is it?' he smiled as he wiped, resolutely buoyant.

'It's your idea.'

'Only if you promise not to treat me the way that girl treats your brother.' We all looked at Etienne, who appeared to try to wave. 'How about Saturday, then? I should be able to get away in good time.'

'Whatever. I'm just here, you know.'

It was agreed.

'Where will we go?'

'That would spoil the surprise, my dear. Always take a woman by surprise.'

'You ought to know.'

He glanced at me then, from beneath his lids, as he resumed feeding, plying two large potato chunks into his mouth, and his eyes were almost triumphant.

9

On that mid-August Saturday, as he had left for the hotel before I drifted down from my room, and made no sign of life all day, I bitterly assured myself that he had forgotten, that at seven, or eight, the phone would ring and he would announce, with no trace of guilt, that he had last-minute business to attend to. I did not allow myself to hope; although already, the day before, I had had Fadéla iron my favourite dress, a cream polished cotton with cap sleeves and an unwieldy shawl collar, acquired the previous summer before all the trouble, that fell in a mousse of gathers over my dimpled knees and made me feel like Marilyn Monroe. ('It's the very devil, this dress,' Fadéla had complained. 'A laundress's nightmare. What do you need it for?' 'I just need it,' I'd snapped, unwilling even with the maid to let my anticipation show.)

At seven, with still no word, I retreated to my room and shut the door, flopped upon my bed in my salty T-shirt and pretended to sleep. I told myself I had been right to despise him, that he treated my mother and me alike, fed us false promises and kept his gifts for strangers. I told myself he was disgusting, reviled the image of his plump and oily chin, the dapper roll of his nape with its shiny, wisping tendrils that had formerly been a site of my particular childish affection. I loathed his hairy knuckles, the thick wedding band, the press of his belly against his starched shirts, the curl of his lashes and the curl, too, of his ears, those dainty close-to-the-head appendages which I had inherited and was generally proud of. I boiled in my fury, and boiled him in it, as if he were one of the damned on the dining room wall, and I satisfied my rage by leaking hot tears onto my pillow and into the roots of my hair. 'Oh Etienne,' I said to my brother – who was far away, being fed in the kitchen by the stout and unsmiling nurse – 'You're so lucky, not to know that he's evil. An evil monster. And I wish he'd just disappear.' Which was, of course, the very antithesis of my desire.

At eight, or shortly past, I heard the muffled sounds of arrival,

the faint flute of my mother's voice in the hall and my father's
oboe in reply; then steps upon the stairs (I sat up); then a knock,
but timorous, on my door (I brushed my cheeks and blinked,
and ran my fingers through the tangle of my head).

'Yes?'

My mother, outside, crooned, 'Sweetheart, are you ready to
go?'

'Where?'

'You didn't forget? Your father's waiting.'

'But he's so late.'

'He's here now, chickadee. How long till you're ready?'

I opened the door and presented my crumpled, sweaty self to
my mother's scrutiny. 'A little while. I've got to take a shower.
I didn't think—'

'Of course he didn't forget,' she chided, with such conviction
that I knew she, like me, had expected the worst of him.

'Will he be cross?'

'I don't think so. Just hop in the bathroom and get going. It's
what women do, you know: keep men waiting. It's not such a
bad idea.'

I got ready, with as much care as if Thibaud stood in the
front hall below. I surveyed my hair and, upon consideration,
left it unwashed, because I didn't want it to drip on my dress. I
soaped my boils carefully, without scrubbing, so that they
wouldn't seep. I powdered my armpits and scented my neck. I
put on a hairband and took it off again, tried instead to tousle
my shorn locks. I chose my newest bra, lacy, with a bow
between my breasts. I buttoned the dress carefully, adjusting the
collar in the mirror several times when I was done. I fastened at
my neck a pink quartz necklace of my mother's, and applied a
sheen of baby-pink lipstick. A crease in my cheek remained
from where I had lain, and my left eye was puffy, but I could
do nothing about these flaws. In the gloom of the unlit
bedroom, I hesitated over my shoes; I wondered about carrying
a purse. My mother came to check on me.

'Now,' she said, 'be ready, or he might be annoyed. It's a
quarter to nine, you know.'

I dithered.

'These shoes,' she said, holding up a pair of pink ballet flats. 'No purse.'

'But those shoes are – they're a kid's.'

'And you're a kid. Come on. You look lovely.'

I followed her downstairs, as nervous as if indeed on my way to a ball, patting at my lined cheek in the hope the mark might fade. My father stood in the living room, swaying to jazz from the stereo, a scotch and soda fizzing in his hand.

'Hey, gorgeous,' he grinned, suddenly handsome to me again, in his sober suit with his greying curls and his brown-skinned solidity. 'Your mother's got you in training, I see: keep 'em waiting. Well, it was worth it.'

I smiled, unbelieving, shy. 'The shoes look dumb.'

'The shoes are just fine. The dress is – what's the word I'm looking for, Carol?'

'How about "divine"?'

'The dress is divine. Quite right. Etienne,' my father called to my brother, who was about to be wheeled up for his bath, and who jerked his head sleepily as my father gripped his shoulder, 'have a look at your beautiful sister! My sister never looked so good, I'll tell you that!' He put down his drink. 'Hang on a minute – ' he headed for the kitchen ' – I've got something for you.'

I looked at my mother, who smiled, a genuine smile.

'Was this your idea?' I asked, suddenly sure it had been.

'His very own.'

Another panic beset me, clamming my palms. 'What will we talk about? Maman?' I tried in vain to remember a time I had spent alone with my father, and could think only of that dishevelled January afternoon. 'We've got nothing to talk about!'

'Don't be silly! He's your father. You're just having date anxiety. Perfectly normal.'

I wanted to scream: surely it was not perfectly normal, to know one's father so little. Becky could never feel such anxiety about Ron, I thought; and then it struck me that Becky and

Ron would never do such a thing, risk an evening without Rachel and Eleanor, an evening out; Ron, of the nervous laugh, who permitted so much, would never allow it. I raced through possible topics as I stood, marooned, in the middle of the *salon*: all seemed dangerous: the hotel, my grandparents, my mother, his mistresses . . .

My father returned bearing what looked like a cake box, the size of a pastry. 'For my date.'

'We're starting with dessert?' I broke the seal with a chewed forefinger. Inside, on a crinkly bed of tissue, lay a single glorious gardenia, yellow, each matt petal moistly spread before me, precise and perfect. Its perfume rose from the box like a vapour.

'Let me pin it on.' My father leaned over me, his fingers fumbling slightly (I wondered if he was nervous too), and chose a spot on the wide swathe of my collar. I could feel his exhalations on my throat, and eyed the medusa sheen of his crown beneath my chin. He pressed the flower to the cloth and worked a glass-headed pin around its stem, close to the bud, so that the gardenia floated there, seemed to breathe upon my breastbone, above my heart, and bathed me in its scent.

'Now let's look.' He put his hands, warm, on my shoulders, and stepped back. 'Beautiful.'

Any vestigial resistance evaporated (I had thought it a well and found it but a puddle): I felt beautiful for the first time in almost a year, in the liquid embrace of his gaze, and I was grateful. 'Shall we go?'

In the car, my fingers against the buttery leather, my dress glowing over my knees in the blue dusk, the roof open to the first, admiring stars, we did not speak. Music (it could have been the fateful Debussy) rolled over us with the breeze and the hum of the engine: my father smirked at the road ahead, and occasionally, from the corner of his eye, at me. I – like so many faceless others, I was aware – felt the power of his enchantment, and willingly succumbed.

He took me to a restaurant in a village by the water, not far away. The evening streets were quiet, but the *auberge* was bright, the dwarf trees outside it decked with winking fairy lights and the blaze from its windows as radiant and yellow as my flower. The maître d'hôtel seemed to know my father and ushered us, with exaggerated deference, to a table from which we would see the garden and feel, through the open casement, the whisper of the night air. My father ordered for me, while I admired the oil paintings on the wall, the stiff napery, the silver flute of orchids, and leaned my head to the quiet chatter of the prosperous, in couples and small gatherings around us. Our waiter was a crimped-haired youth with pimples along his chin, and an impervious calm, whose whisking, steady gestures and quiet nods could only have been the result of emphatic training. Feeling lovely, I half expected him to note my beauty, to smile conspiratorially, admiringly, as I was, in the room, closest to him in age; but whether from education or actual indifference, he seemed not even to see me, slipping artful delicacies before my eyes with an impersonal stealth, and I was left to bask in my father's – and only my father's – attentions.

Conversation proved effortless. In my sudden apprehension I had disregarded the fact that at this, at least, my father was a master, a paragon of charm, here in his element, who averted all discussion of his own psyche as efficiently as the waiter served our food, and discoursed instead upon the restaurant and its chef, upon the art around us that I so openly admired, and upon the seventy-five-year-old Russian exile who had painted it, setting up his easel on this adopted coast and capturing its light; upon the lessons my father had observed in the Bellevue kitchens, which led to such wonders as the platters before us – the lobster ravioli in its pinkish scallop broth, the lamb chops with their dainty wings of bone and succulent medallions, the mould of ratatouille that perched on the *jus* like a little fortress by the sea. He alerted me to the origins of the wine, from vineyards around Avignon as old as the French popes: I clasped my ruby-washed glass and observed its colours dancing in the light, saw that it made my fingers, through the liquid, stretch into bones finer and more elegant than they were, a glorious illusion of adulthood. And when my head was swimming with images of swarthy peasants plucking the ancient vines with their gnarled hands; and of the Russian in his smock, spilling ash on his palette while he worked; and of the white-hatted young chefs-in-training beating sauces – in sum, with the heady wealth of life that blossomed around us in that very room, he asked me, it seemed for the first time, about my dreams for my future – uncertain as they yet were, but predicated on my recent, feverish studiousness – and wondered whether I might care, eventually, to study abroad, in the United States, perhaps. Which led to a discussion, mellifluously guarded, about my mother and the hopes she entertained, he claimed, for my American heritage, of which I had not been aware.

Fortified by the surroundings, by the rich taste of tannin in my throat, by the sophisticated odour of the burgeoning gardenia, I wanted, suddenly, to ask my father questions in return, to ask about the stories – my mother's and my grandmother's – through which his life had been constructed for me . . . and yet the very thought of asking brought a fluttering in my chest, a faint breathlessness, and I postponed the moment again and again, through the almond soufflé and the bitter sludge of coffee, which he chased with cognac in its domed glass, until the moment was past. That, the one moment when he was all mine, as I wished him, slipped away unexploited because I was afraid to find, yet again, that my ideals were mere misconstructions.

We walked after supper in the full night, to the end of the block, where the sailboats clattered at their moorings like restive horses and the moon rose over the sea. From the lone café along the waterfront emerged strains of band music, the jaunty overtones of an accordion, and my father, suddenly, clasped me to him and broke into a dance, my bosom pressed against his chest, the flower crushed between us as we waltzed up and down the pavement. I could only throw back my head and laugh as I was spun, vaguely aware of my white skirt ballooning at my knees and of the pressure of the asphalt through my soles, conscious of his guiding pressure at the base of my spine and of the warm, liquorish cloud of his breath. He was laughing, too; he wanted this too. We were both eager, and free, and as we

slowed and gasped and I giggled, still, I was simultaneously aware
of being – so briefly – in love with him; that this was all he
wanted of me; of any woman; and all he knew how to do; and
aware of being duped, of being – for all the beauty of my dress
and the particularity of my flower, for all that he had made me
and could see on my head his own fine, small ears – as faceless as
a mannequin, as readily replaceable. But I did not want to see
this latter truth, as my mother had not, as no woman could want
to; and resigned myself to his illusion as swiftly, surely, as did all
his conquests, so that as we ambled back to the car, still slightly
breathless, his arm over my shoulder emanating heat and reassurance, I screwed my eyes shut and stepped blind alongside him,
willing myself to remember this dream, to know in every
darkness, when my mother railed and wished against him, and
when I did myself, that this, too, was my father, and a gift.

10

The very next morning, as I resumed the lonely pattern of my
days (although not for much longer, as it was August), I was
already conscious that this memory was precious, dizzyingly
private. To my mother, on our return, I had said only, and
cheaply, that it had been 'fun'; but at breakfast I asked her,
tellingly, how it might be possible to preserve the gardenia,
which had wilted on my nightstand; and had ruefully submitted
to its pressing, in a volume of the vast dictionary, at the page (I
insisted) of 'pleasure', by which we all might, later, retrieve its
flattened significance. I did not know quite how precious the
evening was to be, nor that it would resurface in my dreams for
years, sometimes as a whirl of bliss and other times as my most
dreadful nightmare: a petrified perfection, a poison in every
glorious instant, in which I was aware that if I asked, if I could
only find the right question, I might preserve my father (as I did
the flower), and yet always unable to deduce, and I knew,
sinkingly, beforehand, that I would be unable to deduce, what

the question might be; and each time I remained silent, as I had in fact remained silent, hoping, mistakenly, that the wine and the silver and the twirl along the waterfront would be sufficient to keep him always with us, with me.

But the imaginary life that this one exotic outing assumed was not enough to alter the everyday; and for my father, whose aim undoubtedly had been to win me unconditionally to his side, it must have seemed a failure. I moped and skulked still, and although for an evening or two I made efforts at conversation in memory of the event, I could not retain its sheen, and at my father's first absence lapsed back into my mother's shadow, again picking stubbornly at his excuses, and coming to believe that for a night I had been bought, and simply addled by luxury, as I had fleetingly suspected at the time.

II

I turned my thoughts, then, gratefully, to school. I attributed the resurgence of my skin troubles to a healthy anticipation, and told myself my back would clear, finally, with cooler weather and with classes. I assembled my textbooks a week before the lycée opened, in tidy piles at the foot of my bed, and stacked a half dozen new notebooks (the fruit of an expedition, with my mother, to the largest stationer in town, the one in front of which I had ambushed Frédéric so long before) beside them, with my name and my various subjects carefully lettered inside their pink and orange covers. I took a new and conscious plunge back into my own life, as if the summer had been a sentence or a cure not unlike my grandfather's, due suffering for my accumulated and unconfessed crimes. I foresaw a period of choice; I believed I spied the future at not so great a distance. Change, I told myself, would come about in my own quarter, at my own hand; I would will it.

I wasn't free of my anxious waking nights, and still occasionally hallucinated violent endings for each member of our family.

I noted that a calm had settled over the LaBasse clan, in which only events I considered 'normal' seemed to take place. My brother was growing; my mother was praying; my father was losing his flush of enthusiasm for the Bellevue, bucking against his own father's clandestine yoke, fretting joylessly about its accounts (the economy was bad, the recession told on the receipts). My grandmother took to trembling, a habit which affected the force of her character not at all and was later to be diagnosed as incipient Parkinson's – but this, too, could be deemed normal: grandparents, being old, were expected to be ill. They were not, however, expected to be criminal.

In mid-September, the stout, beaky nurse left our service to marry a naval cook and was replaced by a smooth-skinned West African woman of my mother's age, named Iris, in whose capable ebony arms Etienne, the lover of skin, thrived and clucked. I kept an intermittent eye on the workings of my family, but focused my attentions upon life beyond, thirsty for it. I discovered the dowdy twins, Aline and Ariane, gratefully, in the first week of classes. In their gangly reserve, they weren't thrilling company, but they didn't know, or knew first from me, of my family's recent history (the beads of the story mine to fashion, the ellipses mine to select), and they basked in my eager attention. I gathered that back in Chateauroux, from where they had come, they had been teased for their skimmed-milk pallor and the redness of their hair, and had relied, by and large, on each other's company. They wanted above all to do well in school, considering an occasional ice cream at the stuffy parlour behind the library a risqué interruption of their work, for which they were grateful to my naughtiness and my pocket money.

As my mother put it, I perked up: I ventured, on occasion, to the twins' house, on weekends, and politely praised the lean lunches their mother provided. She was a small, tense creature with her daughters' red hair, but faded and lacklustre, and a habit of holding her mouth open, a dismayed O among her freckles, a woman of whom my own mother would have approved on principle, as industrious and unthreatening, although the modesty of their family situation did not encourage a parental encounter. Their father, moreover, was no likely companion for my parents, a beefy, wall-eyed brute forever hidden behind the sports pages, who emerged only to criticize his wife and daughters with a lopsided scowl that set them all shivering. He acknowledged me only in order to make occasional, hostile references to the comparative comfort of my upbringing ('I'm sure you're better fed at home than here, am I right? Oysters and caviar, is it?'). They inhabited a sad-eyed pink stucco house on the hill at the back edge of town, where Monsieur, having embarked upon *bricolage*, found he lacked either the energy or the time to complete it, so that the weedy back yard was stacked with bricks for an unbuilt porch, the living room with piles of flossy insulation material wrapped in brown paper for an imagined extension, and the bathroom walls were only half tiled. No progress was made with these improvements in all the time I visited the house, and I never saw Monsieur so much as wield a trowel.

From this hideousness I considered the twins' emergence – their survival – to be impressive, and I was relieved to find company whose dermatological fragility outstripped my own. They were asthmatic in the bargain, equipped at all times with blue plastic inhalers which they whisked from cloth pouches their mother had embroidered with their names, and which lent them, for me, a particular mystique, that of ailing nineteenth-century heroines.

Aline wanted to be a doctor, and when at last I invited them for an afternoon at my house, they did not gawk at the statuary or even appear to notice the Bay of Algiers on the living room wall, but were rather, genuinely and unabashedly, interested in Etienne, with whom Aline sat for an hour or more, talking quietly and examining his limbs in a pseudo-scientific fashion. Etienne, heartily accustomed to medical inspection, idled passive and cheerful in his chair throughout, while his nurse came and went around him, rolling her eyes in amusement at Aline's questions about the boy's bowel movements and his capacity for mastication.

In short, the twins were in every way a relief. They admired even my brother; they considered me prettier than they (as, to be honest, did I); they were very good at mathematics and welcomed my help, in return, with history and French. And above all, they fought a domestic dreariness that seemed to me more impenetrable than my own: they thought my concerns glamorous, and larger than theirs (again, secretly, for all my protests, I concurred); they seemed convinced, as I so wanted to be, that I must be destined for a greater future (I was half American, had been to New York) and when I compared our lives, relieved, I was inclined to agree. They made me feel that my friendship was a favour, and I prized the feeling.

At Christmas they presented me with a pair of pillowcases they had sewn, evenings, side by side in front of the television (their father had it always blaring, when he was home: although their house was small, sets dominated both the living and dining rooms, and there was another, I had been informed, beside his bed), with multicoloured daisies and with my initials, in large, looping script, threaded in baby blue. I was delighted that such effort had been made on my behalf, yet could not help but notice that the cases, a blend of synthetic and cotton, had the slinky feel of cheap hotel sheets. Nobly claiming them too precious to use, I folded them and retired them to my underwear drawer, where they lay untouched, until, much later, they accompanied Etienne to his ice-green room, as a reminder of me, and of home; and were used there week after week, boiled in the institutional laundry, until the daisies blanched and the threads unravelled and my visiting mother, in a spasm of guilt at my brother's incarceration, disposed of their ragged remains. I gave them each, in return, a pair of earrings, little green stones for Aline and little pink ones for Ariane, purchased in haste from the costume jewellers' in the shopping mall, and the girls gushed as though I had bestowed on them pearls without price.

12

It is small wonder, perhaps, that in the thrill of such pliable and devoted companionship, I failed to gauge my father's disintegration, to note that, not merely a foil for our miseries, he had embarked alone, and ploughed a furrow more isolate and determined than any of the rest of us, towards his own destruction.

The event, in all its television drama, came, at the time, as a shock only because I had for so long been vigilant against disaster, aware of its potential from the moment of my grandfather's gun – or from the moment, indeed, that Etienne arrived in our lives, his delay in my mother's womb a matter of so little time and yet of such ineluctable import. I considered that I had antennae for disaster – our household prophesied gloom in the Gulf when the press buzzed in congratulation at the efficiency of the Western assault, and was not surprised by subsequent footage of Kuwait's oil wells aflame: I had been trained to anticipate, even to feel relief at, the worst, because the worst always came and it was safer to know it – and yet my wariness had lapsed in the pursuit of my own, seemingly innocent, existence, at the library and the ice cream parlour and in the living room of two dingy, earnest girls whose inoffensiveness was extreme to the point of parody.

Which is to say that when my father killed himself, the act was not, in some absolute way, a surprise; but that its timing – in a valley of apparent quiet, so long after the era of tribulation had settled, and my little life had begun to sprout, seemingly, its own patterns, for the first time not wholly dependent, in submission or reaction, on the patterns of my family – was. In the intensity of my unilateral engagement, I had wished my father dead; just as, paradoxically, I had believed that that engagement, that very wishing, was the certainty that kept my parents safe. And although all reason had told me my will had no part in their story, that the practical demands of Etienne, or of my grandfather, might hold the family together, but not I, with my fevered but impotent imagination, once that will had been diverted from the present, from the past – from their lives – onto the future, and my own life, it seemed that some central, invisible force that had kept the LaBasses in organized orbit had vanished, flinging each of us, and my father furthermost, out into the ether alone. As long as I was wishing for it, or against it, as long as all my wishing was bound up in it, our family had retained its family-ness; and then?

My father's death came in the springtime. It had been almost a year since my grandfather's release. It was only a few weeks to my sixteenth birthday (I wondered how he could not have wanted to see that, and then remembered the year before, the rattling of my doorknob, and my father's thundering insistence that there would be no locked doors in his house; when in fact I had spent my time learning that life was but a succession of such doors, the very image of a corridor an illusion because nothing, and no one, could be anything but alone). It was twenty years since he had met my mother on the boulevard in Aix. It was springtime. (Who, without expertise, would have guessed that this was suicide season, that the very signs of nature's hope were enough to kill some people?) The submarine had come up for air. How could the seamen, tiny but visibly waving in their delight at land, not have given him pause? How, in the maze of uncertainty, of possibility, could my father have found the resolve for such an act? And was it, like my own embrace of life, a departure after his own star? Or was it, as all my other acts had been, a frenzied mothlike beating in the web of the LaBasses, a petty but fatal reaction? Or again, was it a meeting of wish and will, a poisonous confluence in his brain, like my hallucinations of all our deaths, but one which had spilled, unbidden, beyond the realm of fantasy?

The abiding question, too, for me, was this, and remains this: was it fate? Is our ending inscribed in our beginning – and, if so, in whose beginning? In his own, or mine, or Etienne's? Or in his father's, or in the very distant footsteps of Tata Christine, who returned to France and could not abide it, who retreated to the mountains of Algeria, become African in her very soul?

Was my father locked in a destiny, visible or invisible, from which no turning could have spared him? Was it that tense which locked him, perhaps, the pluperfect: the turning before he knew there was a turning, the choice made before he had known there was such a thing as choice, so that any future he might have wanted glimmered in that unreachable place, the might-have-been?

I dream that I could have saved him – if I had been a different daughter, if, that night in the restaurant, I had so much as knocked on the door of his heart, tried its handle, asked; but would I not have had, rather, to enter the watercolour of the Bay of Algiers, to try to change the course of history from long before his birth, a feat impossible even in the imaginary realm of childhood to which I had long ago lost access? And even then?

How is any of us different from my brother, I am led to ask; and the obvious answer is, for all our stories, not at all.

Nine

I

In the immediate wake of my father's death, however, the questions were far more practical. His body was still unburied when, home from school on account of the tragedy, I overheard my grandmother and my mother arguing, in hushed voices that hid nothing, about the possible catalysts for his deed.

'Everything was all right, now,' my mother said. 'It makes no sense, now. It's the *now* I can't figure.'

'Jacques and I have discussed it, and he's most concerned, he's meeting with the bankers this minute. Because the only reason we can think of—'

'No,' my mother hissed.

'The Bellevue has been less than half full for months, headed for debt – not his fault, poor lamb, or not entirely, I'm sure, although Jacques always doubted his business sense, but he so wanted to upgrade, he was desperate for that fourth star . . . We have to be sure he didn't enter into contracts without telling us—'

'This is your son! He would never do – would never have done – such a thing.'

'Never entertain a mistress either, I suppose? He was avid for a double life, a bigger life. Poor boy. It made him feel real.'

'That's absurd. You said it yourself, the women were about sex, that's all. The hotel – he lived for the hotel, he thrilled to run it, properly, his own way, at last, and if your husband hadn't interfered—'

'It is my husband's hotel, my dear.'

'Let's not argue. The last thing we need now is to argue. But I swear to you, he would never have gambled the Bellevue, not now, the way things are going. He saw that fellow, over in Cassis, fold last fall – he knows – he knew – that the couple in Carqueiranne are hanging on by the skin of their teeth – he wouldn't risk the hotel now.'

'We'll see. We'll hope not. He wanted new bathrooms throughout, a complete redecoration. He wanted the restaurant revamped. He talked about closing next winter for the work to be done; and if he meant it, if he was prepared to push ahead in spite of Jacques and common sense, behind his father's back – who's to say he wouldn't have signed contracts we know nothing about? He had meetings with architects, with the bank, with contractors, even – just from his secretary's datebook we can tell that much—'

'I don't believe it. You'll see. I can't – how can you – you slander your own son – and his corpse is barely cold!'

'You don't have a premium on grief, my girl. You, who were prepared, as I recall, to decamp at the first sign of trouble, over some fatuous little encounter or two—'

'How dare you! Never! Please – I think we should leave this alone now – we're upset, of course we're upset, and we say things . . .'

There was a silence. I, through the wall in the kitchen, hardly dared to breathe.

'If not that, then what?' my grandmother asked, disconsolate. 'That at least would be a reason. Then we could forgive him. Otherwise – I've racked my brains—'

'As if I hadn't? As if I've slept? The only one sleeping in this house is Etienne, who can't understand, who just can't understand—'

'Didn't the doctor give you something?'

'I don't want to sleep,' my mother said. 'I want – for God's sake, I want to wake up.'

'Could it have been a woman? Do you know? Was there someone, lately, someone new?'

'They weren't special. You said it yourself. They were never special. *We* were special. Besides, we never discussed it. Not since last spring. A year ago. Not since then.'

'But there might have been — I don't know — blackmail — some woman, some secret — a child — I don't know.'

'And he was afraid I'd find out?' My mother laughed, a bitter clip. 'Do you really believe he would fear that? A year ago, when I was still in ignorant bliss, I might have accepted that. A year ago, though, he thought he was invincible. If there'd been kids — even a dozen of them — he would have told me. It would have been a source of pride. That's the frame of mind he was in. And now? Now I knew, and he knew I knew, and we went on as if we didn't, but I can't believe, I can't accept—' My mother's voice was pinched. 'What does it matter, anyway, why? It's done.'

'If it was on account of the Bellevue, it may matter a great deal, to all of us, and for a long time to come.'

'It's that he's gone — that's what will matter, regardless. There's no answer to that. We all failed him somehow—'

'Nonsense.' My grandmother's voice was shrill. 'It is he who failed us.'

'We're angry. It's natural that we be angry, the priest said so only this morning. But we shouldn't look to blame, he said. We should pray—'

'We pray, we always pray, we'll continue to pray because that's all we can do — but there are facts, too, to contend with—'

'He was depressed, that's the fact. He was alone, some-how—'

'You're his wife.'

'I should have known.' My mother began to cry, her breathing loud and ragged.

'Who could have known? What is necessary, now, is to find a way forward. That's why the facts are important. We can't lose the Bellevue — it would kill Jacques, it would be the last straw—'

'You demon!' My mother cried in a burst of rage. 'It's that man and that bloody hotel that killed Alex!'

The silence was icy and absolute; and then my mother's voice came again, in an entirely other register, entreating. 'Don't go —

please, Madame! – Monique – Please. I didn't mean it. We're all upset – beyond upset – I just don't know how – there's no blame – but please, don't, please don't blame Alex.'

'Don't you?'

2

In the kitchen, my cheek against the cool paint of the dining room door, I realized that, intended or no, whatever its reasons, my father's suicide was his one great and defining action, the defiance of his weakness. A raging, faceless beast unleashed to bring change (how we had all longed for change) on the family, it was his Frankenstein, a living thing that would haunt each of us for ever, the spectre of his will. My father as a ghost had greater influence than his own father could ever have dreamed of; the single curling of his forefinger at the trigger would shape and sunder us as we could never have imagined, or, in all our wishing, wished. It had a life of its own. This moment in the kitchen was the first time that I realized my father was truly dead, that I glimpsed the enormous gulf between the imaginary and the real, when it dawned on me – confusedly, still – that the latter had ultimate power over the former, rather than the other way around.

We had lived, always, in a world of belief; in which stories created from the past had the weight of truth, in which our pessimism was the bulwark against disaster and our most privately husbanded hopes the food on which our unlived futures fed. We had believed – in God, in country, in family, in history – and thought faith sufficient; thought that the world, if our faith were astute enough, would bend to it. This in spite of Algeria, in spite of Etienne, in spite of the force of law, the unforeseen obstacles sent by a silent divine, to test us. After all, Jacques had anticipated the fall of French Algeria, and moved his family to safety. Alexandre had built a home for Etienne's preservation from the wider world. My grandfather had founded the Bellevue upon rock, and he, and we, and it, had survived the report of the first gun and its repercussions.

But my father, in truth, had lived only as if he believed; his faith had stayed with his grandmother and his country after all the other LaBasses had left, and had foundered with the sinking coffin. My father, like his cousin Serge, had been only half salvaged, too late, his only abiding belief in the might-have-been. Which we are always without, as I would always, hence-forth, be without my father. He had had nothing, in the end, to cling to but fact, of which death was the ultimate affirmation. Stories, the fragments shored up against his ruin, were merely that: fragments, words. And all the telling, which lulled my grandmother and my mother and even me, did not point, for him, to a future; that was a place we were left to seek without him.

I cannot travel to Algiers today. Even if I could, I would not find my father's, my grandfather's, beloved city, even in its traces. It is not merely that the street names have changed, that French statues have been replaced by Algerian ones, the geog-raphy altered by construction; it is that I would seek an imaginary city, a paradise conjured of words and partial recollec-tions, a place that never, on the map, existed: just as the Bellevue, today, is not the place it was to my fourteen-year-old eye, although all its landmarks are the same.

3

When my father died, I began to wonder, to dream, about my almost-uncle, about the shadow-man turfed from the LaBasse home before he was born. He, too, had a life, or had had one, a life which, for all I knew, continued still. His life, like my father's, must have been touched by fate; his story (another dropped bead) limned ours; his was the unmentionable ghost (had my father even known about him? I suspect not: my grandmother would never have told him, and my mother

CLAIRE MESSUD

assured me that she did not) that walked alongside my father's, Jacques's sin made flesh, the choice in my father's life made before he had known there was such a thing. Theirs was, perhaps, a might-have-been that could have changed the family stories, the family reality, altered its course even up to my father's last day.

In the beginning, when first this ghostly image appeared before my mind's eye, I wondered whether he walked, quite literally, beside us, whether Khalida's son, a bastard with green eyes, had been packed, by his distraught mother, off to France at the tender age of eleven or twelve, in the company, perhaps, of his youngest uncle, then himself a lad of little more than twenty. This uncle had been a boy, doubtless, known peripherally to my father at the lycée in Algiers, an indigenous wunderkind a few years ahead, bespectacled and sallow, with a downy smudge on his upper lip and a thoughtful manner, who had begun his studies – engineering, most likely – at the city's university at the height of the troubles and, in despair, had sought the advice of an admiring tutor, whose finest deed was salvation of this brilliant Berber student and the finagling, for him, of a place on a course in the tutor's native Lyons. And when, worn by years of solitary striving, by the disapproval of her family and by the strife into which her son was growing, Khalida – more like an aunt than a sister after all, the force responsible for her youngest brother's education – when she learned that he was leaving, seizing opportunity where the moustachioed French mathematician had offered it, she begged her kin to take Hamed with him, to free him from her sinful yoke, his fatherlessness, and to settle him in a good school in Lyons, where she might follow as soon as her finances (the money scrimped from mopping and cooking, the extras from her mending work) permitted.

And so, at the airport, at around the same time as Jacques, Monique and Marie took flight, beneath a winter sun that in its icy brilliance spared no crease or fissure, the trio stood near the check-in counter among the milling hatted Europeans and their girdled wives, alongside the clique of Air France attendants lounging in their pressed uniforms, as the rotors of the airplane roared their practice run outside the terminal. Khalida, wrapped in her frayed, fringed shawl, pressed her green-eyed boy to her bosom, his paltry cardboard case beside them on the ground, and wailed softly from her belly, her tears falling into his hair, while his uncle waited, eyes averted to the tarmac and the greasy plate glass that separated him from it, stroking his downy lip and blowing cigarette smoke through his nostrils like a dragon.

Little Hamed, in his short trousers, beneath which his scabbed brown knees trembled imperceptibly, submitted to his mother's embraces with his eyes open, not knowing what the parting meant, not knowing whether to cry ('Be brave, my little one,' his mother murmured, by which he deduced that he should not, but that he should want to). He tried to imagine what might lie ahead, and unable to, seeing in his mind's eye schoolbook images of snow-covered gables and crenellated castles, wondered what French air would taste like, whether he would find there the familiar smells of cypress, dung, the sea.

Installed in a cold-water flat on the outskirts of Lyons, uncle and nephew did not talk often, and then never of home. Hamed yearned for his friends, for his mother's touch – for the murmur of her voice – while his uncle, immersed in his studies, forgot, or did not know, to perform the simplest parental duties, like prepare a solid meal or set a fixed bedtime. The little boy grew hard and resourceful, foraging for cold supper and amusing himself in the apartment after school, a quiet, fierce child, all but friendless among the towheaded, taunting Catholics who were his classmates. He endured school as well as he was able, a place where teachers expected little of him and peers still less; he lived without, in every sense.

Khalida did not – could not – come. With the help of other brothers, she wrote, occasionally, in French, to her newly French son, stilted, formal encouragements and exhortations that divulged little about the state of the city, about the FLN threats and the new-minted, marauding OAS. Hamed's young uncle guardian raised his head from his books only to lament the divisiveness: he lived in a pure world of numbers and graphs, and preferred to stay there, knowing that neither France nor Algeria was, at that juncture, a fit place for a brilliant Berber uninterested in politics, but that in France, at least, he could hide for a while from the revolutionary call of his generation.

After the peace accords, after the French had retreated from Algeria, Hamed's French life grew worse, not better, a life in which he was marked for misery by the crimp of his hair and the tinge of his skin; but he had become savage enough to contend with it. Savagery is far from schoolwork: he excelled, instead, at fistfights and shirking, at avoiding the lycée where he had been jeered at and pelted with pebbles. He located other boys like himself, marooned far from home, and they banded together. As soon as he could, his voice broken, his own lip darkening, his arms sturdy and muscled, he abandoned the schoolyard and signed on as a mechanic's apprentice, willingly condemning himself to a fate of blue monkey-suits and oily spanners. His uncle, by then respectably employed by the city at his professor's recommendation, pursed his lips in vague disapproval but did not intervene. There were girls, there were cafés: they constituted pleasure of a kind, and Hamed, to his distant mother's dismay, did not see or did not want to see that this, as a Muslim in France without a raft of diplomas, was all there would be, for years to come.

Eventually, and early, there was a wife, children. The pieces had fallen into their immutable places: this was his life. And perhaps, just possibly, when my own father's car broke down on the outskirts of Lyons, on its family way to a long weekend in Paris, the green-eyed Algerian who slid, belly-up on a stained dolly, beneath it, was my uncle. They might have met and never have known. I, a child of eight, may have been sulking in the back seat, sticky-fingered, with a comic book, Etienne strapped in tight beside me, dozing, and may barely have noticed the coveralled mechanic, eagle-browed and tough, wiping his hands on a rag while speaking to my father about fan belts and radiators.

4

Or maybe it was not at all like that. Maybe Khalida kept her boy at home – when her brother offered to take him to France she said, after long deliberation, 'No,' unable to envisage a life worth living without Hamed, her little protector, the only relative who had never cursed her, standing sternly at her side. He, rambunctious like all children, played truant, and fell in with the groups of restless ululating urchins on the edges of the FLN, making a local name for himself as a rabble-rouser, anti-French. In consequence of which, targeted for his green eyes and his cockiness, he fell to an OAS bullet in the madness of early '62, while a passing car beat its horn in the tattoo of '*Al-gé-rie Fran-çaise*' and the Europeans in the afternoon street looked away, witnessed nothing, as his lithe little body, on the cusp of puberty, crumpled in the gutter, his cheek bruised against the kerb and his green eyes wide open, as his blood, in a viscous stream, puddled beneath his frame and dribbled into the road-way, attracting the attention, primarily, of a band of lazy horseflies. It would have been hours before Khalida came home to find him missing, and hours again before she discovered him, untouched, his limbs stiff and his clothes crisp with dried blood, in the purple dusk, as the headlights of cars passed over him and continued on their way.

Or maybe he stayed home and was lucky. Perhaps his family forgave his mother's sin made flesh, and rallied around her, around him. Perhaps, with his mother's guiding hand, Hamed navigated the turbulent years and attended the Lycée Bugeaud after all, once its name had been changed, dogged only by taunts about his green eyes and insufficient Africanness, for which he compensated by hard work and a gentle disposition, a quiet boy trotting along to the mosque with his uncles, his kinky hair flattened with water and the soles of his feet brown and hard as leather. Perhaps, then, he went on to university, as his mother wished, and shone there, a disciplined mind, trained in secular intellectualism, and emerged in Algiers as an academic or journalist, proud emblem of his new country, with an eye on the future and the sheen of hope around him like a halo. In which case the moment of decision came later, at around the time of his unknown brother's death, when, on account of his life's work, Hamed awoke to find a price on his head (because this is what happened, in riven Algeria, at the turn of the century's final decade), facing the choice between flight and terror just as he had as a child, at the hands of the French. And if he stayed, and lived, then for how long? Sooner or later the masked men would have found him, in his car on his way to the university, or in his office, or at home, in bed, while the sun struggled to rise over the white city and the bay; and we would have read of his death in the newspaper, one among so many, overshadowed by the assassinations of Europeans, and would never have known that we had lost a relative; would never have mourned.

In flight, perhaps, if he had been willing to sacrifice his homeland for his life, to choose the suitcase over the coffin, as the rest of the LaBasses did, then he may have turned, as I have done, to the New World, gathered up his wife and sons and daughter and flown, while there was still time, to Washington or New York, where he sought work worthy of his training and former eminence while driving an unsprung, clattering taxi through the city streets to pay the rent. In which case I may lately have peered at his nape through the milky screen, from the back seat, and glanced at his licence with its mug shot, the name typed in capitals, wondering at the green eyes, muttering under my breath about his slowness with my change. If he was listening to the French radio station, then we may even have conversed – as I have been known to do – about America, in French, about how he finds it and whether his children are thriving, about how he misses home, the casbah with its stairwells and alleys, the countryside of his distant school holi-days, the groves of citrus trees and even the rare swarms of locusts that descended to gorge on his grandparents' farm when he was a boy. The French language would have been a bond, rather than a division. And still, in our meeting, we would never have known that we were bound by blood, that we were family; and had either of us been aware, with the choices made for us so long before, we might not have acknowledged our communion, deeming the gulf too great, the mistrust too profound. There would not be words for what links us and separates us at one and the same time.

5

But if I reach back further, and ask not what may have been, but instead what might have been, had choices not been made as they were, before my father and my almost-uncle were conscious of such a thing as choice, I can imagine Khalida still under my grandparents' roof and Hamed – hardly younger than my aunt – playing with Alexandre and Marie in the echoing, ill-paved courtyard of the apartment building, three solid little children squealing over soccer, or cops and robbers, the boys joined in a hunt for beetles to drop down Marie's dress; and on weekends slipping together to the saltwater swimming baths, Hamed my father's protégé and boon companion. And later, at school and at the lycée, even, the two of them, their satchels strung on their backs, racing side by side among the sedate grown-ups to the candy store and wandering the alleys idly, arms linked, in the waning afternoons, each reluctant to break away and head for home, engaging in the time-tried rituals of boyhood friendship, becoming blood brothers (as they already were, without perhaps knowing it, living as if they were what they actually truly were) by their pricked thumbs and the mingling of the ensuing wet beads; fighting each other with sticks for swords; pilfering fruit from the market to share in the Jardin Marengo, beneath the leafy trees, and dragging back home to hide their juice-stained tongues from their respective, stern-faced mothers.

And when the trouble came, in their intimacy they might have resisted it. Or they might not, but each would have been forced to see his shattered world differently, through the eyes of his dearest and oldest friend, and that would have shifted, however minutely, the temper of the era. And if, a thousand or a million times, such alternatives had been chosen, by my grandparents' peers, and by their grandparents, and by their grandparents in turn, perhaps the troubles would not have come as they did, or when they did. Camus' dream – the city of white stone flashing in the sunshine while its life, a fully lived, multichromatic life providing common succour to every shade and faith and diverse history of the Mediterranean basin – might then have been possible.

After all, Saint Augustine was a half-caste, fourth-century son of a Berber and a Roman; and Camus himself, although French, was a Spaniard by descent; and my grandfather's own mother, originally Italian, had a sister who married a Maltese. And myth, or perhaps fact, would have it that at the turn of the nineteenth century a ship carrying nuns to the Antilles foundered at Ténès, on the coast of Algeria, just west of Algiers. Ravaged by illness, the small town where the nuns found refuge had few living women left; and at the orders of their Mother Superior, these sisters followed God's calling out of celibacy and into Muslim wedlock. They settled and propagated, uniting their European, Christian blood and culture with that of their husbands and hosts; and their Superior, the town's saviour, was revered for her actions as a marabout, under the name of Lalla Mériem Binett. If two hundred years ago this was possible, it should have been so a century later, and even now, in Africa as it is in France, or in America.

In truth, I know better. My French ancestors, as far back as Tata Christine, landed on blood-soaked soil, and nothing could undo that beginning. But Tata Christine's isolate path, against the temper of her times, led her into the mountains, where she may, indeed, have delivered Khalida's mother or father into this world. The turning away from utopia – the turning from a city of God on earth – was made time and again, in gestures of all magnitudes, some so slight as not to seem like decisions at all, just as my brother's lingering in the womb, by the measure of the clock, was so slight a matter; and by his fate in the world, so great. Hamed, I imagine, is the key to my father's heart that was never presented to him, the possibility of a different life. It might have altered nothing for them to have known and loved one another as brothers; but I doubt it. I live as if this might-have-been existed, shimmering in the imaginary; and if it is but an 'as if', I have learned, then it is none the less real for that.

6

The casket, at the funeral, had to be closed; upon it rested a photograph of my father squinting and grinning, as if, instead of fragments, that grinning figure lay within. Why my father shot himself, we cannot know. He had not gambled the Bellevue, for all my grandparents hoped it – as a punishment, perhaps, for the blame they felt they bore; if so, they never conceded blame. The hotel, it was true, had fallen on lean times; but so had most others in the region. Alexandre had not secretly been diagnosed with cancer. No lover came forward to press her claim, no unheralded LaBasse children were found squalling at his grave-side, their palms out for money. He and my mother had not argued; nor had my grandfather tyrannized his boy any more directly than was usual. Nothing among his papers shed light on his plans, no scribbled memos or bank transfers indicated the careful premeditation that might, even partially, have explained this act. He left no note.

The local newspapers nonetheless had their day: above a picture in which, black-clad and sombre-faced, we stood assembled on the church steps (but for Etienne, in motion as the shutter snapped, a smirking blur), they ran the headline 'A Family Doomed to Disaster'. Inevitably, they recounted the trial, and elaborated on my brother's disability; and they did their best to imply a sinister mob-link to my father's death. My mother, stocking-footed, fell tiny and sobbing into my arms at the sight of the article, while my grandmother shook her head and grimaced, whether at the press or at my mother's weakness she did not say. My aunt Marie, lately arrived, stood by blinking and bovine.

'We'll prove them wrong,' my grandmother assured the rest of us, her cheek ticking in annoyance and her hands atremble, 'and we'll do it by raising the hotel to new glory, and by sticking together. That's what the LaBasses do.'

My grandfather shifted on his feet, and sighed.

'Such filth is like water off a duck's back,' my grandmother continued, 'unless we give in to it.'

My mother struggled to right herself and restrain her tears. 'We'll see,' she said. 'We'll go on, to be sure. It's just a matter of how.'

'We'll go on as if this hadn't destroyed us,' my grandmother said.

My grandfather coughed, a dry, old-man's cough. Aunt Marie blinked furiously and turned to the window.

'I'm not sure that's possible,' my mother replied, her hand in the small of my back, where my father's had been when we had danced, months before. 'What's best for the children is what matters.'

'Quite,' said my grandfather at last, but vaguely, as though he had not heard my mother's words and wanted only to be on his way, out of his son's tainted living room and back within the safe gates of the Bellevue. 'My retirement, it seems, was short-lived. I haven't been to the office for two days. I think, perhaps, I must—'

'Of course.' My grandmother reached in her purse for the car keys. 'I think – will you be all right?' She turned again to my mother, who glanced at me, and nodded.

'We'll be fine. You'll come for supper?'

'Naturally.'

7

I remember those days as a grainy flickering of curiosities: my aunt twisting her high heel in the mud at the cemetery and emitting an inappropriate yelp; Marie-Jo's voice on the telephone, which I recognized at once and pretended not to, saying of myself, 'She's not here right now, but I'll have her call you back,' before hastily hanging up; the twins stopping by with a casserole from their mother and all the notes from the classes I had missed copied out in their neat hands, doubtless in front of the television in the evening; the radiant sun rising day after day as if nothing had happened, the breeze kissing our cheeks and forearms in supreme indifference to our fate. One afternoon I hid in my father's closet, hunched on his shoes, wrapped my head in his suits, smelling him, the traitor cologne that I had taken for so long as proof of his adultery, now all that remained. One night I climbed into bed alongside Etienne and stretched my body out against his, curling my feet beneath his feet as if we were lovers, while he bucked, a little, and snorted in his sleep. And again, in bed, with my mother, at her request, aware that my back lay in the shallow left by my father's.

It was springtime. The first tourists were arriving, cheerfully oblivious. The water sparkled. The traffic on the main road whooshed and grunted as it always had. Daily I scanned the horizon for rising submarines, and saw none, and wondered if their absence was a sign. At my own wish, I returned to school after a week, surrounding myself with Aline and Ariane as if they were bodyguards, flinching so visibly at voices of sympathy that my fellows backed away. Instead of home, I haunted the twins' grim little house, putting off, and off, the return to our villa, where my mother, wan and frail, excelled as the widow.

She and I spoke a great deal, in the evenings. In honour of my father, she played his music on the stereo and sat, hollow-eyed, in her armchair, with her hands folded in her lap. We did not speak about him, although he was always with us, and although each of us struggled mightily with our guilt (Had we so hated him, then, and had he known it? What would it have meant to have loved him as we ought, not to have counted the cost of his sins and wished, so many times, that he would go?), we dwelt instead on the minutiae of our days, living as best we could as my parents together had lived, pretending. It was posed in this way, me on the sofa, but straight-backed, my feet firm on the floor like a soldier's, my mother opposite in her nacreous austerity, that the prospect of departure was first mooted.

'I've been talking to your Aunt Eleanor today,' my mother ventured, passing a bloodless hand through her hair, and seeming to shiver.

'Oh yes?'

'She – it was her idea, really, but it's not without merit, I think. I wonder – she wondered – whether a change might not be the best thing for you.'

'For us?'

'Well – you see, my life – Etienne – no, for you.'

'I don't want to go live with Aunt Eleanor and Uncle Ron. Maman, don't be silly. I want to be with you.'

'That's what you think, first off, but I want you to give the idea some thought—'

'I know that I couldn't—'

'Besides which, it's not a question of you living with them.'

'Then what?'

'I thought – well, the idea was of boarding school.'

'Boarding school? Where?' In my world, such exile was only for the stupid, although I was faintly aware of boarding schools for the children of gentry, little titled snobs who said 'vous' to their parents.

'Oh, not here, sweetheart. Not in France. You're half American, remember. My half.' She laughed, mirthlessly, and spoke in English. 'The half you have left.'

'It must be incredibly expensive.'

'That's not for you to worry about.'

'And Grand-père and Grand'-mère – what do they think?'

'I haven't asked them. I'm asking you. They believe in turning over a new leaf, or they did, for themselves . . .'

'But Grand'-mère said, and she's right – we've got to stick together.'

'Is she? Right? I don't know. Think about it. Think about the future.'

In subsequent days, I did; and realized that, in spite of everything, I never truly had before. The accordion of my life (so long and so short both, a life) had never been a question. I had not thought of myself as a person who could choose. Freedom was a terrible prospect, exhilarating and terrible. I was on the cusp of sixteen: adulthood was no further in front of me than the summer of Thibaud, my grandfather, and America was behind me; and my mother was leaving it to me to decide.

8

It was a family story told of me (my own, and almost my earliest, bead) that when I was a child of four, one November afternoon, I was taken by my parents, with the infant Etienne in his carriage, for a walk in an unfamiliar park. I was bundled in a fur-trimmed camel coat with leather buttons, a matching fur-trimmed toque upon my tightly braided hair. I wore woolly black tights, the crotch doubtless drooping near my knees, and patent leather shoes with straps. I skipped ahead of my parents, arms out, crying out to the park at large that I was a princess, turning back on occasion for adult approval of my antics. At the centre of the green we came to a fountain, in the middle of which squatted Neptune with his trident aloft and, at his ankles, a clutch of open-mouthed fish, from whose orifices, in summertime, water gushed abundantly. It was then winter, however, and the fishes merely gaped, their goggle eyes on me, while beneath them the silty pool lay quiet, a wistful leaf or two adrift upon its stagnant water. I hopped up onto the fountain's marble border and proceeded to trot round and round, insisting to these figures that I was indeed royalty, my arms outstretched, my eyes intermittently catching the approaching, colourful blur of my parents; when suddenly, to their consternation, I appeared to pause, and then jumped, tights and coat and toque and all, into the water up to my waist. Hauled, bedraggled and chattering, from the murk by my bellowing father (his arms still, then, the safest refuge), I was asked why I had done it. I announced – and it was true; I remember precisely the instant of teetering – that, aware that I was going to fall willy-nilly, I had assumed my fate by making it my intention. What I actually said was simpler, of course: 'I was falling, so I jumped.'

Already at four, from somewhere, I had faith in intention – as if the fact that it had been willed altered the quality of my wetness, and the cold that ensued (three days in bed with soup and stuffed toys). And that, always, was the lesson of my family's stories, of my great-aunt Estelle, of Tata Christine, of my grandparents, of my mother. My father's youthful experience merely reinforced the belief: departure was offered to him, not chosen, and then thrust upon him, with perilous, some might say fatal, consequences. The implication was clear. Severance, departure, once mooted, must be seen as inevitable: that has always been my unquestioned belief. If choice is illusory, the aim must be to keep the illusion intact. With this corollary: there is no returning. We need the might-have-been because we know it will not ever be; the imaginary is our sustenance, but the real is where we live, a reality of fragments. We move the pieces when movement is possible, because possibility and necessity, on some plane, are one; because what is fated and what will be are inescapably the same, and the illusion our only choice, choice our illusion.

And so, because I had to, I chose to go. Aline and Ariane were at once impressed and horrified at the prospect ('America? But people there are so shallow, no? And everybody drives cars everywhere. Will you go to New York?'). My grandmother, tight-lipped, could hardly restrain her contempt, while my grandfather seemed barely to absorb the information, so preoccupied was he with the columns of red ink that laced the Bellevue's monthly accounts. (My mother did not explain how the school would be paid for, but I gathered, eavesdropping, that she had hoarded her share of her parents' small legacy and husbanded it well, and that the funds were to be drawn from a hitherto undisclosed American store.) I asked Etienne, repeatedly, what he would think of my leaving, and he merely giggled and rolled his eyes, stretching a hand, or a foot, as much as to say 'I am here. I will always be here. Here are my limbs.' Foolishly, I believed him.

9

The choice of school – it seemed at a cursory glance that New England was thronged with such institutions – was limited by the tardiness of my application (it was June by the time the decision to proceed was formally taken), and consequently centred upon places where Aunt Eleanor could tweak a connection. In this way, and to my chagrin, I was presented with only three options, two of them single-sex schools – one to which girls were invited to bring their own horses – and the third a formerly all-male establishment on the outskirts of a small town in New Hampshire. The brochure portrayed ruddy youths trudging along snowy paths, their backpacks sagging and their teeth agleam; and again, similar groups sprawled with notebooks in the spring, beneath flowering trees, while behind them a white spire glinted in the unblemished azure sky.

The catalogues for all three schools, on glossy stock, bore lists of student-to-teacher ratios, of ethnic minority and international attendance, of colleges chosen by graduates in recent years. Smiling alumni peered out from the pages, alongside ebullient quotations about their experiences. Teachers were shown in concerned attitudes, monitoring students over Bunsen burners, or writing on blackboards; or, whistle in hand, at the edges of autumn fields, upon which blonde girls with strong thighs and flying tunics wielded hockey sticks with fierce determination.

'Is this what school was like for you?' I asked my mother, bewildered at the sleekness and enthusiasm of it all.

'I went to the local Catholic high school, dear,' she said. 'So, no. But college was, a little. A little like this.'

'It doesn't look like school at all.'

'It'll be fun.'

'That's my point.' I pointed at a photo of a school play, elaborately staged and costumed. 'What's that got to do with school?'

'It's a different approach, that's all. You don't have to go, you know.'

But faced with these seductive plates of golden youth (not a parent, not a family in sight), I could not fail to succumb. 'I want to. I can be – anyone – there, can't I?'

'I suppose you can, if you put it like that.'

'Who I am, it doesn't travel, does it?'

'What do you mean?'

'Nobody will know, except what I tell them.'

'No. Nobody will know.'

I selected the co-ed boarding school, in spite of its remote location ('Show me New Hampshire on a map,' I entreated my mother), largely because I saw a face in their catalogue that resembled Thibaud's, while all the girls at the other two schools looked confidently alien, like escaped guests from the Spongs' cocktail party on Cape Cod.

The selection made, I bragged to Aline and Ariane about it, conjuring for them my Boston summer, as they sat, rapt, cross-legged, in their spoiled back garden. They turned the catalogue pages again and again, till they were grimed with fingerprints, and marvelled at the banks of computers, the microscopes, the quaint chapel.

'So you won't sit the *bac*, then?' asked Aline, wrinkling her pale brow.

'I don't suppose so. Not there. I can always come back after a year and—'

'So you'll become American?'

'Don't be silly.'

'But I mean – for university – you'll go to university there?' She seemed appalled.

'I don't know. Maybe. It depends—'

'But you'll have to, won't you?'

'I don't have to do anything.'

She shrugged. 'Well, otherwise it doesn't make sense, does it? Because if you just have to come back and prepare the exams here, then why go?'

'Because I can. Because I want to.'

Her sister sighed. 'It's beautiful, Sagesse, but it just seems so – remote, you know. I guess it's hard for us to understand. I mean, you're American, so—'

'I'm not American.'

She blinked. 'Well, half American, then. You're not French, anyway, not the way, say, we are . . .'

'What's that supposed to mean? Of course I'm French.'

'Sort of.'

'Not sort of . . .'

'I think,' Aline interrupted, 'all Ariane is trying to say is that we would never belong there, so it seems strange to us.'

'I won't belong there either, you know.'

'Then why go?'

'Because I don't belong here.'

'Precisely,' said Ariane. 'You're different.'

10

When I reported this conversation to my mother and grandmother, my grandmother rumbled with disgust.

'That's the French for you,' she said. 'Small-minded.'

'But Grand'-mère, you're French.'

'I am, it's true, in a way. But I've always disliked the mentality of metropolitan France. In Algeria, we weren't like that. When I think of our ancestors, struggling so hard for the glory of France – for this, only to be told that we don't belong—'

'But you wanted to come here—'

'We wanted to because we had to. And they treated us like dirt. And the *harkis* – betrayed by this country, both here and in Algeria – they treated us all like dirt.'

'Then surely it's good for me to go to America?'

'America? As if there were anything for you there!' My grandmother blotched and quivered. 'The LaBasse family survives by sticking together. We always have. This is where we belong: together. And your mother knows it. Or you ought to, Carol. By now.' She turned, fierce, upon her daughter-in-law. 'You plan to send this child off into the wilderness – no family, no structure, no context. And for what? To a cesspool of violence and McDonald's, the Styrofoam culture, the land of packaging—'

'What exactly,' asked my mother tightly, 'would you have us do? In favour of what do you stand? Not of France, apparently. So I've offered my daughter a chance to start again. You'd have me send her off to Algiers, I suppose, in honour of some vague nostalgia?'

'Oh honestly!'

'No, I mean it,' my mother persisted, 'What is she supposed to believe in? If Alexandre had believed in something, then—'

'Then what?'

'Never mind.'

'I want to believe in the future,' I said, in a joking tone, trying to avert the friction. 'That seems like a good thing to believe in.'

'The future doesn't exist,' retorted my grandmother sourly.

'Maybe the past doesn't either. Maybe nothing does,' I waffled. 'Maybe only Etienne knows what really exists, because that's what he does, that's what he focuses all his energy on – existing. But he's not giving away any secrets.'

'Nor is he heading off to some overpriced summer camp that some marketing manager calls a school. He's staying right here. And so should you.'

My mother took a deep breath. 'And when Alexandre wanted to stay, in Algiers, and you were leaving—'

'That was different. And, as we know now, a bad mistake.'

'It was his choice.'

'Was it?'

'Come on,' I tried to intervene. 'What does it matter now? We can't do anything about it.'

Both women glared at me.

'We can, we ought to do something about what's happening now,' my grandmother said.

'But I want to go, Grand'-mère. Maman isn't forcing me.'

'As if you knew what was good for you! You're just a child!'

'Maman doesn't think so. She trusts me. Don't you?'

My mother nodded, wearily.

'So that's that.'

II

'Let me tell you something.' My grandmother shivered in her seat, as if a painful ripple ran through her spine. She composed herself; then spoke. Her hands, veiny, spotted, were crossed in her lap. She reminded me of an iguana: ancient, somehow primitive.

'When your grandfather first flew over here to look at land, he didn't tell me what he was doing. He just said it was a business trip. I thought he'd been sent by the St. Joseph. I had no idea. And when he came back, and sat me down, and your father and your aunt beside me, in a row in the living room, and marched up and down in front of us waving his hands, rattling the china, and told us that he had signed the papers on this patch of scrub in some unknown little burg in France, I cried. I simply dissolved. Your father, all of fourteen, younger than you are now, stood up and stormed out. He turned white, the purple vein at his temple throbbed, ready to burst. Just a boy. He didn't take a jacket. In his shirtsleeves, he slammed the door.

'The row he precipitated was unending, terrible. Always between them. There was no meal where it didn't hover over us like a swarm, where it didn't bubble through the conversation, through the simplest words, like lava. Eventually, Alexandre more or less ran away from home. He spent more and more time at his grandmother's house – and how could we condemn that? – and less and less with his family. He'd come home in the afternoons, and leave again before supper, like a visitor. Sneaking home to bed like a thief. Believe me, I cried about it. By myself, in private, when my husband was at work and my daughter at school. Within the year, he asked my mother if he could live with her altogether, and she was delighted. She even came to me to plead his case – a vulnerable stage, she said. My own mother. Important not to disrupt his education. Fine. He and your grandfather had been at loggerheads for months by then. Although in truth it had been, perhaps, since for ever. It had always been difficult between them.

'Your grandfather was – well, an old-fashioned father. He'd had to do without one, himself, from a young age, and he felt it was important to be firm, important that a son obey. But adolescent boys, they don't want to, do they? So it was almost a relief when Alexandre went away. Evenings were so much calmer. No roaring and stomping, no slamming doors. It was better for Marie. And he wasn't far away, in that last time. I saw a lot of him. He came by after school. And he seemed calmer, too. He and his grandmother shared a special bond.

'But that was later, and it's by-the-bye. I wanted to tell you about my time. I was no less distressed than Alexandre, you understand, at Jacques's news; but I couldn't turn heel and run away. I had responsibilities, to my husband, to my daughter. Family. I don't know how to explain what that time was like. In '57, we had endured – it was awful – war, on our doorstep. Outright war. The cafés, the airport, the casino – bombs, everywhere; children, teenagers, mutilated and killed . . . and the stories from the countryside were even worse. Families – women, infants – slain in their beds, dismembered. Grotesque. The city was swarming with paratroops, the casbah was sealed off with barbed wire. Everyone lived in fear – not so much for

ourselves, even, but for our children. And we didn't know
where this terror had come from, how it had escalated. Each
new governor they sent from France gave us hope, for a little
while; and in time we had won the battle in the city. The
paratroops did nasty work, I don't deny it, but they had no
choice, and they did it well. They flushed out the terrorists,
squashed their cells, made the city habitable again. People now
talk about torture, but it was on all sides. It was war.

'And let me be clear on this: the Muslims, most of them, felt
as we did. I'm sure of it. We all just wanted our lives back,
wanted life to be as it had been before, in that beautiful city.
Wanted to be able to go about our affairs in peace, under the
trees and in the squares, to go to mass or the market or the
cinema – the wonderful old Majestic, say – without listening
for gunfire and passing truckloads of soldiers, without looking
askance at every brown face, wondering if this young woman,
or that scruffy boy, hid explosives in their bags . . . And for a
while, that seemed possible. It seemed, after the Battle was won,
that we could resume where we had left off. After the madness
in May '58. Which is when Jacques first came here. It seemed
possible.

'From the terrace of our apartment, you could glimpse the
water – we were on the hill, and could see over other buildings.
And at dawn, before anyone else was awake, I would stand
there and watch the sea change with the light, a vast mirror,
and listen to the city starting, like a motor, the hum of traffic,
and the *boulangerie* below opening its shutters, and I'd spy on
the greengrocer's boy as he set out the stands on the sidewalks,
all the beautiful colours, the artichokes and pomegranates, the
apricots, the lettuce, in pyramids against the grey pavement, and
the sky bleeding and then blueing . . . sometimes I'd see ships,
or boats in the harbour, making their way, and I'd chart their
wakes, like ripples in silk, and it was the world I'd always
known, and I loved it. To you, what is Algiers? Nothing – an
unknown, a regret, a dream. But to me, it was life. That
moment, in the morning, was the purest happiness for me. I
thanked God for it, every day. And then I'd waken your

grandfather, and the children, and the day would begin, and I'd know that the rituals – of breakfast, of school, of the house, of our friends; in short, of our lives – kept us safe. And in '57 and early '58, we'd thought we might lose that for ever; and we hadn't. We had triumphed. There was order, more or less, and I can't tell you the relief I felt. It was physical, as if my lungs and nerves and arteries were opening again after some hideous hibernation.

'And into this came your grandfather with his plans and his contracts, and he said that we had to go. He had no faith in de Gaulle. When the General made his promise at Mostaganem, in June of '58, and I said to Jacques, "It's not too late, we can still stay – sell that land back, and we'll stay" – he shook his head and claimed it was a lie. I didn't want to believe him. I tried to persuade him otherwise. Marie tried, too. It enraged me, his stubborn refusal to see that the city was still standing, that we were still living in it. I wasn't a child; I wasn't hopelessly naive; and I knew what I wanted. I wanted to stay. Over a year later, when the apartment was up for sale and the movers ordered, I threatened to stay, with the children, to let him go off alone. It was a dreadful thing to do. We didn't speak for a week. It was worse than the fights with Alexandre, because it was *I* who was betraying him. Can you imagine? In retrospect, I'm stunned at my behaviour. And I prayed. I prayed morning and night for God's guidance, for some sign . . .

'And when the sign came, I regretted asking for it. It was in the late autumn of '59, when that fat peasant Ortiz set his *ultras* marching through town like the fascists that they were, in their khaki uniforms, with their Celtic crosses. I was on the way home from lunch with a friend, and was stopped by their *défilé*, a veritable militia of men with murder in their hearts, and that great fat Spaniard at the helm. I knew, when I saw them, that there would be no peaceful end to it all, when the men on our side had become terrorists like the others, when they had sunk as low. And later, I heard him, that Ortiz. I felt it in my bones when he said it was "the suitcase or the coffin" – that slogan the FLN had been spitting at us for ages, by then – and I knew that Jacques was right. I couldn't know what was to follow, but I knew it was true. The suitcase or the coffin: is that a choice? But it was true, and it was all we had.

'Up till that moment, I had hoped; things had been better. But then I knew that my will was foolish and insignificant; and I told Jacques that we would go. Together. As a family should. It took another year and more, but we went. And from then on, it was bad to worse. From then on, it was the end. It came more quickly than we might have expected, when it came; and God knows what Alexandre and my mother lived through and witnessed in the time after we left. But he didn't want to come with us. If it hadn't been so bad with his father, I would have persuaded him. As a mother, I feel now that I should have. I could have protected him, even a little. From his father, perhaps, as much as anything. But he was already far from me, from us. Because of the row, because of their wills.

'For me, when I remember home, I can still stand on our terrace in my mind's eye, and feel myself a part of the day beginning, and know that it was bliss, while it was; but that was lost to my boy, because he thought he knew what he wanted, and we let him stay until it was all rubble, until the very death of it.

'I'll tell you, the truth is, I'm lucky: I don't live nostalgically. Every morning, I wake up and look out my window at the Mediterranean sea, vast and creeping, and I smell the pines and the heat on the breeze, rising up the clifftop, and I'm in Algiers again. I live, still, in my heart, in Algeria. And that was burned out of Alex, razed in him for ever. And now, still, I ask myself, who knows how it might have been different, if he had been spared that death, if we had travelled together?'

Her story finished, my grandmother perched awkwardly on her chair, looking neither at my mother nor at me, but at Etienne, from whose slightly parted lips a tendril of saliva was slowly stretching. He sneezed.

'You couldn't have known,' my mother said, at last. 'You couldn't have forced him, even if you had known. He wanted to stay.'

'The suitcase or the coffin,' repeated my grandmother. 'For Alexandre, it was both.'

'That was a long time ago. That has nothing, necessarily, to do with his – passing.'

'It marked him.'

'Maybe so. But so did many other events, later events, and probably earlier ones, too. We can't keep asking why.'

My grandmother turned. 'Of course not. But I'm telling you because I know, in my heart, that it was a mistake. And you're about to make another.'

'The situations aren't comparable.'

'You think not, but in some ways . . . It's a matter of moorings.'

'I agree absolutely,' said my mother. 'That Sagesse needs precisely that; and right now, I think boarding school may be the best place to find them.'

'You're a fool, my dear,' my grandmother chided. But her voice hung with resignation and regret.

'If I hate it, then I'll come home. Won't I, Maman?'

'Nothing stands still, Sagesse. You should know that by now,' said my grandmother.

'And there's no turning back,' I finished for her. 'But I have to go. I have to. Maybe I'm like Grand-père, not like Papa. Maybe I see the right way forward.'

'If there is such a thing.'

'The only way forward. Maybe that's what I see.'

12

The remaining months before my departure were dedicated to preparation, and to my family. My bedroom floor was piled, in July, with all my winter clothes, with boots and jackets and woollens that my mother and I crammed into a steamer trunk to be sent ahead by ship. I packed my teddy bear, and a pile of photographs; and when my mother enquired whether I would like to take anything from the house – anything at all – with which to decorate my room, I asked for the watercolour of the Bay of Algiers. She did not hesitate; she seemed glad to be rid of it. It was wound in a ream of bubble wrap and hidden among my pullovers in the heart of the trunk, to hang on an institutional wall in a cinder block dormitory in rural New Hampshire where, had I but known it, I would sit and stare at its sunlit crests and hear – but as clearly as if I were within its frame – the soughing of the Mediterranean against the shore; and I would find conjured in my mind's eye, in the still night hours when my wispy-haired roommate lay sleeping, motionless as a bolster in the bed opposite, my own imaginary city, half Algiers, half home, with alleys and promenades and beaches at once familiar and a revelation, and as real as any place I had ever been.

In some ways, preparing to leave felt like preparing to die, not least because the break with the known was absolute, the new beginning unimaginable. I emptied drawers, discarded papers, just as down the hall my mother emptied my father's drawers and pored over his files. She sent his suits to charity, gave his shoes to Fadéla for her husband, along with a little-used felt hat and some unworn shirts. I took the grey angora sweater of the time of the trial, in tissue, to Aline and Ariane as a gift. I sat on the floor and reread old diaries while purporting to clean out my desk.

I wrote to Thibaud, with whom my correspondence had dwindled almost to nothing over the year. He was awaiting the results of his *bac*. I told him I was leaving France for New Hampshire: he replied at once. Somewhat less mystified than the twins, he was nonetheless taken aback: the routes to his future, the hurdles, were so clearly defined and reassuring, and those of the United States so apparently arbitrary and irrelevant. He had heard about my father, and wrote about that, too, in a strange, formal, elliptical way, about memories and the spirit surviving and God's will and courage – mine, naturally.

He seemed to see my departure as a flight from my father's ghost – which it was, to be sure, in part – but what amazed me in those busy months was the degree to which the earth had closed up over my father, the way his traces flitted in the air (I kept thinking that I heard his voice, downstairs at night, among the notes of his music) but did not tarry, as though he were always on his way home, nearly with us, and yet not solidly absent.

My mother, in her widow's grief (if such it was), took refuge in organization: of my father's estate and accounts; of her own clandestine money; of my brother's medical supervision; of my life to come. She kept moving, always: the expression used, of such women, is that 'she came into her own'. She grew firm with her mother-in-law for the first time. From the day after the funeral until the day I left for Boston, I did not see her cry.

In emulation of her fortitude, I attempted to put my old life in order. I rang Marie-José and asked if I could visit her; which seemed, to my surprise, not to surprise her in the slightest. After a subdued lunch with my grandparents – my grandfather, present but distracted, drummed his fingers on the table intermittently throughout and spoke little, while my grandmother volunteered halfhearted anecdotes about Titine and her housekeeper, about Madame Darty, about the church charity drive, and lapsed again and again into silence, during which only mastication and Zohra's distant kitchen movements were audible – I tiptoed down the stairs to Marie-José's apartment and rang the flickering bell.

13

There is little to tell of our stiff hour in her old pink room, familiar but somehow smaller, like something from a childhood dream. When I arrived, she hugged me tight in silent expression of sympathy over my father, but I felt as cold as if sawdust rather than blood floated in my veins; and when she tried to pin my eyes with her own tear-shined orbs, I merely looked away, like a guilty cat, and padded down the hall to our old sanctuary.

'I hear you're going to America,' she volunteered, settling

her long, brown frame against her white-painted bed, and wriggling her bare toes. 'Lucky you! How wonderful to escape!'

'I suppose,' I said. 'I just wanted to thank you for calling, and to say good-bye.'

'I've felt so terrible, you know,' she fluttered. 'About everything that happened.'

'Sure. Well, never mind.'

She offered a drink, a snack; I declined. She had evidently envisaged an emotional reunion, and did not know how to respond to my disaffection.

'School will be weird without you,' she observed.

'I doubt it.'

'I'm so scared about this last year. I don't know if I can pass the *bac* the first time.'

'You've got months to study.'

'That's what my mom says, she says studying makes the time pass just like anything else – only it's more productive.'

'M-hmm.'

'You've been working hard, haven't you? Hanging out with those twin girls, the grinds. Bet they're good for copying homework off, eh?'

'They work hard.'

'Not like that skanky bunch you were consorting with last year. That creepy druggy guy and his friends. And Frédéric. Jeez. What a bunch of losers.'

'They're all right.'

'Thierry is thinking of preparing the exam for naval college, did you know?'

I shook my head. Marie-José proceeded with unbroken strings of gossip, a chatter as light and as constant as a brook, while I sat and looked at her, up close. This was what I had wanted, why I had called: to see her, to memorize her, to measure whether she had changed. Her features had altered their proportions, slightly: her nose seemed faintly broader, her left eye rounder. Her mane of hair remained the same, its gilded streaks shining and faintly stiff, like raffia. Her breasts were fuller. I wondered if she was on the pill, after her escapade.

Her tongue had a new way of flicking the corners of her lips, self-consciously, when she paused. She seemed emphatically womanly, ripe as a fruit, a creature to whom school had become a childish and obsolete distraction. I waited for her to mention my father, or even my grandfather, directly, but she did not; she skirted around them, around me, as if I were any vague acquaintance. I felt cold, in my extremities. She had grown as foreign to me as someone else's abandoned doll, a human approximation. I could not quite believe what we had shared.

After a while, at a breach in her flow of verbiage, I enquired, 'Did you have anything you wanted to say to me?'

'Me?' She was suddenly wary, her oval eyes narrowing. 'What do you mean? I don't – no.'

'Because you called, that time. That's all. I thought you might have wanted to say something.'

'Oh, no, nothing specific. It was just – I'd heard, about, you know, your dad, and I thought, well – you know.'

'Yeah. Thanks. Listen, I'd better be going, I think. My mother's expecting me.'

'Sure.'

'So, good luck with everything, huh?'

'And you.' She hugged me again, more gingerly this time, as we neared the door. 'Send us a postcard from the States, okay?'

'Right,' I said. 'Sure.'

The marvel, for me, of the encounter, was how firmly that door of my past had been shut, how little I yearned to return to what I had long thought of as the innocent days of our friendship before my grandfather – so long ago, by then – had fired his gun. I could not muster even a twinge of my former affection for my former friend; I could not imagine the person I had been to hold her so dear, to see her as anything other than fatuous and gabbling. I felt as if, in watching her, I had at last seen her clearly, in her womanly ordinariness. She had become what she would be, and she would be that always (I was not far wrong; within three years she would be married, to a man ten years her senior, a salesman met through her brother, and expecting her first child), whereas I, like an old woman and a child at once, felt freighted by my knowledge of precariousness, and wholly uncertain of my path. I might, I thought, become anything; but not that, what she was. She did not even know (nor care to) that there was a veil over things, let alone that it could be torn away.

14

The other call I made, in those last weeks, was to Frédéric. He agreed to meet me at the café on the beach where, in another life, I had sat with Thibaud, before our first, tremendous stroll along the sand. I was sunk in a plastic chair, scanning the menu for the umpteenth time while the late afternoon sun beat upon my brow and the hordes of bathers jostled and shouted along the sand, when he rode up, on a new motorcycle, a fully fledged Honda, with rearview mirrors like antennae and a sleek vermilion frame. He had cut his hair very short, so that it stuck out at right angles to his head, accentuating his unstuck ears, and he carried his cigarettes rolled up in the sleeve of his white T-shirt, like a 1950s rocker.

'Quite an entrance,' I observed, as he slung into the seat opposite, after pausing, barely, in his fluid slide, to kiss my cheeks. 'New wheels?'

'I promised my mother they'd make me study harder.'

I laughed. 'Right. As if.'

He frowned. The stubble grown artfully along his jaw caught the sun. His skin was a colour from my childhood American pencil box: 'Indian red'. 'Seriously. I am. Studying.'

'At the beach, it looks like, if your tan's anything to go by.'

'Yeah. Well. What about you? Really? Are you okay?'

'Hanging in. Just about.'

'Or not? Tell me honestly. You've had a hell of a time. I wanted to call, but—'

'But it seemed too strange. I know. I got your note. Thanks.'

'When something like that happens – none of us knew what to say, you know?'

'It was sweet of you. There's nothing much to say.'

'Lahou cried, you know. Seriously. She sobbed. She really was upset. I don't know if—'

'She spoke to me. At school, on the last day. I didn't – I mean, it's hard. I don't really want to talk about it.'

'Sure, of course. Sorry.'

'I'm grateful, but it's too strange. It doesn't always seem real to me, even.'

He ordered a *citron pressé*, I, a coffee, although I was sweating in the sun in my white shirt, which I had worn because it covered me fully. My skin was no better – if anything it was worse: a little rash had sprouted between my breasts.

After the waiter left, Frédéric watched a hive of coffee-skinned girls pursuing one another in circles in the sand. They wore Day-Glo bikini bottoms and their flat nipples sat like American pennies on their bony chests. They were wholly free in their movements. The rules of their game were not clear.

'Adorable, eh?'

'You pervert! They're about ten!'

'They'll grow up. Quickly, too. Look at the one in pink – a real little Lolita.'

'Is this what you do all summer? Ogle babies?'

'I told you, I'm studying.'

'No girl?'

He shook his head, lit a cigarette.

'Still carrying a torch for Lahou?'

He brushed as if at a fly, but did not answer.

'She and Sami still together?'

'Yep. One abortion on.'

'Not really?'

'Don't sound so shocked, my girl. What do you think they do when they're alone? Hold hands?'

'Shit. That's rough. Poor Lahou.'

'I was the first person she told. Before Sami.' Frédéric sounded proud. 'He had some crazy-ass notion she should have the kid, that they'd set up house, play families. She knew he would; that's why she talked to me straight off. "Get rid of it," I told her. "You're too young." It was what she needed to hear.'

'Who paid?'

'He did. In the end. He's still dealing, in a little way. He's got a job now, too, with his old man.'

'In the bakery?'

'Terrible hours. Up before dawn. He smells like burnt sugar all the time.'

'How long will that last?'

'Not long. He hates his dad. Not long.' Frédéric lit another cigarette off the end of the first.

'You're smoking too much.'

'You think you're in America already?'

'So you've heard?'

'This town is small, sweetheart. Are you excited? You're doing it, getting out, seeing the wider world, leaving the dopes and cretins behind.'

'It's not like I'm going to New York or anything. It's a boarding school, in the middle of nowhere, in the country.'

'Hm. Your mom make you?'

'I want to. She just had the idea.'

'It's a long way.'

'You're telling me.'

'I think it's great, Sagesse. Seriously. You'll blow them away.'

'Or vice versa.'

'You'll be the French girl. It'll be cool. It's much cooler to be the French girl in America than the American girl here.'

'Thanks a lot.'

'You know what I mean. Or than your nasty old grandfather's offspring.'

'Or than my dad's?'

Frédéric poked with his spoon at the congealed sugar at the bottom of his lemonade. 'I didn't mean that. You know I didn't.'

'I know.' I peeled my thighs from the chair and stuck my hands under them. Leaning forward, so that my hair fell over one eye, I was aware that my face was pink, that sweat had beaded unbecomingly along my upper lip. 'I wanted to ask you a favour. A going-away favour.'

'Anything. Ask away.'

'We're friends, right?'

'You bet.'

'So you won't laugh at me?'

'Try me.'

I spoke with my eyes on the sea, my chin out. 'I wondered – I thought – well, because you're a friend – I wondered if you'd sleep with me.'

Frédéric snorted. 'Come again?'

'You heard me.'

'As in "make love"?'

'You can say no.'

He was quiet, fiddling with his cigarette box. Marlboros, red, like the motorcycle. 'Why?' he asked, after a time. 'It's not that I don't – but we're not – it's a – God, you're weird sometimes.'

'That's no, then?' I couldn't look at him.

'I didn't say no. I just asked why. It's out of the blue – I mean—'

'I'm not asking you to pretend you're in love with me or anything. I'm asking for a simple thing. I thought you were burning for it, all you guys.'

'Maybe you should ask Jacquot.'

'Thanks. A ton.'

'I don't get it. Explain. Elucidate.'

'It's like—' I had considered my request for days, and its reasons were so clear to me; but when called upon to present them I found that the words were hard to find. 'My American cousin has a phrase, it's that someone "screams virgin". I don't want to. The best way is not to be one. If I'm going to start an adult life, a new life, I feel like I want to get it over with.'

'Couldn't you just pretend? Just lie. Tell them what you like. Who would ever know the difference?'

'I would.'

'But what if you met some guy, over there, say, even in a

couple of months, and you didn't – I mean, you wanted it to
be the first time, and it wouldn't be . . .'

'Well, I could just as easily lie about that, couldn't I, as the
other way around?'

'You're not making sense.'

'I've thought a lot about it. It's not for anyone else. It's for
me, so I won't be afraid.'

'There's nothing to be afraid of. But I think – you're upset,
about your dad, maybe, or leaving, I don't know. I just don't
think—'

'I'm not asking you to think for me. I'm just asking a favour.
You can say yes or no and that'll be that.'

'But we're friends, you know? It's not – don't get me wrong
– but we're not – I'm not—'

'Okay. It's no. Forget it. It was just an idea.' I tried again to
picture taking off my clothes in front of him. I tried to see how
we could perpetrate the act without him being aware of the
boils on my back, the rash on my chest, without him being
repelled by them, by me. I couldn't. I had imagined asking, but
hadn't been able to imagine any further. By which I should
have known that it was not to be.

'I'm really flattered.'

'Shut up. Leave it alone, now. It's like my father. We won't
talk about it any more. It was a dumb idea.'

'What happened to that guy from Paris?'

'That was ages ago. He's in Paris, anyway. Drop it, okay? Just
please – please don't go telling anyone I asked?'

'I won't.'

'Promise?'

'Sure. Want another coffee?'

We sat together for a while, and Frédéric held forth about his
plans, his mother, a party he'd been to the night before. He was
gracious: he asked more about the boarding school, about my
American cousins. I didn't want to talk. The skin on my back
prickled, and the heat of the sun oppressed and aggravated me;
but neither did I feel I could leave, until my embarrassment had
been sufficiently swathed and bundled in the fabric of banal

conversation, and I at least might pretend to myself that Frédéric had forgotten. And still, when at last we parted, he held my chin for a moment and said, with a hideous, avuncular tenderness, 'Don't worry. Everything will come right at the right time.'

15

I had asked because I had begun to have dreams – or rather, nightmares – about sex. They seemed always to involve my father. I dreamed that I stumbled upon him and a woman I did not know, writhing, naked, in the sheets; I dreamed that he stumbled upon me, that I looked up from the arms of – it was from Frédéric's arms, indeed – to spy my father in the doorway, smirking, his arms crossed, mouthing 'Marie-José'. I dreamed again that the unknown man who licked my nipples, who reached his hand down to my groin, transformed, suddenly, into my father, with hair on his back and the old odour of his cologne in my nostrils, and I awoke to find my own hand between my legs and a thrill, like a current, running through me, that was terror and ecstasy at once. In my waking ruminations, I had somehow determined that only the act itself would free my sleep, and I had decided – it seemed so reasonable – that the presence of Frédéric's naked body in my imaginary bed was an indication, a sign that I should entrust my defloration to him.

Of my father's presence in these dreams I could make but little; I only knew that I would have preferred his ghost to visit me under other, more decorous circumstances, as precisely the guiding hand everyone seemed to feel I required in that time, rather than as the hand directed at my sex. And yet – there would surely have been no one better to oversee my education in that sphere than a man to whom it had been so vital, the man who in waltzing with me along the pavement had made me feel, for that fleeting instant, so eminently and irreplaceably desired.

Walking home that afternoon from the beach, I hated my father for the freedom he had taken for himself, and the freedom he had forced on us. Following my mother, I had railed against the prison of our family; but with my father's disappearance, the bars around us, too, had melted away, the bonds loosened: so, consequently, had the place of belonging evaporated, like a castle in the air. My grandmother insisted that the LaBasses should stick together; but my mother was not a LaBasse, had never been one, for all her efforts, and my brother and I were her children, foremost. Without my father, the very notion of a family seemed a poor chimera, and all our history like so many arbitrary stories.

It is a terrible thing to be free. Nations know this; churches know this. People, however, seek to skirt the knowledge. They elevate freedom to a Holy Grail, disregarding the truth that constraints are what define us, in life and in language alike: we yearn to be sentenced. When my mother had thrown up the pieces of her youth, she had wanted them, above all, to land in formation, to provide her with a family and a home and the rituals of living. In unhappiness, she had stayed put, because the meaning of her life was there, in its outlines, and the pleasures, or dismays, were merely incidental squiggles in the pattern. Now, in my turn, I clutched a handful of fragments, for the first time uncertain whether they were even mine to hold. (Had I a brother, or did he not merit the title? Had I a home? Had I a history? And if, in America, I were to suppress these facts, would they become less true?) I was about to throw all to the wind, to see what might land around me; and perhaps I would find myself with nothing at all, in a landscape bare of grass or trees, a landscape in which I, alone in my pustulated body (the one, marred thing I could not leave behind, the one thing that would not leave me: the only and inadequate definition of my 'I'), would stand, and begin again, from nothing, to imagine a life.

And how many times would I stand thus, in a lifetime, now that there was nothing around me to hold on to, or believe in? And when I asked myself the question 'Is life worth living?' would the answer ever come to me, as it had, in some darkness, to my father, 'This life? No.'

Ten

I

I am American now, or passably so – as much, my Aunt Eleanor insists, as anybody else is. I have, through boarding school and university, accrued the topsoil and sprouting shrubbery necessary to make a landscape mine, as much as anyone's. Aunt Eleanor and Uncle Ron stand like old oaks at the edge of my vista, scarred and reassuringly laden, while Becky and Rachel are sturdy saplings in their parents' broad shade, almost invisible, but rooted there. Before them, reaching towards me, ripple the long grasses of my years in this place, dotted here and there with larger outgrowths, some neglected (acquaintances and even friends along the way, relationships of circumstance and time that have, of necessity, withered) and others flourishing, faithful, never dying. It is not a broad acreage, that floats in my mind's eye, but it is sufficient, and watered, and it grows.

One of the first foreign students I met in New Hampshire, not long after my bewildered arrival there, she older and preparing already to leave, was a round-faced Indian girl from Kenya, with a shiny black braid and loose, jewel-coloured wrappings, who wrinkled her fine nose, in the curl of which a speck of diamond twinkled, and informed me that being American was simple: 'The one requirement,' she sniffed, 'and there is only one – but one I cannot bear – is that you believe in America, that you believe it is the best place.'

I believe, at least, that it is real, and that I am here. But I have taken her at her word: I would not ever openly profess disbelief, and that, thus far, has been enough. In other regions, out in the country's vast wavering plains and valleys that I do not know, I worry that my disguise would be blown from me

353

in a strong wind, that I might stand revealed; but I do not venture there, and so have stayed safe. In the city there are millions like me, of all hues and of hidden histories. We keep mum together and are believed. Sufficiently so.

I rent a studio apartment on the Upper West Side, the same four walls and constantly running toilet (like a brook of my own) and exposed brick trim, the same galley kitchen and scuffed floorboards that I claimed in my second year at Columbia and have kept mine since. I believe – this is a faith – that the air inside my apartment is different, that my hidden history lingers there as a faint flavour on the back of the tongue, indescribable but familiar. In this room, with its intermittent shafts of sunlight and its smeared panes, its low trickles of music and tappings and raised voices from other apartments, above and beside mine, is a place that is my own. It contains few accumulations – a double bed, quilt-covered, scattered with pillows to resemble a couch; a long desk made of a door, sanded and laid upon trestles, atop which rest notebooks, papers and the bland face of my computer; a tufted chintz armchair, in which I rarely sit, and then only to catch the breeze from the broad windows; a dented filing cabinet, which serves also as a coffee table; a scattering of rugs; some lamps; a picture or two (*the* picture among them); a cheap bookshelf; a bulletin board. At the end of my bed rests my old steamer trunk, still decorated with the fraying stickers of its Atlantic crossing, its rows of brass studs dull now. The blinds at the window are pink, slatted plastic: they preceded me here. I have a hallway, a storage cupboard. I have plywood cabinets in the kitchen, the doors of which hang unevenly, and a countertop open to the main room, against which sit two once-fashionable chrome bar stools. I have a shower curtain of clear plastic, decorated with a map of the world, the countries so dispersed as to satisfy a bather's modesty.

To a visitor, these rooms give nothing away; they are not meant to. They reveal themselves only to me. I have been in rooms – have glimpsed them, too, along the very corridors of my building – in which the secrets of a life spill forth, in piles and jumbles, rooms cluttered to the ceiling with the debris of years; and I am scornful of them, as of a life that cannot be distilled, and carried, quiet, in the heart.

Is my own life carried quiet? Probably not, within; but it is carried nonetheless, in another, private language, in the French cadences that echo in my sleep. Being American, I live, in the world outside, in English, as many years ago I longed to do, in the broad, twanging vernacular and exuberant elisions, in the vacuous shorthand ('How ya doin'?' 'Good thanks. You?') of which the greatest proportion of my exchanges is comprised. Outside my windows, the city buzzes, honks, thrills and stinks. Like the Bellevue, it has its seasons – the steamy, urine-pocked draughts of summer, haze-clouded, sweating, a weighted sheen on the flat of my cheeks for months; the crisp of autumn, in which the masses step more spritely; the subterranean steam of winter, when great bowls rise up through the asphalt and dissipate in the bitter, clear air, in which the corner vendors' sugared almonds, and pretzels, and sausages, ring in the nostrils like musical notes. I move through the city, after all this time, like a spy, hoarding the sensations, hoarding myself, garbed and disguised even in the movement of my eyes. Raised in a nation of frank stares, I have learned to observe without looking, to use the watery edges of my vision as precisely as a magnifying glass, to know, like a language, the minute gestures of aggression, or fear, to pick out the lunatic fringe in the apparently gentlest of faces. All this transmits without words: Etienne could have learned it, too; but he will never come here.

My mother visits me every year, once or twice. When she telephones, I do not recognize her voice. That is to say, I recognize it as the voice belonging to the woman who is my mother, but it bears little resemblance to the voice of my recollection, the voice of the woman who raised me and was married to my father, who railed against the LaBasse family and the Bellevue, the voice whose hands braided my hair in childhood so tightly that my eyes watered, whose pointed chin puckered and trembled so violently on the cusp of tears, whose frail and spiny shoulder blades fluttered beneath my adolescent embrace. Flensed, that mother did not survive. The woman who emerged, in time, brittle and clasped, reconstructed (or was it a truer self emerging?), is wholly other. The better for her. She has done things of which my earlier mother would never have been capable. She has eggplant-coloured hair, and unabashedly contemplates plastic surgery.

I had no idea, at the airport in Nice, sixteen years old and trepidatious, arrogant, armoured (or so I thought) – I had no idea of what I thought I knew. Of what was over, of what death really was. I knew there would be no turning back, but I knew it the way I had known about death before my father's came, when I believed, somehow, in permanent change as a temporary measure. And although I thought I knew to be careful what I wished for, I didn't, perhaps, know the meaning of 'too late'. Even now, when I lock myself out of my apartment, and yet can see, in my mind, the exact position of my keys on the kitchen counter, ready to be snatched up – I cannot quite accept that those keys are inaccessible to me, that in the instant in which I slammed the door they became irretrievably, unsalvageably distant, on the other side, in the might-have-been, the ought-to-have-been; and it is only belatedly and with greatest reluctance that I summon the super, or the locksmith – depending on the hour – admitting thereby that I cannot will the keys – and yet I see them, so exactly, and can feel their slippery coldness, their jagged runs – into my present pocket; that my error cannot be undone.

2

The boarding school, when finally I arrived there, deposited by Ron with bursts of anxious laughter and an awkward hug, consumed me, as it was supposed to do. The clattering cafeteria breakfasts, the worn stone stairwells, the whirling frenzy of the activities so beautifully frozen in the catalogue – these novel routines spun like coloured pinwheels, devoured my days. I had a roommate, a lumpen midwestern girl whose bones I failed, in a full year, to locate, even her wrists and shoulders were so discreetly couched in the floury paleness of her flesh. Her hair, too, was pale and sparse, an infant's down on her post-chemotherapy skull. She had had leukaemia as a child, and survived; for which, in principle, one admired her; but there was little to love in her slothlike stillness, her grainy, breaking voice, her faint seaweed smell. The swiftest thing about her was her pet gerbil, a sleek little monster at its squeaking wheel, which creature she freed, on occasion, out of pity or malice, so that several times I discovered tiny black droppings on my pillowcase and once, to my alarm, the very rodent crouching there, its eye glittering with defiance.

This roommate and I were not destined to be friends. We were civil – a courtesy on which I congratulated myself, particularly after the gerbil incident – but sought companionship elsewhere. I joined a book club, tried my hand at amateur dramatics, volunteered my services tutoring French to struggling pupils. I skirted personal revelation, in the late-night common room sessions – conducted in flannel nighties with copious doses of watered cocoa to hand – by feigning, initially, a lack of comprehension, and then by outright lies. They came more easily in English: I was an only child, I said, whose father had succumbed, suddenly, to an allergic reaction. Sometimes he had taken medication, sometimes he had been stung by a bee. When I learned of nut allergies, I had him felled by a contaminated pie crust. These things all seemed possible; they seemed to satisfy. I managed, too, to undress only within locked shower stalls or under cover of darkness, thereby concealing the persistent ravages of my back, all the more abhorrent among girls of pink and glowing dermatological perfection. I thought of myself as a young Muslim, faithfully bound to modesty. And at times it amazed me, how persuasively I skittered along the surface of a life, befriended, involved, unknown. Or rather, more accurately, it amazed me how incurious my peers proved – they who told all, about their drinking mothers and raging fathers, who cata-logued in endless detail their parents' divorces and their siblings' brushes with the law.

On Sunday evenings before chapel, when she could get through (there were only two telephones for forty of us in the house), my mother called; and she wrote, too, every week. But she, like me, played games of omission and revealed to me essentially nothing of her day-to-day, or of Etienne's; and still less about the faltering Bellevue and my grandfather's attempts to fill it. At first, the twins wrote also, stiff, mundane missives on flowered paper (doubtless composed in front of the television), closed with protestations of their affection. But I could not begin to answer, my existence as remote as the Amazon, and these communiqués soon petered out.

I did not miss them. My days were too absorbing, the lurch into a translated life (maths and the sciences were most befuddling) too thorough a demand for me to question it. Was I happy, unhappy? It did not matter. The question was not germane. I was learning, a new self and a new way, broken, with a resounding snap, from the old. In time I bought American clothes, styled my hair in an American cut, chewed gum with the best of them, determined to master my guise more enchantingly than my mother had hers. I was younger, more adaptable, and the society in which I moved more welcoming, or at least less attentive to difference.

As for boys, they had no place, in the early days, in my geography. Their dormitories lay across an open field, which seemed, most conveniently, to mark their distance. When, towards the end of my senior year, I lost my virginity, it was to a former history teacher, a married, moustachioed man in his thirties, no taller than I was, who thrilled to my virgin-ness and, though solicitous and tender, doubtless chalked the conquest of my hymen upon a lengthening list of same, while never for an instant considering me over his Quaker wife, with her Mona Lisa smile (she was one of the school nurses, as it happened, and would, had I asked her, have furnished me with condoms for her spouse's infidelity; though he took care of the matter), and his two rubicund and cherubic infants. Nor was it, for me, a matter of love; I used the opportunity as I saw it, and was grateful that it preceded my graduation by only a couple of months, allowing for several trysts, or practice runs, in which sex did indubitably improve (for me, at least), before I embarked, and freed us both from further obligation. He was called Mr Wilson, and although in our rushes of intimacy, he must have revealed to me his given name, I can no longer summon it, however clearly my upper lip recalls the silky bristling of his moustaches.

But that was much later. In those first months, I looked, occasionally, from my scattered notes and sleepy hours of study, towards Christmas, and home, and thought the prospect gilded. I was, as I have said, too frantic to be homesick, but still, as I had with my aunt and uncle and cousins, I regarded this adventure as a temporary displacement, and heard the genuine ticking of my life's clock from afar, its mechanics firmly embedded in Mediterranean soil. As the holidays approached, I gloated, picturing my roommate's glum return to some clapboard farmhouse snowbound on a pancake plain, and my newfound companions drifting off to the slushy suburbs of New York and Washington, D.C. Some, the farthest-flung, whose parents served time in Dubai or Karachi or Accra, had to make do with others' Christmases – as I, had I but known it, would the following year find myself at Ron and Eleanor's, kneading chestnut stuffing alongside Becky and recalling our distant weekend on the Cape. But that first Christmas I was going home; a journey that impressed my fellows, and even me.

3

When I spotted my mother behind the partition at Nice, I began to bob and wave. And when, as I drew near to her, I glimpsed my brother grinning in his chair (it was an effort, considerable, for her to have brought him), I found my eyes instantly, unwillingly wet, and my cheeks damp as if they, too, had sweated out tears. At a run, I tried to encircle both mother and brother in a single swoop, and succeeded in banging my stuffed handbag against Etienne's pearly ear, hard enough to make him yelp.

My mother was girlish in her glee. On the way home, she turned at every red light and gasped again at how I'd changed, how well I looked, how much I had been missed. Stunned by the flight, the hours in Paris, my lack of sleep, I nonetheless tried to answer her zealous questions as lightly, as fully as I could: about the campus, the roommate, the teachers, the food. But what I wanted to do was peer quietly, from my window, at the crystalline winter light, at the red 'Tabac' signs and green pharmacy crosses, the branching lanes and occasional ambling peasants, at the red-tiled roofs and knobbly vineyards, at the barren blue rise of the mountains.

'The cars look so small, so white!' I exclaimed. She laughed, and Etienne with her. And when, on the highway, I rifled for change at the tollbooth, we both smiled at my fistful of useless quarters and dimes.

Of her own news, my mother was circumspect. 'When we get home, sweetie. There'll be plenty of time to talk about everything when we get home.'

I sighed at the palm-lined boulevard, and noted the fresh paint on the Bellevue's gates as we passed. I marvelled at the new traffic light on the brow of the hill. I felt my lungs fill to bursting as we turned into our familiar street.

'It's home, Etienne! We're really here!'

And he, by way of calm acknowledgement, mumbled, 'Graw.'

'He's so pleased. He missed you, too. And he's had such an autumn – a lung infection, you know, quite bad. He's only just got over it.'

'You never told me.'

'Sweetie, what would've been the point? He wasn't in any danger. And you would just have worried, all that way away, over nothing.'

'What else don't I know?'

'Don't be silly. You're here now. There will be plenty of time for everything.'

'Two weeks isn't plenty of time.'

'Don't be like that.' My mother closed her hand over my wrist, and the heavy gold bracelet she wore lay cold on my skin.

'New?' I asked, fingering it.

'That's another story, dear. All in good time.'

I had never before remarked how meanly the tyres of Etienne's chair squeaked on the front hall's marble floor; nor had I remembered the hollowness of my own step in the entryway. The house felt different, chilled and quiet, as though we three were intruders upon a long-enclosed emptiness.

'It feels like you don't even live here,' I said. 'It's strange. My voice almost echoes.'

'What nonsense,' my mother chided. 'You've just forgotten. Your memory must be pretty short. Now, leave your bags – we'll get them later. Fadéla has left us some lunch, I think, and we can eat right away. Then you can sleep, which is what you most need. I thought we'd put off your grandparents till tomorrow, give you a chance to catch up. And then—' as she was speaking she wheeled Etienne, pale and scrawny, through the salon to the dining room, where the table was set for three, with a large jug of water and a baguette in a cloth-lined basket. My place, however, was set at my father's seat; and while my mother chattered, I set about moving it, place mat and cutlery, glass and napkin, back to its rightful position.

'You can't pretend he'll come back, dear,' my mother said. 'You might as well sit in the armchair.'

'I don't want to.'

'As you like, then. But it's not healthy. Now, as I was saying—'

Over shrimp and avocado salad and Chablis, while Etienne contemplated an empty plate and me, with a gaze in which I discerned, or believed I did, relief and devotion, my mother unfolded the facts of their months without me. Etienne's illness – initially a rumbling cough, which had deteriorated to spouts of greenish phlegm that had threatened to choke him – had necessitated his hospitalization for a fortnight. I marvelled, and was furious, at the smooth conversations my mother had directed over the long-distance lines, at the careful ease of her lying. Again, she maintained that she had done right to keep the news from me.

'But what if it had got worse? What if he'd been dying?'

'You're being melodramatic, sweetie. He wasn't in danger. And if he had been, of course I would have told you, and you would've come straight home.'

'How do I know? How can I trust you?'

'You'll just have to. I'm your mother. You're making such a fuss about a little infection—'

'Two weeks in hospital, Maman!'

'You had enough to contend with, a new environment far from home, not to mention the burden of everything else, of your father. And I was taking care of your brother. And all the doctors, and Iris too. You're not responsible for him; I am. You have a life to lead.'

'He's my brother.'

'He's my son. I would do the same again.' She was quiet for a moment, playing with the breadcrumbs around her plate. 'But it was, you know, it was killing, all on my own. You can't imagine . . . And it's made me think—'

'What?'

'I've been talking about it – with friends, with a friend—'

'With whom? What?'

'Don't get all upset. I've been wondering if it isn't too much to ask, of all of us, for Etienne's well-being – I mean it, above all, for him—'

'What are you getting at?'

'There are places – you know this – equipped, better equipped than even this house can ever be—'

'You aren't!'

'I've just been talking to people, that's all. You know your brother—' we both looked at him, and he grinned. 'He loves people, and attention. He loves being made a fuss of. And now—'

My mother went on to explain that her resources were not unlimited, that there was to be no life insurance payment because of my father's means of death, that she was, in short, looking for a job. 'And if I'm out all day, and back only after Etienne's bedtime, that leaves him all the time with Iris. And she's wonderful to him, to be sure, but that would double her hours, and the expense – you have to understand, it's unrealistic not to consider, for his welfare—'

'Grand-père will pay for it, you know he will.'

'That's another thing we need to talk about. I don't – I'm not – relations between your grandparents and me are not – they're not easy. I don't want to upset you, it's just the way it is. Your father never crossed them, you know. They've been coddled – that's the word: coddled. So that now, when we disagree, they can't seem to – and they're under strain, and—'

'Is the hotel doing badly?'

'It's not a good time for the business, that's part of it, and your grandfather has had to work very hard, and for a man of his age, coming out of retirement – but it's not only that. I think they can't – I think your father's passing has been extremely hard for them.'

'And not for us?'

'It's been hard on our relationship, then. Theirs and mine. Your grandmother thinks it very wrong that you're away, and now—'

'But they'd want to help, for Etienne. To stick together. Have you even asked?'

'I don't want to ask, Sagesse. That's the bottom line.'

4

It was not, of course, the bottom line. The gold bracelet, clunky and ostentatious, speckled with rubies and sapphires, was the bottom line: my mother had a boyfriend. It took her days – almost half my holiday – to work up to the news. Information about Titine's death in October, about Iris's eldest son's engagement, about the new priest in the parish, a young man with, she said, 'bedroom eyes' – all were more pressing revelations than the arrival on the scene, scant months after my father's death, of a suitor, a divorced businessman in his early fifties whom she had known socially for years and never mentioned, but to whose ardent attentions she had swiftly, even eagerly, fallen prey.

'He's wonderful with Etienne,' she assured me, her cheeks bright and her eyes aglow, as I stared stonily out the window. 'He's a kind, gentle, patient man. But strong. Not like—'

'Not like my father.'

'He's very stable.'

'I'm sure.'

'And independent.'

'No doubt.'

There was a silence.

'How could you?' I asked.

'I'm grieving too, Sagesse. Paul is respectful of that. But you, of all people, ought to understand.'

'I?'

'We've talked – at least, we did, when your father was alive. I have a life, too. I'm entitled to one. We have to change. Things change. Can you give me that much?'

I shrugged.

'His children are grown up. He's free. He's in love with me.'

'And you?'

'It's too early for me to know.'

But I prised from her the truth that the 'friend' who advocated Etienne's removal to an institution was none other than Paul, who also advised my mother to sell the house and move into his villa in Nice; that he slept in my father's bed; that he was offering her a position in his firm. 'He wants me to be independent. Not like your father's family. He sees that it was the problem with his first marriage, that he and his wife grew apart. He's very liberated.'

'Marriage?'

'He said marriage, not I. He's patient. You'll like him, I promise.'

'Is that why you sent me to boarding school?'

'Don't be obscene.'

'Who's being obscene? I ask you.'

I wondered how it could never have occurred to me that such a thing might happen. Never, in all the wishing before my father's death, never, in the cloud of guilt and sorrow afterwards, never had I imagined – although, with detachment, I could see the logic of it – that my mother's transformation, our transformation, could involve leaving behind all of it, all of us, the Bellevue and my grandparents, and, above all, me and Etienne. My brother, in his intransigence, the one who would not change, was still, to the last, to have held us, to have remained at our core. Our house had been built for him, our lives patterned around his needs. And if I had been horrified at the ease with which my father had closeted my brother, that long-ago afternoon, in the elevator, and at the ease with which I had left him there, then what was I to feel at my mother's readiness to shunt him, to shuck him off, to hollow him from our lives like the pit from a peach, and wheel him off to an institution more truly imprisoning than the LaBasse family had ever been?

5

The afternoon of this exchange, a brittle, grey day just before Christmas, I went, on foot and of my own accord, to visit my grandmother. We had all had supper together the night after my arrival, a polite and formal affair at their apartment, but neither she nor my grandfather had stopped by the house in the intervening days. She greeted me at the door (Zohra had already left), and her hand on my shoulder was so cold that I could feel it through my sweater. My grandmother looked older to me, the pattern of her cheeks crazed, like old porcelain, with new lines and furrows. Her eyes burned in their sockets, and although she smiled at me, I felt no warmth from her gaze. I felt like a traitor.

We sat opposite one another at the dining room table, the site of so many stiff meals and, for me, of such quiet dread. Outside, a haze enveloped the horizon and the sea churned in its steely broth. The pool below us lay sprinkled with dead leaves, abandoned for the season, its turquoise water stagnant and forlorn. The room, like my grandmother, was cold: a draught seeped around the window frames and scuttled along the floor, in eddies around my ankles.

'So your mother has told you about her paramour?' My grandmother's nose trembled with disdain, and her Parkinson's sent erratic shivers through her.

'I suppose she has.'

'And how do you feel about it?'

'I don't know. I haven't met him.'

'Is that all you can say?'

'How do you and Grand-père feel?'

'It would seem it is none of our business. I feel – I am horrified, for your poor father. At the error of his choice of wife, which is only now clear. Now, perhaps, I understand why he did what he did.'

'That's a horrible thing to say.'

'Your mother has succeeded, in a matter of months, in dismantling a family. A family that had stayed together in spite of terrible trials, for a long time. She is a wicked woman.'

'I don't know that—'

'I feel sorry, above all, for you and for your brother. Although you don't seem to mind, off gallivanting in America. Etienne's happiness is apparently of no importance to you. But at least you are a child.'

'I'm not really, any more.'

'Your mother is the person responsible. I don't blame you. You're my granddaughter, and I'll always love you, and you'll always have a home here. But that woman—'

'She is my mother.'

'If you feel that way . . .' My grandmother made an exasperated swoop of the head.

'Is this guy so awful?'

'I don't know him. I don't care to. He's a Gaullist, for one thing.'

'Yes, but—'

'And I can't condemn him for trying his luck, albeit with unseemly haste. But your mother seems to have welcomed him into her bedroom without batting an eye—'

'It's hard, being alone.'

'What would you know about it? And she was never alone. You didn't have to leave – she sent you. And your grandfather and I, what are we? Nothing? And Etienne?'

'But she doesn't belong. She's never belonged.'

'Then that's been her decision.'

'But you've never liked her.'

'Have I ever said such a thing? Has your grandfather?'

'What about me, then?'

'You'll always belong here, with us, if you choose. That's up to you.'

The apartment's silence weighed, the moribund rooms with their trinkets and doilies pressed upon us, the cold air so thick it felt like matter between us. There was a faint smell of frying, left over from lunch, and of the soap with which Zohra scrubbed the floors.

'Thank you,' I said. 'I'm grateful.' But the choice – is it not always? – had already been made.

6

My mother was out when I got home. Iris sat in the living room, in the rose velvet love seat which illuminated her dark skin, knitting, while Etienne, covered in his plaid rug, dozed near the window.

'He likes to look out and see the day,' she said. 'Even when it's not a particularly nice one. I know it's colder over there, but it makes him happiest, so I bundle him up warm and let him have what he wants.'

'Has he been for a walk?'

'Too brisk, today. With his lungs, now, we want to be extra careful. A recurrence would be an awful thing.'

'What was it like?'

'He can't tell us, can he, poor love? But he was pale as spaghetti, and as limp, and the cough just tore through him. Chills one minute, burning up the next. He lost weight, you can see even now. Couldn't muster the energy to eat. You could see in his eyes, he was scared. Plain scared.'

'Did Mother stay with him in hospital?'

'She came every day.'

'And at night?'

Iris stopped knitting and looked at me. 'Two weeks is a long time. You can't easily be sitting up all night in a chair for two weeks, especially if you've got other things on your mind.'

'So he was alone.'

'Sometimes I stayed. There were always nurses on call.'

'But Etienne can't call.'

'He's all better now, that's the important thing. We just need to be careful, in the winter.'

I'm not sure why it was worse to think of Etienne all alone in the dark in a strange place. In one way or another all of us were, after all. But there seemed to me something particularly rending, particularly true, about my brother's isolation. I wondered whether they had strapped him down, at the wrists and ankles, so he wouldn't dislodge his IV, and worried about whether they had left on a night-light, somewhere, even far away, so that he didn't wake up and crane his neck and, seeing nothing – no looming shapes, no shadowed walls – doubt, with a thundering heart, that he had woken at all. But perhaps it was like the time in the elevator: perhaps he did not fear the absolute dark, as I did, but merely floated in it, invisible and free of deformity. I often assumed – I still do; how could I help it? – that we are the same, except that I have voice for our terror and anguish.

But maybe this is wrong: maybe Etienne didn't mind the hospital bed, with its bars he couldn't fall through and its enticing array of sweet-skinned nurses. Perhaps he did not miss my mother when she left, nor my father, nor even me, but was content in his present, whatever that was, so long as he was not in pain. We believe about Etienne the things that we need to. Our vessel, he accepts them all, each projection, each inconsistency: joy, tragedy, history and its loss, nullity, wholeness – and why not? And who can say?

And yet if this is so, if he enfolds and embodies our every need, is it because he is himself without a self? I know this isn't so, although I know so little what a self is, nor for how long, whether a matter of flesh or spirit, of the past, or of dreams – but all these things are incontestably scored along his skin and in his heart. He has lived them all, as I have.

In studying the brain, I learned in college, a Canadian scientist probed his conscious subject's exposed grey matter with tiny needles, here and there, dredging up thereby (but she could give voice to them; the subject was a 'she') specific and forgotten days of childhood – an ordinary afternoon in a canoe, upon a June lake; a winter evening at the breath-misted window, eyes on the silhouetted copse at the bottom of the hill, the fire spitting in the grate behind – each brilliant, gemlike, overflowing. Everything was there, each brush of flannel at her father's elbow, each speck of grit on the tongue, each dog-shaped cloud scampering overhead and ripple on the water. All this, each instant, hour, day, we carry; somewhere; as does Etienne, just the same.

And if it is so, that he has room to be himself, in all its particular secrecy, and yet is capacious enough uncomplainingly to shoulder all that we require of him, all need and fear and innocence, everything – as he is the repository of all the memories trapped, unsalvageably, in the webbings of our own brains (no scientist awaits to jolt mine back to the surface; nor would I necessarily desire it), then what is he? Then Etienne Parfait, *plus-que-parfait*, is not less than me; he is, in his silent wisdom, infinitely more vast.

And still, I hated to think of him alone. That night, the night before Christmas Eve, I lowered its bars and crawled again, as I had used to do, into his narrow bed, where he lay sleeping, so that we might be together, one. I settled his smooth forehead in the hollow of my clavicle, curved his body to the line of my own, stroked his fine hair (my mother kept it almost as long as a girl's; he winced at the sight of scissors) and breathed in time with him. He seemed so light, almost hollow; and safe within his skin, as if he permitted, rather than needed, me there. I did not protect him. If anything, my brother protected me, although I had so long sought to escape him.

I fell asleep with his head tucked under my chin, and woke before dawn, when the first bird called in the trees outside and the earliest shades of day crept blue along the floor. Etienne, in my crook, was hot, his brow damp, his breathing phlegmy and full. He smelled of sweat, a man's, not a boy's, sharp and seamy, and his penis was pressed hard against my leg, like a little limb. I had forgotten that he was no longer a child, had wanted to remember him that way, had wanted him to be one. Aghast, and aghast at my dismay, I slid from beside him, and he moaned, a little, but did not waken. My own bed was too tightly tucked, chilly; but I slept at once, relieved to be alone.

7

When the aged Augustine breathed his last, papery and feverish in his bed in Hippo, at the end of the summer of the year 430, he had not yet seen his earthly home destroyed. But he knew its destruction was imminent: the Vandals were at the gates. Within the year, Hippo was in flames, all that he had found familiar flattened to oblivion. Its library – its stories, Augustine's words – was spared; and in this way, his world, his Roman, Christian Africa, a life's work, would live in the imaginary still.

Camus, too, predeceased his homeland, his French Algeria; but he, too, looked on in horror at its death throes, the murder and torture within, on both sides. And he died, that absurd January afternoon in 1960, twenty-four kilometres out of Sens

on the Nationale 5, in that crumpled Facel-Vega, with his
words on the pages in his briefcase in the trunk of the car, to be
salvaged and passed on.

That they knew their Algerias were dying mattered no more,
in the broad continuum, than that they died themselves, men
guilty of harm as well as good, who loved societies guilty of
more harm than good. Because a country, like the Phoenix, like
the soul, survives its conflagrations. But it mattered, surely, that
they spoke.

8

I am American now: it is a life which has, like that of many
others, like my father's, or my grandfather's, the appearance of
choice. And in time, America becomes a home of a kind,
without the crippling, warming embrace of history. I finished
school; I enrolled at Columbia University; I followed a path as
logical to my classmates, to my dowdy roommate Pat, as
Thibaud's path, or Aline's and Ariane's, had been to them. I
kept Becky and Rachel in my sights, American cousins leading
their unquestioned lives, and strove to emulate their readiness. I
slid easily into the tumble of the city, grateful for its indifference.
In a gesture of perversity, I studied history, as an undergraduate,
the wild idealism of the Founding Fathers, the piling, stone
upon recent stone, of a culture notable for its interest not in the
past but in the future; a different, an American, way of thinking.

For a time, I shared my bed with a hollow-cheeked graduate
student, a Yeshiva rebel with persistent dark circles beneath his
eyes, a man obsessed with film theory in zealous abscission from
the terrible weight of his own family's history. We talked about
ideas, about *suture* and shot-reverse-shot and notions of feminine
narrative; we discussed professors and students and the landscape
of New York (with the exception of Brooklyn, his birthplace,
which smacked, to him, too much of home); we sought
out ethnic restaurants and sampled exotic cuisines and talked,

pretentiously, about them too. And when the time came that we could digress and postpone no longer, when we ought to have opened the locked cases of our own stories (it is something, surely, that most courting couples undertake from the outset), we baulked, both of us, and withdrew, little by little, until our chance encounters in the library or at ill-lit wine-filled gatherings were excruciating, our stiffened exchanges freighted by all we knew we did not know about each other and had not wanted to reveal.

After that, I kept my liaisons brief. I lied. I shed my father's death, my brother, to be sure; but also the twisting paths of my family's history; I hid my private, all-too-real, unseen Algeria. Many times I have told men whose smells commingled with my own among the wilted sheets that the watercolour on the wall was but a trifle from a junk shop in the Village, or a random gift from a long-forgotten friend. I did not – I do not – answer questions; which is not difficult, because most do not ask them. And when pressed, I fabricate, aware as I do of my life's puzzle pieces drifting, mutable in language if not in fact, changing shape in the room around me.

I have been, most often, French; but also French Canadian, or simply American (the Robertsons' home is useful in this regard, as it gives texture to my lies), and upon occasion, Argentinian or Venezuelan, for kicks. I felt particular fondness for the man who listened, wide-eyed, to my description of the pampas, who strolled with me down the avenues of my imaginary Buenos Aires. I had met him in a bar, had spent a long weekend mooning along the shores of the Hudson and folding myself against his narrow, virtually hairless, chest; and, in embarking upon my South American fantasy had decided, after that afternoon, never to clap eyes on him again; which, of course, he could not know. I covered him the more tenderly and fulsomely with my kisses, that he might always recall his Argentinian lover as gentle and expert, and not detect the untraceable fleck of pity in her eyes.

9

Last August, my grandfather had a stroke. Mademoiselle Marceau discovered him, crumpled at his fine, broad desk, in the middle of the afternoon, his cheeks blue, his livered hands still grasping a sheaf of papers that were damp in the summer heat. The hotel was full to capacity, the pool splashing with a new generation of rambunctious youth, whose parents sipped drinks on the parasol-shaded terrace. My grandmother told me, over the telephone, in a voice that wavered like her body, and as she spoke I was visited by the blinding glare of the Mediterranean sun, by the vast, silvered, twinkling expanse of the sea that had once shaped my whole life.

It was up to me to inform my mother, the knowledge describing the earth's arc not once but twice, along the mysterious airwaves. She, in her grand villa in Nice, awaiting Paul's return as she once awaited my father's, betrayed no emotion, but sighed, and said, 'I suppose Etienne should be taken to see him.'

'I'm coming,' I said. 'I'll take him. I know how it is for you. Don't worry about it. I just thought you'd want to know.'

Paul paid for my ticket, but I spent only one night under their roof. I stayed instead with my grandmother, at the Bellevue, in the bed that had been my father's, when he arrived, so long ago, the prodigal without a coffin. My aunt Marie was there, too, in her old room, in her pillowy bulk, leading with her great bosom, fatuously bustling and bossing the hunched Zohra, bullying my grandmother to eat and to sleep. We visited my grandfather's hospital bed together, the four of us, women with so little to say to one another. He could not speak. He lay supine, one lid drooping, the left side of his body a dead weight and the right scrabbling, minutely, painfully, to live. But with his good eye, the same eye, the one that still held himself, he fixed me, as he once had across the ocean of brown carpet, and he knew me, owned me, as he had always; he insisted, the last but one to do so, upon my historical self.

I intended to take Etienne to visit him, but found I could not. My grandmother would not do it of her own accord; my aunt, who did not think my brother wholly human (and never had) considered it a futile and acrobatic undertaking, better avoided. My mother did not emerge from her new life to offer assistance. It was up to me. And as I sat, sweatily grasping Etienne's slender, fronded hand in the dappled garden of his own institution, the stark smell of his room coming off him in waves, as he eyed me, bird-like, from his juddering head and seemed, wetly, patiently, knowingly to smile, I knew I could not bring these two men together (for there was no doubt about it, then: Etienne, too, was a man), each to look upon the other, so alone, and see himself reflected.

I stayed an afternoon with my brother, and talked to him about my life in New York (he seemed – perhaps I willed it – to nod deliberately in his smiling), and fed him, spoonfuls of chocolate pudding that dribbled, mingled with spit, brown along his pale chin. But I declined to bathe him, when the moment came, not wanting or able to see his man's body unclothed, and left him giggling coquettishly at the attendant, stopping only to bury my face in the top of his head and extract, in my nostrils, to the back of my throat, the true smell of him – not of his surroundings, with their sickly masking perfumes, but of him, part of myself, whom I had always known. It was like drawing deep from a spring that you know can sustain you, remote in the mountains, and whose sustenance must last indefinitely, perhaps forever, because the journey is so arduous that you may never be able to make it again, not in your lifetime, nor perhaps in that of the source. The source, after all, like anything else, may dry up.

My grandfather now has his own institution in which to rest. It stands outside Geneva, a stern nineteenth-century mastodon overlooking Lac Leman. My grandmother, ailing herself, has gone to live with her daughter, her less-favoured child: the LaBasse family must, after all, stick together. Thierry's father has been appointed the interim manager of the Bellevue, while its sale is

negotiated; and it flourishes again, my grandfather's house built
on rock.

10

The century, the millennium, is drawing to a close. Scattered,
alone, each of us waits in our corner for the chiming of the
hour, for the new leaf, for the next move, for the coffin – we
don't know what it will be, but all of us know we are waiting.
Soon there will be no one left to tell the stories, no one but me
and Etienne.

And yet, they aren't our stories alone. They seep outwards.
Hairline seepage, perhaps, but perceptible, if you look closely.
To the suicide of Mitterrand's loyal lieutenant Pierre Bérégevoy,
for example, in the spring of 1993, in which I picture not the
former prime minister of France, but only my father, walking
alone along the river outside Nevers, beneath the overhanging
grey sky, the burgeoning alleys of trees mourning, in their
delicate dance, his imminent demise; and the quiet rush of the
brown water, interrupted, for only an instant, by the terrible
report of the gun. And to the War Crimes trial, much later, of
Maurice Papon, former secretary general of the prefecture of
the Gironde, about which I read in the American newspapers.
The blurred old man in the photographs, a *pied-noir* like my
own kin, his eyes wide, his hair fluttering around his weathered
cheeks, his expression at once haughtily defiant and afraid – he
is, to me, my grandfather. He is my history, what I am, no
matter how I elide or disguise it. He, too, is inescapable, he is
part of my story.

As a graduate student, my field is the 'history of ideas', a neat,
evasive term that covers thought, not fact. I have opted for
centuries of reflection over centuries of action, as though the
two were separable. But the visions of the mind, more than
the rubble of cities and the bones of men – the life behind the

eye is what lingers. I am groping for a thesis, panic-stricken that its subject, like a religious vocation, has found me in spite of myself, or would, if only I would listen.

The effort to shut out the truths, my truths, is all the harder, in these past months; not simply because the university showers me with deadlines and forms, but because there is, now, a man I want to know. Not to caress and to pity, nor to lie to, or lie with, and abandon; but to know. I see him in the library, glimpse him in the delicatessen or the Polish pastry shop, his slender, old-fashioned briefcase dangling at his side, his cuffs too short for his bony wrists, his lonely brow furrowed in the effort of translation. We have not yet met, but I have asked about him, and I know what must somehow transpire. He is younger than I am, by a little, and lanky, and his black hair moulds like astrakhan to his finely shaped skull. His skin is dusted, as if by dark sand, and his eyes, beneath their curling lashes, are green as the sea. Not long in America, he has washed up here like Phlebas the Phoenician, but alive, from the wars of his home-land – and of mine – of a home that exists only in the imaginary. His name is Hamed. How to tell him, who might have been my cousin, the stories I know? How to avoid it?